Upside Down in a Laura Ingalls Town

A Novel

Leslie Tall Manning

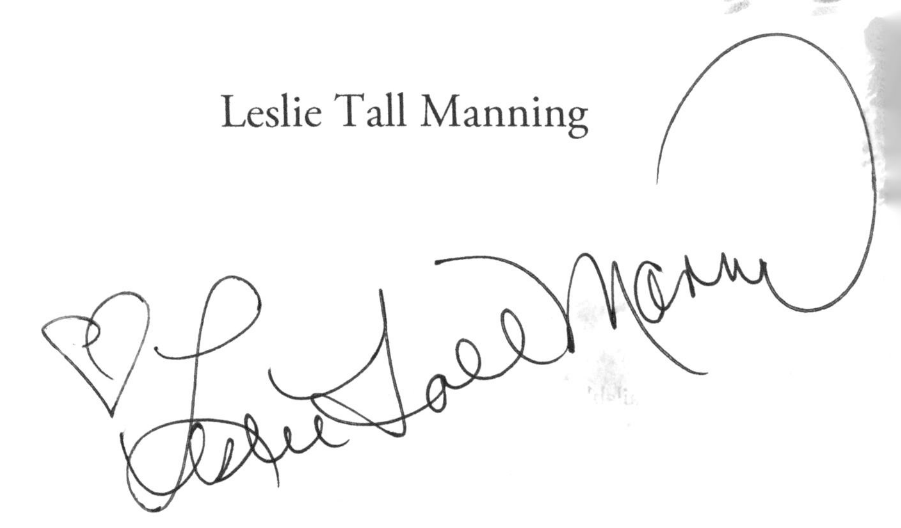

ISBN: (Mobi) 978-0-9961306-4-6
ISBN: (Paperback) 978-0-9961306-5-3
ISBN: (Audio) 978-0-9961306-6-0

Cover design by J. Kenton Manning Design, Inc. Copyright © 2015.
Formatting by Polgarus Studio.

Available from Amazon.com and other book stores.

For Laura Ingalls Wilder

And for all the young women who have spent at least one moment standing in Laura's shoes.

'Tis the gift to be simple,
'Tis the gift to be free,
'Tis the gift to come down where we ought to be,
And when we find ourselves in the place just right,
It will be in the valley of love and delight.
When true simplicity is gained,
To bow and to bend, we will not be ashamed
To turn, turn, will be our delight,
'Til by turning, turning, we come 'round right.
~Where We Ought to Be
~By Shaker Elder Joseph Brackett, Jr., 1848

CHAPTER ONE

I stumbled onto the porch, trying to suppress the giggles as I reached my house key toward the lock. The truck inched away from the curb behind me, and I turned to wave, even though I couldn't remember at that moment if it was one of Libby's brothers or some other guy. I swung my keys up high like little metal flags, and then they were suddenly soaring through the air and landing with a thud in the planter, where spring tulips were just starting to bloom.

"Shit."

As I bent over to dig out my keys, the front door opened.

Rebecca Lynn stood there in her pink nightgown, her hair flat on one side like she'd ironed it. This made me laugh, picturing my ten-year-old sister ironing her hair. That weed Libby's friend shared with me made even the most stupid things seem funny.

My sister held the storm door open as I managed to recover the dirt-covered keys and step into the hallway. The house was dark except for the staircase.

"Dad's asleep," she said, shutting both doors and locking them behind me. "Gross, Brooke, you smell like Grandpa."

I wasn't sure what she was referring to—the smell of smoke or booze.

"Shut up," I told her. "You aren't my mother."

She gasped. "You shouldn't say things like that. I'm telling Daddy."

"You're smelling badly?"

"I said, I'm telling Dad."

"Yes, you *are* smelling bad."

"Stop it," she said, putting her hands on her hips like a grownup.

"Stop it."

"I'm serious."

"I'm serious."

"I hate you," she said. "You are the worst big sister in the whole entire universe."

She turned, hiked up her nightgown like an angry Cinderella, and marched up the steps two at a time.

If I was lucky, I'd make it up *one* at a time.

Someone had found a large rock and was banging it against my head.

"Brooke," my dad's heated voice said from the other side of my door. "I want to see you. Pronto."

I clicked the button on my cell phone: eight a.m. On a Saturday. Crimony. I crawled out of bed and realized I'd slept in my clothes. I kicked off my heels, then put on my bathrobe and opened the door a crack.

"Morning, Dad," I said, offering a fuzzy-toothed smile and pushing my pink and black bangs from my sticky forehead. I thought for sure my head had split open the night before and half of it was left behind at the party.

"Oh, Brooke." Dad shook his head sadly. He stared at the hoop in my eyebrow. He was always staring at it. Like it was a pimple he wanted to pop but didn't have the nerve. "Come downstairs for breakfast. I have an appointment this morning, and I need you to watch your sister. And take a shower first. You smell like your grandfather."

I struggled through all of it: taking off my clothes; turning on the water; stopping the soap from slipping away from me; squeezing the bottle of shampoo. It was all I could do not to curl up in a little ball under the hot spray on the bathtub floor.

Presentable enough in jeans and a Life is Good T-shirt, I went down to the kitchen. Dad and Rebecca Lynn were eating pancakes at the table. Just seeing the syrup threw my gag reflex into overdrive.

"Sit down and eat," Dad said.

"Not hungry."

"I didn't ask if you were hungry. There are people on this planet who have nothing to eat this morning. Pretend you appreciate what you have."

I sat as he put a pancake on my plate, and then plunked the syrup bottle next to my orange juice glass. As I stuck a piece of soggy pancake in my mouth, he started in.

"I checked on you around midnight. You weren't home yet."

"Yes, I was. I was hanging out in the garage. I fell asleep out there. On the futon."

He held up a finger. "Strike one."

I was smart enough not to respond.

"Another lie and I will take away your car keys for the remainder of spring semester."

I had reason to be skeptical. Dad never followed through on any punishment he threatened me with. He interrogated me the only way he knew how: quietly and methodically, his voice super soft, like a priest in a confessional.

"Where was the party?" he asked.

"In Greenville."

His eyes grew large. "That's forty-five minutes away. You're too young to go that far for a party."

"Hell-O…sixteen. Besides, I can't help where the party was."

"How much did you drink?"

"Two cups of punch."

"What was in it?"

"Not sure. Something sweet."

"Was Libby with you?"

"Yes."

"How many people were at the party?"

"About a hundred."

"She's lying, Daddy," Rebecca Lynn said. "Parties don't have that many people."

Tool.

"She's right," I said. "It was more like a hundred and fifty."

"Were the parents there?"

"Uh, no," I said, laughing. It was a frat party. A *college* party. *Sans chaperones.*

"What's so funny?" Dad asked.

I took a chug of OJ. "Nothing."

"Who drove you home?"

"A friend of Lib's." *I think.* "A really nice boy."

The word "boy" was a stretch, since he was probably more like nineteen, and I couldn't remember his face, let alone whether he was especially nice or not.

"What time did you get in?"

I didn't know so I shrugged.

Rebecca Lynn said, "Two-fifteen. I saw it on the microwave."

"You broke curfew, Brooke," Dad said.

"Whoops. My bad."

"And you're too young to drink. Especially hard liquor."

"You drank when you were sixteen," I reminded him.

"I tasted beer with my father, who brewed it for a living. Not the same thing."

I smashed my pancake into a wet, syrupy mound. "So, what's my punishment?"

"Keys...for a week."

This didn't matter to me. Libby could drive me to school, and there weren't any good parties coming up. Dad wasn't very creative when it came to sentencing. Though I had to give him credit for trying.

Now, he reached across the table and placed his hand on top of mine.

"Brookie...I think your mother would be proud if you could grow into the woman she always dreamed you'd be. And that doesn't include getting wasted or taking rides from strangers. Your mother wanted you to be the best person possible. Do you understand?"

I nodded and sat at the table picking at my food until Dad left for his appointment. Rebecca Lynn decided to crank up her Miley Cyrus CD, and if I hadn't had an awesome pair of earbuds to block out the noise, I would have clocked her upside the head.

Libby drove to school since my keys were locked away in Dad's office desk. Her truck was old and bumpy, a hand-me-down, and made my handwriting go haywire.

"What are you working on?" she asked.

"That history essay on Civil War crap. It's due today."

"Ms. Bernard wants everything done on the computer. Times New Roman, twelve-point font, double-spaced. And you had two days to do it."

"Didn't have time."

"Didn't *make* time."

Libby was our school's popular party girl, but she still got awesome grades.

"You're just lucky to be born smart," I told her.

"Don't be a douche. You wouldn't have gotten into this school if you weren't smart. You just don't try."

"Wow, if you didn't wear a bra, I'd swear you were my dad."

"Brooke, you are way smarter than me. It doesn't take a brain surgeon to manage their time. I do my homework in study hall. On Saturdays, while my brothers are at their boring basketball games, I reread whatever chapters we did in class, and I review my notes on Sunday nights before bed. I manage my time. And I don't complain about it. It's school. Big freaking deal. There are worse things I could be doing, like making biscuits at

Bojangles, or writing in the dirt with a stick. You're just being a martyr. M-A-R-T-Y-R. It's one of our vocab words this week. Look it up."

CHAPTER TWO

Dad put the bucket of previously jailed chicken and the environmentally unfriendly Styrofoam bowl of mashed potatoes on the table. I poured three glasses of milk and Rebecca Lynn grabbed the paper napkins.

"It's nice to have all of us around the dinner table for a change," Dad said.

He was talking about me. That if he hadn't asked in advance for a family dinner, hadn't grounded me, or at least thought in his own mind he'd grounded me, I would have taken a paper plate of chicken up to my room and eaten at my computer while pretending to do my homework.

"I want us to take a road trip," Dad said as he handed me the bucket. I grabbed an extra crispy leg and passed the bucket to my sister. "The three of us."

"Where are we going, Daddy?" Rebecca Lynn asked in her nauseating baby voice.

She'd started using that voice around the same time Mom got sick. Dad said to let her do it, that she would grow out of it, so I never said anything. But it still made me grind my teeth.

"To Charlotte," Dad said. "All day Saturday."

Charlotte was a long, boring, five-hour drive from New Bern. I'd have to miss getting my specialicious red nail polish at my monthly pedicure.

"What for?" Rebecca Lynn asked.

"An interview."

"With who?" I asked.

"*Whom.*"

My dad worked as an engineer for a local phosphate company. I couldn't imagine *with whom* he'd have an interview, especially so far away. And on a weekend. *My* freaking weekend.

Dad dropped his extra crispy thigh onto his plate, and I noticed he'd barely taken a nibble. My dad loved his bucket of chicken. It was his weekly carbo splurge. But now he was staring at that thigh like it was a chunk of phosphate. He wiped a napkin across his mouth, even though there wasn't any grease there.

"We have…an opportunity. Maybe. If we're lucky."

"Are we moving out there?" I asked, my stomach dropping. "To Charlotte?"

I pictured being dragged away from my neighborhood where I had known most kids since kindergarten. Away from the river, the Atlantic Ocean, my school. Charlotte was *The City*. With tall bank buildings and freeways infested by gobs of people, moving around like a bunch of hyperactive ants.

It was my turn to put on the baby voice. "Dad?"

"We have an opportunity as a family to be part of a television reality show."

"What's a reality show?" Rebecca Lynn asked.

Flashes of *Big Brother*, *Real Housewives of Orange County*, and *Survivor* crashed into one another in my head.

"A reality show," Dad explained to my sister, "is a show where the participants are filmed doing everyday things."

"There'd be cameras in our house?" I asked.

I thought of my messy bedroom, the acne meds on the bathroom counter, the gazillion stuffed animals covering nearly every inch of space…

"I don't know all the details yet," Dad said.

"Then why are we going all the way out to Charlotte?"

"It's only for an interview."

"Thanks for asking us first, Dad."

"I want to be on television," Rebecca Lynn chirped.

I shot her a nasty look and she shoved a chicken leg into her mouth.

"It's not a big deal," Dad said. "I saw the ad in the *Observer* and thought we'd be good candidates."

"Why?" I asked.

"They're looking for hardworking, honest families. I sent them a letter. And they responded."

I fingered the hoop in my eyebrow. "What did your letter say?"

"I told them about the adjustments we've had to make this past year. I'm hoping you'll be on board." He looked directly at me when he said this. This is The Curse of the Oldest Kid: giving permission to a parent who has already made up his mind.

"You sent a letter without our agreeing to it," I scolded.

"I did it on a whim."

"What about your job?"

"I'll work it out."

"But what if—what if they pick us?"

"There will probably be hundreds of families to choose from."

"But what if they like *us*?"

"Then we'll be on television."

"Doing what?"

"That's what we'll find out this Saturday."

"I hope we get to do it," Rebecca Lynn said. "My friends will think I'm cool."

"I want to be on television," Rebecca Lynn said from the back seat.

I gritted my teeth. "You've said that, like, a hundred freaking times today."

"So?"

"So, you sound like a broken record."

I did my best to ignore my annoying sister while Libby's texts kept me company on the drive to Charlotte.

Five hours later, we pulled into a parking garage. Dad grabbed the little white ticket. After parking, he said, "The letter says no cell phones allowed, Brooke, so leave it in the car." I tucked it in the front console. We walked out of the garage and onto a sidewalk toward a tall glass and metal building.

"Fifth floor," Dad said, holding the letter in his hand as we walked through a marble lobby. We stepped into the elevator. I pressed the number five.

"Do you think I'm dressed alright?" Rebecca Lynn asked.

"We don't even know why we're here," I told her. "Who knows if we're dressed right or not?"

I knew my face was pulled into a sneer, and Dad glared at me.

"What?" I asked, putting on my regular old face again.

The little bell rang, the elevator doors opened, and my first wish was that I'd snuck in my camera.

Under the flickering fluorescent lights was utter chaos. Mobs of people covered every inch of pale blue carpet or faded couches or folding chairs; other families, moms and dads and sons and daughters. One family was dressed identically, all four members wearing green and white striped shirts with freshly ironed khaki pants. Another family dressed like they were headed to a funeral, head to toe in all black, including their shoes. Still another looked like they belonged in a Harley commercial, the youngest boy with a Mohawk and his older sister donning at least four tattoos, none of them as pretty as the panther on my lower back.

I wore jeans, a pair of high-heeled black boots, a black and white top, and a bunch of chunky bracelets. Dad wanted me to pull my eyebrow ring out and get rid of the pink stripes in my hair, but I'd fought him on it. If it was true families they wanted, then I was going to be honest about my fashion choices. As would be expected, Rebecca Lynn wore a plain blue dress with tights and her hair was pulled back in a headband, and Dad donned a tan collared shirt and a pair of brown corduroys.

Compared to these other people, we were straight out of a JCPenney ad.

I straightened my spine, threw my shoulders back, and raked my fingers through my hair. For just a moment I felt the twinge of competition.

Then I snapped out of it. I didn't care about any of this. I should have been sitting in one of those relaxing massage chairs at Happy Nails with my feet soaking in paraffin.

A young black woman wearing a headset, complete with tiny microphone against her mouth like a hip-hop star, came up to us.

"You all here for the audition?"

"Audition?" I asked. "I thought this was an interview."

"Oh," the woman said. "We just call it an audition so it feels, you know, like Hollywood."

"Hollywood," Rebecca Lynn cooed.

Dad said, "Last name's Decker. Tim, Brooke, and Rebecca Lynn."

"Great," the woman said, checking off her list. "Room three. They'll call you for your aud—*interview*—in a little bit."

She spoke into her headset as she zipped away.

Dad grabbed Rebecca Lynn's hand and I followed behind as we worked our way through the horde of reality TV wannabes. Another family had just left the pea-green couch in the corner. We took their place. The smell of must rose up.

"What's that boy doing?" Rebecca Lynn asked, pointing across the room.

The boy, no older than five, was trying unsuccessfully to do an imitation of a robot. His body remained stiff as his arms and legs moved spastically. His parents egged him on, clapping each time he made a strange beeping noise.

"Maybe he's having seizures," I said.

"He's just being silly," Dad said.

"Are we supposed to act silly?" Rebecca Lynn asked.

Dad shook his head. "Absolutely not."

I was about to ask Dad for the umpteenth time what in heaven's name would make him want to do this—my dad, the NC State graduate; the boring engineer; the weekend golfer; the man who owned more Dockers than jeans—when the gal with the headset called out, "Decker!"

As we stood up, Dad grabbed my wrist, squeezing it a little too tightly. His upper lip was sweating. "Please, Brooke, make me proud."

"Dad," I said, following him into the room, "you're freaking me out."

But Dad didn't respond. Two bright lights shone on us as a skinny man with a scruffy graying goatee stuck a camera in our faces, and the door closed behind us.

CHAPTER THREE

"I'm Ricardo Gonzales," said the smiling man behind the desk. He had long dark hair tied in a ponytail, and his hands were folded neatly in front of him like he ran a country. His words held on to the traces of an accent. Next to him sat a large woman with short, curly red hair and a T-shirt that said, *Roll 'Em!*

"Have a seat on the couch over there," Ricardo said, pointing with his head, "and we'll begin the audition."

Why did everyone keep saying that word?

We sat with Dad in the middle, me on his right, Rebecca Lynn on his left.

"So," Ricardo said, "no one has told you anything about the actual show, is that correct, Mr. Decker?"

"Correct."

"What makes you want to be part of a project you know nothing about?"

"Our family could use a little—diversion."

"What's *diversion*?" Rebecca Lynn asked.

Dad explained, "Something to take our minds off what we've

been through."

"And what have you all been through?" Ricardo asked.

"Their mother passed away last summer. It's been a long haul."

"Oh," Ricardo said, his smile tipping. "Right. You wrote about that in your letter. I'm sorry for your loss."

He said he was sorry, but I caught a slight twitch in his eye as he glanced at the fat woman next to him.

"So," Ricardo said, "if you were chosen for this venture, you feel, after what you've been through, you'd be able to handle adverse situations?"

"Of course."

"And your girls?"

Rebecca Lynn said, "Daddy showed us how to be strong."

"That's awesome," Ricardo said. Then he turned to me. "And you? Do you think adversity makes a person stronger?"

"I don't know." I started to play with the ring in my brow, but stopped myself.

"Do you think you could live for a time without certain things?"

"Like what?" I asked.

"Makeup? Hairspray? Jewelry?"

Why was this Ricardo guy asking me such stupid questions? I looked at Dad, but he was staring at the camera.

"And what about the mall?" Ricardo went on. "Your cell phone? Your social media? Could you live without those things for a long period of time?"

"I can," piped Rebecca Lynn.

But Ricardo didn't care about my sister. He was waiting for my answer.

"How long is long?" I asked, the spit in my mouth drying up.

He shrugged, not like he was bored, but like he really didn't care how his answer affected me. "Four months."

I laughed, but it was just a spurt of nervousness, not a LMAO kind of laugh.

Ricardo waited.

"Well, no," I said. I could feel Dad's body stiffen next to me, but I didn't care. "I could never go that long without those things. They're a part of life. Where does this show take place, on an island?"

Ricardo didn't answer my question. "The show would require your family to leave behind the modern accoutrements you have become accustomed to. Like soda, fast-food, television. For four months, you'd have to give up your friends, your social networks, your favorite iTunes, your boyfriends, your weekend slumber parties—"

The large woman next to Ricardo, who had stayed silent up to this point, said, "Your high heels and deodorant. All the creature comforts."

I was beyond nervous now. I didn't know where the television show was going to take place, but I did not want to do it. No freaking way, no freaking how. I would have to make too many sacrifices. Shit. I had already sacrificed my mom. Wasn't that enough?

My dad patted me on the knee again. "Those kinds of things aren't important to us."

"Yes they are," I said.

"No, they're not. We've learned as a family what it means to do without."

He was lying. We hadn't done without. If anything, since Mom had died, Dad was buying more crap than ever. We had every new gadget known to modern man: a Kindle; a Nook; the latest iPhone; iTouch; iPad; i-*Everything*. We had three PCs collecting dust, two laptops, and a 3D television. Last October, on my sixteenth birthday, Dad bought me a brand new Explorer with heated leather seats. We took a trip to the Bahamas for Thanksgiving, Christmas looked like Macy's exploded in our living room, and we spent New Year's skiing in Vail. He never said a word when I added pink to my hair, or when he spotted the panther tattoo on my lower back while swimming at the country club. He never showed any emotion when I went for that dark eyeliner look, almost, but not quite, Goth. I never heard a stink about quitting the track team. And he still gave me money when report cards came out, even though my *A*'s had dropped to *C*'s, except for Gym which was a *D+*. At the end of last semester, as he handed me a fifty, he said, "I know you'll find your way back."

Now, my dad's face seemed desperate. He wanted this. I didn't know why he wanted it, but I wanted it for him. For *him*. But not for *me*. Maybe I could live with relatives while Dad and Rebecca Lynn went off to this strange land where no one used deodorant or checked out Youtube videos.

My stomach rumbled and my heart raced as pictures of a labor camp popped into my head, the three of us dressed in gray coveralls, a six-digit number stamped on our forearms, barbed wire surrounding us.

"Is this a prison reality show?" I licked my chapped lips and waited for the answer.

Ricardo smiled and said, "We can't disclose exactly what it is until you pass the first round. If you make the cut, then you'll be told. For now, we have to keep the details as quiet as possible. Too many ears in Hollywood looking for a good reality show. Know what I mean?"

My head nodded yes even though I had no clue what he was talking about.

Ricardo continued with the questions:

"Okay, then. Do any of you have any habits you can't quit for a few months?"

Like making out with cute boys or pounding Jell-O shots on a Friday night?

I watched with horror as my dad and sister shook their heads.

Ricardo jotted something down on the paper in front of him. "Anyone who makes it through will receive a full physical, but to save us some steps, do any of you require regular medication?"

Like pot brownies?

Again they shook their heads. Dad nudged me until I did the same.

"Any pets that will be difficult to leave for any length of time?"

Rebecca Lynn said, "My goldfish died."

"How did that make you feel?"

"Sad. But I didn't cry. We flushed him down the toilet. He's with Nemo now."

Ricardo leaned forward. "What are your fears?"

My dad spoke first. "Something happening to one of my daughters." He put an arm around each of us and squeezed. "Or something happening to me."

"And you?" he asked Rebecca Lynn. "What scares you?"

"Zombies. And ghosts."

Ricardo nodded. "Me too."

Rebecca Lynn smiled.

"And Brooke," Ricardo said. "What frightens Brooke Decker?"

Well, let me tell you, culo burro *Ricardo. Yesterday it would have been getting caught sleeping in history class, having Dad find out I'd snuck beer onto my school's field trip to Charleston, or getting a speeding ticket out in Greenville. Now, my fears are having a camera in my face, the incessant grin on that fat woman next to you, and the way you keep staring at me, like I'm going to be the reason we either will or won't make the cut.*

"Nothing," I told him. After seeing my mom suffer through a double mastectomy, watching her wither away from chemo, then floating to her death on morphine, I believed at that moment I was telling the truth. I raised my chin a notch. Dad's pride filled the room. "Nothing frightens me."

"Very good," Ricardo said, nodding slowly, marking a sheet in front of him. "Thank you for your time. We'll be in touch."

We were quickly escorted out of the room, and just as the door was about to close behind me, I saw Ricardo fist bumping the chubby lady beside him, her pudgy smile in the center of that pasty face turning her into a redheaded Pillsbury Dough Boy.

CHAPTER FOUR

During the two weeks following the interview-slash-audition, Dad didn't mention it once. I figured we were axed. Boring until they were snoring. I wondered if the family with the robot kid would be picked. At least the kid was entertaining.

But I guess we weren't too boring, and when the producers called to announce we'd made the first cut, Dad jumped around like he'd won the lottery. On the morning of our home interview, he totally lost his mind. His alarm went off at six. I heard him take a shower, and then his feet were thumping through the house.

I came out of my bedroom wearing pajamas, my hair jutting out in sharp angles all over my head.

"Get dressed," he said. "Crew is going to be here soon."

He'd said 'crew' like it was a friend of the family.

I went back to my room to dress and came out a few minutes later to the smell of bacon. Downstairs, Dad stood in front of the stove. Rebecca Lynn was sitting at the table eating scrambled eggs. I slid onto a chair opposite my sister.

"Coffee?" Dad asked me.

"Sure."

Dad let me drink it some weekends. Having to be up this early on a Saturday, he owed me one. After adding cream and sugar, he set the New Bern mug in front of me. He plucked the bacon from the pan and placed it on a folded paper towel. "What are you girls wearing today?"

"This," Rebecca Lynn said, patting the collar of her frilly white dress. She looked like an underage bride.

"And you, Brooke?"

"I'm wearing it."

I wore my faded jeans, a tight blue T-shirt tucked in, and a leather belt with flowers on it. My tan Ugg boots were still up in my bedroom, so I was in my socks.

"Wear a dress. And take out that brow hoop."

"Why?"

"Because I want us to look nice."

"Are you saying I look like crap?"

"Don't use that language at the table. Or in front of the cameras, if you can help it."

"Dad, for all we know, this show takes place in the middle of a dump site."

"Why are you fighting me on this?"

"Fine," I said. "I'll wear a stupid dress."

When we were finished eating, Dad grabbed our dishes and put them in the dishwasher.

"Rebecca Lynn," he said, "put on an apron before you dust the living room. Brooke, I need you to sweep the front porch before you change."

He poured himself another cup of coffee and grabbed a handful of paper towels and a bottle of Pine Sol from under the sink. He headed to the guest bathroom.

"Let's get this place shipshape," he said over his shoulder. "I'd hate to lose this gig because we can't keep a clean house."

At one o'clock the doorbell rang. Rebecca Lynn ran to the door like the house was on fire. Dad and I waited in the living room.

"You didn't take out your hoop," he said.

I was saved by Ricardo's voice in the hallway.

"Well, if it isn't Miss Rebecca Lynn Decker. A movie star name if I ever heard one."

My sister skipped into the living room like stupid-ass Goldilocks, followed by Ricardo and the same cameraman from the audition. The lady with the red hair and weird grin wasn't with them, and for that I was grateful.

The cameraman's name was Carl. With his skinny arms and neck, and that *Swamp People* goatee, I pegged him as more of a "Bubba," or "Skeeter," but I didn't say anything.

"Please, sit down," Dad said.

He fanned his arm to the two overstuffed chairs across the coffee table from the couch. Ricardo sat, but Carl the cameraman, whose camera was already on, stood behind Ricardo.

I thought it was best to jump right in. "Are you going to tell us what kind of reality show this is?"

My dad shook his head. "Brooke—"

"It's alright," Ricardo said. "That's why we're here." He sat back in the chair and crossed one leg over the other, making himself right at home. The bottom of his leather sandal was scuffed. "There are moments in time that can never be understood, at least not fully. Times we only read about in history books, or see in movies, barely a re-creation of the truth. But it takes more than reading about it or putting on the costumes to understand what history really means." He sounded like a PBS host. "This is the opportunity to go back in time."

Carl the cameraman inched closer to my dad's face, but it should have been my face, since I was the one who was about to freak out.

"Ever hear of Laura Ingalls?" Ricardo asked.

"I have her books!" Rebecca Lynn shouted excitedly. She started counting on her fingers, "*Little House in the Big Woods, Little House on the Prairie*—"

"Sit down, Rebecca Lynn," I whispered.

Ricardo turned to me. "Do you know who she is?"

"Of course I do."

I thought of my mom, sitting on the sofa on a rainy Saturday afternoon, watching cable reruns of her favorite *Little House on the Prairie* series. Sometimes she'd cry. She would hold onto a tissue, and she would sob as she sat there on the couch. I asked her once why she was crying. She told me it was because the show made her happy.

Ricardo wiggled his fingers at Carl, who moved with lightning speed to my side. I could feel the camera sending invisible waves through my cheek. It took all my strength not to flip off that large glass eye.

"It helps that you know who she is," Ricardo said.

My dad cleared his throat and clicked his neck. "The show is about modern-day pioneers?"

"Not exactly," Ricardo said. "It has nothing at all to do with *modern*. In order for us to mean what we say when we call it a *reality* show, we plan to keep it as true to the era as possible."

"Which era?" I asked, even though I knew the answer, and even though I knew I would have to do whatever it took to get Dad to see that these people were out of their flipping minds.

"The mid-1800s. Eighteen-sixty-one, to be exact."

I started doing the history lesson in my head: mid-1800s meant no electricity. Without electricity, there would be no lights, no television, no computer...

"You're going to shut off our electricity?" I asked, shocked that this could be legal. I pictured our king-size suburban house gutted of all its modern appliances. "You can't—"

"No," Ricardo said. "The show won't be filmed *here*."

"Then where?" Dad asked.

"I can't disclose all of the information until we narrow down the participants, but the families selected will be part of a community in the North Carolina backcountry."

"Laura Ingalls didn't live in North Carolina," I smugly told him. Didn't these people do their homework?

"The lifestyle is comparable," Ricardo said. "Historians have accurately detailed the way it was then, and we've followed their guidance to a tee."

"Dad—" I whispered, the panic creeping into my throat.

Ricardo kept on yapping. "We are choosing families from different backgrounds, and giving each of them a different backstory, mostly for variety."

"Like Williamsburg," Dad said.

"Except that at the end of the day, you won't take off your costume and go home to a microwave dinner." Ricardo laughed and I wanted to slug him.

"Dad," I said, pulling on his arm. "We can't do this."

"Brooke, not now."

"But—"

"When does it begin?" he asked Ricardo, cutting me off.

"Third week of May. So you have time to become acclimated to your new home before you plant your crops."

"Crops?" A horrifying picture of the three of us picking cotton under the afternoon sun slid through my brain.

"You'll be responsible for growing much of your own food," Ricardo said. "Have you ever had a garden?"

"My wife," Dad said. "She had an amazing green thumb. I think we can figure it out."

"No, we can't," I said.

"Yes, Brooke," Dad said, never looking at me. "We can."

Rebecca Lynn said, "I want to be like Laura Ingalls, Daddy. Can I? Can I be like Laura?"

"You can if we get chosen."

My sister was smiling, my dad was smiling, and Ricardo was smiling. I faced the cameraman. Behind his creepy goatee, Carl was smiling too!

But I was not. My smile had crawled into a hole and died.

"Dad," I said. "I'd miss my friends."

"You'd make new friends in the backcountry," Ricardo said.

I ignored him.

"Dad, please. You can't be serious about this..."

Ricardo interrupted again. "This is the chance of a lifetime. It's the opportunity to—"

"Shut up!" I screamed. Carl shoved the camera in my face, but I didn't care. "This is asinine! Do you hear yourselves? How can you all think this is something I'd want to do?" I stood up. Tears ran down my face. I knew there were long black streaks on both my cheeks, like a Goth who'd just discovered that vampires are make-believe. "I don't want to do this. Please, Dad, I'd miss junior prom. Plus, I only have this summer and next before college." I had sort of forgotten about college over the last few months, but now it seemed like the most important thing in the world. "Please."

No one said anything for a moment. The tiny red light on the camera held steady.

Dad took my hand. His voice was so quiet I could barely hear him. "Sit down, Brooke."

I did as he asked. I wiped my cheeks with the backs of my hands. My bottom lip wouldn't stop trembling. My dad took my chin and turned my face toward him. I tried to say "please" again, but it wouldn't budge.

And then the words flew out of him like venom from a snake. "I'm doing this for *you.*"

"What?"

Ricardo said, "In your father's letter he told us how things have been since your mother passed away. How hard it's been, especially on you."

My head jerked hard toward Ricardo.

"What the hell do you know? You don't know anything about me. Or our family. You're just creeping for some freaks to put on your show. You think I don't know how reality shows work? How they deliberately try to make people look like idiots?"

"That's not what this show is about—"

"You only do it to make money. Everybody knows that."

"This is a shared venture," Ricardo said. "Everyone involved loves history and wants to share that love with an audience."

"I want an audience, Daddy," Rebecca Lynn said. She was crying now, too.

Ricardo stood up. "Why don't we take a little break? Let things cool down. We'll come back in a few."

Ricardo and Carl left the living room. I heard the front door close.

Dad stood up, and for a moment I thought he was going to hit me. My Dad bragged about the fact that he had never, ever, in his entire life, hit another soul, so this idea frightened me more than anything else.

"Stand up!" he ordered.

I did, but I took a step back.

"Why are you jeopardizing this?"

Rebecca Lynn stood behind him, sniffling. She grabbed onto his hand.

"I really don't want to do this, Dad. I don't—I don't think it's fair—"

"Fair? You're talking to me about *fair*? You girls lost your mother. I lost my wife. So don't say anything to me about fair."

"I know you think you're doing this for me, somehow, but…I don't want to live in any time but now. I don't want to live on a prairie, or in the woods, Dad. I don't want to leave where we are." I started bawling, choking on the words. "I'll—

I'll do better in school, and I'll start doing more around here. I won't hang out with Libby anymore, or her friends from ECU. Is that what you want?"

Dad let go of Rebecca Lynn's hand and pulled me to him. I could smell the spicy aftershave he hadn't worn since before Mom died. He hugged me tightly as I cried into his shirt. But his hug told me the decision was already made; that I was a case of "too little, too late."

"Brooke," Dad said as he held me. "We've lost so much already...I don't want to lose anything else."

"Like what Dad?" I said in a muffled voice. "What are you afraid you're going to lose?"

He squeezed me harder, and the words he chose bore a hole through my heart.

"*You*, Brookie. I'm afraid of losing *you*."

Carl and Ricardo came back into the house and resumed their positions, Ricardo in the overstuffed chair and Carl with that one-eyed bird on his shoulder. Dad sat with his hand on mine as if to anchor me.

"So," Ricardo said. "Get things ironed out?"

Dad nodded.

Right away, Ricardo started asking questions, one after the other, like he'd never left; like I hadn't just had a personal meltdown.

Ricardo: "What religion are you?"

Dad: "Episcopalian. But we don't go very often."

Ricardo: "How physically active are you on a daily basis?"

Dad: "I enjoy taking walks along the river."

Me: "You haven't taken a walk in a long time, Dad."

Dad: "Maybe you're not home enough to witness it."

Rebecca Lynn: "I ride my bike. And I jump rope."

Ricardo: (Handing me his stupid smile.) "And you?"

Me: (Shrugging, defeated.) "I go to gym class at school. And I walk down to my friend Libby's house a couple times a week. It's a few blocks."

Ricardo: "What activities do you do over there?"

Me: "Hang out. Play pool. Watch Netflix. Junk like that."

Ricardo: (Scribbling on the sheet.) "What do you know about the Civil War era?"

Rebecca Lynn: (Shouting like a contestant on *The Price is Right*.) "Abraham Lincoln freed the slaves!"

Dad: "I've read a few books on the subject."

Ricardo: (Smiling, moving a finger along the edge of the sheet.) "Any specific skills you'd like to share?"

Dad: "Skills?"

Ricardo: "Anything that could make your family stand out from the others. Like weaving. Or tanning."

Me: "What does tanning have to do with Laura Ingalls?" I pictured myself in a bikini, my winter skin soaking up the rays out in the middle of a wheat field. It was the first time that day that laughter rose up inside me.

Ricardo: "Tanning is making leather."

Dad: "I never did any tanning, but back in my teens I helped grow collards."

"You did?" I asked, surprised.

"With your Great Uncle Mitchell. He owned a farm out in

Boone. I spent a couple of summers there, and he taught me how to plant and harvest." (To Ricardo.) "I also learned to brew beer. But that skill I learned from my father. He owned a few breweries. I have what you might call an eclectic family."

"But you chose to become a chemical engineer," Ricardo said.

"Yes. Well. Real life beckoned."

Ricardo: "Would the family be open to a physical?"

Dad: "Of course."

Ricardo: "Can any of you sew?"

Dad nudged me.

Me: (Mumbling.) "I sewed a pillow once."

Dad: "It's beautiful, with velvet trim. As nice as Pier 1. Her grandmother keeps it on the sofa in her living room."

Ricardo: "Can any of you cook?"

Another nudge.

Me: (Sighing.) "A little."

Dad: "Brooke did everything around here when her mother was ill, including the cooking. She made meatloaf, burritos, lasagna, chicken and rice. She's a wonderful cook."

Ricardo: "Any of you know how to ride a horse?"

Rebecca Lynn: "I like dogs better than horses."

Dad: "Brooke?"

Me: (Fiddling with my eyebrow hoop like a kid with OCD.) "I took riding lessons for three years during middle school."

Ricardo placed the paper in a beige folder and closed it.

"Why do you think you should be one of the families chosen for this venture?"

Before I had time to add my two cents, Dad said, "We understand hardship and know what it takes to overcome that.

When we have disagreements, we work through them. We can also offer humor and creativity to the project."

"*Venture,*" Ricardo corrected.

"Venture," Dad repeated.

"And you?" Ricardo asked Rebecca Lynn.

"It would be fun to dress up like Laura Ingalls. Could we have some pets?"

"Yes, ma'am." He turned to me. "How about you, Brooke? A little while ago, you wanted nothing to do with any of this. What made you change your mind?"

The way Dad's voice had trembled. The way he held me so tightly he almost cracked my ribs. The way his panicked words told me he was afraid of losing me, even though I'd been afraid of losing myself for nearly a year.

Welcome to my world, Dad.

Ricardo stared at me, waiting.

It occurred to me no matter what I said, or how I said it, it wouldn't matter. If our family, even after all my stink and tears, ended up on the show, I would not be shipped off to a relative's house for four months. There would be no shopping at Peacock's Plume for the perfect prom dress, no sitting in a stretch limo with my bestie, miniature bottles of vodka and rum tucked inside our sparkly purses. I would not spend the summer tubing on the river, or hanging out at Libby's beach house in Emerald Isle. I'd miss my kitchen, my bedroom, my house, and everything in my life that was as different from Laura Ingalls' life as one can imagine.

And it also hit me that no matter how much I wished it, Mom would not be able to save me.

"My dad wants change," I told Ricardo, trying not to cry again. "I guess this is the only way to give him that."

"*Us*," Dad said. "This is for all of us."

But it's because of me, I thought, clinging to the outside chance we wouldn't be chosen. I secretly crossed my toes and silently pieced together what I remembered from the *Our Father* prayer.

Dad asked Ricardo, "Did we make it in?"

"The videos still have to be reviewed by our producers. Their decision won't be made lightly, but we'll let you know ASAP. We want to give our families enough time to prepare, both mentally and emotionally. A venture like this will be life changing—for everyone involved."

CHAPTER FIVE

Libby had a huge FROG—Finished Room Over Garage—which her totally awesome parents let her and her three older brothers turn into a hangout room, with an old plaid sofa bed, a bunch of beanbag chairs, a huge flat screen, and a pool table that had seen a lot of use. A bunch of us neighborhood kids met over there at least once a week, and we hung out until dinnertime, when her mom told us to go home and eat with our own families.

"You'll understand why this is important when you have kids of your own," she'd say as Libby and her brothers set the table.

When I returned from Lib's the Monday after the home interview, I heard my dad's voice coming from the den.

"I understand," he was saying. "Thank you, Ricardo, for taking the time to call."

I stepped into the arched doorway of the den. Dad looked up from his leather recliner. The cell phone sat on the coffee table. Channel 13 News was on the television over the fireplace, but the volume was turned down. The ticker tape that ran along the bottom of the screen told me there was a thirty percent chance of rain.

"That was Ricardo?" I asked.

Dad nodded but didn't say a word.

Either way, I was afraid to hear the answer. If we got on the show, the next four months of my life would be destroyed. If we didn't, I was sure my dad would try to find another way not to "lose" me. Like by sending me to some creepy all-girl boarding school where American Pecking Order Stats was a required course. Or to Outward Bound where I'd have to live in the wild and feast on tree bark.

"Go get your sister," Dad said.

Rebecca Lynn was doing her math homework at the kitchen counter. A pot of spaghetti sauce simmered on the stove.

"Dad wants to talk to us," I told her.

"Okay," she said, jumping down from the stool.

I grabbed her by the wrist, hard, so she'd know I wasn't messing around.

"Ouch!"

"Shut up and listen to me. Dad got a call from Ricardo."

"So? You don't have to break my arm."

"If we didn't get picked, Dad is going to be really upset. I just want to prepare you."

"If we didn't get picked, it'll be your fault." She pulled out of my grasp and ran into the den.

Dad leaned against the leather chair arm, his arms folded across his chest. "I have some news."

Rebecca Lynn hopped from one foot to the other like she had to pee.

"Ricardo said the turnout at the audition was more than anyone expected. They're only choosing a select few..." He looked at the muted television as if the words he needed were scrolling across the bottom along with the weather. "Well...so...he and the producers agree that the Decker Family...would be an asset to the show."

My mental dictionary looked up the word "asset" and my knees nearly buckled.

"Daddy?" Rebecca Lynn said. "Did we, or didn't we?"

Dad suddenly jumped to the center of the room, danced a jig like a drunken leprechaun, and scooped up Rebecca Lynn in his arms. "We did we did we did!" He swung her around in a wide circle. After he put her back down, he said, "You girls ready to go back in time?"

"I am!" Rebecca Lynn squealed.

"How about you, Brooke?"

I didn't answer. I held my fist against my mouth like I'd just witnessed a murder.

"She's crying again, Daddy," Rebecca Lynn said.

"You should be proud," Dad told me. "We beat out hundreds of other families." He took the remote control and turned off the television. "Why don't you go upstairs and process this? I'll call you when dinner's ready."

I barely felt my legs as they took me up to my bedroom, where posters of Bob Marley, Katy Perry, Pink, and other cool singers covered my walls. Where my laptop sat ready and waiting, my light blue pillow shams and bedspread and curtains matched a perfect Eastern North Carolina sky, and my closet full of not-yet-worn summer clothes seemed to sigh with sadness.

"Ricardo said I can have pets," Rebecca Lynn was saying downstairs. "Do you think he'll let me have a pig?"

I kicked my bedroom door shut before I heard the answer.

CHAPTER SIX

Ricardo came to our house the next day accompanied by a man dressed in an expensive suit and shiny leather shoes. Carl the cameraman tagged along. Rebecca Lynn and I followed the men into the living room.

Ricardo introduced the man in the suit as Burt Novak, the show's executive producer.

"I know this is a lot for your family to take in," Novak said as he sat on the sofa before anyone asked him to. "We're here to answer any questions you may have."

"I have a question," I said. "Why did you choose the 1860s? Why not a fun era, like the Roaring Twenties, or the 1960s?"

I pictured my hands and head stuck in the stocks like an accused witch, or on my dress a red letter "A" for "Adultery" for being unfaithful to the venture.

"We made the decision in a very unconventional way," Novak said. "Our team sat at a table at the Red Lobster, put a bunch of dates on scraps of paper, and threw them into a hat. Eighteen-sixty-one was the winner. The name of the show is

Upside Down in a Laura Ingalls Town. I think the title says it all, really. The town will be filled with other families, just like yours. Though there will be individuals who are on their own, for the sake of keeping the town feeling real."

"On their own?" Dad asked.

"Like the town sheriff. The reverend and his wife. There may even be a passerby from time to time, to keep things authentic. We want to stay true to the events of the day."

"Like what?" I asked, way too lazy to go through the American history timeline buried somewhere in my brain.

"Like the Civil War," he said. "There may be a few reenactors roaming about, along with a some other surprises."

Civil War reenactors were nothing new to me. New Bern, North Carolina, my hometown, is steeped in Civil War antiques, yearly encampments, blacksmithing, and re-created duels. There are even stories of cannon balls buried in the mud on the Neuse River floor.

"Let's get to the rules," Novak said. "Each family will be strictly monitored. You do something against the grain, and the cameras are bound to catch it. You do something a little extra 1800s-ish, and the cameras will catch that as well. Our camera people will seem intrusive in the beginning, but you'll get used to them. The videos are sent to the producers on a consistent basis. But you don't need to be bothered with that. Just worry about *not* getting kicked off the show."

"Kicked off?" I asked, a little too enthusiastically. "What would get us kicked off?"

"Sneaking in something that wasn't yet invented. Speaking like a modern girl instead of one from 1861..."

Rebecca Lynn said, "I can talk like a girl from back then." She stood up. "Papa, there are turkeys over yonder!" She giggled and sat back down.

"Wonderful," Novak said, grinning like a dipwad. "Each family will arrive at different times to establish the town. Your family will be the last to arrive. Some are already there. Like the mercantile owners, for instance, who set up weeks ago."

I was relieved we didn't own a mercantile.

Novak said, "And each family will have their own MO."

"MO?" I asked.

"*Modus operandi.* It's Latin. Basically, it means, where you came from, why you moved there, and so on. Your backstory."

Ricardo added, "But all the backstories are different."

"Right," Novak said. "That way the show has layers. You'll find out yours the day your venture begins. Until then, we recommend doing some research. Might help you acclimate more easily. At the end of your stay, our team of historians will be reviewing all of the videos, evaluating the condition of your homesteads, as well the general condition of each family member. They'll be looking at things like animal health, cleanliness, food supply, money left…"

"So, back to the rules for a second," I interrupted, my wheels turning. "What else would get us kicked out?"

Dad shot me his rarely seen, super nasty face, the one where his lips pull tight together and disappear.

Novak said, "Physically hurting townspeople or their animals—"

"That would never happen," Dad said.

"Stealing from your neighbors—"

What could anyone possibly own in 1861 worth stealing? A pair of bloomers? A coonskin cap?

Novak added, "Or deliberately sabotaging the venture."

Dad said, "You can be assured none of those things will happen. Right girls?"

"Right," Rebecca Lynn said.

I gave a noncommittal bounce of my head.

"Good," Novak said as he opened a folder. "We take contracts very seriously in the television industry. Now that everyone is on board, let's get your father's signature."

Dad took the pen and grinned as he scrolled his name on the line.

First Libby cut my hair to my shoulders to get rid of the split ends, and then she dyed it back to mousy brown to cover the pink stripes, per Novak's request. Afterward, we drank Dairy Queen milkshakes spiked with dark rum, and Libby made a toast to me, clicking her plastic cup against mine.

"Here's to my best friend. I hope she doesn't get hoof and mouth disease or come back with a belly full of baby."

We got one of her brothers, Tripp, to drive us to the new 3D movie that was so stupidly funny, especially when you're tipsy. He kissed me on the lips when he dropped me off at my house later that night, and even though he is a year younger and I'd never once thought of him as cute, the rum sort of made him look okay. I didn't let him stick his tongue in my mouth, but I did kiss him back. The way I saw it, it was going to be my last kiss for a very long time, and I would take what I could get.

My dad asked me to call Florida and tell my mom's parents about the show. After Mom passed away, Dad didn't talk to them much. I think that's because Grandma sounded just like her.

"Your mother would be proud of you girls," Grandma told me over the phone. "She would have jumped at the opportunity to do something like this. When will the show be aired?"

"Just after Christmas," I told Grandma, my stomach rolling in a tidal wave toward my throat. I couldn't think about being aired on television without feeling sick.

My dad's parents, who lived out in Banner Elk, said they'd take care of our house while we were gone. They were retired and could use some time away from the mountains. Grandma Jen thought Dad had lost his mind, but Grandpa Paul said, "I knew my son was more than just a left-brained engineer."

CHAPTER SEVEN

We were driving out to a farm in the middle of nowhere where we would spend one night. The next day, we'd be taken to our new homestead. I glanced at Rebecca Lynn in the back seat, her favorite stuffed dolphin on her lap. I cranked up my iPod and watched the unfamiliar countryside zip by as my dad followed the directions to a town a few hours away, out in the Piedmont area, where the flat land turns hilly and pigs turn into sheep. As we parked the SUV in the clay and gravel driveway, we were met by a tall thin woman who looked like a man, except for her flowered shirt. Behind her stood a cameraman, not Carl with the goatee, but another guy, this one with a big belly who looked like he'd be more comfortable at a Star Trek convention than out in the sticks with a camera on his shoulder.

"I'm Martha." The tall woman shook my dad's hand as a pair of excited dogs came and sniffed our shoes. "This is Rusty, one of the camera people who will be part of your venture."

He mumbled a hello. I noticed a ketchup stain on his T-shirt.

After the introductions were made, Dad followed Martha's

husband, a man she called Bug, toward a barn. Rebecca Lynn and I followed Martha through a back door and into an ugly old-fashioned kitchen. Martha poured us each a glass of sweet tea as we sat at the scratched wooden table.

"Let's get to it," she said, sitting across from us. "First, Brooke, the average 1800's woman, especially a pioneer, did not wear makeup. Or earrings. And certainly not *that* thing." She pointed to her own eyebrow for emphasis.

The cameraman zoomed in on my face. I deliberately fluttered my lashes for the camera. Then I said to Martha, "It's only a little eyeliner." And liquid base, powder, mascara, eyebrow pencil, and blush. It was how I rolled. I could have passed as a ten-year-old boy without makeup.

Martha said, in a stern voice, "It won't matter what you look like. Plenty of farm women didn't even own a mirror. Now, then. I will be going over some important details about the show."

The word *show* conjured up images of a circus family. With the camera following me like a giant eye, I felt like I was smack dab in the middle of the ring: *Step right up and get a good gander at the pissed-off teenager. Watch with awe as she deliberately sabotages the show…uh…venture…so she can go back home and party with her bestie, buy a dress for the prom, and a new skimpy bikini for those glorious summer days of surf and sun at Atlantic Beach!*

"The contract is very specific," Martha said. "No electricity. No indoor plumbing."

"What about toilet paper?" Rebecca Lynn asked.

"Toilet paper was invented in the 1850s. That's the good

news. The bad news is it didn't become a hit until the 1870s."

"How will we live without TP?" I asked.

"Everyone's gonna have to deal with difficulties, but it's gonna be especially hard for you two. Y'all are going into this venture with a single father. So you girls will have to do the work your mama would have done. You'll churn butter. Collect firewood. Keep a clean house. Tend to the animals. You'll pickle and jar goods, cook in a fireplace, and so on. Won't be nothing you'll do that wasn't done back in 1861. Any questions so far?"

I said to Martha, out of the side of my mouth as if the microphone wouldn't be able to pick up my voice, "What about, you know, that time of the month and all?"

"I'm glad you asked. Rebecca Lynn, if you could step onto the porch for a moment, so I can talk to your sister in private."

She had asked my sister to leave, but it was okay for the cameraman to stay.

As soon as Rebecca Lynn stepped outside, Martha grabbed a bag sitting on the kitchen counter. She sat beside me, stuck her hand in the bag, and handed me a crude imitation of a sanitary napkin.

"Thanks anyway," I said, putting it on the table. "But I use..." I lowered my voice. "Tampons."

"Not in 1861 you didn't," she said, sliding the pad back to me. "For various health reasons, pads were the better choice."

"So, what am I supposed to do with this? There's no sticky side."

"You safety pin it to this belt." She handed me a cloth contraption with a couple of pins. "You're very lucky. The safety pin had just been invented."

"You've got to be kidding me."

"You take the pad and pin it like this," Martha demonstrated. "Then you put the belt around your waist."

"That's disgusting."

"Go into the bathroom and try it. You'll want to know how to do it ahead of time."

In the bathroom, after pricking my fingers and swearing under my breath like a sailor, I managed to get the belt tied around my waist and pin the pad to the belt. I felt like I was wearing a diaper.

"This is awful!" I cried through the closed door.

Martha responded, "You won't even know you're wearing it after a day or two."

My periods lasted six days. With four months ahead of me, I'd have to deal with this mess at least twenty-four days.

I removed the archaic pad and stepped back into the kitchen. "If I'm going to be stuck wearing these, I'll need at least twenty-four. But forty would be a safer bet."

"You'll be supplied with two."

"Two!"

"You'll have to wash them."

I stood there with the pad and belt dangling from my hands, my throat closing around the awful words I wasn't allowed to say.

"All settled then?" Martha said, ignoring the panic eating up my face. She called my sister in from the porch. "Let's get y'all into your proper clothing. In a little while you'll be molded into the perfect imitation of a mid-nineteenth-century family."

CHAPTER EIGHT

My sister and I followed Martha into the guestroom. Two large boxes sat in the middle of the floor with each of our names in black letters across the side.

"Who wants to go first?" Martha said.

"I do!" Rebecca Lynn shouted.

My sister opened the flaps and dug through the box. "A dress!" She held the brown flowered dress up to herself and fanned it out like she was ready to strut along a catwalk. The dress had long sleeves and a rounded neckline, perfect for choking a person. She plunged her hands into the box again. "A slip! And an apron! And a bonnet! Look, Brooke!" She dropped the clothes to the floor and put on the pale green bonnet. It was made for a horse and covered the back of her neck as well as her head. Her face was hidden somewhere inside, but I could barely see it. She stooped down and pulled out a pair of black low-heeled boots and a pair of black wool socks.

"Your turn," Martha told me.

"I was hoping to keep the suspense going."

She did not respond to my sarcasm as I opened each of the four cardboard flaps on my special box.

I pulled out a long flowered dress. "It's gray." Who would go out in public in such a dreary color? Even with the flowered pattern the thing looked like a rain cloud. Next, I pulled out a short-sleeved cotton slip, a yellow bonnet (ugh, yellow!), and a white apron. My hand dug back inside and landed on something hard. I pulled it out of the box.

"Your corset," Martha said.

I had pictured myself wearing one someday, like to seduce my husband on our wedding night, or dress up as a sexy cat on Halloween. I ran my hand along the white material, feeling the stiff vertical supports beneath and the thin ribbon looped in and out of rows of tiny holes. I held up the corset and placed it against my front.

"I think it's too small."

"It's supposed to be snug," Martha said.

I dropped the corset onto the floor next to the other things, and pulled a pair of black leather boots and wool socks out of the box.

"That's it," I said.

Rebecca Lynn said, "What about toys?"

"I hate to break it to you, sunshine," Martha said. "Farm kids back then didn't have too many toys. Maybe a dolly made of fabric scraps, or a chunk of wood carved into a figurine. Some kids had clay marbles. Won't be too much time for playing, anyhow."

"What about Snappy?" Rebecca Lynn asked.

"That's her stuffed dolphin," I said. "She won it at the State Fair."

"Anything modern is gonna have to stay behind," Martha said. "Your things will be safe until y'all get back in September."

Rebecca Lynn's lip trembled and I placed my hand on her back. That day at the fair had been an awesome day. One of the last family trips before Mom found out how sick she was.

"Why don't you help yourself to Wanda?" Martha pointed to an ugly zombie-like doll leaning against a pillow on the bed.

Rebecca Lynn stared at the doll but didn't answer.

"We'll have an early supper meal," Martha said, "and an early bedtime. In the morning, we'll wake at sunrise. You'll be helping us around the farm before you head on to your new home."

Morning came fast. Rebecca Lynn and I were told to put on our regular clothes for now and were given large aprons. After a hardy breakfast that felt more like death row's last meal, Dad went with Bug out to a field. Martha handed me a metal pail. My sister and I followed her out to the barn where a large black and white Holstein, her udder nearly touching the ground, waited to be milked. She stood in a stall, munching on dried grass.

Martha pulled a low stool to the cow. Up close, it looked like Nature had taken a Sharpie and drawn black clouds on her udder. "First thing you gotta do is relax her, like this, with your hands stroking to let the milk down. Do not yank hard. The milk will come real easy if you don't stress her out. Open both your hands and put your fingers together, thumb in front of the teat, four fingers behind it. Clamp it off with your fingers so her milk can't go back up. Whatever you do, *do not pull.* You *squeeze.* Like this. The milk will start out slowly, then get faster as she loosens up. Be sure to alternate between teats. Okay. Now it's your turn."

She stood up and plunked me down on the stool. She guided my hands. The teats felt rough and soft at the same time, and very warm. In no time, milk was squirting into the pail. The cow turned and shot me a dirty look.

I pulled my hands away. "Am I hurting her?"

"She's just curious about who you are," Martha said. "It would hurt her a lot more if you didn't milk her at all."

"I want to try," my sister said, nudging me off the stool.

"How often do we milk?" I asked.

"Twice a day, about thirty minutes each milking, depending on your cow. You might get as much as seven gallons at a time, so you'll want to split the milking into two buckets."

After we finished milking the cow, Martha showed us how to collect eggs from the chicken coop. Rebecca Lynn collected three and I collected two. They were wet and gross, and I couldn't wait to wash my hands.

When the eggs were cleaned and dried, we were told to take a shower—the last one for a long time, I thought sadly as I stood under the water for twenty minutes. Afterward, I dried my hair and by rote put on my makeup.

When we were done, Martha came into the guestroom. "Brooke, please follow me."

I followed her back into the steamy bathroom. She handed me a square jar and a stiff washcloth.

"You may not redress until your face is clean. And take out that hoop."

She left me standing at the sink. After a few deep breaths, I pulled the hoop from my brow and tucked it in the front pocket of my jeans. I wiped my face with the remover until there was no trace of makeup left. I was horrified by the girl glaring back at me. Even the mirror seemed to gasp in fear.

She can wash her own damn washcloth, I thought as I dropped the stained rag into the sink.

"Brooke will get dressed first," Martha told Rebecca Lynn when I stepped back into the bedroom. Our clothes were spread out in two separate piles on the double bed and our ugly black boots sat on the floor. Rebecca Lynn sat on corner chair.

"After you put on your socks," Martha explained to me, "you'll need to put on your underpinnings. This includes your chemise and corset. After that, your dress and apron."

"How will I go to the bathroom?" I asked.

"In an outhouse."

"I mean, *how*? With all these clothes?"

"Pull them up and around your waist. Believe me, you'll be careful once you start doing laundry."

I took off my jeans and top. I pulled up the ugly black socks and stood there in my underwear.

"Turn your back to me and take off your bra," Martha said.

Reluctantly, I did as she asked.

"Now hold up your arms."

The slip came down over my head, my arms passing through the short sleeves. It hung down just below my knees.

"How come I don't have petticoats?" I asked.

"Too cumbersome and way too hot. The hoop skirt became the replacement."

"Why don't I have one of those?"

"Hoop skirts were for women who pretended to faint while their servants did all the work."

I pictured the beautiful ball gowns from *Gone with the Wind* or *Great Expectations.* Even though it would be ten times harder to move around while wearing something fancy, I felt cheated.

Martha told me to take off my modern-day underpants.

"What will I wear instead?" I asked.

"You'll be *alfresco*."

"What does that mean?"

"No undies."

"Are you serious?"

"You want one more thing to worry about when you take a trip to the outhouse?"

"What about, you know, when I get my monthly?"

"That's what the belt is for. To hold the pad in place."

Again, Martha turned her back. I instructed my sister to close her eyes. I pulled my panties out from under my slip and shoved them into the paper bag along with my other modern clothes. I silently bid my underwear goodbye, biting down on my lip to keep from crying. By the time this venture was over, my bottom lip would be chewed away.

Next, Martha fitted my corset around me, the loose ribbons dangling in front.

"Can I look yet?" my sister asked.

"I don't care."

"That's pretty," Rebecca Lynn said when she opened her eyes. "Where's my corset?"

Martha said, "Not until you turn fifteen."

"Be thankful you're too young," I told my sister.

Martha helped me situate the corset. "Let some air out."

As I emptied my lungs, she pulled the ribbons into a small tight bow above my heart.

"I can hardly breathe."

"You'll get used to it. Millions of women did."

Once I had the corset in place, I turned this way and that in the floor-length mirror. I didn't look sexy at all. The corset was on the outside of my slip. I looked like a three-year-old who had dressed herself for the first time.

Next, it was boot time. I sat on the edge of the bed.

"This is how you lace them up," Martha said, guiding the black laces through the holes, looping them around the hooks, and tying them in a knot.

I stood up. The tightly laced boots, which gripped my legs a few inches above my ankles, were as uncomfortable as the corset.

"Put on your dress and apron before helping your sister get settled," Martha said. "I'll be right back."

She left the room.

I put on my dress which buttoned up the front, and then I tied my apron in the back. I helped my sister get into her things.

"You still happy about being a movie star?" I asked as she sat on the edge of the bed. She didn't answer. I laced up her shoes, pulling them tightly like Martha had shown me.

"Ouch! You're hurting me."

"Then stop fidgeting."

Martha came back into the room. With a comb, she showed us how to part our hair in the middle and pull the sides into weird doughnuts above our ears. We clipped them back with metal hair pins. We both looked like Princess Leia from *Star*

Wars. If they let us keep these costumes after the venture was over, and I decided not to burn them, maybe I would wear mine to a Halloween party.

Halloween made me think of pumpkins. And pumpkins made me think of fall. And fall made me think of summer. And suddenly I was crying.

"If you don't want to do this," Martha said, placing the yellow bonnet on my head and tying it in a bow to the right of my chin, "then why are you?"

Rebecca Lynn spoke for me. "Daddy wants her to learn things."

"Well," Martha said, wiping one of my wet cheeks with her thumb. "Brooke isn't the only one who's going to learn things."

"What'll we do for fun?" my sister asked.

"You might play games in the evening after dinner, or in the morning before chores."

"We can play on Sundays," Rebecca Lynn said.

"Sundays where you're going are for church and socials."

"Sundays back home are for sleeping in," I said through a stuffy nose.

Martha handed me a white handkerchief and I dried my eyes. When I tried to give it back, she said, "Tuck it up your sleeve in case you need it again."

With our bonnets tied correctly, and uncomfortably, I will add, Rebecca Lynn and I stood side by side in front of the mirror. She squealed and clapped her hands. But I was silent. The yellow bonnet threw a shadow across the top half of my face and gave my eyes dark circles underneath. Pimples on my chin that had been carefully hidden by Maybelline were now visible. And the light freckles I had camouflaged for the last two years were suddenly right there for the whole world to see. I turned away from my ghastly reflection, sickened by the ugly girl in the mirror.

No wonder 1800's women didn't own mirrors, I thought.

In the living room, we waited for Dad. When he stepped into the room, everyone, even Martha, laughed.

My dad had turned into an overgrown Tom Sawyer. He wore a white collarless long-sleeved shirt, a pair of high-waisted brown wool pants tucked into tall leather boots, brown suspenders holding up his pants, and a brown hat with a round top and a wide brim. All he needed was a piece of straw hanging from his lip.

"You're totally going to miss your Dockers," I told him, shaking my head.

"Look, Daddy," Rebecca Lynn said. "I'm Laura Ingalls."

She spun around once, then looked down at her footwear. "My new shoes hurt," she said in her baby voice, pouting.

"Maybe she has them on the wrong feet," I suggested.

"These shoes aren't made for left or right," Martha said. "You can wear them on either foot."

"You'll get used to them, honey," Dad told her.

Martha said, "Please, everyone, sit down."

As we sat on the sofa, she went to a desk in the corner. She picked up a piece of yellowed paper with a circle of red wax sealing it shut, and handed it to my dad.

"What's this?" he asked.

Bug said, "Your new life."

Dad held up the letter. "Check out this beautiful handwriting."

I stared at the tall thin loops, the fancy waves, and hooks between letters.

He read:

"'Dear Decker Family: Welcome to your 1861 venture. The period-style clothes you are wearing have been hand sewn. Take care of your clothes, as each of you will start out with only one set. You will also be given a one-month supply of canned goods, preserves, and—'"

"One month?" I asked. "That's not enough food."

"We're not going to have enough food?" Rebecca Lynn asked.

"Of course we will," Dad said. "The producers would never let us starve. This is a venture."

"Or a scientific experiment," I said, fighting hard not to make a rat's face and suck on my teeth like a rodent, just to prove my point.

"A *venture*," Dad said again, holding up the letter. He continued:

"'Your family's background is as follows: You are relocating from New Bern to a town in the backcountry called Sweet Sugar Gap. Yellow Fever has been spreading rapidly through your port town, and your father feels this is a safer place to raise a family. You have thirty dollars left after the purchase of your new homestead.'"

"*Thirty dollars?*" I asked.

Bug said, "Money back then didn't spend the same as today."

"'This allotment will be spent judiciously. Your homestead sits on nearly one hundred acres of land, most of it forest, three acres fertile, which you may cultivate any way you wish. Your family will receive upon entering the township a solidly built house, complete with outbuildings and a nearby creek.

"'This era takes place at the start of the Civil War. You may see or hear things pertaining to this time in history, and are asked to respond accordingly. Under no circumstance is any member of the Decker Family allowed to break character or bring contraband into Sweet Sugar Gap. This includes, but is not limited to, all tech gadgets, check books, credit cards, modern currency, modern clothing, jewelry, weapons, soaps, toothpaste, toothbrushes, shampoos, lotions, cosmetics, or anything found in the modern world not invented yet, or was not a common item found in the mid-1800's backcountry. The truer you are to the era, the better this venture will be for everyone involved. We want our audience to experience the wonders of the mid-nineteenth century right along with you, and we want your time to be one of discovery, education, and excitement.

"'We wish your family safe travels as you journey back in time. Sincerely, The Producers and Staff of *Upside Down in a Laura Ingalls Town.*'"

Dad placed the letter on the table. "We'll do exactly as our ancestors did, and exactly as the producers want."

"I don't have a clue what they want," I mumbled.

"I don't like my shoes," Rebecca Lynn said. "And my socks itch."

"I can barely see with this yellow sack on my head," I added.

"Enough complaining," Dad said. "Martha, Bug, thank you for everything. We owe a lot to you for helping us get ready for our new life."

But I knew something that Bug, Martha, Dad, and Rebecca Lynn obviously did not know: No matter how much training I got, no matter how much they forced me into looking the part, I would *never* be ready.

CHAPTER NINE

At nine o'clock that morning, a car horn beeped outside. Rusty and his camera followed us as we stepped onto Martha's porch. In an instant, thoughts of my diminished peripheral vision, overly tight shoes, and lack of underwear disappeared. In the gravel driveway sat a large black SUV with dark tinted windows, straight out of *MIB* or *Mission Impossible.* But it wasn't the SUV that made me anxious. It was the horse and wagon parked behind it.

Burt Novak the producer and Carl the skinny cameraman with the goatee stood in front of the SUV. I nearly laughed at Novak's tailored suit and thousand-dollar tie as he stood only inches from cow dung in his Italian leather shoes.

At the helm of the honey-colored wagon sat a man wearing a cowboy hat and boots. Rusty stepped off the porch and walked over to Carl. They shook hands like old college buds and stood by the wagon discussing the best camera angles and other tech junk.

Cowboy jumped down from the wagon and followed Novak

to where the three of us stood by the porch.

"Amazing," Novak said, as his eyes moved from bonnets to shoes to suspenders. He introduced us to the cowboy. "This is Pete Lowry, one of the show's consultants."

Cowboy Pete shook Dad's hand. "You all look just like a mid-1800's family."

"But we aren't," I said loudly. "Not *really*."

Novak said, "But you will pretend to be."

"But still, we won't be."

Novak lost his grin and took a step toward me, barely missing the cow patty. He said, "The second you get to Sweet Sugar Gap you will no longer be a girl of today. Everything you do, everything you eat, everything you say will be monitored."

His grin came back just as quickly, like we'd just won a trip to Cancun, complete with umbrellas in our drinks. "This is where your venture begins. Carl and Rusty will be with you from six a.m. to at least eight p.m. every day. There will be other camera people stationed throughout the town, but these two you will get to know best." He rubbed his hands together like it was the coolest thing in the world to be stalked by paparazzi fourteen hours a day.

"Why don't y'all follow me to the wagon?" Cowboy Pete said.

"Where's the cover?" I asked as we walked down the gravelly driveway. I remembered pictures from our history books of the famous covered wagons used during the Westward Expansion, back when pioneers thought it would be romantic to move to a place as foreign as Hogsmeade Village.

"Since you'll only be traveling short distances, you'll be using a smaller uncovered wagon. This is known as a farm ranch wagon."

The two-wheeled open cart had a high seat up front just behind the stocky white horse. The seat, I noticed, was short in length. I wondered if Dad and Rebecca Lynn and I could all fit on that bench at the same time. I moved my hand along the side of the wagon. The wooden wheels were taller than me. I pictured Rebecca Lynn accidentally getting her skirt caught under one of those wheels, and I moved to stand beside her. Dad inspected the packages piled in the back, almost to the brim. When he was through, he walked to the front of the wagon and rubbed his hand along the horse's neck. She snorted and shook her head up and down.

"What's her name?" Dad asked.

"Willow," Pete said. "A strong mare. She knows me better than anyone, so I will be coming along for the ride to teach you the ins and outs of buckboard riding. Want to make sure you can handle her."

"Where will we sit?" Rebecca Lynn asked, staring at the seat built for two.

"You won't be sitting," Pete said. "You'll be walking."

"*Walking*?"

I could feel Carl's camera zooming in on my poor sister's face. Rebecca Lynn reached for my hand, and I let her.

Cowboy Pete said, "Should only take a few hours. Lots of families took weeks, even months, to hike all the way to their new homes."

Dad climbed onto the wagon and took a spot on the seat, which bounced up and down under his weight. "This is awesome," he said, peering out from underneath his wide hat.

Bug and Martha dug through the back of the cart, examining

the jars and bags and boxes. Martha took my sanitary pads and belt wrapped in a piece of clean linen and put them into a wooden box. She opened up a tin box with "Wilmington Black Tea" printed on the side, took a deep whiff, and shut the lid. Then Bug held up a small box. Across the top were the letters "AAA."

"I don't think these batteries are supposed to be here."

Novak grabbed the box and tossed it into the SUV.

While Bug and Martha continued to go through our provisions, Rebecca Lynn said, "I need to use the bathroom before we go."

I followed her into the house for one last visit to the porcelain god. I let her go first. She spoke to me from the other side of the closed door while she tinkled.

"Do you think Daddy will let me ride in the wagon if I get tired?"

"Maybe..."

"What if I get blisters? What if they pop?"

"I don't know..."

I wasn't really paying attention. I was busy digging out my contraband from the bottom of my paper bag. I stuck my iPod deep in my apron pocket. Next, I dug my eyebrow ring from my jeans pocket and dropped it next to the iPod. I dove back into the bag and pulled out a select group of makeup containers. As soon as Rebecca Lynn came out of the bathroom, I headed in. I locked the door behind me, went to the vanity, and laid the containers in the sink. If I was going to have a camera zooming in on my face, I needed to give the audience a reason to tune in. First, I put tiny dabs of liquid base on my pimples. Next, I took the black eyeliner and outlined my eyes. I was already feeling normal. I ran the mascara brush over my lashes. After a little blush, I touched the hole where my eyebrow hoop used to be, and frowned. Wearing the hoop ring would be overkill, so I left it buried in my pocket. Next, I unbuttoned my dress at the top, pulled the sleeves down around my shoulders—shoulders that would miss an entire summer of sunbathing—and tucked the tiny makeup tubes and containers into the narrow spaces of my corset. Totally uncomfortable, but well worth the suffering.

When I came out of the bathroom, I stopped one last time in front of the full-length mirror. I could see Rebecca Lynn behind me, sitting on the rocking chair, hugging her stuffed dolphin. As I retied my bonnet, I heard her sniffle.

"What's wrong?" I asked, eyeing my reflection.

I knew what was wrong. She was starting to understand what I'd known all along: Dressing up like Laura Ingalls is only fun when you're going to a Halloween party or singing in a western musical.

"Tell Daddy I changed my mind," she said.

"He signed a contract."

"I don't care. Go tell him we don't want to do it." She put Snappy up against her face.

As much as Rebecca Lynn got on my nerves, I did not like to see her cry.

"Just pretend we're playing dress up," I told her, turning away from the mirror. "You like dress up."

She lowered Snappy to her lap. "What if my feet get sore?"

"I'll tell Dad to let you sit in the wagon."

"You will?"

I nodded.

"Okay," she said, drying her eyes.

"Drop Snappy in here," I told her, feeling like Harriet the Hypocrite, holding out the brown bag like one of the show's producers. "Take Martha's doll instead."

Rebecca Lynn looked at the doll sitting against the bed pillow. The eyes were made of brown stitched X's, and the mouth was a black button. The only way you could tell it was a girl was by the dress and bonnet.

"She's ugly," Rebecca Lynn said.

She looks just like us.

"Take it anyway. It might be the only toy you have for the next four months."

My sister dropped the stuffed dolphin into the bag headfirst, and I folded the edge before placing it on the floor by the bed. Then she grabbed the doll by the yellow yarn-hair sticking out from the bonnet and left the room. I followed.

Martha stood in the kitchen as I passed through.

"These are for your lunch," she said, handing me two burlap sacks. "One is fried chicken. The other is filled with peaches and sweet breads for—"

She took my chin in her hand. I felt like I'd just been caught smoking weed on the high school catwalk.

"Might take you a while to understand, child, but that stuff on your face won't be nearly as important as you think."

I pulled away from her and hurried through the door.

A short man wearing a baggy black suit and bowtie was standing near the wagon. On a nearby table sat a large suitcase. Next to the suitcase sat a wooden box. When he opened up the box, it turned into an accordion with a brass and glass lens in the middle.

"Photo time," Novak said. "It may take a little while to get a good picture, but you'll get to see it before you leave."

For nearly twenty minutes we stood as still as possums in front of the wagon as the man fiddled with the freaky camera. The sun caused me to squint even with the bonnet, sweat poured down the back of my legs, and my corset rubbed my ribs until I started to feel like a piece of tenderized pork.

The photo was grayish brown like it had been taken a hundred years ago. I was impressed with how perfectly the talented photographer captured my scowl.

After the photo session, Rebecca Lynn and I waited as Pete showed Dad how to handle the reins. Soon we were on our way, waving goodbye to Martha and Bug in their faded jeans and Mr. Big Time Producer in his overly pressed suit as they watched us head down the gravel driveway. Rebecca Lynn and I trudged behind the wagon as it started out along the dirt trail leading to the green hills beyond, and the mystery town known as Sweet Sugar Gap.

It wasn't until twenty minutes into the trek, tall trees sprawled out on either side of the road and Martha's farm like a speck of dust behind us, that I realized I had forgotten to use the toilet one last time.

I sighed.

At least my face looks good for the camera, I thought as I held in my pee.

CHAPTER TEN

We hiked alongside the slower-than-molasses wagon for what felt like days. My calf muscles contracted with every step, and my heels felt bruised. The mid-May humidity seemed heavier than usual, especially with the layered clothing. I kept swatting at bugs that dipped inside the shade of my bonnet like it was a hole in a tree. Rebecca Lynn swatted the air in front of her face, too.

We weren't the only ones walking. Carl and Rusty walked along with us, only they had to carry their cameras.

"Why didn't you ride in a car?" I asked Carl.

"We get better shots this way. More personal."

"We're not supposed to talk to the participants," Rusty told Carl.

"Sorry, Brooke," Carl said. "Pretend we aren't here."

"For four months?"

Carl didn't answer.

"What do you think our house will look like?" Rebecca Lynn asked me.

"I don't know."

"Do you think we'll make some friends?"

I shrugged.

"You might meet someone like Libby."

"Doubt it."

She held the front of her dress in a bunch as she hopped over the ruts.

"My feet hurt, Brooke."

"Mine do too." I had already tripped a few times, much to the pleasure of our cameramen. Out of spite, I decided not to fall anymore.

"Tell Daddy to let us sit in the wagon," Rebecca Lynn said.

"We've only been walking a little while."

"You promised to tell him when I got tired."

I hiked my skirts up to my knees and jogged up to the front.

"Dad!" I called.

Pete helped Dad stop the horse.

"Something the matter?" Dad asked.

"Rebecca Lynn's tired. She wants to know if she can climb up there with you."

Pete said, "Not while I help your father handle the horse for the first time."

"Can she sit in the back?"

Pete took off his hat and repositioned it on his head. "Up to you, Mr. Decker."

Dad jumped to the ground, moved some of the packages around in the back, and helped Rebecca Lynn into the wagon. She squeezed in between the bags and boxes like a seventy-pound sack of potatoes.

"Sorry there's not more room, Brooke," Dad said as he climbed back onto the front seat.

"How much farther?"

"Four miles," Pete said. "But we'll be stopping in a little while next to a creek. We can have lunch there."

The fact that I didn't faint was a tent-revival miracle. I didn't have my vitamin water or my Gatorade, and I had to pee so badly I thought my head would explode. Just when I was contemplating throwing myself in front of the wagon, we came to a place where ancient tree branches hung over the road in wide arches.

"Creek's up here," Pete said as he helped Dad steer the wagon to the side of the road. The sound of the babbling brook made my bladder cringe.

"I have to pee," I told Dad, running into the thick trees.

I ran until I could no longer see the horse, yanked up my dress, and stood with my feet wide apart. Within seconds I was filled with the kind of relief that only peeing can give a person.

As I squatted, I gazed up into the trees. A small stream of light made its way through a tiny crack in the canopy and fell across my face. When my bladder was finally empty, I didn't move. I realized I had nothing to wipe myself with. In a panic, I checked out my surroundings. Leaves were all around me, but I didn't know the difference between any of them. I knew the saying, "Leaves of three, let them be," but what if there were bugs on the safe leaves? Or microscopic things that were smaller than bugs? I nearly shouted for Rebecca Lynn but was afraid that Rusty or

Carl might think there was something out here worth filming.

Then I remembered what I had in my sleeve. I pulled out the handkerchief and thanked Martha under my breath. When I was through, I stepped away from the muddy puddle, gently folded the hanky, and tucked it in my apron pocket, where the iPod and my eyebrow ring still hid in the bottom.

Dad, Pete, and Rebecca Lynn were sitting on a large blanket near the stream. Carl was filming the picnic and Rusty stood by the wagon eating a power bar.

"Going to wash my hands," I said. I knelt down by the creek's edge and rinsed out my hanky in the cold water. Once it was washed, I brought it back to the wagon and hung it over the side to dry.

The chicken was wonderful. And so was the peach.

I was ready to relax, cool off my screaming feet in the stream, let my tired legs rest a while. But we had barely finished our lunch when Pete said, "Time to mosey. Gotta get you settled before bedtime."

"Bedtime?" I asked. I could tell by the sun's position it wasn't even noon yet.

"You'll be retiring when the sun goes down."

I laughed. "Why would we go to bed so early?"

"No lights."

"What about candles?" Dad asked.

"Sure, you got candles. And oil lamps. But you don't want to be using them up the second you all get to your homestead. You'll want to save 'em for a rainy day. Besides, you'll *want* to go to bed early. In 1861, everyone in the backcountry did."

We finished our lunch, buried our chicken bones in the dirt

like Pete showed us, and washed up in the creek. Within minutes, we resumed our trek, Dad and Pete handling the reins, Rebecca Lynn gripping that ugly doll in the back of the wagon, Rusty and Carl in their hiking boots trailing close behind, and me, growing more apprehensive with each step I took, kicking up dirt as I worked to keep up with the wagon.

CHAPTER ELEVEN

What amazed me most as we rounded the last bend were the white balls of fluff covering the hillside.

"Sheep!" Rebecca Lynn called out.

The breeze brought the bleating right to my ears.

"Your place is up here a quarter mile," Pete said. "It's a big homestead. You all can't miss it."

Like Super Mario, I shuffled back and forth behind the moving wagon so I could see what Pete was talking about. My stomach fluttered more than ever as I caught sight of the house on the hill in the distance, the sun shining over it like a spotlight. "Look at me, Brooke!" it seemed to shout. "I'm your new home!" And what a palace it was! The grand house was painted light blue—the same color as my bedspread back home—with black shutters and a silver tin roof. I counted two chimneys, but I was certain there were more on the other side I couldn't see. A wraparound porch swept across the front and sides like a petticoat, and a long dirt road led up to it through a grove of giant pecan trees. I looked at my dirty shoes and ugly dress. No way was I going to wear this old rag in a beautiful house like that. I wondered briefly if the sewing machine had been invented yet. Either way, it didn't matter. If I could sew a pillow by hand, I could stitch my way through a few dresses.

My thoughts were interrupted when Pete said, "There she is. In all her glory."

Dad slowed the horse down and parked the wagon in the shade of some broadleaved trees.

"Let's go up the driveway," I said. If someone had told me I'd be jumping with excitement at any given time on this venture, I would have called them whacko. But here I was, tingling from my bonnet to my pointy shoes.

I took the lead. If they wanted to sit on the dirt road all day, so be it. I, for one, was tired of walking. I was ready to stretch out on that wonderful plantation porch, put up my throbbing feet, and drink sweet tea with fresh lemon.

The sheep on the hill let out the occasional bleep as they chewed the grass. This didn't seem so bad. The sheep fed themselves. So I'd be collecting a few eggs, and making butter every once in a while. So what? Maybe I could learn to live without *NCIS* and Facebook after all. Maybe...

Dad and Pete jumped onto the road and stood next to each other on the other side of the wagon. Why weren't they over here with me? Why was I still alone on the driveway?

They weren't even looking in the right direction. They were looking in the opposite direction, as a matter of fact. I walked around the back of the wagon. My eyes tried to see what they were seeing, but all I could make out was a tilted cabin sitting on the left side of a wide clearing the size of a football field. A long log fence, the beams crisscrossed like the fences in the Gettysburg battlefields, divided the property from the road. Someone had tried to make the shack seem fancier than it was by adding a swinging gate with a trellis above. Wild roses grew up and over the trellis.

Unfortunately, this *Curb Appeal* addition only made the cabin look worse. A few other rickety buildings were scattered across the property, and a thick spooky forest hugged the back and sides in a semicircle. To the right of the shack, a collection of tree stumps covered the earth like round wooden seats, and next to one of them sat a large wood pile with an ax stuck in the middle of a log, like someone had been chopping moments before we arrived. I had just stepped into Middle-earth. I waited for a hobbit or an elf to come skipping out of the trees.

"Did you girls think it would be this perfect?" Dad asked.

What's perfect?

"Help me down, Brooke," Rebecca Lynn said.

I didn't take my eyes off the building—if you could call it a building—even as I helped my sister onto the ground.

"Dad," I said, laughing nervously. "That's not our house. Our house is up *there*. The one on the hill."

"No, darling," Pete said, shaking his head and smiling sadly.

Oh my God, he just gave me a pity smile!

Rusty shoved his camera in my face. With my hand I tried to shoo him away like the flies buzzing around my bonnet. Carl stood next to the road, filming the shack and the grounds.

"I don't understand—"

"*This* is your house," Pete said.

I didn't have anything against log cabins. I'd even stayed in a few while skiing in Aspen, or on family vacations in the Appalachians. But those cabins were huge, and perfectly built. They came with gorgeous wrought iron lights, awesome kitchens, manicured hedges, comfy porch furniture, and hot tubs.

This thing was made by a mentally challenged giant with oversized Lincoln logs. The front had a crooked door in its center, and one glassless window on the left had shutters that would probably turn to sawdust if you forced them closed. And something told me the nearest hot tub was a hundred miles from here. Not to mention a hundred years.

"My *bedroom* is bigger than that," I said, holding on to the edge of the wagon, not brave enough to step any closer.

No one responded.

"I'm claustrophobic." I placed a hand on my chest for emphasis. "I'll suffocate in there."

My imaginary plight was ignored.

"How far from town are we?" Dad asked.

Pete said, pointing with his thumb, "About five miles."

Five miles?

"Sweet Sugar Gap," Dad said like he was cooing over a newborn baby. "Our new home."

"Sweet Sugar *Crap*," I said under my breath.

Rebecca Lynn heard me and grabbed onto Dad's hand as the two of them followed Pete through the squealing gate.

In a daze I trailed behind them, and the cameramen behind me. My lip trembled and my throat grew tighter with each step through the dirt yard. I glanced up at the pretty house on the hill, then back to the shack. *Our* shack.

"Just look at those logs," Dad said in wonder. "They're hand-hewn."

"What's that mean?" Rebecca Lynn asked.

"The logs were shaped by hand, with the hard blows of an ax or chisel."

"How do you know?" I asked in a pissy voice.

"I did some research like the producer suggested."

"I looked up chickens, Daddy," Rebecca Lynn said. "Only hens lay eggs."

I hadn't bothered to do any research. What was the point? All the research in the world wouldn't have turned this dead gray shack into a pretty blue mansion.

"I'm glad you know about chickens," Pete told my sister. "We got y'all six laying hens."

"What about the other animals?" she asked.

"They'll be delivered in the morning." Pete nodded toward the roof. "Got some strong cypress shingles there, Tim."

"It even has a front porch," Dad said, like he'd just discovered a pot of gold and not a crooked porch that made me lean a little to the left like I'd smoked some bad weed.

"The chinking has been done for you, so you don't have to fill the cracks yourself," Pete said, leading us toward the back of the building. "Got a nice stone chimney as well."

The chimney leaned almost as badly as the porch, only in the opposite direction. I stared at the gray flat stones piled one on top of another. It wasn't nice at all. Actually, it sucked. The cabin was the complete opposite of the blue palace on the hill. It was as gray and foul as a rat and squatted there in the grass like it was taking a dump. I was suddenly caught in the middle of a Brothers

Grimm fairy tale, standing in front of the same house where the mean old witch bakes little children in an oven.

Then the sour smell came to me, swirling around my head and thrusting its way through me. When I was out cruising with my friends I didn't mind it so much, because it made me think of fresh vegetables and summer vacation. But with that rancid odor so close to what Pete was calling our house, I wanted to toss my cookies right there.

"Where are the chickens?" I asked, swallowing hard.

"Just over there," Pete said, nodding in the direction of the barn which sat only a few yards from the house. "So you won't have to go too far to collect your eggs."

I put a hand against my nose and tried to keep my lunchtime peach from climbing into my throat.

"I can't wait to see the inside," Dad said, as he and Pete headed up the tilted steps and onto the front porch. Rebecca Lynn skipped behind them. I didn't feel my feet move as my boots thumped against the rat-shack steps.

Pete opened the front door.

"Wow," Rebecca Lynn said, running into the cabin.

I followed the three of them inside, and Rusty followed behind me. Carl stayed out on the road.

The rectangular room was a dark cave, about sixteen feet wide by twenty feet deep. The low ceiling and walls were made of rough beams, extending from front to back.

"Pine and cypress," Pete said, as if telling us the names of trees would make the room look better.

In the room's center sat a long table with a bench and two chairs. Along the left wall hung long shelves lined with tin plates and cups, mixing bowls, lanterns, skillets, glass containers, and utensils straight out of a torture chamber. On the right was a low wood counter that ran half the length of the wall. Under the counter sat a large wooden bucket, and on top sat a pile of white linens, neatly folded. Above the counter was a second window matching the glassless one facing the front. A third window sat directly across the room from the counter.

I ruffled through the pile of linens. They felt coarse, like they were made of burlap.

Pete walked to the other end of the room. "Here's your fireplace, also known as your oven."

The fireplace took up most of the back wall and sat square in the center, with the stones climbing up to the ceiling. A rickety stool sat on either side. A long-barreled gun hung over the mantel. On top of the mantel lay a Bible.

"This is where you girls'll be spending a large part of your time," Pete informed us, "cooking your meals and boiling water."

"Boiling water?" I asked, staring at the fireplace's cold mouth.

"For cooking and doing laundry, mostly."

"Where's our bathtub?" I asked.

"Nature is your tub. Stream's thataway." He pointed his thumb in a direction behind the house.

While Pete showed my dad the details of the room, I spotted a wooden ladder in the corner to the right of the fireplace. Rebecca Lynn came over to where I stood with a foot on the bottom rung, peering up into the dark.

"What's up there?" she whispered.

"How should I know?"

I pulled my skirts into one hand and slowly climbed the ladder. I stuck my head through the rectangular hole at the top. The ceiling up there was the actual roofline, so the only place to stand without whacking my head was in the center of the small room. On the floor sat two boxes low to the ground, a single mattress shoved into one, and a full-size in the other. I was older and taller, so I chose the bigger one. Each bed was positioned under the low slanted eaves and covered with a checkered quilt and flat pillows. Thin streams of light seeped in through tiny fissures in the walls and spilled across the beds. A square hole used as a window sat just above the bed I chose for Rebecca Lynn.

My makeup was jabbing me under the corset. I pulled out the tiny containers and hid them in a dark corner where one of the beams met the roofline, then put the iPod next to it. I took the hoop ring and gently laid it beside the iPod. I readjusted my dress, pushed the bonnet from my head, and let it fall along the back of my neck. It was hot up in the attic. And beyond stuffy. And it smelled like squirrel pee.

"Well?" Rebecca Lynn asked from below.

"Well, what?"

"I want to come up."

"So? No one's stopping you."

"That the bedroom?" I heard Dad say from somewhere downstairs.

Won't be any secrets in this house, I thought.

"Yes," Pete told him.

Next thing I knew, the four of us were clustered in the tiny attic. Rebecca Lynn and I each sank down a few inches when we tried out the uncomfortable mattresses, and Dad and Pete stood hunched over like they had severe cases of scoliosis. Rusty stood on the top step, filming us.

Dad said, "Not too bad."

"Where are you going to sleep?" I asked Dad, for a moment feeling sorry he might have to sleep in one of the outbuildings, or on the floor downstairs.

Pete laughed. "Your dad will be sleeping up here. With you girls. You're sitting on his bed, Brooke."

"What? No way. We can't share a bedroom. Dad…"

Dad said, "This is how they did it back in the day."

Rebecca Lynn said, "It'll be like a slumber party."

I know there's really no comparison, but for a moment I was reminded of Anne Frank.

"You might want to put a piece of fabric or cheesecloth in your window there," Pete said. "Will keep down on the flies and other vermin."

"What other vermin?" I asked, horrified of what might creep into our room while we slept.

"Mice…bats…"

"Daddy," Rebecca Lynn whined.

"Don't worry, honey. I'll take care of it."

Dad's forehead was crinkled, and part of me was satisfied to see him worried. But another part of me didn't like that look at all. It was a look I'd seen twenty-four-seven when Mom was sick; a look that said he didn't have any control over the situation.

By the time we had climbed back down the ladder, I was sweating profusely. My antiperspirant had worn off, and I hadn't snuck any in. I was so worried about my face, I hadn't thought about the way I might smell.

Rebecca Lynn was doing a potty dance.

"Dad," I said, "I think she has to go."

"Not just number one," she whispered.

"I'll show you where the outhouse is," Pete said, leading us out a narrow back door next to the fireplace. He pointed to a wooden bucket beside the small back stoop. "Grab that bucket, Brooke. You'll be using it for all your laundry."

I picked up the bucket. It yanked on my back muscles, and it wasn't even filled with water yet.

The outhouse, which was about as elegant as our totally awesome house, stood twenty yards from the back door, hidden among some bushes and saplings. We would have to hike out here, rain or shine, day or night, just to use the toilet. Something ran through the brush a few feet away, and I jumped.

Pete opened the outhouse door, which had a cutout of a quarter-moon. "Brand new."

"They should have built a new house to go with it," I said.

Pete ignored my comment. "You can keep the smell under control by pouring in some lye. You're lucky to have some in your provisions. Lots of folks ended up making their own."

"Daddy," Rebecca Lynn said, staring into the hole. Rusty's camera followed her gaze. "What if something's down there?"

"Nothing's down there, sweetie. Just dirt."

"But I don't have any toilet paper." Tears welled up in her eyes.

Here we were, next to a creepy forest, discussing toilet paper and outhouses, with Rebecca Lynn too afraid to go. This was when it all became real to me. We were living in another time. We had a log cabin with a crooked chimney, we shared a bedroom, and we used a freaking outhouse. For four months this is how things would be, and the cameras would be filming it all. I wondered how many embarrassing scenes would end up on Youtube.

"Stay with your sister while she goes," Dad said.

"But Dad, she's got to do more than tinkle."

"Please, Brooke. Just until she gets used to it."

Pete said, "I'll go find you a rag."

"What'll I do with it when I'm done?" Rebecca Lynn asked, still staring into the hole.

"That's what the bucket's for," Pete said, walking back to the house.

Rebecca Lynn hopped from one foot to the other until Pete returned with a large square of white linen the size of a tablecloth.

"We'll tear this into three strips," Pete said, like it was an everyday thing, ripping up pretty fabric to use for wiping. He took out a knife and cut three equal strips out of the fabric. He pointed through the oaks and pines beyond the outhouse. "Follow the path to the stream when you're all done."

Pete and Dad went back to the wagon while I, along with Rusty's camera, helped Rebecca Lynn get over her fear of outhouses. I handed her a strip of fabric.

"Stand outside the door," she told me, drying her eyes.

I swatted flies and no-see-ums with the extra pieces of linen while I waited.

"You still there?" she asked after a moment, her voice panicked.

"Duh. Where else would I go?"

After a few minutes, she came out of the outhouse. The dirty rag sat on the floor. Rusty had the nerve to pan his camera over it.

"Hey!" I told my sister. "Don't be a pig."

She started sniveling again as she picked up the soiled rag.

I held out the bucket. "Drop it in." I scrunched up my nose. "You can wash it in the stream."

"But it's gross."

"Your poop-o is not my *problemo.*"

I carried the bucket by the handle and the three of us entered the forest of pines and cypress and oaks. We made our way down the path to the creek. The clear water moved quickly over the smooth rocks. I stooped down and filled the bucket. Within seconds my hands were red from the cold water.

"We don't have any soap," I said as I dried my hands on my apron.

Dad appeared on the path carrying a rectangular piece of wood with ridges of metal taking up two-thirds. "Found a washboard. You take your dirty things, dip them in water, and scrub them hard against the metal."

Even if Dad hadn't explained how to use a washboard, it was sort of a no-brainer.

"And here's some lye soap."

He handed me a chunk of what looked like brown cheese. It felt soft in my hand. I put it to my nose. It smelled like a wet dog. "Yuck."

"It's also harsh on your skin," he said. "Be sure to rinse your hands well afterward."

I didn't want my dad standing there while we washed, especially something this gross. It was embarrassing to have him watch us do such lowly work. Bad enough to have a camera taking it all in, but my dad…

"I think we can handle it, Dad."

After he headed back toward the house, I told my sister, "Let's keep a bucket of water and some soap next to the outhouse. We are each responsible for washing out our own rags, and we'll take turns dumping the dirty water down the hole. Dad included. I think that's fair, don't you?"

She nodded.

"Okay then. You ready to play *Little House*?"

She nodded slightly, took her dirty rag, and began to scrub.

"Good."

I was relieved my little sister didn't give me any grief about following orders. At least for the moment. But then, this was only the first hour of our effed-up life in the backcountry.

If my math skills were intact, and I was pretty sure they were, we had nearly 3,000 cotton-picking hours to go.

CHAPTER TWELVE

"Let's show Willow her new home," Pete said as he showed Dad how to release the horse from the unloaded wagon. Carl hung out near the edge of the property and panned the woods with his camera. Rusty stayed with us. He was starting to feel like a pet bear.

We walked Willow down a narrow path between blades of high grass to the large barn. Dad and Pete opened the double doors. The barn was filled with bales of hay, and a horse blanket hung over one of two stalls. The first thought that hit me: *This is twice the size of our cabin!*

"Keep your animals in here if the weather turns sour," Pete said, removing the bit from Willow's mouth and the saddle from her back. She nodded her head and moved freely around the small corral beside the barn. "Plenty of room inside and out for them to be comfortable."

We left the barn and walked around back where the smell from earlier got a whole lot worse. A horde of white and rust-colored hens came running out of a little house on stilts, down the ramp, and up to the chicken wire fence. Rebecca Lynn bent down and stuck her fingers through the hole. One of the chickens went for her bonnet, just missing her nose, while another pecked at her fingers.

"Ow!" She pulled her hand back. "He bit me!"

"*She*," I reminded her.

"Y'all have some chicken feed in your provisions," Pete said. "At nighttime, you'll want to get them hens into the coop, close the door, and take down the ramp. Keep 'em safe from predators."

He led Dad up the next hill while I negotiated with my sister.

"How about I do the laundry, and you feed the chickens? They can be your pets."

Rebecca Lynn patted one of the chickens on the head, and this time it cooed under her hand. "Okay."

We made our way up the small hill where Pete and Dad stood next to a tiny building.

"This here is your smokehouse," Pete said.

"We aren't allowed to smoke," Rebecca Lynn said.

Dope.

"This is where you'll keep your meat."

Dad stuck his head inside the doorway. "What meat?"

"Plenty of wildlife out here."

I laughed. "You're going to hunt?"

Back home he'd grab a napkin and give old daddy long-legs a flying carpet ride outside. I'd never seen my dad kill anything, except mosquitoes.

"I don't want you to shoot animals, Daddy," Rebecca Lynn said.

"Is there a place where I can buy meat?" Dad asked Pete.

"From the mercantile in town. But whether you buy it or get it on your own, you'll have to preserve it."

Next, we followed Pete back down the hill to a stone building growing out of the earth. The wooden door was made for trolls.

"Got a natural spring here in your springhouse," Pete said. "Water flows into a channel so you won't have to go all the way to the creek. This room will also keep your perishables fresh."

"Like a refrigerator," Dad said, peeking inside.

Except this refrigerator was made of mud and stone, sat fifty yards away from the kitchen, and was missing an automatic water dispenser.

"I feel like I'm visiting in the Last Homely House," I said.

But as soon as I stepped inside, the sweet hobbits disappeared. I was suddenly reminded of *The Ring*, the scariest movie in the universe, with the dead girl who climbed out of the well her mother had thrown her into. I took in a deep breath. The cave smelled like wet earth, the way I would imagine a tomb would smell. Maybe I'd take a hike down to the creek for my water instead.

"Where will our crops be planted?" Dad asked.

"Over here."

We followed Pete to the widest open space on the property. Rusty panned the empty field with his camera.

"Hasn't been used in the last fifty years or so," Pete said. "A lot of clay, but if you till enough you'll find some nice soil. It's gonna take some effort to plant and water." He turned to me. "Once they come up, you and your sister will help harvest."

"Hoo-ray."

Pete walked us back to the cabin. "The sun will be setting in a few hours. Need to get your house squared away before there's no outside light left. First thing to do is get the fire going in the kitchen. There's a tin of safety matches in with your goods. It'll be warm in the house, but keeping that fire lit is important." He looked me square in the eye. "You'll also need to decide what to make everyone for dinner."

As we followed Pete back into the house, I grew nervous again. I hadn't thought about dinner. We had cleaned Rebecca Lynn's rag (totally disgusting), hung our personal rags on twigs I shoved between the cracks in the outhouse (I should have snuck in toilet paper, smack-in-the-forehead duh), then stood with my sister as she fed the chickens and collected eggs (two small brown ones, whoopee). With all the time spent doing other things, dinner had never crossed my mind—especially the fact that I would be the one chosen as *Top Chef.*

In the kitchen, Pete helped to start a fire in the fireplace and then spent the next two hours helping us get organized.

I stared at the open shelves. "Why don't we have cabinet doors?"

"Less chance of mice getting into your food if you don't keep your goods in the dark."

The earlier thought of vermin crawling over my body while I slept was replaced by the more disgusting thought of tiny mouse brownies decorating our meals.

We went through our packages, organizing them on the shelves. The heaviest of the supplies were four large sacks we placed on the floor under the shelves: buckwheat flour, Irish potatoes, onions, and rice. A smaller bag was filled with walnuts.

There were tins filled with spices, like cinnamon and salt and pepper. A burlap sack held large chunks of dried ham. Jars were labeled "lard" or "molasses." A funny cone-shaped package had the word "sugar" on the side. I did a happy dance when I found a container labeled "Soda" until I realized it was the kind used for baking.

"Keep all your cooking things near the fireplace for easy access," Pete told me.

I wished he'd stop singling me out. Was I the only one in the room capable of boiling water?

Whenever we came across a foreign kitchen item, Pete either demonstrated how it worked, or told me to find a picture in a large book entitled *The Encyclopedia of the Home*. I looked up at least a dozen objects: a funny drilling machine called a cherry picker; a butter mold with a stamp; a laundry paddle; baskets for collecting eggs, berries, and vegetables. We now owned a collection of earthenware (called crocks) for preserving some of our food, with wax for sealing the crocks; a butter churn; a tea kettle; and a coffee pot (NOT the Mr. Coffee kind from Target!) It took Pete twenty minutes to show me how to brew coffee over the fire, and when it was done it tasted like clay.

There were a few cookbooks. All four of us went through them, trying to find the easiest meals to make with what we had in our possessions. Pete informed me I would be cooking for him *and* Carl *and* Rusty.

When I stared longingly in the direction of the kitchen knife for reasons other than cutting food, he added, "For a night or two. Then it'll just be for your family."

We continued scanning the cookbooks. All of the pictures

were hand drawn, and the type was barely readable in the dim firelight. I held a book close to the fire, which made me sweat. Most of the recipes sounded strange and gross, and almost all of them used lard. I pictured my thighs turning into sacks of grease by the end of the venture. For our first dinner, we all agreed on slices of ham, fried potatoes, and fried okra. I could handle the potatoes, but I'd never fried ham in a heavy skillet before, and I couldn't stand okra, even though it's pretty much a Southern law to love it.

God knows I was way too tired and way too hungry to argue.

"The most important job out here is chopping wood," Pete told my dad. "Without wood, you have no fire. No fire, no meals. Back before central heating, firewood had to get you through some long winters. You wouldn't want to be chopping down trees in the middle of a snowstorm."

My dad's arms were skinny and fleshy white and he'd never had calluses in his life. I couldn't imagine him chopping wood. I could barely see him swinging an ax.

Pete sent Rebecca Lynn and me to gather some logs, which we dragged to the back door and into the cabin. He grabbed a heavy black skillet from a wrought iron hook on the side of the fireplace and placed the hook on one of two iron rings built into the fireplace floor, a few inches above the ground. He got the fire going and pushed some burning embers under the ring until it looked like a campfire.

I stared at the flames. "I'm going to cook our meals in there? How will I know how to adjust the fire?"

"You'll understand it soon enough," Pete said, as he jabbed the flames with the poker. "Go fetch some water before it's too dark to see."

Go fetch? What was I? A dog?

I told Rebecca Lynn to come with me, but Pete shook his head. "It should never take two people to do a simple task like fetching water."

I grabbed the large bucket beside the back door, and just before I left I pictured myself hitting Cowboy Pete in the head with it.

The sun seemed to set earlier in the backcountry because of all the trees. Staring across the property from the back stoop, the springhouse rose up like a dragon with a square mouth. On one hand, that mildewed cave was a lot closer than the creek. On the other hand, that dead girl from *The Ring* might decide to pay me a visit.

I chose the creek, wishing for the first time that one of the cameramen had come along. But they were busy filming the Incredible Fireplace Episode in the cabin. I ran past the outhouse. By the time I found the creek, dusk was falling. I dipped the bucket into the cool water. As I heaved it back up the overgrown path, I wondered if another girl, one from long ago, had been expected to do this kind of work. Had she been happy living out here, hiking for water and living in a shack in the middle of nowhere with that pretty blue house snubbing her from up on the hill? Had she wished she'd lived in another time? Maybe in the future?

By the time I got the water to the cabin, slices of potato were sizzling in the pan. My mouth watered.

"I helped cut the potatoes," Rebecca Lynn said.

I put the bucket beside Pete.

"Never let your skirts near the fire," he warned Rebecca Lynn and me.

He poured a little water into a deep black pot hanging in the fireplace from an upside down L-shaped post.

"Keep this pot filled with water, Brooke, no matter how many times a day you have to get it." He nodded toward a smaller black pot on the floor. "That's your stew pot. You'll be eating a lot of stew. And soup. And cornbread."

"How will I bake cornbread without a real oven?"

"Before modern ovens, they had Dutch ovens." He pointed to another black iron pot sitting on the floor near the fireplace. This one was shallow, with three small feet and a silver handle. He removed the lid and put it back. It sounded heavy. "If you slow cook in this, you can make almost anything you like: bread, biscuits, cake…"

"Cake!" Rebecca Lynn said, staring at me like my cooking skills would be the thing to keep her happy.

But Mom had been the baker in our house. I couldn't compete with her in our kitchen back home, so I didn't get my hopes up using a Dutch oven.

"Tim," Pete said, "cut up some pieces of cured ham. Use that knife over there, and slice it thin. Gotta get 'em into the pan before the potatoes burn."

Dad scraped the pieces of ham from the cutting board into the hanging skillet. "I like all of us cooking together."

"Well, don't get used to it," Pete said. "Tonight's an exception. Your daughters—namely Brooke—will be the cooks in this household. You'll be dog tired by dinnertime. Preparing meals will be the last thing on your mind."

In the flickering light of the fireplace, I saw Dad frown.

Pete ordered, "Girls, set the table."

I was just about sick of Pete bossing us around. If those stupid cameras hadn't been in my face, I would have told him to set the table himself.

While Rebecca Lynn and I grabbed misshapen tin cups and plates, and super skinny forks with super pointy tips, Carl went outside, and Rusty put his camera on the table and took a seat.

When my sister and I were through, I stood back and gazed at the table, with two thin candles sitting in tin holders in the middle, platters of food covered with towels, plates, cups, and forks. It could have been a photo straight out of *Garden & Gun Magazine*.

Within minutes, we were all sitting together at the table.

"Tim, you can do the honors," Pete said.

"I'm sorry?"

"Grace." Pete folded his hands, closed his eyes, and waited.

Dad bowed his head. "Thank you, Lord, for this opportunity to share such a unique experience with my family. Keep us healthy and happy, and allow us to grow. Amen."

And keep me from jumping on Willow's back in the middle of the night and hightailing it out of this God-forsaken place. Amen, Hallelujah, and can I get a witness?

I wolfed down two chunks of ham, a handful of potatoes, and even a few pieces of okra, which Pete had added spices to and didn't taste half bad. I washed it all down with water from the creek, which tasted fresher than anything from a bottle.

When I asked Pete to pass the platter so I could have seconds, he said, "No seconds."

"But I'm still hungry."

With the only light coming from the fireplace, I could barely make out a sly smile.

"Well, darling," he said. "Welcome to a popular complaint of the 1860s."

CHAPTER THIRTEEN

There was a vaguely familiar sound drifting in through the open window. Car alarm? Cell phone?

Groggily, I sat up, rolled my head around in circles, and rubbed my eyes awake. In the twilight, I felt around for my end table, but of course, there was no end table, only floor boards, and I instantly remembered where I was. Exhaustion covered me. In the middle of the night, a scratching sound woke me up, and I had a hard time falling back to sleep. Now, my flat pillow smelled like sweaty socks, and tiny flecks of dust were stuck to my eyelids. My legs itched from the straw-filled mattress. I wiped my cruddy eyes again, rubbed my stiff neck, and scratched my dry legs as tiny streams of light filtered in through the window. Dad had nailed up a large piece of cheesecloth to stop the bugs from visiting, but it didn't stop that high-pitched screech from stabbing at my eardrums.

I shook Rebecca Lynn by the shoulder, but she didn't budge. Her arms were wrapped tightly around Martha's zombie-doll.

Dad sat up in his bed. He had slept in his short one-piece

underwear. Rebecca Lynn and I both slept in our slips. I had just about cried with relief when I took off that devil-loving corset.

"What's that noise?" I asked, licking my lips, running my tongue across my fuzzy teeth.

"If memory serves me right," Dad said, "it's a rooster."

"Is it ours?"

"I don't know." He stood up too fast and bumped his head against one of the low, slanted beams. "Damn it!" He stooped over and rubbed his head. "I'll get dressed downstairs. Get up and help your sister."

"It's still dark outside."

"We go to bed when the sun goes down, and we get up when the rooster crows. That's the way it works."

As he went down the ladder, I shook Rebecca Lynn harder. She slowly sat up. I lifted the cheesecloth from in front of the window and wrapped it around a nail, letting in the bluish morning. Outside I spotted the outline of that ruthless rooster sitting on top of one of the fence posts. "We're up, you stupid bird!" He ignored me and kept cock-a-doodle-doodling. I think he was laughing at me.

It took us nearly twenty minutes to help each other dress, our eyes barely able to see in the dim morning light. In less than thirty seconds, my corset dug into my skin and the toes of my shoes rubbed against day-old blisters.

As soon as we got downstairs, Dad said, "Let's start with some coffee."

"I don't like coffee," Rebecca Lynn said.

"Drink some tea," I told her. Then I turned to Dad. "What should we have for breakfast?"

"How about some eggs?"

"They only laid two," Rebecca Lynn said.

"Go see if they laid some more," I told her. "And feed them while you're out there." I handed her a basket for the eggs and the tin cup to dip into the feed bag.

After holding my breath for three minutes in the outhouse, I washed out my rag in the bucket and went down to the creek for some fresh water. I was squatted on the bank when a twig snapping grabbed my attention. I scanned the looming forest on the other side of the wide stream.

"Rusty? Carl?"

No one answered.

I filled the bucket quickly. Even if it was only a raccoon or a deer, I didn't have any desire to meet a wild animal up close and personal.

By the time I dragged the smaller bucket back to the house, the sun was heating up the day and my neck was already sweating.

In the cabin, Dad helped me stoke the fire. Next, I started the coffee. I tried to make it the way Pete had shown me, but it boiled through the spout and into the fire, sizzling as it turned the ashes to mud on the fireplace floor.

"Sorry."

Dad sighed and then turned toward the front door. "Did you hear that?"

Shaking my head, I followed him onto the porch.

Out on the road in front of the house stood a couple of men dressed like Dad, only way dirtier. They were talking to Pete. Rusty and Carl were filming what the men had brought with them: a skinny black cow with a bulging pink udder, an old grayish mule, and a Barbie-colored pig digging its snout in the dirt. All were loosely tied to the fence with a rope. Nearby, the rooster paced back and forth pecking at the dirt.

"What do we have here?" Dad said as we stepped through the gate.

Pete said, "Mule's to help get your field plowed. Rooster's a welcome-to-the-neighborhood gift. And a pet, as promised."

As if on cue, a small brown mutt came running up the road. He jumped onto the pig's back, and they rolled around in the dirt. I got the feeling they knew each other. I bent down and rubbed the dog's belly. I let him lick my face. For the first time in two days, I actually smiled.

As I squatted next to the dog, I caught movement out of the corner of my eye. I stood up and walked to the edge of the road, gazing up the hill rising beyond the two long rows of pecan trees. A bunch of people stood on the porch of the blue house. I couldn't make out whether they were men or women, young or old. Were they looking in my direction at the same time? Did they know a family had moved into the ugly shack down the hill?

Dad asked me to go inside and try making coffee again.

"She burned it the first time," Dad told the men.

"She'll get it right," Pete said laughing. "She's gonna have to, especially with extra men to cook for this morning."

I stormed up the porch steps and slammed the front door behind me. While I concentrated on making the coffee—this time without burning it—Rebecca Lynn came through the back door carrying the egg basket in her arms, cradling it like a baby.

"Look!" she said. "Seven eggs! And four apples!"

"I didn't know hens could lay apples."

"No. In the apple trees. Most are up too high, but there are lots of blackberries, too, if you want to help me pick them." She placed the basket on the table. "Where's Daddy?"

"Checking out our new animals."

"Oh!" she squealed. "I want to see!"

"Wait!" I told her, grabbing her by the arm before she got away. "First, you need to set the table. We've got eight people to cook breakfast for."

I didn't care how bitchy I sounded. I wasn't about to have my sister playing around while I was in the hot kitchen working my ass off.

Rusty came into the cabin just as I was putting Martha's sweet breads on the table. While Rebecca Lynn set the table and cut up slices of apples, I cracked the eggs open, dumped them into a big ceramic bowl, and stirred them with a fork. I poured the mixture into the pan with a little bit of lard, but the fire was up too high. By the time all of the men were seated at the table, including Rusty and Carl, the scrambled eggs were more brown than yellow. Once I pulled the pan from the fire, I spotted the mud tracks leading from the front door to the table.

"Watch it with your dirty boots," I told the men. "I'm not your mother."

One of the grubby men laughed. "Your cook's a little spitfire." He grabbed a cup and held it in the air. "I'm ready for some coffee."

The men, including my dad, left no room for Rebecca Lynn or me at the table.

My jaw clenched as I grabbed the coffee pot with the pot

holder, poured myself a cup, and put the pot on the table on a folded up towel. I dished out eggs for everyone and put the salt and pepper on the table. I sat on a stool on one side of the fireplace. My sister sat on the other.

Rebecca Lynn said, "I want some orange juice."

"No orange juice," Pete said with his mouth full.

I put down my plate and went to the cone-shaped package on the shelf. "I can't reach the sugar," I said. At this rate, I was never going to eat a hot meal. I might not have a seat at the table, and I might have to serve these filthy men like I was their freaking slave, but if I was going to enjoy a cup of coffee, I at least deserved a little sugar.

Pete stood up and grabbed the package. "You'll have to use sugar nips to cut it."

"Sugar nips? That sounds like a country band." I started to lay the package on its side.

"Keep it standing, like a Christmas tree," Pete said, pulling off the wrapper, exposing the stiff white cone. He grabbed one of the strange tools hanging on the wall. They looked like pliers, only way sharper. "Use these nips to cut off how much you need. It's a ten-pounder. Should last you a while if you're frugal."

I cut the sugar into weirdly shaped chunks, plopped a lump into my own cup, and put the rest on a plate in the middle of the table. The men emptied the dish in an instant.

I sat on the stool again and ate my cold burned eggs.

"Daddy," Rebecca Lynn said, "what animals did we get?"

"We got a cow—"

"A super skinny one," I said.

"And a pig—"

"Totally obese," I added.

"And a dog."

"A dog!" Rebecca Lynn left her half-eaten plate of eggs on her stool as she ran out the door.

Without thanking me for breakfast, and without cleaning up their places, the two helpers went out the front door, followed by Carl and Dad. Rusty stayed at the table and kept the camera rolling as Pete downed the last of his coffee.

My tongue was getting sore trying to dig out pieces of egg from between my molars.

I said to Pete, "Please tell me people brushed their teeth in the 1800s."

He went to a shelf, grabbed three plain brown boxes stacked one on top of another, and placed them on the table. "This one's your father's." He opened the lid. The camera zoomed in on the contents: a straight razor with a bone handle, a comb, a beastly toothbrush intended for dinosaur teeth, a jar with the words "D.R. Harris and Co. Ltd." scrolled across the top, and a small round shaving brush.

"This one is for you girls," he said, handing me the box.

I lifted the lid and peeked inside: a soft bristle hair brush, a small hand mirror, two more of those prickly toothbrushes, a plain porcelain jar, and the two sanitary pads, a gift from Martha.

"Tooth powder," Pete said, pulling out the jar.

I unscrewed the lid, dipped a finger into the powder, and tasted it. "Gross! It tastes like chalk."

"The better tasting stuff won't be around for thirty years. But this will do the trick."

Inside the third box I found white and black thread, a few

needles, a thimble, and a collection of mismatched buttons.

As Pete left me to play with my new toys and headed toward the door, I asked, "What are we supposed to do all day while my dad's plowing? Stare at the walls?"

Pete stopped in the middle of the room and turned to me. In a very clear, very monotone voice, he said, "Fetch more water to bring out to the field. Your father and the men are gonna need it. Then come back and wash them dishes. After that, you'll tend to the outside chores before the day gets too hot: milking your cow, brushing the horse, checking her hooves. You'll feed your dog. Introduce your pig to her pen and feed her. Then you will make sure they all have fresh water."

Rusty's camera zoomed in on my stone face.

"Next, you will collect berries and apples for preserving, and once you grow your vegetables you will preserve those, too. You'll bake bread. If you all want butter or cream or cheese, you'll have to make it yourself. We put a crock of raw milk out in your springhouse to get you started. You're gonna have to decide what to make for breakfast, lunch, dinner, and dessert each day. Planning meals will be a big part of your life out here. You're gonna sweep the house. Including the fireplace. You need to start a trash heap since there won't be any garbage men to haul it away. Be careful where you put it. Too close to the house, you'll attract all kinds of bugs and animals. Bears included. Now, back inside the house, you need to reshape your beds. If you don't, they'll get mighty uncomfortable. You'll spend some time mending whatever rips you get in your clothes. If your clothing gets soiled, you'll do some washing. If you have any time or energy left after the sun goes down, you can make pretty things for your home: curtains, table centerpieces, and the like. The next day it starts all over again. You'll tend to the animals, make the coffee, prepare breakfast for your family..."

Pete's voice droned on and on like my tenth grade math instructor, who should have been a hypnotist instead of a teacher. When he finished rambling, he walked out the front door, leaving me standing in the cabin, the heat from the fire causing sweat to drip between my shoulder blades, the camera marking my every move. My eyes took in the dirty dishes on the table, the greasy pans in the fireplace, the mud tracks all over the floorboards, and the heavy pot near the hearth that already needed refilling. The tears were rolling down my face before I was aware I was crying.

Rebecca Lynn came back in, skipping across the cabin floor. I wished she'd skip right into the creek.

"Daddy says I have to help you—" She stopped in the middle of the room when she saw my face. I turned toward the dying fire and jabbed at the cinders with the poker.

"Don't cry, Brooke," Rebecca Lynn said. "We just got a dog."

I didn't respond as I threw down the poker, grabbed the water bucket, stormed out the back door, and made my way to the springhouse, even though it smelled like the pool house at the country club. And if that creepy dead girl from *The Ring* was out there, who cared? I may as well have been dead too, thrown into a well and left there for seven days until my body rotted and my fingernails fell off and my soul escaped, because this place was no different than hell.

CHAPTER FOURTEEN

Getting water was less scary with Dad and the other men nearby in the field and Rusty trailing behind me. Still, I kept the door open while dipping the bucket into the dark pool. Back at the cabin, Rusty sat at the table filming as I tore up a rag and used it to wash dishes, but it hardly did the job. While Rebecca Lynn dried and put the semi-clean dishes back on the shelves, I noticed that fireplace ashes had made their way to the middle of the room.

"How the hell am I supposed to sweep this place without a broom?"

"You're not allowed to cuss."

As if I give a rat's ass, my brain replied.

"Go see if there's a broom in the barn," I ordered my sister.

She ran off like I'd just asked her to hunt for Easter eggs, and this time Rusty chose to follow her.

With the two of them out of my hair for a bit, I went upstairs to reshape the beds, but even the smaller mattress was too heavy to move. Underneath the mattress was a rope net instead of a normal box spring, so the mattress kept bouncing around as I tried to maneuver it. Finally, I lay across it like I was making a snow angel, matting down the straw inside and doing my best to smooth it out. As I bent over to pick up the quilt from the floor, my corset jabbed me in the ribs, taking my breath away. Within minutes I was holding that awful fashion mistake in my hands. I shoved it through the netted rope under my mattress and breathed a sigh of relief.

Back downstairs, I tried sweeping the fireplace ashes into a pile with a wet rag, but the rag turned black with soot and made things worse by creating a pattern of black swirls.

Rebecca Lynn came in through the back door, Rusty still behind her like a stray dog.

"No broom," she said.

I couldn't imagine what the already dingy cabin would be like after a few weeks of mud and fireplace soot devouring everything in sight. If someone had told me that one day I'd miss my vacuum cleaner, I'd have called them nucking futso.

"Come to the barn with me," Rebecca Lynn said. "I named our cow Gretchen."

I didn't care if she named her Queen Elizabeth.

In the barn, I slid an old stool over to Gretchen while Rebecca Lynn played with Sully the dog. Rusty stood in the corner of the barn filming as I pulled on the warm teats like Martha had shown me. Sully came over and stuck his head underneath the cow and swooshed his tongue against her udder.

"Gross," I said, shooing him away. "Rebecca Lynn, you need to feed your dog."

"Feed him what?"

"Whatever you can find that a dog would like."

Pete popped his head into the barn just after Rebecca Lynn left.

"Be sure to put that milk in the springhouse to keep it cool," he said. "Use a crock and seal it good. Don't forget to grab the crock that's already out there. Should be enough to get ya'll started on your butter."

I finished milking Gretchen and let her loose in the corral to hang out with Willow the horse. They seemed to get along well, eating from the same pile of green hay. With black flies swarming around the milk buckets, I took two trips from the barn to the house where Rebecca Lynn was rationing dried ham to Sully in exchange for doing tricks. I split the cream between two large crocks, and my sister and I carried them to the springhouse together.

Out in the middle of the field, Dad and Pete and the two helpers tilled, the mule grunting in front of the old-fashioned plow. Sweat poured down Dad's face and neck, but as spent as he already seemed, he looked like he belonged out there, stumbling through the muddy earth.

As we walked back from the springhouse, which wasn't scary at all with my sister along, Rusty headed out to the field.

In the cabin, I dragged the butter churn across the floor and put it beside the table. The narrow barrel stood as high as my hip and had what looked like a broom handle sticking up through a hole in the wooden lid. I opened one of the big kitchen books and read the section out loud to my sister. In between sentences I pointed to the items we'd need.

"'This is your first endeavor making butter for your family.

Once you have mastered this skill, your family will have a nutritious meal and they will owe it all to you! Here are the items you will need: raw milk, either from cow or goat…'"

"Goat?" Rebecca Lynn laughed.

I continued reading. "'Cheesecloth (also referred to as cream cloth), and a butter churn with paddle…'"

My sister wiggled the handle.

"'Retrieve your cream pot from where you have kept it at sixty degrees Fahrenheit for at least twelve hours. The best time to churn is in the coolness of the morning.'" I opened the crock Pete had started for me. "'Strain cream through the cheesecloth.'"

Rebecca Lynn held up the cloth.

"'When you can hear the cream has turned solid, take off the lid and scrape the sides of the churn to prevent waste. A wasteful kitchen is a lonely kitchen!'" I shook my head. The book should have come with a warning sticker: *For Lame Asses Only*. "'Next, pour spring water into the churn. Turn the handle for two to three minutes. Pour away the excess water, then pour in fresh again. Keep turning the handle in this fashion until the milk has turned solid. It may take twenty minutes or more. Once the butter is made, place it on a board. Take the cheesecloth and placed it on top, pressing out all of the moisture. Finally, you may add salt according to pleasure.'"

"Can we do this on the porch?" Rebecca Lynn asked.

"Don't see why not."

After skimming the cream off the top of the crock, we poured in the milk, and together carried the churn onto the front porch. I sat on the top step and began churning with the barrel positioned between my sister and me. Sully lay on the dirt at the bottom of the steps watching us. Soon, Rusty was standing in the front yard filming us instead of out in the field. I wondered if the producers of *Upside Down* would appreciate his scene choices.

I pumped my arm up and down a few times and peered into the barrel. "No change." After five minutes, my shoulder was screaming. "I know you're dying for a turn," I told my sister.

As Rebecca Lynn struggled to find a rhythm, a woman came walking down the dirt driveway belonging to the blue house. As she got closer, I saw that her face was nearly ebony and shiny with sweat. She wore a gray dress matching my own except mine had flowers, and a large white apron covering the front, all the way down to her shoes. On her head she wore a stark white bonnet. In her hands she carried a large basket.

Rusty ran over to her and moved the camera in on her face, but she didn't seem to notice. I stood up and waved. She waved back and gave a wide smile as she approached our gate.

"May I?" she asked.

My sister and I nodded.

She made her way to the porch. "You folks the new family?"

"Yes, ma'am. I'm Brooke Decker, and this is my sister, Rebecca Lynn."

Rebecca Lynn said, "This is our dog, Sully."

"I'm Nanny," the woman said. "I been asked to welcome you. From the whole Miller family."

She handed me the basket. I lifted up the pretty cloth napkin and made out a collection of colorful pastries underneath.

"Donuts!" Rebecca Lynn shouted.

"*Scones,*" Nanny corrected. She put a hand on Rebecca Lynn's arm. "Child, you can't churn thataway. Put some man's muscles into it or you ain't never gonna get no butter. Like this."

She handed me the basket and dragged the churn into the shade of the porch. Then she sat on one of the rockers, placed her hand on the top part of the stick, and rocked the chair forward and back as her hand moved the paddle handle up and down. Rusty stood on the porch taking it all in.

"You see?" Nanny said, ignoring the camera. "You be here all day if you keep a-goin' the way you been."

I liked Nanny right off, and not just because she was helping to churn. Her Deep South accent made me feel like I'd stepped into a time machine.

"I want to try it," Rebecca Lynn said, taking Nanny's place on the rocker.

"There," Nanny said, patting my sister on the head. "You be fine. Now, in about twenty minutes you feel it get real firm, then you pour off that cream and pour in some cold water. Do that a handful of times and you be all set. You got some water ready?"

"I'll get it," I said. I ran into the cabin, but before I put the basket on the table, I tore off a piece of scone and nearly died with ecstasy. When I stepped onto the porch again, Nanny was churning.

"My arm got tired," Rebecca Lynn said.

"S'alright, child. Don't mind none."

"Can we make cheese?"

"Oh, yeah. Farmer's cheese is good eatin'. You got a cookbook to show you how?"

Rebecca Lynn nodded.

"How old are you?" I asked.

"About thirty," she said, moving the wooden stick up and down with ease.

"Are you related to the Millers?"

"Lawdy, no, child! Ain't no relation!" Her straight white teeth glowed against her dark skin as she laughed. "I be theys house slave."

Okay, so we all had special storylines to follow, and pretending to be a backcountry girl totally sucked. But signing up to be a slave? I wondered if the producers would give her extra points for bringing us homemade scones.

"Do you live with the Millers in their house?" Rebecca Lynn asked.

"No'm. I lives in the quarters behind it. With my husband, Josiah. He works with the Millers' horses and tends to the grounds, mostly."

I took over the churning as Nanny leaned against the porch railing.

"What do you do up there?" I asked as I rocked back and forth the same way Nanny did. My tired fingers could sense the liquid growing firmer.

"Sweep, dust, cook..."

"Sounds like us."

"But I also take care of them Miller children—"

"They have kids?" I asked. "How many?"

"Prudence, she be about seventeen...Herbert, he twelve...Elijah, he the youngest—"

"What's Prudence like?" I asked, suddenly craving a girlfriend more than ever.

"Well, she rich, and she smart. She speaks the French language like they's do in New Orleans, and plays the piano, and sings, and reads as good as a preacher."

"Is she nice?" I asked.

A voice from far away rang out: "Nanny!"

A girl with bouncy brown curls marched down the driveway toward the cabin. Carl and his camera followed alongside. Her dress was a shiny, pale blue thing and she held it up off the dirt with both hands. It swayed back and forth like a lamp shade, because underneath the dress she wore a hoop. Beneath her sheer bonnet was a clean and shiny face that would have been pretty if it weren't for the scowl.

"Nanny, I've been looking all over God's green earth for you!" the girl said, standing on the other side of the open gate.

Nanny hurried off the porch, mumbling under her breath, "Yes, Miss Prudence, yes, ma'am…"

I told Rebecca Lynn, "Stay here. And keep churning."

As I followed Nanny, and Rusty followed me, I heard the girl say, "You are as slow as a mule. Mama only asked you to take a basket of offerings."

"That's what I done, ma'am."

"Hi," I said, walking through the gate.

The girl looked behind me at our Leaning Tower of Logs, and then moved her eyes up and down my body. I swear she took a sniff, like she believed I was the one causing that rancid smell, even though a person with the tiniest bit of brain would know it was chicken poop. My laughter at how silly she acted was replaced by the idea of how disgusting I must look. My appearance had been forgotten while doing the mountain of chores. But now, with another girl besides my sister to compare myself to, it hit me that I must look like a pig, or at least someone who hangs out with one. I fiddled nervously with my bonnet. I hadn't showered or brushed my teeth in over twenty-four hours. Mud covered my boots and a brown ring decorated the bottom of my dress. Dirt was caked under my nails. My day-old mascara probably made me look like a raccoon.

"You must be the new family," she said.

"We arrived yesterday," I said, trying not to compare my mud-stained dress to her shiny one, or my ugly side buns to her head of curls. "I'm Brooke Decker, and over there's my sister, Rebecca Lynn."

"I'm Prudence Beatrice Miller. Of the Raleigh Millers. Did you get the scones? They were made from an old family recipe in London. That's in England. They're made with cream cheese, but you've probably never heard of that. Where did you say you're from?"

"I've heard of cream cheese. And we're from New Bern."

"The port town? I think I passed by there once on the way to the Atlantic for a holiday. Equally filled to the brim with sailors and lice, isn't it?"

"Actually," I told her, never skipping a beat, "Raleigh wouldn't be on the map if it wasn't for New Bern, the original Seat of North Carolina. We chose to come out here so we could become autonomous. Oh, I'm sorry. *Autonomous* means *alone. Independent.* In case you've never heard the word."

I was thrilled to see a little smile appear on Rusty's face. I had to stop myself from offering him a fist bump.

Prudence turned to Nanny. "Well? Why are you still standing

here? You've got bows to tie."

"Yes, ma'am," Nanny said. Carl turned his camera in her direction as she hiked up the hill.

"She'll do anything to get out of work," Prudence said before Nanny was barely out of earshot. "But she's got to get my hair ribbons done before tomorrow. My father has hired a man to come and take our panoramic photographs. Have you ever heard of photographs? They are very expensive."

"Uh, yeah, I know what photographs are."

"Of course you do," she said, in a voice so snotty I imagined myself pushing her to the ground and smearing mud on her perfect blue dress that matched her perfect blue house.

But before I had a chance to obey those thoughts, Rebecca Lynn shouted to me from the porch. "Brooke, my arm is dying."

"I'll let you get back to your churning," Prudence said. "You will be attending church on Sunday, won't you?"

"I guess so."

"Of course you will. We can talk afterward at the picnic."

"Picnic?"

"And if you ever want a break from churning butter, come up for a visit. My house is the one—"

"I know which one it is."

Duh. There were only two houses as far as the eye could see: one built for a perfectly dressed princess to throw lavish parties in, and the other built for smelly farm girls who churned milk to make cheese for parties they'd never have.

"Very well," Prudence said as though she were suddenly bored. "I will tell my mother I have met you, and that the Decker family is simple and pleasant."

Even with two cameras panning us, I couldn't help myself. "Are you freaking kidding me? You're going to act like this for an entire summer?"

But my questions didn't matter, because Prudence ignored them.

"See you on Sunday," she said. "Don't forget to wear your best."

I didn't have a best.

"I shall wear my green satin dress," she added, pausing for Carl to follow before closing the gate. "The one with laced sleeves and twenty-two pearl buttons. My mother says that's God's favorite."

As she strolled up the rise to her house, she flipped her curls with her fingers like she was headed to a coming-out party, her dress swaying back and forth as she moved, Carl's camera taking in every bit of the dramatic scene.

CHAPTER FIFTEEN

We made butter! The milk had magically turned into a solid mass of creamy white goodness. It wasn't yellow like our Harris Teeter margarine at home, but it was still butter, and we had made it ourselves. It wasn't a lot, considering how much milk we used and how long it took, but a baseball chunk was better than nothing. I added some salt and let Rebecca Lynn have the first taste.

"It's yummy!" she said, clapping her hands together.

I scooped a lump with my finger and tasted it. It *was* yummy. I never knew I could get so excited about butter. "Taste this, Rusty," I said, handing him a small knife which he dipped and then ran his tongue along. He smiled and nodded, which was all I needed to know we had created a miracle.

I ran the crock out to the springhouse to keep the butter cool, making sure the lid was tightly sealed. Not once did I think about the dead movie girl in the well. Instead, with my tongue rubbing itself over my fuzzy teeth, I thought about something else entirely.

Back at the cabin, I told my sister, showing her our box of toiletries, "I'm not about to lose my teeth out here, especially on television."

After Rusty filmed us leaning over the dirt near the back door as we brushed our teeth with dirty chalkboard toothpaste, my sister and I planned lunch and dinner, stoked the fire, and continued with our chores. Later, while Rebecca Lynn played fetch with Sully, I went to the corral and brushed Willow. I forced the brush through her matted mane and cleaned her hooves of debris.

While stroking her neck, I realized my hands were even dirtier than they'd been that morning. Black gunk was caked under my nails and around my cuticles. Disgusted, I headed back to the cabin for a piece of linen, grabbed the tiny mirror from the wooden box, bribed Rusty to stay behind with my sister—"I'll make you a special batch of butter"—which he reluctantly agreed to, then I headed down to the creek. I dipped my hand in the chilly water and shook out a shiver. It would have to do. We had no tub, and no sink to speak of. All of our washing would have to happen here at this cold creek, or in the house using the small bucket, which would have to be filled up before bathing and dumped out after. At least I was cutting down the amount of work I'd have to do in order to get clean.

I put the tiny mirror on a tree stump and stripped down to my slip, hanging my clothes from a low branch near the stream. First, I washed my feet, which were unbelievably filthy. How on earth did dirt find its way through a pair of leather shoes and wool socks? I scrubbed my feet the best I could, careful not to rub too hard against the blisters sitting on each of my pinky toes.

Next, I took the edge of the linen, soaked it, and rubbed my face. When I pulled the cloth away, it was black. I washed my legs, snagging the linen on the stubble. I felt my underarms. Bristly hairs poked through. My mom had been part Italian, so the hair on my head was naturally thick, but the hair on my body was, too. There was no BIC or Gillette razor in my box of goodies, and it was beginning to seem like I'd be spending the next four months adding up the things I should have snuck in. By the time I was done with the rag, my skin matched a plucked chicken's. But I didn't care. I would take a frozen clean body over a warm filthy one.

I slipped my hair out of their buns and picked up the little hand mirror, turning it at different angles, trying to see more than four inches of me at a time. I rubbed my fingers through the ends of my hair, snagging them on knots. Somehow, sand had made its way to my scalp. I bent over and dipped my hair into the water, wishing for my Moroccan Argan Oil Shampoo. I'd have settled on a thimbleful of Walmart Great Value. No wonder the girls wore bonnets in the old days—they didn't want to die of embarrassment. Shivering, I dried myself with the flimsy linen, and redressed. As soon as my toes were tucked away inside my socks, I could feel the griminess already attacking my freshly washed feet. Sighing, I put the bonnet back on my head.

As I stared at myself in the mirror again, forcing back tears of hopelessness, a rustling from across the creek bounced along the rocks, followed by the snapping of a tree branch.

I froze.

For nearly a minute I stood there, peering into the forest, but all was silent. The rustling had stopped, and now all I heard was

Rebecca Lynn calling my name.

"Brooke!" Her voice meandered down the path. "We need to make lunch!"

Tucking the mirror in my pocket, I ran back to the cabin, glancing nervously behind me into the trees across the stream, but at least feeling a little bit cleaner.

The men smelled like they'd been rolling around in cow dung all morning. Not one of them said a word until they'd wolfed down apples and baked beans and scones with homemade butter.

"You made the butter yourselves?" Pete asked.

"Yep."

"Nanny made the scones," Rebecca Lynn said.

"Nanny?" Dad asked, guzzling his third glass of water. He had lowered his suspenders from his shoulders, and they hung at his sides. His hair was all cockeyed from sweating under a hat all morning. In less than twenty-four hours he had morphed into a farm boy.

"Nanny is the Millers' slave," I said, trying not to laugh. It sounded ridiculous saying the word out loud.

Rebecca Lynn said, "She helped us churn the butter."

"She shouldn't be doing your chores," Pete said. "Not if she works for another family."

"We did our own chores," I told Cow Patty Pete. The list of things I'd done so far could wrap around the earth, and it was barely noon. My hands were raw, my feet were throbbing, and I had wet greasy hair tucked up under a bonnet that felt like a diaper. We had kept the fire going, made sure fresh water was available, and had just made a fine lunch for a bunch of cowpokes who smelled like old wet tennis shoes. I didn't need the leader of the pack accusing me of laziness. "Nanny just showed us a better way to churn. So you all could have some real butter."

"Be careful," Pete said. "You don't want to be getting that slave girl into trouble."

I thought Pete was joking. What kind of trouble could Nanny get into? She wasn't a *real* slave.

"You couldn't pay me to be Prudence's pretend slave. Or her pretend friend. She's a total skank."

Dad dropped his spoon and it clanked against the bowl.

"What?" I said. "Girls didn't call each other names in the nineteenth century?"

The table remained silent as we finished eating, then the two helpers headed back outside with Carl behind them. Rusty stayed with us.

Dad said, "Thank you, girls, for such a wonderful lunch. I'm proud of you both." He looked at me when he added, "Let's remember how important it is to stay in character."

Rebecca Lynn gave him a hug, stepped back, and put her hand to her nose. "Gross, Daddy. You stink."

Dad laughed as if stinking up a room was the coolest thing in the world.

I watched him then, as he headed toward the door, stopping to pick up his wide-brimmed hat and putting it back on his head. He seemed tired, but at the same time, he bounced with extra energy. Like a basketball star who just made the championship shot in overtime. It was incredible to me that my dad had taken time off from work and traded in his PC and pie charts for an ax and a plow. We had everything back home. We each had our own rooms; real kitchen cabinets and an overfilled side-by-side refrigerator; unlimited electricity, hot water, four toilets to choose from, all of them *inside*; cell phone alarms instead of an annoying rooster; cable television; and a stove that didn't need firewood.

As Dad left the cabin it occurred to me that maybe he was sick of all those things. That he liked the plow. And the suspenders. And the stink. Maybe all these things helped him forget a little of the previous year. Maybe he wanted to forget what our family used to be, the life we used to have. Maybe he was different from me in a way I never knew until now.

CHAPTER SIXTEEN

In my dirty slip, I lay in the dark stuffy attic on my second night in the mid-nineteenth century, and I cried. I cried for my mom, who would have been a wiz in our country kitchen, who would have made our stay out here easier, and maybe even fun. I cried at the pitter patter of tiny feet which grew louder and closer in the dark as they scurried across the attic floor. I cried over Prudence Miller, with her perfect cinnamon-colored curls and pretty blue dress that matched her pretty blue house. I cried about how hard I would have to work every day for the next four months. The constant stream of work that would never end. I felt like that Greek mythological guy, Sisyphus, doomed to carry a boulder up a hill, but every time he makes it to the top, the rock rolls back down and he has to start all over again, pushing it up the hill, knowing the whole thing is pointless.

If every day turned out to be as endless as this last one, I would die.

Here are the things I did *after* lunch: I washed the dishes with cold water and a rag. Then with a rag tied to the end of a stick I mopped up the men's muddy boot tracks. With help from my sister, I picked more apples, brought in three piles of firewood, and went to the springhouse two more times so the men would have water while they planted. Rebecca Lynn and I made cheese, boiling the milk until it curdled, separating the curd from the whey, ending up with a blob the size of a hockey puck. I mended the bottom of Rebecca Lynn's dress when she ripped it on a nail sticking up out of a floorboard near the table, then I grabbed the Bible from the mantel, put it on top of the nail, and stomped my foot on top of it until the nail went back into place. I milked Gretchen again. After that, I brushed out Willow's mane, even though it didn't need it, but it was more for my own entertainment than hers. I brushed out Rebecca Lynn's tangled hair, too, going slowly so she wouldn't cry. Three times in three hours I re-bunned it and retied her bonnet.

I checked out the *Handbook for Overland Expeditions* for menu ideas. For dinner I made rice. Dad suggested I cut up tiny bits of bacon and dried vegetables, and by the time I added a little butter and some pepper, it tasted almost like the Number Six Rice Bowl from Golden Wok—only without the egg rolls. Or soy sauce. Or hot mustard. Or a fortune cookie. After dinner, I mopped the muddy floor again and washed out the filthy rag. A little while later, I sat in the outhouse, hiking up my dress, holding my breath, trying to go as fast as possible, knowing that not only my family had used the toilet, but the workers and the cameramen had as well. As I sat there, I thanked God my special rag was still clean and hanging on the nail.

So. Those are the things I did. Here are the things I did NOT do:

I did NOT watch *America's Got Talent* and wouldn't know who had won until after summer, and by then I wouldn't care. I didn't wash my hair with my expensive shampoo, file my chipped nails, check my Facebook page or update my status ("Totally awesome scraping the shit off my boots!"), like or dislike some viral Youtubes, throw some pics up on Instagram ("Showing off my brand new bonnet while yanking on engorged cow titties!"), or study for finals, which I was forced to take early and barely passed. I didn't text Libby one hundred and twenty times, didn't chill out with friends at her house, pass around the guitar, or sneak a couple of brewskies from the garage refrigerator. I didn't cruise up to the Dairy Queen for an Oreo Blizzard. There was no twenty-minute shower, no putting on my Hello Kitty pajamas, no grabbing a bedtime snack of string cheese or a couple of Dove chocolates. I didn't take inventory of my new summer dresses or bathing suits or sandals or earrings or ANYTHING.

As I rolled over on my side with my head against the flat stinky pillow, I fell into a troubled sleep where all I could dream about were the things I no longer had. Things like my *Mad Men* table lamps from Target, the IKEA candles in my own bathroom, my posters, my body pillow, my seashell night light. But the one thing I missed the most was the light blue comforter Mom had bought at Bed Bath and Beyond, the one that was way too childish and totally faded, the threads starting to unravel, that I still didn't have the courage to donate to RCS. And right now I wished I could curl up inside my old comforter like a caterpillar in a chrysalis, until summer was over and this whole damned show was behind me.

Throwing a pity party for myself only made things worse. With my brain constantly reminding me where I was, I slept less than three hours, and when the rooster crowed outside our window, I wondered how he'd taste with gravy.

Dad sat up and pulled on his dirty trousers. He still stank from the day before, only now the smell had sort of settled into the air around him, like the cloud that hovered around Pigpen in the *Charlie Brown* cartoons.

"I want you girls to see our field," he said.

"Will the men be here for breakfast?" I asked, wincing from the pain in my lower back as I sat up.

"No. They left early this morning."

"What about Rusty and Carl?"

"They mentioned something about sleeping in."

I pictured the cameramen, my only connections to the outside world, even if they didn't do more than nod or grunt. Did they get their own rooms? Real beds? Sleep with Egyptian cotton sheets and fluffy pillows under their heads? Would they be pigging out on a huge Southern breakfast, one that Nanny cooked for them? Wiping their mouths with fine linen napkins?

After Dad went downstairs, Rebecca Lynn and I helped each other dress. It took us less time than the day before because my rib cracker stayed hidden under our mattress.

"What about your corset?" Rebecca Lynn asked, winner of the prestigious Hall Monitor Award.

"I'm a suffragist," I told her.

"What's a suffragist?"

"A woman who thinks wearing a corset is bullshit."

We climbed down the ladder. Dad had already started the coffee.

"I want orange juice," Rebecca Lynn said for the millionth time.

Dad poured two cups from the pot and handed one to me. "No oranges, remember?" He made my sister a cup of tea, then took his coffee cup to the table.

My sister and I cooked up a ham and egg scramble, which we inhaled like we hadn't eaten the night before.

After breakfast, we followed Dad out to the field, Sully tagging along at Rebecca Lynn's heels. As we stood on the edge of the dewy landscape, the sun was barely peeking through the forest, thin patches of fog hovering over the tiny mounds of freshly tilled dirt.

"I can't believe you did all this in one day," I said.

"One helluva long day," Dad said. "But isn't it beautiful? We've got eggplant over here, collards over there, and carrots and tomatoes over there..." He stood with his thumbs hooked beneath his suspenders like he'd been wearing them for years. "The soil here is like the stuff you buy at Home De—" He stopped himself. "Like the stuff you might buy at the local mercantile."

"No cameras yet, Dad," I told him. "I don't think you have to worry about what you say."

"I just don't want to do anything that could—take me away from all this." He turned back to his field.

"I'm going to start my chores," Rebecca Lynn said. "Come on Sully. You can help me feed the chickens and collect their eggs and feed Bambi."

"Who's Bambi?" I asked.

"Our pig. And I named our rooster Clyde, so you'll know what to call him." She skipped away from the field toward the barn.

"I think your sister likes it here," Dad said. "How about you?"

I shrugged.

"Brooke," he said. "It's going to get easier."

"How do you know?"

"Because I just spent fourteen hours plowing and planting, I haven't had a shower in two days, and I feel like I'm on top of the world. If you don't fight it, everything will ebb and flow." He bent down and touched the soil. "Now I know what they mean by God's Country. Can't you feel your mother out here? It's like she's all around us."

No, I could not feel Mom out here in the middle of this God forsaken field. She was back at home. She was in the kitchen, baking her famous Amish cakes and sharing them with the women in her book club; in front of her vanity brushing through her dark wavy hair; in the SUV listening to NPR or some other radio program while patiently waiting for Rebecca Lynn or me to come out of school. She was screaming my name to the point of embarrassment as I soared over the hurdles. She was feeding the homeless down at the shelter or greeting guests as a volunteer at the History Center. Mom was home. Back in New Bern. And we had left her behind…

"Brooke?" my dad said, standing up and leaning his lower back into his hands. "You okay?"

"Just thinking of all the chores ahead of me."

"Well, today's your lucky day. I'm going to help you and your sister."

"Help us?"

"So we have more time to spend in town."

"Town?" I nearly jumped up and down with excitement.

"I knew that would make you happy."

He was right. This news did make me happy. I barely felt my blisters as we headed back to the cabin.

CHAPTER SEVENTEEN

By the time Round Rusty and Skinny Carl had made their way down the Millers' hill, our morning chores were done, and the wagon sat ready for town. Rusty was coming with us. Carl held a Nikon and planned to stay behind to take some still shots of the property.

"These are for shopping," Dad said, placing two small baskets in the wagon.

Rusty sat up front with Dad, and Rebecca Lynn and I sat in the back. Dad shook the reigns and we were off. I figured sitting in the back of the wagon would be more comfortable than hiking alongside, but my body was tossed around like that ugly doll Rebecca Lynn slept with.

We passed by two farms along the way, the hillsides between them scattered with cows, sheep, and cotton. One of the homesteads on the right had a sign at the end of the dirt driveway: Doctor Hensel. A while later, we passed a small square building sitting in the middle of a pretty meadow. One of the trees next to the building had a small wooden swing hanging from a branch.

"Over there is the schoolhouse," Rusty said.

I observed the tiny crooked structure, thankful it was summer.

Thirty minutes and a thousand bumps later, we made our way to the top of a rise. The wagon halted.

Dad shouted, "Girls, look!"

Rebecca Lynn and I rose to our knees in the back of the wagon and followed his gaze. Down in a valley sat a real life ghost town. A handful of wooden buildings lined up in a short row on one side of the dirt street, a narrow space between each. Like our cabin and the school and the farmhouses we'd passed along the way, each building was unpainted, so the town looked like a ghostly watercolor made up of grays. The sidewalk wasn't a sidewalk at all, but a boardwalk that ran along the front of the shops, connecting one to the next. Across from the row of buildings was a field. Beyond the clay center street was a hill with a pretty white church halfway up the rise. The sun shone brightly on the bell hanging in the steeple, and clusters of leafy trees surrounded the building. The scene was straight out of one of those old-fashioned country calendars, the kind they sell at Mitchell Hardware.

Rebecca Lynn and I sat back down as Dad took the reigns and carefully steered the horse down the hill and onto the street. Up close, the buildings were more than just ghost town façades. Each one had a sign hanging from the eaves of the porch: Murphy & Sons Goods and Seed; Murphy & Sons Tannery; Wrightman's Bakery & Confectionary; Sheriff's Office; Blacksmith; and Sweet Sugar Gap Carriage Works.

Dad made a U-turn at the end and came back up the short street. In front of Murphy & Sons Goods and Seed, he directed Willow to a shady spot. Rusty panned the street with his camera while we got out of the wagon and Dad tied the horse to a wooden post where she drank water from a trough.

"Okay, girls. I want you to behave like mid-nineteenth-century women. No modern slang, no modern references, no modern anything."

"Do we at least get to shop like modern girls?" I asked.

"One dollar each is your limit," Dad told us as we grabbed our empty baskets.

I couldn't imagine what in the world I would buy for a mere dollar. In the modern world, one buck might get me a half pack of Stride gum or a kid's hot dog at the Moo Cow Café.

Rusty kept his camera on my face as we entered the store, and with good reason. As soon as I stepped over the threshold, my jaw nearly hit the floor. Move over Myrtle Beach, I had just entered a shopping paradise! The entire room was packed with more nineteenth-century crap than I ever knew existed. Large signs hung everywhere, pointing to baskets or drawers or shelves: Ladies Shoes, Men's Work Shoes, Tobacco, Coffee, Horse Medicine. There were Spices from Exotic India, Real Haitian Sugarloaf, Best Ever Soap Flakes, Pipe Stoves: New and Improved! Some items weren't priced, but other things were: Barrel Of Flour, 2 Cents; Cornmeal 100 lbs, 2 Cents; Bread One-Pound Loaf, 5 Cents; Coffee, 25 Cents; Tea, 47 Cents; One-Pound Bacon, 18 Cents; 60 Pounds Potatoes, 2 Cents; Dried Beans, 8 Cents....

Drawers labeled Nails, Small Farm Tools, Kitchen Tools,

Rubber Stamps, Buttons, Colored Thread, and Sewing Needles took up entire walls behind the long cluttered counters. Chairs, lanterns, rakes, and other tools hung from the beams overhead. Glass front cabinets reaching as high as the ceiling were filled to the brim, the items on top crammed under the eaves. Each side of the room had a ladder on a track behind the counter to make reaching the higher shelves easier. One wall was dedicated to Fine Men's Hats, Fine Ladies' Hats, Fine French Parasols, Fine Fans, Fine Purses, Fine China, Fine Oriental Slippers, and Fine Hoop Skirts. If I'd used the word "fine" that many times in my essays at school, I would have flunked English.

Rusty stood next to Dad while he showed our list to an older man behind the counter, and Rebecca Lynn and I wandered around. We both spotted the candy right away, long sticks with swirls of green or red or brown: "Five for a penny!"

"Grab twenty," I told her, my mouth watering.

As Rebecca Lynn picked out her favorites, I stared up at the hoop skirts sticking out from the wall like reassembled skeletons: Thomson 20-Spring Heavy Wire, 62 cents! I let my eyes scour the fancy hats and parasols, then the items on top of and beneath the glass counters. There were rolling papers and pipes (for tobacco only, I assumed), a leather-bound pocket drug kit, Pinaud Talc, Mrs. Boyd's Almond Oil Hand Cream, tiny round spectacles, matches, slates, white chalk, Gideon's Bibles, and books like *Lullabies for All Ages*, *Modern Homeopathy*, *The Hand Book of Etiquette*, and *A Guide to the Usages of Society with a Glance at Bad Habits*. I saw a women's magazine called *Godey's Lady's Book*, a deck of playing cards, postcards, parchment paper, and ink wells. There were dolls made of cornhusks and rags. Next to the dolls, pine toy soldiers filled a large wooden bucket.

With my basket in my hands, and working hard to keep my eyes from popping out of my head, I found myself amazed that even as far back as 1861, people craved this much junk.

I was standing in the middle of a nineteenth-century Walmart.

There were Dainty Ladies' Gloves, stacks of ceramic ware, tin cups, silverware, and bottles of lamp oil. Mounds of bags containing salt, oats, grain, rice, and Rogers and Smith Chicken Feed were stacked five feet high in the back. There were candles, aprons, mousetraps, pails, canned and jarred goods, a tall wide barrel crammed to the top with giant green pickles, bins filled with seeds of all kinds, brooms, The One and Only Newly Patented Can Opener, straight razors like the one in my dad's toiletries box, toothbrushes, "Love Among the Roses" perfume, pumice stones for nails, orange wood sticks for cuticles, and flowery soaps. There were pencils—"Now with Rubber Erasers Attached!"—slates, rakes, pails, aprons, calendars, hairbrushes, silver-framed hand mirrors, lace handkerchiefs, lace bonnets, shawls, mother-of-pearl combs, dried flowers in sachets, checker boards with wooden checkers. Bolts of Calico, plaid, and even silk fabric were displayed along one of the side walls. Against a glass cabinet leaned a pair of Tom Walkers, better known as stilts, and next to them a couple of wooden fishing poles. Under the glass I found clay marbles and one of those games with a tiny ball attached to a cup by a string. In front of one of the counters sat a wide metal bathtub: "Built For The Whole Family!" Next to the tub was a stack of washboards. Beside the washboards, a sign reading, "Dollies and Dashers to Make Laundry Agreeable!"

offered freakish wooden devices to help me enjoy the sport of churning dirty socks and soiled petticoats.

The average kid would turn ADHD in a place like this.

I finished eyeing everything under the glass and started picking out a few things. Into my basket went a small soap that smelled like old lady perfume (anything was better than lye), a box of laundry soap flakes, a pumice stone for the calluses my palms were developing, and an orange wood stick for pushing back my cuticles. I gazed up at the hoop skirts again when I bumped into a crate filled with sheet music. I ruffled through the stack, reading the silly song titles under my breath: "Old Dan Tucker," "Mary Blain," "Gaily the Troubadour," "Turkey in the Straw," and "Miss Lucy Long."

As I finished reading through the ancient top ten Billboard list, I spotted something in the corner, sitting up high on a shelf. Something that made me forget there was anything else in the room. Up there on that shelf, like it had been waiting for me for over a century, sat a guitar. It was made of yellow wood, and smaller than the one Libby's oldest brother let me tool around on. And it was beautiful.

"Pretty guitar, huh?"

I spun around to find a boy about my age, with a mop of dark hair and green eyes. He wore a large white apron—well, one that I assumed used to be white but was now spattered with who knew what—that fell below his knees, a white long-sleeved shirt with a pair of brown pants, those oh-so-popular suspenders, and boots. Fuzzy sideburns traveled along his jaw line like a couple of giant caterpillars.

"Yes," I agreed.

I looked back up at the guitar and spotted the camera in the corner to the right. Behind me, another camera hung from the ceiling by the front door. I didn't have to know history to understand those glass eyes weren't a true part of the 1800's shopping experience.

"You new in town?" the boy asked.

"Two days ago," I said.

"You all come out here for the mining?"

"Mining?" I laughed. But the boy didn't see the humor in his question. "Oh. No. My Dad's contract says he has to be a farmer." I lowered my voice and rolled my eyes. "As part of the *venture*."

"Well, I guess living out here is an adventure. This is my family's store. We're the only mercantile for miles. So anything you need, just ask." He pointed to a sign on the wall and read it out loud: "'Your One-Stop Mercantile Shop.'"

I checked to see if he was smiling. If maybe he was giving me a little wink to prove he was playing along for the sake of reality television; for the sake of the millions of viewers who watched more hours of cable than they spent outside. But the boy wasn't smiling, and he wasn't winking. He just stood there like a nineteenth-century goofball.

Well, then, fine. Acting all stupid and Laura Ingalls-like was better than being back at the cabin cleaning up horse crap and fetching water.

I said, "What about a guitar pick, sayeth you, oh, kind gentleman?"

The boy laughed.

Goofball has a sense of humor after all.

"Just use your fingers like I do."

"You play?"

"Some."

The guitar stared down at me. "How much is it?"

"Hey, Pa!" the boy shouted, making me jump. The man looked up from Dad's supply list. "How much is the guitar?"

"Four dollars fifty, son." Then he said to my dad, "I try to get him to memorize the prices, but what can you do?"

The boy shuffled his feet and chewed on the inside of his cheek.

I cleared my throat. "Is four dollars and fifty cents a lot of money?"

He shrugged. "For some it is."

Rebecca Lynn skipped up to me and held out her basket. "I got all this stuff for less than a dollar. I got twenty sticks of candy, a ball for Sully, a deck of cards, and a bag that smells like flowers. Smell it." She held the sachet up to my nose. It smelled like a used dryer sheet. "Who are you?" she asked the boy.

"My name's Wendell. And you are?"

"Rebecca Lynn. I'm ten. Brooke is sixteen."

"Seventeen in October," I added.

"We're the same age," Wendell told me as he brushed his thick hair from his forehead.

I didn't care how old he was. He smelled like hay and dirt, and his goofy smile seemed even goofier now that I knew his age.

Dad walked over to us.

"Mr. Murphy says to give him thirty minutes to gather the things on our list." He extended his hand to Wendell. "I'm Tim Decker."

"Nice to meet you, sir. Wendell Lee Murphy."

"One of the sons in Murphy & Sons?"

"Yes, sir. I'm the oldest of four."

I tried to picture the four of them at the Charlotte audition, wrestling each other, maybe singing a boy band tune for the producers.

Rebecca Lynn said, "Look what I picked out, Daddy."

"Put them on the counter next to that crate." He glanced at the things my basket. "You find everything you wanted?"

"Are you kidding? I want everything in the store."

Wendell said, "Oh, this isn't everything. We have a wish book you can order from. Might even have one of those picks you asked about."

"A pick?" Dad asked.

"For the guitar." I pointed to the instrument up on the shelf, staring at the camera, wondering if it was a live feed, if the producers in Los Angeles were watching us at this very moment. I was tempted to stick out my tongue, but with Dad and Wendell standing there, I decided against it.

"We can't afford a guitar, Brooke."

"But it's only four-fifty—"

"This is 1861. We don't have that kind of money."

"The producers should have warned us we'd be the only ones starting from scratch." I turned to Wendell. "At least you get to have a store. We got a shack and a barn."

"Brooke," Dad said, grabbing my wrist. "This is neither the time nor place." He let go and turned to Wendell. "Could you add some paper to our list? Maybe my daughter can let off some steam by writing letters."

"We can send letters?" I asked.

"You can also get them," Wendell said, pointing to a small sign over a doorway in the back of the store: Post Office.

The only time I went to the mailbox back home was when Mom was too weak to make it to the end of the driveway. It seemed like she got a hundred cards a week. I would read them to her while she lay in bed, especially when her eyesight started to go. She said that was her favorite time of day, when I read her those cards. On the days when no cards came, I'd reread some of the best ones. I don't think she ever noticed they were the same ones she'd heard a dozen times before.

"You'll need a quill and some ink," Wendell said.

"And a broom, please," I said. If I wasn't allowed to have the guitar, I may as well sweep to my heart's content.

"How much are the brooms?" Dad asked Wendell.

"Thirty cents."

"We can't afford one, Brooke—"

"But a *broom*, Dad. I don't have any other way to keep the cabin clean."

"If you want to give up some of the things in your basket..."

I stared at the laundry flakes and the hand soap like they were my best friends. "I need these things."

Wendell took the basket from me. "You could always make a broom yourself. Plenty of branches and straw around."

"Good idea," Dad said.

I shot Wendell a "Thanks for nothing" look, but he had walked away to get us our letter-writing stuff, so the dirty look hit the back of his head.

"Who wants to check out the town while we wait?" Dad asked.

"I do!" Rebecca Lynn said, heading to the door.

As I started out the door behind my sister and dad and Rusty, I glanced back at Wendell, standing behind the counter, adding up the things in my basket. He winked at me, like we suddenly shared a secret; one that said we totally agreed how lame all of this was. But then he rubbed his eye like there was dirt in it, and I shook my head as I left the store.

Next door to the mercantile, we walked up the steps and into Murphy & Sons Tannery, where they carried saddles and chaps and cowboy hats. The camera panned my hand as it stroked the beautiful saddles. Rebecca Lynn laughed at the chaps. My dad tried on a cowboy hat, but it made him look like a dork.

Next, we stopped in front of Wrightman's Bakery and Confectionary. Cake plates sat in neat rows in the window below beautifully scripted signs: Delectable Chocolates! Sugar Cookies! Fruit Pies! We stepped through the doorway simultaneously breathing a loud "Ahhhh." Just smelling the baked goods made me feel more lucid.

In front of the counter, a woman stood with twin girls around Rebecca Lynn's age. The mother was being handed a package by the plump older lady behind the counter. The older lady had a streak of flour across her cheek and globs of chocolate on her apron.

Rebecca Lynn went up to the little girls. "What did you get?"

"A peach pie," the first little girl said. "For Sunday supper."

"You eat pie for supper?"

"It's for *after* supper."

"I live up that road," my sister said, pointing.

"Us too," said the second little girl. "We got a tobacky farm."

"We got a cow and a pig and some chickens," Rebecca Lynn said.

The child's mother finished paying at the counter. When she turned around, I noticed her perfect posture, and that she wore her corset. I stood up straighter.

"I'm Mrs. Duffy," she said. "And these are my girls, Beth and Tina."

"Tim Decker," Dad said. "These are my daughters, Brooke and Rebecca Lynn."

Mrs. Duffy smiled politely at the three of us and turned to the woman behind the counter. "Thank you, Mrs. Wrightman."

She nodded to us as she and her children left the bakery. I was impressed with how everyone seemed oblivious to the fat man following us around with a camera in our faces.

"Good morning," Mrs. Wrightman said, wiping her hands on her apron. "Can I get you some cookies? Or perhaps the children would like some treacle."

"What's treacle?" I asked.

"Taffy."

Try to get taffy out of my teeth with my Jurassic toothbrush? I'd bleed to death.

We chose a strawberry pie and three freshly baked croissants.

"That will be twenty-eight cents, please."

I was used to seeing Dad's fat wallet, with his credit cards and driver's license and wad of bills. But out here, he carried a small leather bag filled with coins.

We ate our croissants as we strolled along the wooden

sidewalk and peeked through the window of the sheriff's office. A man with white hair and a white moustache curled up at the edges sat at a desk reading something with a magnifying glass. I spotted the star-shaped badge on his vest. Behind him, a red, white, and blue flag with a circle of nine stars hung from a pole. Across the room sat an empty jail cell straight out of Mayberry.

"Don't want to get in no kinds of trouble 'round here, pardner," Dad said, trying too hard to sound like John Wayne or some other dead cowboy.

Rusty went inside the sheriff's office while we continued down the plank sidewalk. The blacksmith shop stood a few yards beyond the sheriff's office, and finally the carriage works. That was it. That was the town. Aside from all the stuff to check out at Murphy & Sons, there wasn't much more to see here than back at our homestead.

"This is just like a real town," Rebecca Lynn said.

"A real *lame* town," I said, popping the last bit of flaky croissant into my mouth.

"You have to stop saying things like that, Brooke," Dad said, his voice low. "We have no idea how many cameras there are, maybe hidden in places we aren't aware of."

"Like in our outhouse?" I said it jokingly, but as soon as the words left my mouth, I wondered if it was possible, or even legal.

"It doesn't matter where they are, or where we think they are. If we stay in character all the time, it'll be a lot easier to forget we're being taped at all."

Back in front of Murphy & Sons, Rebecca Lynn gave the last of her croissant to Willow while Dad and I sat a porch bench until our order was filled.

"Mr. Decker," Wendell said, poking his head through the doorway. "My pa is ready for you. I'll put the things in your wagon while you settle up."

Inside the store, Mr. Murphy handed Dad a slip of paper. "Shall I put your things on credit?" he asked.

"Is that customary?"

"A man's word is his bond."

"I think I'll stick with cash for now."

Mr. Murphy helped Dad count out stacks of coins before we headed out of the store. Rusty was already sitting on the buckboard when my sister climbed into the back. As Wendell put the last of our items in the wagon, he held out his hand to me. His grip was strong, his hand calloused.

"Thanks," I said, lowering myself onto the floor among the packages.

"See you at church tomorrow."

Dad backed Willow out of the parking space and did a decent job not running over anyone.

As we left the tiny town, I looked back to see Wendell standing in the shade of the storefront porch, his arms crossed like one of those wooden Indians in front of a tobacco shop.

Rusty sat next to my dad, filming behind us as we made our way up the rise. I thought of the woman who ran the bakery; Mrs. Duffy with her twin daughters; Mr. Murphy and Wendell; the Millers with their snotty daughter; even the slave girl, Nanny. All of these people fit into this made-up town perfectly, like Cinderella's slipper when it slides onto her tiny foot.

As we made our bumpy way back to the cabin, it seemed like everything I'd done before coming on this venture was a dream.

That all the chores, the people of Sweet Sugar Gap, the wagon trip to and from the miniature town, was real, and I didn't understand how this could be. It made my brain sizzle just to think about it. So I scolded myself for being unfair to my real life, my real friends. I was being unfair to the modern world I'd left behind. I might not have electricity, or normal clothes, or the computers and things I used to have, but I would only be *pretending* I was one of these people. Wendell and his fuzzy sideburns. Who the hell would grow those things just for fun? Prudence, with her hoop skirt and nasty attitude. And Nanny, pretending to be a slave, for God's sake. They could buy into this bullshit town as much as they wanted. Just a bunch of people who auditioned that day out in Charlotte, an audition that seemed ages ago, in a city that seemed as far away as the moon.

Even if I performed for the camera the way everyone expected me to, I would secretly and constantly remind myself I was not and never would be one of them; that I hated it out here in the sticks, and I didn't give a double fother mucker about ratings or Hollywood or the people of Sweet Sugar Gap.

CHAPTER EIGHTEEN

When Dad shook me awake, I heard tapping on the roof, like a squirrel was sprinkling tiny nuts all over it.

"We'll be late for church," he said, pulling up his suspenders. "Why didn't that stupid rooster wake us up?"

Rebecca Lynn mumbled from her side of the bed, "His name is Clyde."

"What's that noise?" I asked.

"Rain," Dad said.

As soon as he made his way down the ladder, Rebecca Lynn and I dressed.

"I don't want to wear my dress to church," she said. "It's dirty."

"Dad!" I shouted downstairs. "We don't have anything nice to wear!"

"God doesn't care how you dress!" he shouted back.

"But it's raining," I said, trying not to whine like my sister, but finding it hard not to.

Without a response, the back door opened and shut, and I

knew he'd left to use the outhouse. I remembered the pretty parasols hanging at Murphy & Sons and wished I'd bought one of those instead of old lady soap. I didn't own a shawl or a fancy bonnet, and wished I'd bought those as well. I only had my work clothes, my work boots, my dirty nails, and my greasy hair.

I put on my dress and turned my apron inside out so the dirt and food stains weren't so obvious. When I slid on my boots, I spotted greenish mold clinging to the leather. I tried to help my sister with her bonnet, but she grumpily pushed my hands away. "I can do it myself."

Rebecca Lynn finished dressing and headed downstairs; I stayed behind to put on some makeup. Maybe my disgusting clothes would be less noticeable if my face didn't suck. In the nearly dark room with the tiny mirror hanging from a nail, I dabbed on some blush and mascara before tucking the items back in the corner of the ceiling. I grabbed my bonnet and headed downstairs.

Breakfast was a stale scone with butter, an apple, and some coffee—*un*burned, I will add.

"Tend to the animals before we leave," Dad said. He put on his shirt over the dirty long underwear and wrapped a strange detached collar around his neck. His fuzzy face needed a shave. I'd never seen my dad with facial hair before, but here he was, looking almost cool, like a drummer in an Indie band.

Rebecca Lynn grabbed a cup of feed and ran out to the coop. Sully, wet and muddy from the rain, followed. I ran through the drizzle to the barn where Gretchen stood inside, waiting for me, and put the bucket under her. Afterward, I was sure she gave me a smile of relief. I patted her on the head.

As I headed toward the springhouse, the heavy bucket banging against my thigh, my feet slipped out from under me. For some reason I held onto the milk bucket instead of letting my hands catch my fall. Onto my rear I fell, like stupid-ass Jill who tumbles down the hill after Jack. I sat there in the rain, shaking my head as milk soaked through the front of my dress and wet mud seeped through the back.

Like a psychic, Rusty showed up just as the mosquitoes started pecking at my face. He wore a modern yellow rain poncho and a pair of Sperry boat shoes.

"What happened?" he asked as the camera closed in on my face.

"I'm learning how to tap dance. What does it look like?"

Without bothering to help, he followed me as I stood up and carried what was left in the bucket to the springhouse. Wet and shivering, and probably resembling the dead girl in *The Ring*, I poured the milk into two crocks and shut the door behind me.

In front of the cabin, Dad was already sitting on the wagon with the reins in his hands. Rusty climbed onto the seat beside him. In the back sat Rebecca Lynn. She had grabbed the quilt from our bed and held it over her head like a tent. I crawled under the quilt and huddled next to my sister, holding onto the basket that held the strawberry pie.

"You're all muddy," she said, scrunching up her nose.

"Yeah? Well, you smell like chicken poop."

Clyde, our mentally challenged rooster, decided to give us a wakeup call just as we headed onto the road. *Good timing, Cuckoo Bird.* We had only traveled a few yards when another wagon pulled by a stocky brown mule came up behind us. A man with mahogany skin, wearing a wide leather hat and a black coat, sat on the buckboard, handling the mule. Next to the man sat Carl with his camera on his shoulder.

Behind the first wagon came another, only this one wasn't really a wagon at all but an open two-seater buggy, a small canopy suspended over the travelers' heads and held up by a pole at each of the four corners.

Within seconds both wagons passed us. The black man tipped his hat as they went by, and Dad did the same. Carl panned our wagon, and Rusty panned the other two. As the second cart passed, I caught Prudence in the back seat, a thick blanket draped across her lap, a lacy shawl across her shoulders. A canopy protected her head, but she still used a parasol. On her right sat a little boy. In the front seat, a man—Mr. Miller, I assumed—held the reins that controlled a large work horse, and next to him, another young boy. Prudence waved excitedly as she rode past, like we were in a holiday parade. From under the quilt I gave a small wave back, and then the wagons were gone.

The wooden church doors screamed in pain as we pulled them open. The minister on the platform stopped speaking, and the room became a silent cave. A few camera people, including Carl, were scattered throughout the room, panning our pathetic expressions as we entered, as well as the dozen or so faces of men, women, and children as they twisted their bodies around to get a good look. The women and their daughters looked identical in high collars and sheer bonnets, shawls covering shoulders, hair in perfectly round pin cushions on the sides of their heads. Some held onto pretty fans. All wore pretty gloves. The men and boys held their dress hats and wore black coats with dark pants and clean white shirts with collars.

Not only did we look filthy compared to these other families, my dad's musky scent entered the room along with us. I silently prayed that his overwhelming stench was reason enough to kick us out of church *and* Sweet Sugar Gap.

The minister held up his arms like a television evangelist and smiled. "Welcome," he said, his voice echoing through the narrow church.

We chose a spot in the very back. Dad took off his hat and raked his fingers through his oily hair. In the corners of the high ceiling, two more cameras hung like one-eyed spiders.

For nearly an hour, the minister droned on about neighborly love, quoting something from John or Luke or one of those guys. We grabbed a hymnal and followed along as best we could, singing one song and then another. Off to the right, an organ played. When it was time to sit back down, I noticed the person playing the organ was Wendell Murphy. He was dressed in a black suit with a white stiff-collared shirt, a thin black bowtie at his throat. His thick hair was clean and combed and neatly parted at the side. Even his sideburns looked less bushy. He played the organ well, even if the music was like something you'd hear at a funeral.

Toward the end of the sermon, a man from the front row stood up and passed a velvet-lined basket up and down the rows. The entire room was silent except for the organ music and the plink-plink-plink as coins dropped into the basket. When it came back to us Dad dropped in one small coin.

The sun suddenly shone through one of the stained glass windows and fell upon the pulpit. The minister beamed and spread his arms even wider. "It looks as though God would like us to have a sunny picnic."

Everyone nodded and smiled as we rose for the final song.

Behind the church, long wooden tables lined up end to end, with benches on both sides. Camera people moved about, and little kids ran around like free-range chickens. Some of the ladies went to their wagons for their covered dishes. I headed to ours while Rebecca Lynn took off with the Duffy twins and Dad shook hands with the minister.

"Brooke Decker!" came a girl's voice from behind me.

Prudence floated toward me in her green satin dress, face flushed with humidity, Sunday buns perfectly symmetrical under a sheer bonnet, and gloved hands holding a sheet cake the size of a doormat. "What happened to you?" she asked, gaping at my inside-out apron barely covering my stained dress.

"Had a rough morning."

"You must come up to my house. I have some old dresses you may have. And do not thank me. It is more blessed to give than to receive. What did you bring for the picnic?"

"Strawberry pie," I told her as we approached the wagon. I reached in and grabbed the box, then lifted the lid for her to see. One of the cameras zoomed in on the pie.

"Oh, how quaint," Prudence said. "I don't think I've ever seen one quite so small."

As we walked back to the picnic area we sidestepped a wide

mud puddle, and if the camera hadn't been hovering, she would have "accidentally" stumbled into it.

The rain clouds had drifted away; the sun was shining brightly now, and steam rose up from the grass. In the Miller's buggy, the black man still sat high up on the buckboard. He tipped his hat and smiled as we walked by. I smiled back. Prudence ignored him.

"Isn't he coming to the picnic?" I asked.

"A slave invited to a picnic! Oh, Brooke Decker. Your sense of humor will undoubtedly help me get through the tedious summer."

I grabbed her by the arm and put my mouth to her ear, not caring if the microphone picked up my voice. "You shouldn't be rude to someone for ratings."

She didn't respond as she marched a few feet ahead of me to the table. Each place was set with a tin plate, silverware, and a cloth napkin. Platters with towels on top covered the center. If a meal this great was going to happen every Sunday, maybe church wouldn't be so bad after all.

After placing our desserts next to the other dishes, Prudence dragged me to where the children were playing. She introduced me to her twelve-year-old brother, Herbert, and her ten-year-old brother, Elijah. I met Wendell's little brothers, Willie, seven, Welford, eight, and Washington, ten, who all had the same thick brown hair and green eyes. I said hello to the twins we'd met at the bakery, Beth and Tina. Mrs. Wrightman, the woman who owned the bakery, had a six-year-old daughter named Belle, and Doctor Hensel's son, Peter, was fourteen. Including Prudence, Wendell, and my sister and me, the kids made up a baker's dozen.

I scanned the crowd but didn't see Wendell. Not that I needed to see him, but with only one boy and one girl my age, and the summer months looming ahead like an endless gray sky, I couldn't be too picky.

As if she'd read my thoughts, Prudence said, "Have you met Wendell Murphy?"

I nodded.

"His family runs the mercantile," she said.

"I know. I was there."

"Isn't their wish book wonderful? I've ordered a brand new tea set. I shall invite you for a tea party when it arrives."

I was more of a Beartown Java Cappuccino girl, or a red Solo cup lover, depending on the situation, and Prudence was as annoying dog poop on my shoe, but if it meant getting out of a few chores, I would learn to sip tea.

"Brooke," Prudence said, touching my arm like a grandmother, "it's not in my nature to be rude, or to gossip. But I feel I have to say this to you. As your new friend." I waited as she licked her lips in preparation for whatever nonsense she had to say. "It's just that, well, I'm not one to judge, lest ye be judged, but you look like a…*fancy girl.*"

"Fancy?"

"Only fancy girls do not wear their corsets in public." Before I had a chance to tell her to mind her own beeswax, she put her face close to mine. "What is that on your lashes?"

"Midnight Blue Extra Thick."

Prudence held that blank stare. I waited for her to crack up, to say, "OMG, girlfriend, can you believe, like, we're totally on this lame reality show? You are, like, so smart to bend the rules.

And screw that stupid tea party. Murphy & Sons sells papers and corncob pipes, and I know a couple of local Indians…"

But she didn't crack up. She didn't even crack a smile. She was as smooth as a piece of ice as she placed a gloved hand against her chest. She glanced at the camera, ever so slightly. "Really, Brooke, you need to wear your corset or boys won't respect you." She took the silky blue shawl from her shoulders and placed it around my own, tying it into a large knot in the front. "Wear this. Perhaps no one will notice."

A door in the back of the church opened and slammed shut again. Wendell came down the back steps and stopped to talk to some of the men.

"There's Wendell," Prudence said, patting her bonnet and fluffing up her dress. "Hi, Wendell!" she called waving.

Wendell walked over to us. "Afternoon, Prudence." He stared at my clothes. "Afternoon, Brooke. You fall off the wagon?"

"Oh, no, I—"

"I'm going to give her one of my old dresses," Prudence told Wendell. "Isn't that right, Brooke?"

I shrugged.

Wendell said, "That's nice of you, Prudence." The church bell clanged. "I don't know about you all, but I'm hungry."

We followed him to the table. After Reverend Clark gave the blessing, platters of mashed potatoes, sweet potatoes, corn, rice, beets, carrots, and gravies were spooned onto plates in fair portions, as were the meats and breads. Lukewarm sweet tea was poured into glasses. The table grew silent as everyone ate. Soon, platters were passed around again. There was enough food to eat not only two helpings, but three, which I happily did.

Next, apple and strawberry pies, and white frosted cakes were cut into wide slices. By the time dessert was over, nearly every platter was empty.

After the meal, the afternoon sun high in the sky, the children took to running around again, hiding behind trees, somersaulting down the rain-soaked hill. At the table, Prudence and I helped the women clean up while the men sat around and sipped tea or smoked their pipes. Wendell sat with the men, and for the first time I caught the hint of honey blond in his hair. As I leaned over to clear his plate, he smiled up at me, and I smiled back. From the other end of the table, Prudence watched us. I lowered my eyes and grabbed the dishes and carried them to a large barrel by the creek, then helped wash and dry.

"What do we do now?" I asked Prudence when the clean up was finished. I was stuffed to the gills, and as good as the food was, I couldn't imagine a once-a-week smorgasbord was the only fun I'd have out here.

"Come with me," Prudence said.

Together we walked behind the church and made our way up the rest of the grassy hill. I heard grunting as Rusty tried to keep up with us, his face the color of a tomato, like the word "treadmill" wasn't in his personal dictionary. It was a five-minute hike, and the hill was muddy and a little slippery from that morning's rain, but my dress was already soiled, so a little more dirt wouldn't make a bit of difference.

We reached the top. On the other side sat a valley between a pair of rolling hills, and smack in the middle lay a broad river. Trees and rocks lined the river, and from the top of the hill, I could see white caps on the water.

"I could sit up here all day," Prudence said.

We stood together as a warm wind rose up from the river and ruffled the hems of our dresses.

"Prudence," I said, wanting to get the conversation started before Rusty's camera appeared. "Do you worry you might not last out here for four months?"

"No. This is my home now."

"But it's not your home. Not *really*."

"Yes, Brooke, it is. And I plan to keep it that way." She touched my arm like we were lifelong besties. "Oh, look down there. A deer by that tree. Isn't he sweet...?"

The more she spoke in that sugary sweet voice, the more I wanted to smack her bonnet off her head. But Rusty now stood with us, his camera panning the valley as Prudence went on about how perfectly wonderful nature is.

She eventually stopped jabbering, and I glanced toward the townspeople behind us down in the picnic area, Wendell somewhere among them. It was hard to tell one male from another with all the men wearing the same clothes. I turned back to the river where the deer was soon joined by a half dozen friends. They stood nibbling wild berries and flower buds. Standing on the hilltop with a full belly, the sun warming my face, and that beautiful river below wasn't half bad, I had to admit.

And, I decided, Wendell Murphy wasn't half bad either.

CHAPTER NINETEEN

For nearly a week, after Clyde screamed bloody murder, and even on the mornings when he was too stupid to wake us up, I got dressed, started the coffee, and tended to Gretchen and Willow. Rebecca Lynn went to the coop to feed the chickens and collect eggs, then feed Bambi, who seemed to be getting fatter and muddier by the minute in her pen behind the barn. We cooked three meals in the fireplace, churned butter, made cheese, dragged in firewood, washed yucky rags, and poured lye into the outhouse toilet. We even made a broom. Rebecca Lynn found a slightly curved tree branch, and together we collected straw. It took a few hours, and by the time we were done, our homemade broom belonged in a magical game of Quidditch. It left long scratches in the floorboards, but at least some of the dirt came up.

Aside from the daily chores, and aside from having a camera or two in our faces all day, life was pretty uneventful for a girl in the 1860s.

But when our clothes began to look like they'd been pulled

from an alley dumpster, and stank just as badly, I decided it was time to add a little spice to my routine. Yes, the "Holy Day of Dirty Skivvies," otherwise known as "Wash Day," had finally arrived.

Dad's pants and socks were so smelly I had to hold my nose while I dunked them into the bucket of boiling water with a pair of long wooden tongs. And my sister's and my own clothes weren't much better. But we used the soap flakes instead of that awful lye soap, so our fingers wouldn't disintegrate. While our outer clothes soaked in the bucket out back, Dad chopped wood in his long underwear with the top half pulled down around his waist, and my sister and I did our chores in our underpinnings. I took a wet soapy rag and washed our moldy leather boots. Since our socks were also soaking, we stayed barefoot, which was awesome. Even dodging horse and cow paddies was better than wearing those itchy socks and pinchy shoes.

Rebecca Lynn and I strung a line across the kitchen since the humidity was high and nothing would dry outside. Our clothes smelled like a fireplace, but they dried in less than a day.

Dad walked through his garden for hours at a time, watering the seeds with bucket after bucket like he was sure chunks of gold were going to sprout up. On the other side of the barn where the sun hit all day, he planted sunflower seeds. He also started a trash-burning pile at the back corner of the property. But most of the day, he chopped wood on the side of the house.

"Part of the evaluation will be stockpiling our wood," he reminded me. "A few cords a week should do it."

"How much is a cord?"

"Enough to fill two wagons."

The first time Dad swung the ax into the air, he looked like a blindfolded two-year-old trying to hit a piñata. But by the time a week was out, his arms were tan, and the three-foot-high log pile stretched halfway across the side of the cabin. Which was good, since we went through firewood like nobody's business, and it wasn't even winter. It seemed like every time he got the pile to grow higher than his hip, we girls would steal logs for cooking.

By the time the sun started to set each day, we were all too tired to play with our deck of cards which sat in the unopened box on the mantel. With all the blisters from sweeping and churning, I could barely move my fingers, let alone dip a pen into an ink well. The only letter I managed to write was to Libby. I kept it brief:

"This place sucks. Wish you were here to make it less sucky. Love, Brooke."

Two days before our next ride into town, I treated myself to a spa. I did my afternoon chores faster than usual, then snuck away while Rusty hung out with Dad in the field and Rebecca Lynn played with Bambi and Sully. I made my way down the path to the stream with a large, clean piece of linen in my hands. If I was going to see Wendell again, I needed to get rid of this awful stink. Not that he was my only motivation for hygiene awareness, but it didn't hurt to have an additional reason to scrub the nooks and crannies.

After brushing my teeth, and candle-waxing a doubled piece of thread from the sewing box to use as floss, I stood in the creek rinsing, cringing at the site of my hairy legs. My armpits weren't any better. In fact, they were worse than my legs, because along with the stubble, I had no antiperspirant, and little red sweat bumps made my underarms itch. Naked and shivering, I held the tiny mirror in my hands. My reflection had recently begun sporting a uni-brow, like an actress in an Italian prison movie. Blackheads decided my nose was the perfect place to breed, and freckles that Sunforgettable SPF 30 used to keep away were now scattered all over my cheeks like someone had blown cinnamon into my face.

I thought about my makeup, hidden away on an attic eave. That old cowgirl Martha had been right—there was no need for it out here. By the time half my chores were done, streaks of black and tan would be dripping down my cheeks like mime paint. I was Brooke Decker disguised as Plane Jane disguised as Dirty Girty, and I would be for a while.

I dried myself off and re-dressed. On my way back to the cabin, the trees heard me sigh. I sighed because I was dirty, no matter how hard I scrubbed, even with the old lady soap I'd bought at Murphy & Sons. I sighed because even though I brushed every day with that chalky toothpaste, my teeth felt like they were covered by a thin film of plastic. I sighed because minutes after my nooks and crannies were clean, they filled with dirt again. I sighed because I would feel this way until mid-September, with a camera catching me nearly every time I let out a stinky, miserable breath.

On Friday morning, just after breakfast, a knock came to our door. The three of us raced to see who it was, seeing as how visitors weren't exactly lining up to say howdy to the Deckers. It was Nanny, the Millers' fake slave, standing with Rusty behind her, the early sun barely making a dent in the shade of the porch. A bright pink dress lay stretched across her arms.

"Sorry to disturb you, Mr. Decker, sir, but Miss Prudence ask me to come down here and see if Miss Brooke will come for tea today."

"She has chores," Dad told her. "They can visit during church—"

"Oh," Nanny said, shaking her head nervously. "Miss Prudence say I got to do Miss Brooke's chores so's she can go visit." I briefly wondered if Nanny had used that amazing slave dialect during her Charlotte interview.

"Brooke can do her own chores," Dad said.

Nanny's face filled with worry, like she truly believed she'd be punished if she didn't obey orders. She held up the dress. The bottom fell to the floor in a swooping wave. "Miss Prudence say I got to help you dress, Miss Brooke. She want you lookin' nice when you go on up there."

I couldn't give a rat's ass about seeing Prudence, but I was dying to wear a different dress, and I'd get to see inside that awesome house.

"Dad?" I pleaded.

"No one is doing your chores for you, and that's the end of it."

Rebecca Lynn said, "I can milk Gretchen and brush Willow. The animals like me."

"That's a lot of work," Dad said.

"I'll make the beds before I go," I said.

Rebecca Lynn added, "Laura Ingalls would do it for her sister Mary."

For the first time ever, my little sister's brown-nosing was working in my favor.

"You will pay your sister back," Dad told me.

I squealed like I'd just been invited to the prom and kissed my dad on a bristly cheek.

Rusty followed Nanny and me up the ladder and sat at the top of the rectangular hole, his camera panning the room.

"This is nice," Nanny said, standing in the center so she wouldn't hit her head on a beam.

"I have to share it with my sister *and* my dad. Which totally blows. My sister kicks in her sleep and my dad snores like a grizzly."

Nanny laughed. Her teeth were straight and white and her smile was beautiful. Her skin was beautiful, too. She would have been one of those women perfect for the 1800s because she didn't need any makeup.

"I help you turn them mattresses so's you can get dressed," she said as she pulled the quilt from my bed and placed it on Dad's. "You gotta wash that tickin' or the dirt'll start growin' bugs."

"Bugs?" We already had the world's supply of black flies in our kitchen, and no-see-ums swarmed around the outhouse no matter how much lye we threw into the hole.

"Invisible bugs that make your skin itch. Next time you does your laundries, you boil them sheets." She demonstrated how two people together could lift the mattress, shake it up and down, and turn it over. She said if my sister helped it could be done. "If you don't shake it so a few days a week, your bed will get lumpy. Before you knows it, the straw will poke at you like a porcupine."

As we flipped the mattress, something beneath the ropes fell to the floor. Nanny held it up for me to see, accusing me with her eyes. "What is your corset doin' under here?"

"I hate it."

"You don't be wearin' a special fine dress without one." She laid it on the bed next to the dress.

I turned to Rusty. "When we're done making the beds, I'm going to get undressed. Maybe you could film my sister collecting eggs instead of me in my underwear. I'm still underage, you know."

As Rusty let out an indifferent snort and headed back down the ladder, I said under my breath, "Perv." Nanny didn't respond. She was really good at pretending Rusty was invisible. I wondered if I would ever be able to do the same.

"How do you know about this mattress-flipping thing?" I asked her after we'd flipped the larger mattress.

"I learnt it."

"Just for the show?"

"So's you can visit with Miss Prudence."

I helped Nanny lay out the quilt on my bed, and then went to my Dad's. "I hate having so many chores."

"Well, there's lots of things I hate, but I still has to live with 'em."

"You could always make up an excuse to leave."

"I gots a contract with the Millers."

What she meant was she had a contract with Hollywood, like the rest of us. I lowered my voice. "Why are you really doing this?"

"So's you have time to get ready for tea."

"I mean, why are you doing *this*?" I fanned out my arms. "Why are you *here*? What made you want to be a slave for four months? I can't imagine going that long—"

"Listen to me now. I gots strict orders not to talk to you about nothin' that don't have to do with helpin' you get ready for tea."

"Orders from the producers?"

"Orders from the Millers."

"But that doesn't make any sense. They can't tell you what to—"

"Enough!" she said, tightening her jaw and pressing her lips together. Her eyes became black marbles in the dim room. Her fun slave accent vanished. "Do you want to go for tea or not?"

I nodded.

"Fine. Then let's just do what we're expected to do."

I didn't understand why she was getting so upset, but her accent disappearing in a flash made me uneasy, so I dropped it.

Once the quilts were back in place, Nanny held up the pink dress while I slipped out of my ugly one. On top of my slip, I tied up the corset. Nanny held out the dress for me to step into and pulled it up over my shoulders.

As she buttoned up the back, I said, "This would look perfect with a hoop."

"Get yourself one."

"They're too expensive."

"Thatta be the truth. Maybe one day I shows you how to make one." She looked around the room. "Got a hairbrush?"

I grabbed the soft bristled brush from the rafter where it sat above the tiny mirror. "Sorry my hair is so greasy," I said, embarrassed.

"Use some vinegar."

"Vinegar?"

"Lotsa white ladies uses the vinegar. But I has my own recipe: almonds and citronella oil. Takes that grease away and smells fine. Leaves your hair feeling soft. I can make up a paste for you."

"Really? That would be awesome."

She finished brushing my hair, twisted it into those stupid Princess Leia donuts, and spun me around to tie my bonnet.

"Are Prudence's curls natural?" I asked.

"No ma'am, she uses a curlin' iron."

"What? How—"

"I put the iron in the fire, and then I curls her hair."

"Oh."

"It takes time to do it thatta way."

"I wish I had that kind of time."

"Cut up some rags."

"What for?"

"You cut 'em into strips and tie 'em up in your hair like so. Then you sleep in 'em, and in the mornin' you gots curls." She placed a warm hand on my cheek. "They's some red roses growin' on your fence. Take a petal or two and rub 'em on your cheeks. Smell good and you look alive too."

I was growing with excitement thinking about the rose petals until I remembered what covered my feet. I was at least an inch taller than Prudence, so my hideous black boots stuck out like a pair of rotting logs.

Nanny followed my gaze. "I got some extra material for some trim, if you want it."

For some reason, the more I pictured fixing up my new dress

and curling my hair, the more I thought about Wendell Murphy. Even those silly sideburns started to seem appealing.

"You thinkin' about a boy, now, ain't you?" Nanny asked me.

I grinned like an idiot. "No."

As she followed me back down the ladder, I thought to myself, *Nanny is one smart cookie.*

CHAPTER TWENTY

Rusty and his pet camera followed Nanny and me up to the blue mansion. The hill wasn't so steep, but it was long, and the air was crazy humid, so by the time we reached the house, my armpits were sweating profusely beneath the pink dress.

We walked up the front porch steps. They were much straighter than ours, and there were six instead of three. Nanny rang the doorbell. I felt like a trick-or-treater.

The door was opened by a pretty older version of Prudence. And a larger version: Mrs. Miller was pregnant. Her round belly stuck out like she carried a watermelon. Her long, ruffled smock dress was straight out of an antique costume catalog.

"You must be Brooke Decker," she said.

"Yes, ma'am."

"I'm Mrs. Miller. Won't you come in?" She turned to Nanny as we stepped through the doorway. "I want to take a bath this morning, and I want the water warm, not like yesterday when you tried to boil me like a shrimp."

Nanny nodded and quickly made her way down a hallway

toward the back of the house.

Beneath my feet lay a beautiful green and black Oriental rug. Painted portraits hung on top of striped wallpaper, and framed prints of flowers lined the staircase. A round table with scrolled legs sat in the middle of the foyer with a vase of white roses on the marble top. Above the table hung a fixture with oil lights instead of modern bulbs. The entryway was bigger than my entire cabin.

Jealousy rose up in my throat.

"The dress fits you well," Mrs. Miller said, closing the door behind Rusty and me.

"Yes, ma'am" was all I could think to say. To my right a pair of French doors led to a parlor straight out of *Southern Living* magazine. A painting of a hunting dog with a pheasant in its mouth hung over an ornate white mantel. A small piano sat against one wall. Dark furniture—a tall desk, a bookshelf, and a coffee table—matched the wood trim of the two old-fashioned sofas facing one another, each one covered in pink velvety material. In the corner by a large window sat a wide love seat with an ottoman beside it. A leather book lay open on the seat.

"Prudence waits for you in her playroom," Mrs. Miller said. "It's up the stairs, first door on the right."

"Yes, ma'am," I said again. "Thank you."

Rusty trailed behind me and Carl passed us coming down as I made my way up the wide sweeping stairs, one hand lifting the long dress, the other gripping the beautifully polished railing. I felt like Scarlett O'Hara. Without the hoop, of course. At the top of the steps ran a long narrow hallway. Three doors on the right and three doors on the left were all shut, and if it weren't for the open door at the opposite end allowing sunlight to spill into the space, it would have been as dark as our cabin.

Curious, I walked to the end of the hall, the floorboards slightly squealing under my feet. I pushed open the back door and stepped onto a porch, with stairs leading down to a stone path below. Halfway up the path sat an outhouse. Beyond the outhouse was a large stable. A few yards behind the stable, an apple orchard stretched as far as I could see. In the middle of the orchard sat an unpainted wooden outbuilding on short stilts. Smoke made its way out of the chimney.

"Is that where Nanny lives?" I asked Rusty, not expecting an answer, and not getting one.

A girl's humming entered the hallway, so I headed back to the playroom door. I reached out my hand and touched the doorknob. The humming stopped, and Prudence's voice slipped under the door: "A lady always knocks."

I was suddenly standing inside the pages of *Great Expectations,* picturing beyond the door a long banquet table covered in spider webs, moldy food, and a decomposed wedding cake.

I tapped lightly against the wood.

"Entrée vous."

The instant I opened the door, light and color attacked my senses. Four windows stretched from the hardwood floor to the incredibly high ceiling, two on the opposite wall and two facing the front, and each framed by ruffled peach curtains, lace ones beneath, letting in the sunshine. The floor was partially covered by a large blue and peach Oriental rug more elaborate than the one in the foyer. A writing desk sat in one corner, and a chaise lounge in another, a pretty quilt folded across the back. An open toy chest sat in front of one of the windows. Dolls of all kinds—ceramic, stuffed, naked, dressed—were scattered about. Four of the dolls had been set up in fancy clothes at a tiny table near the desk, a miniature tea set ready. A bookshelf with glass fronts held onto at least fifty leather-bound books. A white mantel like the one in the parlor was lined with colorful glass figurines, everything from horses to elk to elephants.

And then there were the walls. The bottom half was wainscoted and painted a lighter shade of peach than the curtains, but it was the top half that really got my attention. Growing up in a Southern river town, filled to the brim with Colonial and Victorian houses, I'd seen wallpaper that would send the average girl tripping. But these walls weren't wallpapered. They were *hand painted.* On one wall sat a knight on a white horse heading up a sage-green hill toward a castle in the distance. On the next, a king and queen sat on thrones, their crowns covered in sparkly jewels. On the third, a mermaid floated on a giant seashell in a bright blue-green ocean. But the fourth wall was insanely awesome. It depicted scenes from different fairy tales and fables. I spotted Cinderella standing on a staircase with the clock at midnight behind her; Snow White in her red cape; the Evil Queen gazing at herself in the mirror; Rapunzel leaning out the window of a high tower, her long golden hair reaching the ground and curling around a tree trunk.

A chandelier was suspended from the ceiling's center, and beneath that a table larger than the one for her dolls sat covered with a starched white table cloth, a chair on either side. The chairs were covered in dark purple velvet, and the wooden backs were scrolled like they belonged in King Arthur's Court.

The black man I'd seen at the wagon's helm on Sunday stood next to the table, wearing a black suit and bow tie. He held no expression and his hands were folded behind him.

In one of the chairs at the table sat Her Highness.

Rusty scanned the scene, and Prudence smiled at me as I crossed the threshold. "Please, shut the door behind you."

She wore a dark green dress with a big bow tied in back and a hoop skirt that forced her to sit on the very edge of her chair. The ruffle on a pair of frilly bloomers could be seen peeking out from beneath the hem. Pale blue satin slippers covered her feet, and a big green bow, not a bonnet, was pinned to the side of her curly head. To go with her dress she had added white gloves that met her elbows. All she was missing was a white cane and a lamb.

I was shocked. Impressed. Pissed off.

Mostly pissed off.

"If you leave your mouth open," Prudence said, "the flies will think you've got honey inside. Come." She motioned to the empty chair with a gloved hand.

I shut my mouth and walked over to the table. The man pulled out my chair.

"Thank you," I said as I sat across from my hostess.

"Tea, Josiah," Prudence told the man.

Josiah leaned over and poured dark tea from the dainty porcelain pot into each of our cups.

"Sugar, Miss?" Josiah asked.

"Sure," I said. "I mean, yes, please."

He raised the lid from a small glass bowl in the table's center and picked up a pair of tiny tongs, plunked one white piece into my cup, another into Prudence's.

"Thank you," I said.

He nodded and stood upright again, like a fake Halloween butler.

"This is sa-weet," I told Prudence.

"You haven't had a sip yet," she said.

"Not the tea. This house. This room. *All* of this."

"Most girls would have thanked me for inviting them here."

"Oh. Sorry. Thanks for the invite. And thanks for the dress."

"I see you're wearing your corset."

She picked up her cup with her pinky in the air, blew on the tea, and sipped it. I tried to imitate her, silly as it looked and stupid as I felt.

"Josiah," Prudence said. "Crumpets."

Josiah went to the writing desk and picked up two small china plates. He placed one in front of each of us.

I stared at my plate.

Prudence laughed. "Don't tell me you've never had a crumpet before."

"These are English muffins."

"That's silly. They aren't muffins at all." She turned to Josiah. "Well? What are you waiting for?"

Josiah bent over and removed the lids from two tiny white bowls. I picked up the little knife from the center of the table and started to dip it in the butter. Josiah looked confused.

"No," Prudence scolded me. "Let him do it. It's his job."

The man bent over again and spread a tiny bit of butter on my English muffin crumpet thingy. "Jam, Miss?"

"Yes, please," I said uncomfortably. "Thank you."

"You don't have to offer him a thank you," Prudence said as she nodded for Josiah to give her jam. "He doesn't expect it."

Josiah finished with the crumpets, took a step back, and stood motionless again.

"He's mostly an idiot," Prudence said, sighing. "But he does pour tea well enough."

She took tiny bites of her so-called crumpet and sipped her tea. As I imitated her, I had to keep reminding myself that all the people in Sweet Sugar Gap, except for me, of course, wanted to be here. Josiah didn't have to do this. He could have said no. Just like Nanny could have said no.

"So, tell me, Brooke," Prudence said. "How do you like living in Sweet Sugar Gap? Don't you just love the smell of grass and fresh flowers?"

All I could think about was the smell of chicken poop and my own sweat.

"I don't have much time to enjoy anything." I gave her the rundown of my life in the backcountry, leaving out the colorful adjectives. "What kinds of chores do you have?"

"I haven't any chores. That's what slaves are for."

I should have been worried about Josiah, but he was a grownup, able to make his own choices, and besides, I couldn't stop thinking about *me.* I worked from sunup until sundown. My clothes were no fancier than Nanny's, not including this pink hand-me-down from Prudence. I had to suffer through baths in a freezing cold stream, my hairy legs belonged to an ape, and I had to share a bedroom with my dad and little sister. I had no privacy, my hands were cracked, and my lower back throbbed. I was no different than a cotton picker, really.

A huge ball of woe-is-me welled up inside me, and I forgot for a moment about Rusty and his camera. "It's totally not fair."

"Excuse me?" Prudence asked.

"You get to live up here and I have to live down in that shack."

"Are you blaming me for your misfortune?"

"No. It's just not fair, that's all. And the Murphys with their store. Hardly an even playing field."

She ignored my whining. "Oh, don't you love their store? I want just about everything in their wish book."

"The only thing I want is their guitar."

"That's a boy's instrument. You should play the piano, like I do."

I laughed. "We wouldn't have anywhere to put a piano, except maybe in our fireplace as kindling. It doesn't matter anyway. The guitar is too expensive. Wendell said it's nearly five dollars." My stomach did a surprising flip-flop at the mention of his name.

"Five dollars is hardly anything these days," Prudence said. "Of course, with war so close...well, if it ends slavery, that will be the end of our orchard, our lifestyle, everything."

I didn't want to play along with this talk of war and an orchard she'd probably never seen up close. I didn't want to sit here with Missy Prissy, listening to her jibber jabber about stuff that wasn't real, like I was back in a boring history class. Actually, I'd rather have been in a history class.

"I miss New Bern," I said, the pangs taking hold. "We're only here because my dad thinks this venture will make me—our *family*—stronger. But we didn't need to come all the way out here. Back in New Bern, I had friends, and fun stuff to do. Why did you all come out here, anyway?"

"My father felt we'd be safe out here in the backcountry."

"Safe from what?"

"The war."

I drank the last of my tea and put the cup on its matching dish. "You're doing a really good job, Prudence."

"What do you mean?"

I was supposed to be careful, especially with that camera just about jabbing me in the ear. But Prudence sitting there all smug in her perfect world…well, without knowing it, she was pushing me.

"Treating Nanny and Josiah that way," I said. "Acting like this world is normal."

"For the next four months, this is my normal world," she said without blinking. Her frozen green eyes made me nervous. "Josiah," she said, never looking at him. "More tea."

Josiah bent over the table like an old willow tree, poured fresh tea into our dainty china cups, and I spent the next hour listening to Prudence talk about a war that no longer existed, and slaves that in reality had been freed a hundred and fifty years before, and I almost wished I'd stayed back at the cabin sweeping out the fireplace or washing outhouse rags instead.

CHAPTER TWENTY-ONE

Saturday couldn't come fast enough. We girls did our morning chores as quickly as possible as Dad readied the horse for town. I grabbed a handful of rose petals and rubbed them against my cheeks. I did the same for Rebecca Lynn. Soon, our wagon made its way up and over the hills until the final descent into town. I stood up as soon as we'd parked in front of Murphy & Sons and jumped down the second Dad hitched Willow to the post. Carl had stayed up at the Millers' place, and Rusty lagged behind with my sister as I straightened out my bonnet in the doorway. Casually, I strolled into the store, my basket swinging next to me.

Wendell stood behind a counter, helping a man with his purchase. When he saw me, he smiled.

I smiled back and pretended like I was interested in the items under the glass.

Dad said, "Fifty-cent limit."

I started to protest but he headed across the room to speak with Mr. Murphy. Rebecca Lynn rooted through the toy soldier barrel. As I grabbed a handful of candy sticks and placed them in my basket, I tried hard not to stare at Wendell, whose apron was freshly washed and pressed, and his chin shaven clean.

I didn't want him to think I was in his store to gawk, so as Rusty moved around the room like a bored ghost, I moseyed over to the pipe stove by the front door and picked up a newspaper from the stack: *Harper's Weekly*. The date at the top was a few weeks ago—in reality it was a few weeks plus one-hundred-fifty some-odd years ago. I sat on a rocker, placed my basket on the floor, and scanned the front page. A grainy photo of a fat bald man stared out. Some military guy named Butler. A few pages in, my eyes fell across a sketch of a young man in a uniform, a tall hat on his head like he was in a school marching band. The soldier had been killed in Baltimore, the first victim of the Civil War. As I scanned the article, I felt someone looking over my shoulder.

"Luther Ladd," Wendell said. "He was our age."

I folded up the paper. "How much is it?"

"Six cents."

Newspapers weren't my thing, but at least it was something to read. I stood up and placed the paper in my basket. My eyes traveled up to the guitar, still sitting high on the shelf.

Wendell said, "You got a letter."

I nearly had a stroke as I waited for him to get it. I glanced up at the cameras staring down from the corners of the room, feeling like a rat being observed by scientists. And I guess I was like a rat, running aimlessly through some weird maze, hoping for a paltry piece of cheese at the end.

When Wendell returned, I stared at the envelope like it had

traveled through a worm hole from the future. On the outside of the envelope, Libby had drawn a smiley face with his tongue sticking out and wild hair on his head.

We paid for our purchases. As Dad and Rebecca Lynn and Rusty headed out of the store, I said goodbye to Wendell before climbing into the wagon.

Rebecca Lynn said, "Can't we buy another pie?"

"Sorry," Dad said.

"What about the church picnic?" she whined.

"Y'all could make your own pie," Wendell called from the doorway.

"Sounds like a great idea," Dad said.

As we backed up the wagon, I could see Wendell standing there, grinning. It wasn't a sneer. It was a genuine grin like he'd just handed me a bouquet of roses, and it made my stomach turn inside out. But, bouquet or not, thanks to Wendell Murphy, I would now be adding pie-making to a daily list that never seemed to quit growing.

CHAPTER TWENTY-TWO

On the ride back from town, I tore open the letter from Libby:

> *Brookie-Wookie! OMG, you will not believe how boring this place is without you. My dad said not to ask him for one dime until fall, so I got this totally dorko job at the bowling alley, which sucks because my tan is already fading. If you only knew how disgusting it is to touch shoes that a million people wore. Shoot me, please! I wish you were here working with me. We could hide some of the bowling pins. Or put Vaseline in the bowling ball holes. Hahaha.*
>
> *Anyhow, that's it from the trenches. My hand is tired from writing this with a pen instead of texting, otherwise I'd write more. I miss you and hope you are living large in 1861.*
>
> *Have you met any cute cowboys or Indians?*
>
> *Love, Libby.*

I folded the letter back into the envelope. Libby was sad she was losing her tan? Grossed out by other peoples' shoes? Dealing with the angst of a tired hand? I had a hard time feeling sorry. Seriously.

When we got back to the cabin, a jar was sitting beside the front door. A tiny note attached said "SHAMPU" in crooked letters. While Dad inspected the garden—hundreds of tiny green sprouts had started poking their heads through the soil—I brought the jar into the house.

"What is it?" Rebecca Lynn asked.

I placed the jar on the table and twisted off the lid. The smell of lemons rose into the air. "Shampoo." I held out the paste for her to smell. "From Nanny."

"It smells good."

I held it out for Rusty who took a whiff and smiled. Then I put the lid back on and gathered up the largest of the flour sack towels, my small mirror, my old-lady soap, and my new hair product. I grabbed the old-fashioned razor from my dad's toiletries box and wrapped it up in a towel. Someone had to put that thing to good use, and Dad, who was beginning to resemble Early Man, obviously wasn't interested.

"I want to take a bath, too," Rebecca Lynn said, pulling off her bonnet.

Engrossed in my own appearance, I hadn't noticed until that moment how dirty my little sister was. Her body was covered in red clay and dust. Little specks of white things were sitting in her greasy hair, and her nails were lined with black. Her nose had been running earlier that day, and tiny streaks of clean went from her nose to her top lip.

"Grab a towel, Half-pint," I told her, referring to the nickname Charles Ingalls had given his daughter.

On our way to the creek, with Sully at our heels, we stopped at the field.

"We're going to take a bath in the stream," I informed Dad, who smiled before turning his eyes back to his plants. Then I told Rusty, "Dude, you can't follow us. Don't be a Steven Stalker."

We left Rusty behind with Dad, and Rebecca Lynn and Sully and I continued on our way, the chickens squawking in their coop as we headed toward the path.

At the stream, Sully lapped at the clean water before lying down on the bank. His eyes moved between the two of us as we readied for our baths. I unboxed the straight razor and placed the toiletries in a row on a log. My sister and I took off our shoes and socks. I pulled off my dress. I undid my corset and waited in my slip as Rebecca Lynn undressed. I showed her how to hang her clothes on a nearby tree branch so they wouldn't get any dirtier. Having to wash all of our clothes and sheets and linens once a week was bad enough; I didn't need an extra day of that lovely chore.

She stepped into the middle of the creek. I filled the bucket. "Get ready, little naked bean sprout, this is going to freeze your bazookas off." She yelped and giggled at the same time as I dumped crystal clear water over her head. She folded her arms across her chest and shivered.

With each vertical streak of black that made its way to Rebecca Lynn's buttocks, I felt guiltier. I remembered back to when she was two and I was eight. Mom had asked me to stay with her in the bathtub for a few minutes while she folded laundry. I took off my clothes and got into the tub. I loved the smell of my little sister back then, so sweet, like talcum powder and fresh air. We played with the magnetic plastic letters, sticking them against the side of the tub. Then I farted and made her laugh. Mom trusted me with her life back then.

Rebecca Lynn said now, "Daddy needs a bath more than us."

"You're not kidding."

I took the old lady soap and rubbed it against the rag. I scrubbed my sister from her shoulders all the way down to her ankles.

"Do your front," I said, handing her the rag. "Don't forget your face and ears."

When she was done, I scooped a chunk of shampoo out of the jar. I wanted to make it last, but her hair was so dirty. The shampoo didn't lather much, so I rubbed it deep into her scalp. "Cover your eyes." I poured water over her head and squeezed out her hair.

"I want to take a real bath," she said through blue lips and chattering teeth.

"I know, right?"

When she was clean, I tossed her a towel which she wrapped around her head. She splashed around in the water as I took off my slip. My sister would see me naked for the first time since we were little. For some reason, none of that privacy stuff seemed to matter out here in the woods. If anything, it seemed like the most natural thing in the world to be standing naked in the middle of a creek on a hot summer day. It felt so liberating to bathe, even though the water was cold. Black and red dirt washed from my skin into the stream and away over the rocks.

"I see tadpoles," Rebecca Lynn said.

"Cool," I told her.

"Do you think there are fish?"

"Maybe. If there are, we'll go fishing."

I heard her say quietly, "Just like Laura Ingalls," and I smiled.

The sun told me it was about five o'clock. Dad was hanging out with his garden sprouts, and a blackberry pie, which I'd baked in the Dutch oven, thank you very much, was cooling under a piece of cheesecloth in the kitchen. The warm air brushed over my shoulders as I stood in the creek, taking in the smell of leaves and soil. This wasn't so bad, really, once everything fell into place. I hadn't thought of *NCIS* or my iPod in a week. I didn't crave McDonald's, or Pepsi, or beer.

And, of course, there was Wendell.

Prudence had a crush on him, but that didn't bother me. This was reality television. Maybe it would turn out to be more like *The Bachelor* than I had suspected, with two girls liking the same guy. Just like it, only without the hot tub. Wendell's face hovered in front of me while I washed my hair, the smell of lemons cascading over my cheekbones. I admitted to myself that if it weren't for him, I'd probably give up on bathing altogether.

I finished rinsing my hair and soaped up my rag. I scrubbed my body, feeling brand new as dirt from my arms and stomach slowly washed away. Like a baptism. I thought of Mom and how proud she'd be if she saw me now, watching over my sister, enjoying nature.

The rustle of moving branches caught my attention. I looked up. On the other side of the stream, a baby deer pulled leaves from a bush. Within seconds, three more deer stood next to the first. They glanced up and went back to eating. Even Sully knew better than to disturb them, as he stayed put on the bank.

"Brooke…" Rebecca Lynn said.

"I know," I whispered. "Aren't they beautiful? Probably the only thing that's cool about this place."

"Brooke!"

"Shut it. You'll scare them away."

I peered down at my legs which were now clean, but hairier than a monkey's. This was going to be my favorite part of the bath. The *coups de grace*, as my mom used to say whenever she put a scoop of vanilla ice cream on top of a warm chocolate brownie. I reached for the razor, but it wasn't on the log where I'd put it. I looked on the bank under the towel, then in the stream. I squatted down, swishing my hands among the underwater rocks to find it. My fingers were nearly frozen and my teeth were chattering like mad. If I didn't shave soon, my hands would be too stiff to hold the handle.

"Brookie…" Rebecca Lynn said like a whining broken record.

"What?" I asked, raising my voice. "What do you want?" The deer scattered and bounded off into the trees. "Now see what you did? Damn it, Rebecca Lynn."

I shook my head and continued to feel around in the stream for the razor, determined more than ever to make my legs silky again. My fingers hit against something sharp, but it was only a twig.

Then everything happened so fast.

Sully jumped into the water and I stood up. He started

barking at Rebecca Lynn. Even though my sister had put on her slip, she was still standing in the middle of the stream in her bare feet, the towel around her shoulders. One of her arms was sticking straight out. Her face was ashen, and she was staring down at something in the water. She shook her head like she'd just seen a monster. The first thing that came into my mind was leeches, and then, even more frightening, water snakes.

"What is it?" I asked, my heart coming up in my throat.

I stepped closer, trying not to slip on moss-covered rocks. As I moved toward her, I followed her gaze downward. There was no monster, and there was no leech stuck to her foot. Blood was pouring from a thin line in her calf.

She stared at me, her brown eyes wide, her mouth in a big open circle, like she was surprised to see me.

I spotted the open razor, the bone handle in her fist.

"It was an accident!" Rebecca Lynn suddenly shouted. "I didn't mean to!"

She screamed then, a blood-curdling scream you only hear in horror films. Sully circled her as he barked. I slipped as I reached out for her and fell on my knees in the creek. I stood up again, my body numb to the cold. I grabbed the razor from her hand and threw it onto the bank.

"What did you do? What did you do…?"

I grabbed her towel, and as fast as I could, wiped away the blood. I'd never seen a slice so straight and deep. It started on the outside of her right knee, and worked its way six inches down the side of her calf. I wiped and wiped, but each time I did, the blood gushed faster.

Remembering what I had learned from Lifeguard First Aid at

camp, I grabbed my apron and tied it tightly around her thigh, just above the knee, as I elbowed the crazed dog out of my way.

"I'm bleeding!" Rebecca Lynn screamed.

"I know! Stop screaming!"

I grabbed my slip and pulled it over my head. Still barefoot and trying not to lose my balance in the stream, I gathered up my sister.

"Stop wiggling!"

"I'm bleeding!" she screamed again.

The water around her feet had turned to an eerie shade of orange.

I cradled my little sister in my arms, made it up the low embankment, and ran. In my bare feet, I stepped on branches and roots, trying not to cry out when they jabbed the soles of my feet. Sully barked like a rabid dog as he followed at my heels. I could feel her warm blood dripping down my arm.

We ran into Rusty at the edge of the woods.

"Get my dad! Hurry!!"

He never let go of his camera as he ran across the yard to the field.

I made my way to the cabin with Rebecca Lynn sobbing in my arms. Dad met us on the back stoop.

"I'm bleeding, Daddy!" she cried.

Dad took her from my arms and tore into the cabin. Rusty panned the dark drops of my little sister's blood as they made a dotted path along the wooden floor.

"What happened?" Dad asked, placing her on the table.

"Your razor," I said.

"Oh, dear God," he said, peering down at her leg. His hands

were covered in blood.

Rebecca Lynn cried harder.

Dad turned to Rusty. "Go down the hill and get Doctor Hensel."

"I've never ridden a horse before," he said. I was amazed his camera never left his shoulder, and thought in one brief moment of insanity that maybe it was permanent, like a goiter, or a second head.

"I'll go then," Dad told him. "You stay here with…" He looked at Rebecca Lynn, then at me. "No. Brooke. You go get the doctor and bring him back with you."

"One-way is a shorter distance than roundtrip," I said.

Dad touched the soaked rag on her leg. My sister screamed. He shook his head, confused. "The ride will make it worse."

"But Dad—"

"Go get the goddamn doctor!"

I didn't have time to argue. In my slip and bare feet, I ran to the corral. Willow came to me before I called her, and without any challenge let me bridle her. I wasn't about to take the wagon; that was way out of my league. I secured the saddle and made sure the bit and straps were in place. I opened the gate, climbed on top, tugged on the reins, and shouted, "Hi-ya!"

With me on her back, she trotted down the dirt road and over the first rise. Crazy things, like Willow breaking a leg, an Indian attack, or a wagon robber, popped into my head. My sister could bleed to death. And now I was riding a horse whose back had never known me, down a barely familiar dirt road, to a farmhouse I'd only seen in passing.

It ran through my head that this kind of thing wasn't in the contract. This kind of thing didn't happen on reality television, unless you counted *Survivor*, where all the OCD bug-eating crazies couldn't wait to witness disaster. Someone fainted now and then on the *Biggest Loser*, or got drunk and overheated in a hot tub on *The Bachelor*, but not anything like this.

This went galaxies beyond the venture I'd been talked into.

Doctor Hensel met me at the end of his driveway in a black buggy pulled by a stocky horse. A man who could have been Jackie Chan's twin sat next to him with a camera on his shoulder.

"I hear you got an emergency," Doctor Hensel said.

"Yes. My sister—"

"Lead me there."

He followed me up the road to the cabin, the buggy close behind Willow and me. Inside the house stood Prudence and Mrs. Miller, along with Nanny.

"We heard what happened," Prudence said. For the first time since we'd met, she didn't seem to be playing for the cameras. She stood next to the table where Rebecca Lynn lay unmoving, her face pale and her breathing shaky. Nanny removed the bloody rag, exposing the cut.

Doctor Hensel placed a hand on Rebecca Lynn's forehead, "Hello there, Sweetie. Just going to clean this up a little."

"I want Brooke."

Prudence and Nanny moved out of the way so I could stand beside the table. I held her hand.

Dad said, "She cut herself with my straight razor."

The doctor pulled a candy stick out of his pocket and gave it to Rebecca Lynn. He put a pair of spectacles on his nose and took a small jar out of his bag. He gently swabbed the sides of the gash with a clean piece of linen.

"She needs stitches," Doctor Hensel said. "There are two ways we can work this, Mr. Decker. One way is to stitch it with what I have in my bag. In the real world, I worked in the ER for twenty years. I have local anesthetic, real stitches, and real antibiotics. The other way is to take her to a hospital. Offsite. We'd send for a car."

"A real car?" I asked. It felt like a century since I'd seen an actual automobile.

"What do you want to do?" the doctor asked.

"What's your advice?" Dad asked.

Rebecca Lynn sucked on her candy as her eyes went from the doctor to Dad.

Doctor Hensel said, "If you decide to take care of this here, you'll be charged 1800's prices for the stitching, but modern-day prices for the medicine. If you choose to go to a modern hospital, that will take you out of Sweet Sugar Gap. For good."

Oh my God, I thought. *This is our chance! Why didn't I think of this before? It would have been worth slicing my own leg in two to get us back to Modern Land.*

I chanted in my mind, *Hospital, hospital, hospital,* like a Duke fan at a basketball game.

"I don't want to go to a hospital, Daddy," Rebecca Lynn said. "I don't want to go home."

Doctor Hensel said, "Mr. Decker?"

No Dad, don't agree with her. I don't want to wash in the creek. I don't want to flip mattresses or sleep on a musty pillow. I don't want to bake bread or pies, or hang out with Prudence drinking tea. I don't even need Wendell, do I? Maybe I only convinced myself I liked him because he's the only guy my age within a hundred miles...

Dad told the doctor, "Take care of it here."

"Very well." Doctor Hensel turned to me. "If you'd get some water boiling, that would be helpful."

Adding insult to injury that we weren't going to run with joy over the hills back to our old life, I was reduced to being the water fetcher. First it was "Boil the water" then "Bring me clean strips of rags" then "Bring some water for your sister to sip."

Prudence followed me out to the springhouse, *sans* cameramen who thought it required three cameras to film the down-home stitching of a little girl's leg.

"I hope your sister's okay," Prudence said.

"Thanks."

Back in the cabin, Rusty and Carl and the Jackie Chan look-a-like kept their cameras zooming, even after the Millers and Nanny had left. Afterward, they dug into the blackberry pie I'd made for church the next day. They were no better than a flock of turkey vultures, waiting to swoop down the second a raccoon gets hit by a car. When Carl had the nerve to ask me for a cup of coffee to go with his slice of pie, I sugar-sweetly reminded him we weren't allowed to talk to one another.

Rebecca Lynn was already asleep on a makeshift bed near the fireplace by the time the doctor was ready to leave. Carl had left with the Millers, so Rusty and Jackie Chan kept the cameras rolling as Doctor Hensel handed Dad a piece of paper. Dad silently grabbed his leather pouch from the mantel, counted out a bunch of coins, and placed them in the doctor's hand.

After Doctor Hensel left with his cameraman, Rusty stayed a little while longer.

I asked Dad, "How much was it?"

"Ten dollars."

"That's not so bad."

He put his leather pouch back on the mantel. "Just how long do you think three dollars is going to last us?"

Not knowing what else to offer, I said, "I'm sorry, Dad."

He didn't respond as the back door slammed behind him.

CHAPTER TWENTY-THREE

The next morning, Rebecca Lynn sat at the kitchen table with her leg propped up on a chair beside her. Leaning against the chair was a walking stick Dad had made from a thick branch. My sister looked like a female Tiny Tim, and posed for Rusty's camera. I was counting the seconds for her to milk it for all it was worth. I didn't have to wait long.

"It hurts, Daddy," Rebecca Lynn whined. "I don't want to sit in a bumpy wagon."

Dad dropped his empty coffee cup into the dish bucket. "Then you and Brooke can skip church today."

I was wearing the dress Prudence had given me. My hair was shiny and smelled like lemons. I felt awful about my sister's injury, so, while Rebecca Lynn slept, I had rolled her hair up in rag curls, and then I did my own. Now, my sister and I could have passed for backup dancers in a Katy Perry video.

"Church is the only time I get to see other people," I reminded Dad.

"You should have thought about that before you let your

sister play with my razor."

"I wasn't playing with it, Daddy," Rebecca Lynn said.

"You were responsible, Brooke," Dad said. "I trusted you."

"Yeah? Well, *I* trusted *you*."

"What does that mean?"

"You had no right dragging us out here."

"We signed a contract."

"*You* signed it!"

"Stop fighting," Rebecca Lynn said.

I could see Rusty's eyes growing wide with excitement, like he was suddenly filming a high stakes boxing match and not some stupid family in an argument out in the middle of Bumflip Nowhere, in an era that had ended before my great-grandparents were born.

"Why did you take my razor to begin with?" Dad asked me.

"To shave my legs."

"Nobody out here cares if you shave or not, Brooke."

"Is that why you don't shave anymore?" I scrunched up my nose to show my disgust for his scraggly beard.

"What I do with my face is my business."

"Well, what I do with my legs, and other parts of my body, is *my* business." I gave him a hefty modern-day chicken neck. "I am going to church," I informed him, dropping my plate into the soapy bucket.

"She likes that boy, Daddy," Rebecca Lynn said.

"Shut up."

"What boy?" Dad asked.

"Wendell," my sister answered.

My cheeks were hot.

"Well," Dad said, "you can visit with Wendell next week. Today you'll stay here and keep an eye on your sister."

He pulled up his suspenders, grabbed his hat from the chair, put it on, and went out the front door. Rusty started to follow but then stopped. He stood in the middle of the room, confused.

"Oh, go with him," I told Rusty. "Church is more exciting than anything here. Besides, without us there, you'll have extra to eat at the picnic."

While the breakfast dishes sat in the bucket soaking, I went upstairs and took off my bonnet, my pretty Sunday dress, and my tight corset, and hung them up on nails next to my work dress. I took off my shoes and socks and put them on the floor under the window. I didn't think about it beforehand, I just did it. I grabbed the Maybelline bottle from my secret hiding place and smeared the beige liquid all over my face, hiding my freckles. I circled my eyes with the eyeliner like I was hot for werewolves, then I used the tiny mirror to help guide the silver hoop through my eyebrow. I ran my fingers through my thick curly hair and shook it out. Finally, I grabbed my iPod and headed down the ladder.

"Why are you in your slip?" Rebecca Lynn asked.

"I'm tired of those clothes."

"But you have to wear them. And you're not supposed to wear jewelry."

"Whatever."

"Daddy's going to get mad."

"I don't care cuz it ain't fair, and I don't wear no underwear."

I went outside, suddenly craving flowers. I walked all over the property in my slip and bare feet as the wind played with my curls. Without that awful dress choking me, I felt weightless. I picked wildflowers growing along the fence. Tiny bees seemed unhappy that I was disrupting their breakfast, but I picked them anyway. Back in the cabin, I put the wildflowers and red roses in every empty container I could find, filled them with water, and put them all over the downstairs. Mom had had a knack for making our home look like it belonged in a garden magazine with the flowers she used to grow. Now, it looked like she'd stopped by for a visit.

"They're pretty," Rebecca Lynn said.

I slid her bonnet from her hair, ran my fingers through her curls, stuck a tiny daisy behind her ear, and did the same to my own. "We don't have to live like moles, you know." I invited my sister to sit with me on the front porch.

"What should we make for Sunday supper?" she asked as she rocked, patting Sully on the head.

"Maybe Dad can pick up some Happy Meals on the way home from church."

Rebecca Lynn giggled a moment but stopped herself. "You're going to get us in trouble," she said. But I caught the flicker of mischief in her eye.

I sat on the other rocker with my iPod buds in my ears, listening to Folk Uke, an awesome band I introduced to Libby a thousand years ago. "Aren't you sick of your clothes?"

My sister shrugged.

"And your shoes?"

"They hurt my feet."

"Exactly. Who says you have to live with sore feet? You already have a sore leg. It hardly seems fair to suffer so much."

She looked at her shoes, thinking. "Laura Ingalls took her shoes off sometimes."

"I know, right?"

My sister untied her laces, took off her shoes, and slipped out of her socks. "The socks were rubbing my bandage."

"Since we're spending the morning enjoying nature instead of church, you don't have to wear your apron either."

Rebecca Lynn stood up and took off her apron.

"Good girl," I said.

"What if Daddy…"

"Daddy Dear is at the picnic. Without us. Chowing on meat and potatoes, and scarfing on all kinds of yummy desserts."

Without saying a word, Rebecca Lynn took off her dress. She folded it neatly and put it on top of the apron on the back of the rocking chair. In her slip she sat again, pulling her cut leg up onto the seat and placing her hand protectively on top of the bandage.

"I feel cooler now."

"Damn straight."

She put her arms in the air as she rocked. "I feel like an angel."

I laughed. We did sort of look like angels, only my wild hair and dark eyeliner made me more of a fallen one.

My favorite Fallout Boy song drifted through the tiny ear buds, and I missed my old life more than ever.

Sully followed me as I jumped off the porch. The clover felt smooth beneath my feet. I said to Rebecca Lynn, "Come here, little sister."

She limped down the porch steps with her walking stick over to where I stood.

I took one of the ear buds and put it in her ear.

"It's loud," she said.

I turned the iPod down and started moving, a little swaying at first, but as the music grew faster I started rocking out, like a spastic sinner at a tent revival. Rebecca Lynn couldn't move as well with her stitched-up leg, but with the walking stick in her hand, she managed to jiggle next to me. Sully moved in and around us, barking, and we laughed as we danced in front of the cabin. I hadn't felt so good, so free, in what felt like forever.

The two of us danced our way through two dozen songs, one just as good as the last. I knew Rebecca Lynn didn't care for my kind of music, but she still had pretty good rhythm, even with a bum leg. With one bud in her ear and the other in mine, we moved like mad women, shaking our crazy curls and laughing hard as we danced. Our faces were red and our feet were filthy, but we didn't care. For the moment we had music, we had each other, and we were having a total blast.

I was imagining we were the witches in *The Crucible*, dancing around a cauldron, when the ground shook violently beneath our feet. We froze.

"What is that?" my sister asked anxiously.

I clicked off the iPod. The rumble grew louder. The ground vibrated harder. "I don't know..."

It wasn't until we saw the dirt flying that I understood what we were experiencing: the thundering of hooves. Carriages and wagons soon made their way around the bend, approaching our house.

At the head of the small stampede were Dad and Rusty.

"Oh, snap," I said, as families parked their wagons along the sides of the road. Dust was everywhere and I started coughing.

Rebecca Lynn hobbled to the porch and inched her way up the steps. She put her dress back on, and worked to put on her apron. I stood transfixed in the front yard, an abandoned mannequin in her underwear.

Dad jumped down from the wagon. He took off his hat and waved the flying dirt away from his face. One by one the townspeople stepped down from their wagons. Rusty and Carl, and two other camera people, filmed the forming crowd as everyone followed Dad through the front gate. The younger kids went up on the porch to see Rebecca Lynn's stitches, which she proudly showed them. Like a small herd they disappeared into the house.

"What's going on here, Brooke?" Dad demanded.

I held onto my iPod with one hand and put the other hand on my hip. Well, I had come this far, dancing like a maniac out here in my slip, listening to music from Modern Land, wearing my raccoon makeup. Maybe this was the perfect moment to get off this crazy ride. My last hoorah. Maybe I wasn't cut out for this crap. I dared myself to do it, in front of the cameras, in front of these people. I would show Dad what dragging me out here had done to my mental stability. With any luck, Producer Dumb-ass Novak and Director Dip-shit Ricardo would come hauling me off the premises like a party crasher at the White House. They would realize I was bad for ratings, and we'd all be sent home. Dad would hate me for a while, but when he realized I only had one year left before college, he'd become guilt-ridden and forget all about Sweet Sugar Gap.

"I'm done," I announced proudly.

"Done with what?" Dad asked.

"With this. I want to go home."

Dad took wide steps until he stood a foot from me. "This is your home."

"No, it's not!" I screamed, making him jump. I didn't care that I was being filmed for television. I didn't care that everyone was watching me, judging me. I didn't know these people. I didn't owe them anything. "This is not my home!" I turned to the townspeople who weren't my real neighbors at all, and shouted, "How can this be worth it to you people? My sister almost lost her leg for ratings!"

Dad stepped closer until the tips of his boots nearly touched my bare toes. "You are going to get us kicked out."

"Perfect."

"If we get kicked out, we forfeit everything."

"I don't care."

All the families stood in our yard now. Prudence made her way to the front of the spectators who carried linen-covered dishes or crocks in their hands. Everyone stared at me like I was the number one attraction in a freak show.

I gazed over the crowd with their perfect nineteenth-century outfits and hairdos, carrying their Early American covered dishes. There were the Murphys, Wendell included, the Millers, and all the other people handpicked to come out here. I wondered, how could they all be so good at this? And why in heaven's name was this venture so important to everyone but me? Was this was a case of mass hysteria? If it was, why hadn't I caught it yet?

I thought about holding up my iPod high in the air; to turn it back on and let my music blare from the tiny ear buds. How would they respond to seeing an actual gadget from more than a hundred and fifty years in the future? Would they deem me a witch? *Let's find out.* I touched my iPod. Wrapped my hand more tightly around it. Started to raise it into the air.

Wendell's face seemed to wonder if I'd be more comfortable in a straight jacket. Then he turned away, as if by embarrassing myself I was embarrassing the whole town.

My eyes connected with Dad's. He no longer looked angry. He looked frightened. Streams of sweat dripped from his uneven sideburns onto his shirt. He said, speaking methodically like he had just learned English, "If we get kicked out, we forfeit the money."

At first I believed I had misunderstood him. That he'd said "bunny" or "honey" and I couldn't imagine what he meant by either of those words. Then he grabbed me by the wrists like he was drowning and I was his life preserver.

"There is a million dollars at stake here." His jaw was clenched like he suffered from Tetanus. "Do you understand?"

"What—"

"If we go home, we get nothing." He took a step back, his face the color of a ripened purple grape. "Not one red cent!"

"I didn't know about any money," I told him, told the crowd. I waited for someone, anyone, to offer an explanation. But no one said a word. "Dad, you never told me."

"Well, now you know."

"You should have told me."

"It shouldn't take a bribe to make you want to work hard, Brooke. To make you want to be a great person."

My eyes moved from his heated face to the crowd standing behind him. I felt like I was surrounded by zombies, staring at me like they were debating whether to eat my brains or not. Except they weren't only looking at my head, which was covered with a rat's nest of hair. They were staring at my dirty bare feet; the modern makeup decorating my face; the hoop earring in my brow; my clothes which, back in the 1800s, were probably equivalent to being naked in today's world.

Surrounded by all these perfect replicas of another century, I stood out like a giant whitehead on a clear-skinned face. I may as well have brought smallpox to the tiny town of Sweet Sugar Gap.

Only a few minutes before, I was brave. I was modern and free and thrilled to have my crazy hair and lack of clothing. But now, with Dad breathing like an angry ox, the townspeople kicking uncomfortably at the dirt, and a collection of movie cameras scanning my underpinnings…

"I…I…"

"I'll take her inside," Prudence said as she grabbed my wrist and pulled me toward the cabin. "It's the neighborly thing to do." She brought me into the cabin and pushed me up the ladder. I couldn't feel my legs.

Prudence said nothing as she watched me wrap the cord around the iPod and tuck the bundle up in the eaves. In silence, she held up the tiny mirror as I pulled the hoop from my eyebrow. This too, I put back on the beam.

When she finally spoke, it was in a whisper. "Your dad is

really pissed."

"I'm the one who should be pissed. He never told me about the money."

I tied up my corset and slipped my dress over my head. I sat on the bed and pulled on my socks.

"I don't think it's so bad out here," Prudence said, sitting on Dad's bed as I got dressed.

"Why would you, when your family gets to live in a mansion and your playroom is larger than my whole cabin? It's easy for you with a bunch of slaves waiting on you hand and foot, and your beautiful dresses. Try living in this shack for a while. Try milking a cow and feeding a filthy pig and washing your private parts in a freezing stream. Let's see how well you play along."

"Don't be jealous."

"I'm not—"

"This is about Wendell, isn't it?"

"What? No."

"I see the way you eye him."

"So? He's not so bad to look at. He also happens to be the only guy around."

"He's not interested in you, if that's what you're thinking."

"How do you know?"

"I can tell by the way he looks at me," she said.

"He'd look at anyone if it meant winning a million dollars."

"Including you?"

I put on my apron and tied it. I was suddenly tired and sad. If everyone else was out here to win money, then Wendell was, too. Even so, I wanted to put Prudence in her place. "FYI," I said. "Wearing a hoop skirt and waving a fan doesn't make a boy want you. Boys like girls who are real. Money or not. I know your type, in any era. You're the snotty type who thinks every guy likes her, like you're entitled to be liked, even though you haven't earned it. You have no idea what it means to work hard, or to suffer."

"You want to borrow one of my slaves? Nanny can do your chores while you run around in your underpinnings."

"She's not a real slave."

"For the sake of this show she is."

"Whatever. I don't want any slaves, real or not."

"Fine. That's the last time I make the offer."

"You know, you're twice the beeotch when the cameras aren't around."

"I don't have to listen to you," she said. "You can stay up here the rest of the day for all I care. I, however, plan to have a wonderful time at our old-fashioned picnic. I'm going to perfect the part of the Southern rich girl from 1861 who pretty much gets everything she wants and doesn't have to apologize for her good fortune."

She headed down the ladder, leaving me in the hot stuffy attic. Slowly, I laced up my shoes.

CHAPTER TWENTY-FOUR

I watched the women as they worked together in my tiny kitchen, preparing the Sunday meal like it was the most important thing on their minds. But the only thing on my mind was the money, and the fact that Dad had lied. Not lied outright, but lied by omission. A trick I had perfected.

Dad ignored me as we prepared the picnic, turning his head in the other direction when I walked by him with one plate or another. Blankets were placed on the low grassy hill near the springhouse. Rebecca Lynn hung out with the younger kids, and Prudence followed Wendell around like a shelter puppy as he readied the fire with the men. We ate while the sun was still high in the sky, the breeze just enough to help stave off the thick humidity hanging over the property. There was ham and wild turkey and cornbread stuffing and gravy; fresh lemonade and tea; homemade biscuits and pies and gingersnaps topped with powdered sugar. After dessert, Dad took the men around to show off the farm while the women cleaned up.

It was business as usual when the picnic was over. I was asked to fetch water from the springhouse. The camera people were busy filming a multitude of scenes, so I took off across the lawn before they had a chance to follow. I entered the stone building, needing some peace and quiet and no longer afraid of ghosts, and sat cross-legged on the cool cement floor. I breathed in the damp smell of earth and thought about what Prudence had said…about me being jealous.

Was I? And if so, of who, or what? Of Wendell? Of Prudence's big house and easy life and pretty things?

Of the fact that she still had a mother?

My hands went to my wet cheeks. It seemed as though tears were always sitting close to the surface, ready to let loose without my say-so. I wondered if other girls who had lived out here a hundred years ago sat in this very springhouse, sobbing over their circumstances.

And why was I crying, really? Was it because I would have traded in a million dollar prize for a chance to spray stinky bowling shoes for the summer? Was it because my dad was angry? Disappointed? Because I had embarrassed myself in front of the whole town? In front of Wendell?

My head jerked at the sound of approaching feet. Wendell ducked his head under the springhouse doorway and stepped inside. I stooped over and filled the bucket, keeping my head down, hiding my red eyes beneath my bonnet.

"You alright?" he asked. He took off his hat and hunched his shoulders to fit beneath the low dirt ceiling.

"I'm fine."

"If it means anything, you look cute in a slip."

I tried to laugh, but only a little snort came out.

"You know, Brooke, I'm homesick, too."

I faced him. "You are?"

"Sure." His voice was softer in here, like we were standing in a confessional together. "I know what you're going through."

I don't want to like you Wendell. Please stop looking at me that way. Stop having pretty green eyes with long dark lashes. Stop pushing your thick hair off your forehead. Stop being more than what you're meant to be: a diversion from this hellhole.

"I don't think living out here for four months is worth any amount of money," I said. "Do you?"

"I'm not out here for the money."

"You're not?"

"My dad thought it would bring us boys down to earth, getting back to basics. As it turns out, things are pretty rad."

"*Rad*? What are you, a backcountry surfer dude?"

"I mean, *splendid*."

We laughed.

Knowing Wendell was also homesick made me feel less lonely, less like an outsider, and less like there was something out there in Modern Land I was missing by being trapped here in the olden days. And the fact that the money didn't matter to him made me feel an even deeper connection. I wondered, as my stomach fluttered, if he felt it, too.

He glanced behind him through the miniature doorway. Carl was heading up the path toward the springhouse. "Listen," Wendell said. "We really can't talk about these things, okay? Just play along. Nobody wants to get kicked out."

"I do."

"Well, your dad doesn't."

"I don't have a problem with him staying."

"But if you go…if your family breaks up…well…that would suck."

"It would?"

"Totally." He smiled, and I nearly melted into the springhouse floor. "Just do what I do. Try to get into the rhythm of things. Like you do when you're on vacation."

"I don't consider working ten hours a day much of a vacation."

"What if I could make things better for you?"

"Better? How?"

"I'll think of something…" He blushed. It was a real blush, the kind that starts at the collar and crawls across the cheeks and along the tops of the ears.

I grabbed the bucket of water and Wendell shut the springhouse door behind us. Carl filmed us as we moved along the path.

"The men are going to shoot targets over at the Millers' place," Wendell said. "The winner gets a turkey."

"Can girls come?"

"Who else will cheer on the men?" A yard down the path, he said, "I like your dress."

"Thanks. Prudence gave it to me."

As if she were a dog with bionic ears, Prudence was suddenly strolling up the path, her hoop skirt forcing her dress to sway back and forth, her curls bouncing up and down against the back of her neck.

"There you are, Wendell Murphy. I thought a bear had come and stolen you."

"He was just helping me with the water bucket," I said, handing it to him. We shared a smile.

"I hope you two haven't been telling each other secrets," Prudence said.

Neither Wendell nor I responded as the three of us walked along the path toward the cabin.

"I can't wait to see you shoot, Wendell," Prudence said as she tried to hook her arm in his, but he switched the bucket to his other hand, separating them. She ignored his disregard and said, "Brooke can take the bucket the rest of the way, can't you Brooke? She's strong. Like an ox."

Wendell said, "But I don't mind—"

"I have no problem carrying my own bucket," I said. "It says a lot about a girl who does her own chores and doesn't rely on free help to do them for her."

Wendell grinned. So did Carl. If the camera had owned a mouth, it probably would have grinned as well.

"Oh, Brooke," Prudence said, offering a fake laugh. "Go along now." She fanned her fingers.

I grabbed the bucket from Wendell's hands. As I trudged along the path ahead of them, I could feel them both staring after me. But I was praying that Wendell was staring harder.

Prudence sat on a blanket on the hill next to her house. Beside her sat her mother, who held her hands against her baby belly. A few yards away, Rebecca Lynn and I sat on one of our bed quilts and watched as the men took turns firing at clay pieces sitting on a large tree stump. Third in line was Wendell. He placed the rifle against his shoulder, aimed, and fired. The clay piece on the stump flew into bits and he lowered the gun. Prudence clapped and giggled like an idiot, and Mrs. Miller patted her daughter on the back as though she were the one who'd made the shot.

Dad stepped up to the line holding the gun from over our fireplace. Mr. Murphy showed him what to do and stepped back as Dad took aim. Another blast reverberated through the air. The bullet didn't go anywhere near the target, but the crowd cheered like he'd blown up the entire stump.

By the time the sun had moved into the western half of the sky, the shooting competition was over, and Wendell and Mr. Duffy had tied for first place. They were each given a live turkey for their winnings, and bowed for the crowd and the invisible cameras.

The families folded up their blankets and put their crocks and baskets back into the wagons. My dad shook hands with those who were leaving, and I thanked the women who had shared their food with us, meaning every word.

"My wife's feeling tired," Mr. Miller said. "I need to get her home." He patted Rebecca Lynn on the head. "Sorry about your leg, but it sure did bring on a nice picnic."

Prudence batted her eyelashes as she said goodbye to Wendell, ignored me completely, and stepped into the carriage with her mother and Carl, following the other wagon holding her brothers and father. They disappeared up the hill.

Wendell's brothers played with Sully in the yard, and Wendell sat with me on the front porch steps while his parents visited with Dad inside. Rusty leaned against the porch rail, his camera on the two of us. Wendell looked toward the camera and brought his eyes back to my face. He licked his lips. I noticed how thick they were. My stomach folded inside out.

"You aren't anything like her," he said.

"I'm sorry?"

"Prudence."

"Oh."

Wendell's Adam's apple moved up and down as he cleared his throat. "I'd like to talk to your father."

"Right now?"

He nodded.

Rusty followed us as we stepped into the cabin. Dad was pouring coffee for himself and Mr. Murphy, who sat at the table. By the fireplace, Mrs. Murphy was helping Rebecca Lynn change her bandage.

"Mr. Decker?" Wendell said, taking off his hat. "Could I speak with you, sir?" Wendell made his way to the table. Mr. Murphy glanced over to where I stood in the doorway. "Mr. Decker, sir, I would like to call on your daughter."

"Call on?" Dad said. "Oh. *Call on*. Well. I suppose..."

"Thank you, sir." Wendell ran back to me, grabbed my arm, and pulled me back outside.

"What was that?" I asked.

"What do you think it was?"

I was too nervous to respond. With the camera zoomed in on us, I felt like I was one of the women on *The Bachelor*. I almost laughed out loud, picturing Wendell down on one knee, handing me the final rose, violin music playing in the background. I saw our photo on the cover of *People*, our nuptials announced on

Ellen, like Prince William and Princess Kate.

As we stood on the porch, Wendell said, taking my hands in his, “Told you I’d make things better.”

CHAPTER TWENTY-FIVE

Dad hadn't said one word to me since my meltdown, and sharing a bedroom didn't make it easy to ignore one another. By the time he'd made sure Rebecca Lynn was asleep on her temporary bed downstairs, I was already under the covers. Now we lay on our beds in the stuffy attic as my sister's light snore drifted up the ladder. The moonlight sent a stream of yellow across the eaves as my eyes adjusted to the dark. Wendell's sweet smile floated in front of me, helping me relax a little.

I whispered to Dad, sure he was still awake, that he would want to talk about what had happened. "Today didn't turn out so bad. I mean, it kind of turned out okay." After a moment, I added, "I'm really sorry, Dad."

"For what?" he asked in a monotone voice. "The iPod? Your underwear exhibition?"

"You should have told me about the money."

"Would it have made any difference?"

I didn't answer.

"What in God's name were you thinking? I've never been so

embarrassed in my life. I can only hope they don't kick us out for what you did…"

I saw myself again, standing in front of the townspeople in my underwear, my spastic curls like cotton candy gone wild. The more I played the scene in my head, the more ashamed I became. "I just thought if I listened to a little bit of my old music…"

"They had music back in the 1800s, Brooke. Your generation didn't invent it."

"I know."

"Where's your iPod now?"

"In the eaves."

"Get rid of it."

"It doesn't matter anyway. The battery's almost dead and I forgot to bring a charger."

In my head I laughed, realizing how silly my last statement was, considering there wasn't any electricity to charge a charger with.

"Keep it out of sight," Dad said. "There's a lot at stake here."

"Don't you lose money by skipping work for four months? Isn't it sort of a tradeoff?" A moment of silence crept by. "Dad?"

When he started speaking, and the words floated along the trickle of light between our beds, the words didn't belong to him. They belonged to the night; had snuck into the room through a crack in the logs. "We're broke," he said.

I let out a snicker. "How can we be broke? We go on trips…you bought me a new car…"

"Brooke…"

"…and what about private school? And all our—"

"Listen to me." He let out a long stream of air, and I grew

nervous. "We're in trouble, Brooke."

"What kind of trouble?"

"We may lose our house."

I sat up, barely hearing the scratching of a tiny critter nesting somewhere close by. "What are you talking about?"

"Your mother," Dad said. "When she was sick. All those experimental treatments. They weren't covered by insurance. The hospital bills were massive."

"But your job, Dad. You have a cool boss. Can't he give you, like, an advance or something? Can't we—" I didn't have the words to describe it, but I knew if you were about to lose your house, there were ways to save it.

"There is no job," he said.

"You quit your job to come out here?"

"I got laid off."

"When?"

Another pause, this one longer than the first.

"When, Dad?"

"Last March."

I swallowed, but there was no spit to go down, and I let out a little choking cough.

"I wanted to give you girls everything after your mother died. I wanted to…fill the empty space."

Tears rolled down my cheeks. I wiped them away and saw my wet fingers in the moonlight.

"You had such a difficult time after she died," Dad said. "I just wanted you to be happy again. I just wanted you…" He stopped. When he spoke again, his voice trembled. "I looked for a job every day, but without moving us to another city…well, I couldn't just up and move you."

"But you did up and move me. You moved all of us."

"Only temporarily. It was the lesser of evils."

"You made me think this was all because of me...that dragging us out to Bumfreaking Nowhere was my fault. How could you do that? How could you make me think that?"

"You were the deciding factor, Brooke. You were falling apart back in New Bern, whether you realize it or not. I wanted to give you this opportunity to get back on track. I truly believed...and still believe...it was a good decision. For all of us."

"What about Rebecca Lynn? Was what happened to her worth it?"

"I knew living this way would be difficult, but losing our home would be harder. Brooke, if we leave now, we may not have a home to go back to. Do you see why I brought you out here? Do you see how important this is?"

I nodded in the dark. I did see. He didn't say it out loud, and he didn't have to: Whether we kept our house or not was up to me. If I did anything else to make us *un*-nineteenth-century-like, we would get kicked off the show, go back to New Bern, pack up the house, and then what? Live in my SUV if repo man didn't come and take it away?

I suddenly pictured the producers poring over the video of my personal coming-out party, my crazy curls and bare feet. I saw them rewinding it, then fast-forwarding it, playing it over and over again, deciding which parts to put on the air, which scene was the ultimate clincher of our expulsion.

Then I figured that maybe coming out here was my fault to begin with. If I'd done better in school, if I'd listened more, spent less time at Libby's, less time partying, maybe I'd have seen enough to put the pieces together. Maybe Dad would have told me the truth sooner. I could have found a job. I could have helped. We wouldn't be sharing a bedroom in a one-hundred-degree attic the size of a closet if it weren't for me. A doctor wouldn't have had to sew up a slash in my sister's leg.

"If we don't win, we'll only be able to keep the house until Thanksgiving," Dad said. "Coming up with the money to pay off the bank is my goal. All I want is a chance. I'm tapped out, Brooke. Dry. Your daddy is an empty tank."

I was crying hard now.

"Your sister doesn't know about the house," Dad said. "And I plan to keep it that way."

"What do we have to do to win?"

"What I've asked you to do all along: acclimate. Convince the producers you are a mid-nineteenth-century girl; that we will do what it takes to be the best backcountry family."

I pictured the townspeople and how they all seemed like they were born and bred in Sweet Sugar Gap. Backcountry folk, just like the early settlers. There was Prudence, twirling around in her pretty dress, curling her hair and sipping tea in that palace. I thought about Wendell and how convincing he was as a simple country boy working in his father's mercantile. And even though he was pretty convincing as a boy who liked me as much as I liked him, I still had my doubts about his motives.

'I want to make things easier for you,' he had told me. Would he have said those words if a camera hadn't been there as witness?

I felt a bit of the old Brooke seeping through—the one before Mom got sick—who loved to kick ass in the women's hurdles, scored third to the highest in her sophomore class on the PSAT, and got accepted into the School of Science and Math. Of course, I never went, because everything in my life had turned upside down…

"My eyebrow hoop," I whispered in the dark. "I took it from Mom's jewelry box. It didn't have a mate. It's the only thing I have out here that reminds me of her." We were silent for a few moments before I said, with complete conviction, "I'll help us keep our house, Dad. I'll help us win."

Dad said, as he rolled over in his bed, facing away from me, "That's good, Brooke. Because we really don't have a choice."

CHAPTER TWENTY-SIX

Nearly every waking second was spent wondering if the hatchet would come down on our family. Had the tape already been sent to the producers? Had we been voted off the show, and they were just waiting for an interesting live-action time to tell us, like during a church picnic, or while washing dirty socks?

I spent the additional seconds trying not to think about Wendell, waiting for him to call on me, worried whether his affections were real or bogus. I wondered how I would compete with him, while at the same time crushing on him, and that thought led me to wonder how on earth two people dated back in the old days. An entire day was taken up by chores. And I was hardly the picture of romance. I didn't wear makeup anymore, and I kept my hair hidden under a bonnet. Was it possible he was actually attracted to me this way?

I became obsessed, wondering if he was for real or not, if he planned to come back to "court" me. I went out on the porch every morning to shake out the bed linens, clean the bottoms of our boots, or sweep the porch steps, just so I could keep an eye on the road in front of our cabin. In and out I went. I got a lot done those days, and the cabin nearly sparkled—at least as much as an old rickety cabin can. But no one ever came up the road.

A few days after the infamous picnic, I found a large sack behind one of the rockers on the porch. I opened it up and smiled. It was filled with scraps of colorful material.

"From Nanny?" Rebecca Lynn asked as I sat on a rocker like an old married woman. I nodded and took the pink dress Prudence had given me, opened my sewing box, and slowly made my way around the hem with a long piece of dark green material. The contrast made the edge of the dress pop. At the bottom of the bag was a handful of white lace, which I carefully sewed around the cuffs and attached fake lace pockets to the hips. By the time I was done, it had turned into the perfect first-date dress.

Now all I needed was a place to show it off. And a date.

Stepping in muck and having hay stick to my shoes no longer bothered me. All of my tasks I did by rote, like eating or breathing or taking a wiz. I was waking up before Clyde began to crow. "Quit your day job," I told Cuckoo Bird as I cut some roses for the breakfast table. While Rusty followed me around like an overfed zombie, I milked Gretchen and groomed Willow. I helped my sister collect eggs and feed the chickens. Even fat pig Bambi got a little of my attention, snorting with happiness when I stopped to pat her head, mostly out of sympathy.

Saturday morning, Shopping Day, as I hung the coffee pot on the hook over the fire, the pot started shaking. Coffee sputtered and dripped into the embers. I stood up. The shelves were shaking, too. The whole cabin was rattling. I grabbed the only two mixing bowls I owned and placed them on the table so they wouldn't crash to the floor.

Dad and Rebecca Lynn hurried down the ladder. Pulling his dirty pants up over his long underwear, Dad ran to the front door and swung it wide. Dust flew into the cabin. Rebecca Lynn and I followed Dad onto the porch.

"Is it a stampede?" I asked as the multitude of horses come over the Eastern rise and sped past the house.

Dad pointed to a wagon with the name "Horely Family Circus" scrolled in bright red letters across the side.

"A circus," I breathed.

We stood and watched as six wagons, some with covers, some carrying bundles a mile high, raced past our cabin. Across the road, Rusty stood with his camera, filming the parade.

"They had circuses back then?" Rebecca Lynn asked.

"Since the beginning of time," Dad said.

I could barely make out a grin underneath all that facial hair.

A man steering one of the wagons tossed a piece of paper into the air as they flew by. The paper floated onto the grass. Clyde pecked at it.

Dad jumped off the porch and grabbed it. He held it up and read: "'Come One, Come All! The Horley Brothers Circus: A Truly Spectacular Show to astound and mesmerize even the most intelligent being! Come and witness Gregory, the fastest juggler east of the Appalachians; Lady Regina, the razor-sharp tightrope walker; Bernard, the incomparable sword-and-fire eater, and many more acts made to thrill!'" Dad laughed. "This is fantastic!"

The flyer told us the performance was the following Wednesday evening, at six pm in the schoolyard. Price of admission: ten cents.

By the time the train of wagons had disappeared, our cabin was surrounded by a thick haze of dust. Rusty joined us as we went back inside.

"Can we go, Daddy?" Rebecca Lynn asked.

"I wouldn't miss it for the world."

Neither would I, I thought, as my stomach flipped with excitement.

As we readied Willow for our trip into town, I made up different scenarios in my head as to how Wendell would react when he saw me, if he would remember what he had said the other night, or if I should just chalk it up to show business. Either way, I was a nervous wreck.

On the way to town, we stopped by Doctor Hensel's to get Rebecca Lynn's stitches out. For being such a trooper, he gave her a ham bone for Sully, which drew flies to the back of the wagon all the way to town.

We passed the white circus tent next to the schoolhouse, a red flag at the very top waving in the wind. The tent was smaller than the ones I'd been to in Modern Land, but that didn't ruin the excitement. Circus people in the school yard milled about, sitting on little stools, cooking on open fires, dogs running around.

In town, we were barely parked when I jumped out of the wagon and sped into Murphy & Sons. Rusty tried to keep up with me as I ran through the store. I spotted Wendell stocking canteens in a cabinet. He smiled and waved, like an ordinary guy crushing on an ordinary girl, not like he was going to win something by doing it. Relieved, I smiled back and took my basket around the store, pretending to take inventory of all the goodies instead of staring at the back of Wendell's head.

Rebecca Lynn came up behind me. "Daddy says we can't buy anything today, especially if we're going to the circus."

I knew the real reason was because of the doctor bill. I nodded, not caring if I ever bought anything again. The circus was in town.

Rebecca Lynn stared at the sweets like a penny candy addict. I looked at the pretty hoop skirts and gloves. I checked out the toys beneath the case to see if anything new had been added. I spotted a collection of oval brass belt buckles with eleven stars around the outside and the letters "C.S." in the center. Next to the case on top of the empty table was a tented sign: Men's Boots Temporarily Sold Out. All Future Orders for Soldiers Only.

I overheard Dad talking to Mr. Murphy. "My crops will be up soon, and I can trade you then. In the meantime, can I at least get some necessities besides the chicken feed? Maybe some salt? And some ham? We only have enough for one more meal."

When Wendell was through stocking canteens, he came over to me. My stomach rolled with waves and I tried to keep my knees from knocking. I pushed my bonnet back a little.

"Not buying anything today?" he asked, noticing my empty basket.

"Not unless you want to sell me that guitar for a few pennies," I said laughing. I glanced up at the shelf, but my smile vanished. The shelf was empty. "Where is it?"

Wendell said, "Sold it."

"Who bought it? Maybe I could get them to sell it to me."

"I doubt it."

"Well, maybe I can order one from your wish book."

This conversation was a waste of time, because even if I did order one, I didn't have the money to pay for it.

"We're only ordering necessities right now," Wendell said. "I'm sorry. Guitars aren't on the list."

"Why not?"

He grabbed me by the arm and pulled me toward the back. He whispered, "Because of the war."

"But there is no war."

"Well, the producers say there is." He raised his voice again, and Rusty turned his camera in our direction. "Anyway, I have a feeling the second we get supplies in, they'll be gone. Soldiers are cleaning us out."

Dad came up to us. "I've placed my order. You and your sister want to wander with me up the street?"

"Can we stop by the bakery?" Rebecca Lynn asked.

"'Fraid not."

"I'll come anyway."

I smiled at Wendell. "I'll stay here."

As Rusty followed Dad and Rebecca Lynn, I said, "I think this war thing is stupid."

Wendell shrugged. "A contract is a contract. The show can do whatever it wants."

"But faking a war…"

If a war could be faked, then other things could be faked as well. Like a boy's feelings.

The cameras in the corners of the store were watching our every move, like a department store looking for shoplifters. But

I didn't care. If I was going to stick this out until the end, I had the right to know.

"Do you really like me?" I asked Wendell, not bothering to whisper. "Really?"

"Of course."

Mr. Murphy stopped what he was doing behind the counter and looked in our direction.

"Prove it," I said.

He touched my arm, briefly, causing goose flesh to move over my shoulders, down my back, and along my legs. "Did you hear about the circus?"

I nodded.

"Go with me."

"Alright. But what about *before* the circus? It's still days away."

"Are you inviting me to dinner?"

"Um...sure."

"When?"

"I don't know..."

"How about tonight?"

"Oh. Okay."

"What time?"

I ran through the limited recipes in my head, thinking about what to cook, and how long it would take. "Six o'clock?"

"Pa?" he called. "Can I go to the Deckers' house for dinner tonight?"

"As long as the stock is put away."

"There," Wendell said. "Dinner tonight, six o'clock, your house."

My stomach moved in spasms, but I kept my voice smooth. "What will we do after?"

"Take a walk. Look at the stars. Talk."

"About what?" I couldn't imagine what there would be to talk about in such a strange world.

"We could talk about fire-eaters."

"And tightrope walkers?"

"Sure. And jugglers."

We laughed together as I shoved all thoughts of fake wars and expensive guitars and pretending to fall in love for money way in the back of my brain where they belonged. There were more important things to think about: like what to cook for dinner when your guest of honor is the cutest boy in Sweet Sugar Gap.

Back home in Modern Land, Wendell and I would have met up at the DQ, or at Union Point Park down by the river. We would have eaten alone, had a private conversation, and made out afterward if I was lucky.

But in Yesterday World, dinner was a family affair.

I hoped Wendell wasn't picky. I prepared Dutch oven cornmeal biscuits and split pea soup with ham chunks. Our tiny cabin held onto the delicious smells, and for a while it seemed more like a restaurant than a musty cabin with a chicken coop nearby. By the time I heard the horse's hooves out front, my stomach was so infested I could have started a butterfly museum.

The second Wendell stepped through the cabin door, Dad and Rebecca Lynn started in. He didn't seem to mind answering their silly questions, even with Rusty focused on him most of the time. And Wendell's answers were quick and funny, like a real old-fashioned boy with a good sense of humor. I got the feeling Mark Twain and Wendell Murphy would have gotten along pretty well.

While I finished setting the table and lighting the candles, Dad said, "So, Wendell, how long has your family been in the mercantile business?"

"As long as I can remember," Wendell said, walking the fine line between lying and ignoring the question altogether.

"Do you have any pets?" my sister asked. "We have a horse, a pig, some chickens, and a cow." She put her hand under the table and patted Sully's head. "And Sully."

"We have an old mutt named Edgar."

"What do you sell most of at the store?" Rebecca Lynn asked.

He paused like he was checking off inventory. "Lots of seeds and grain, jars for preserving, and newspapers. But recently, a lot of boots and rifles, too."

Placing the bowl of biscuits on the table next to the homemade butter, I said, "Soup's on."

"It smells delicious," Wendell said.

I beamed like a brand new star as I scooped out four bowls of soup. This was so different than feeding those stinky men who helped Dad plow. And I knew that this meal was eaten mostly in silence because everyone liked my cooking.

Afterward, as I poured after-dinner coffee into three tin cups, Wendell grabbed his satchel and pulled out a small package. "Straight from Switzerland." He placed a box of chocolates on the table.

I nearly died with ecstasy as the chocolate melted on my

tongue and slid down my throat. It was as good if not better than a first kiss.

Dad said, "I'll clean up. Why don't you go sit on the porch?"

Rebecca Lynn jumped up and headed across the floor.

"Not you," Dad told her. "Just your sister and Wendell."

Wendell and I went outside with Rusty behind us. The night air was heavy and still. We sat on the top porch step and stared into the heavens. A gazillion stars covered the dark sky like a sparkly blanket.

"Sometimes I feel like this is a place where I could stay," Wendell said, "if I had to."

Stay in Sweet Sugar Gap? Now that was definitely something I had not considered.

I wanted to say so many things to Wendell. In private. "Hey, Rusty," I said, suddenly breaking the invisible fourth wall. "Could you get me a glass of water?" I rubbed the front of my neck with my hand. "My throat is super dry."

Rusty didn't answer.

"Pretty please?"

He narrowed his eyes as he lowered his camera, then went into the house. The second the door shut, I grabbed Wendell's hand.

I yanked him across the property toward the barn. Once on the other side, we giggled as we stood like statues in the dark. I could smell the trash heap directly behind us. My dad had been burning our trash every few days, but now the table scraps and other decaying stuff rose into the air in waves. On the other side of the field, a large figure moved along the edge. If it hadn't been for the moonlight reflecting on the camera's glass eye, I would have mistaken Rusty for a bear. I put a finger to my lips as I led Wendell away from the barn and down toward the stream.

It took quite a while in the dark as we stumbled and held onto one another to prevent us from face-planting on the trail, but we finally found the creek.

"You're crazy," he whispered.

"I just wanted some privacy, you know?"

Wendell didn't respond as I took off my shoes and socks and stepped into the water. Shivers ran up my legs and into my spine, and I giggled as he took off his shoes and socks and followed me. I nearly tripped on the rocks, and he caught me. Holding me there, in the moonlit woods, in the middle of the stream, I nearly lost my mind with how much I wanted to kiss him. I leaned into him, pressing my front up against his, tilting my head back just so, but he turned his head to the side.

"No, Brooke."

I wondered if I stank; if maybe I was so used to my awful smell I had simply stopped noticing it. "Why not?" I asked.

"This is 1861. Boys make the first move."

I didn't force it. Some boys are like that, wanting to wait, whether from Yesterday World or Modern Land. But it didn't matter. I had all the time in the world out here.

Even though he didn't want to kiss, I leaned more into him, and we wrapped our arms around one another. But as we stood there, silent except for the sound of water moving over rocks, and his quick but steady heartbeat in my ear against his chest, the thought of cameras and reality shows and money coursed through me, like a cluster of parasites that had been hiding in my bloodstream, but were now crashing into my brain all at once.

I tried to keep my voice smooth, relaxed. "Wendell…how do I know this is all true?"

"True?"

"You. Here. With me. How do I know you aren't just doing this for ratings?"

"How do I know you aren't with me for the same reason? Or because I'm the only guy in town your age?"

He was right. If he could play the game, then I was capable of playing it as well. But I wasn't playing a game. Was I? I really liked him. Didn't I? I tried to picture us doing things together back in New Bern: taking a hayride at Christmas time, hanging out with Libby and her brothers in their FROG playing a game of Eight Ball, or watching a funny movie on a Saturday night. I wasn't faking it, because I could picture us together, and we were having fun. And it made sense that if I wasn't faking it, then neither was he.

"I just worry a lot," I told him.

He took his arms from around my waist and tilted my head back, one hand behind my bonnet, the other against my cheek. "About what?"

"I don't think I'll ever like it out here as much as you. Or as much as the others. I work so hard all the time."

"You're calling this work?"

"What I mean is, you're so good at this. It's like you were born in this world. I feel so out of place compared to you. Compared to everyone. It's like I don't fit."

Funny thing was, I didn't fit in back home either, especially after Mom died. I had become that oddly shaped block trying to squeeze into a small round hole.

"Well," Wendell said, "if it's all the same to you, you make it look easy. Dinner was great tonight. And the cabin by candlelight was totally...I mean, *really* romantic."

"It was?"

"You don't want to admit it, but you're pretty good at this yourself."

Was I really?

"Brooke! Wendell!" My dad's angry voice stormed through the trees.

"Rusty is a big fat baby," I whispered.

Wendell didn't respond. He never responded to my comments about the camera people. Never acknowledged them the way I did. We dried off our feet with the end of my apron and put our socks and shoes back on.

Back at the cabin, after a stern lecture from my dad about our disappearing act, I walked Wendell to his wagon.

"Drive safely," I told him.

"I will." He lit the two large kerosene lamps that hung from the wagon's front and climbed onto the seat. "I had fun tonight, Brooke."

"Me too."

"I'll see you soon."

"Okay."

After he shook the reins and rode off into the dark, I turned to see Clyde rustling around in the plants by the fence. "Cuckoo Bird," I said. Then I sang a song I remembered from my one short year as a Girl Scout: "Kookaburra sits in the old gum tree, merry, merry king of the bush is he. / Laugh kookaburra, laugh kookaburra, gay your life must be." With his beady little eyes, the rooster stared at me like I'd lost my mind.

As I walked up the cabin steps, I realized that hanging out with Wendell that evening made me think of hanging out with him once the venture was over. Of the things we would do together. Of introducing him to Libby and her brothers. And this made me think about my Real Life still sitting out there in Modern Land, and that thought pushed me back into a sad stupor.

Stop doing that, I scolded myself. The less I thought about what was going on in that other world without me, the less I would miss it. Besides, the circus was just around the corner, I had a beautiful gown to wear, and a hottie named Wendell Murphy was taking me as his date.

CHAPTER TWENTY-SEVEN

I had just finished my morning chores the following Wednesday when a set of angry cramps inched across my pelvis. My body had always been in sync with a twenty-eight-day clock, so, as much as I had foolishly prayed for it to hibernate for four months, here it was at last: my *I-am-woman-hear-me-roar interlude*, as my mom jokingly called it. I grabbed one of the sanitary napkins and the belt, (aka *magician's apparatus*), stuffed them into my apron pocket, and headed to the outhouse. It took a few minutes of fumbling around, mainly because I had to hold up my dress and slip while arranging that dang belt around my waist, and pinning the napkin to the belt, and all of this while trying to breathe with a corset choking my middle, but I finally got everything in place.

As I waddled uncomfortably to the front of the cabin, my sister jumped up from the rocker. In her hands she held a hoop skirt. "Nanny left this for you. She said she made it herself."

My fingers rubbed the lightly colored wood. "I can't believe it."

"It'll make your dress really poufy."

I brought the hoop inside, tried it on, and let the dress fall over the bell shape. I showed it off for my sister, spinning like a ballerina on top of a jewelry box.

"Are you going to wear it to the circus tonight?" she asked.

"I am."

"I think Wendell will like it."

I nodded, agreeing with my astute little sister, ignoring the cramps that ebbed and flowed like tiny waves of lava, smiling as I twirled in the center of the cabin.

I had taken a strip of lace and tied it in a small bow on my right ring finger, and had stolen a smidge of coffee to camouflage the scuffs on my boots. I didn't wear gloves or carry a parasol, but with my lemony hair twirled into buns beneath my bonnet and my cheeks pink from rose petals, I felt like a Parisian princess. Like true royalty, Dad let me sit on the front seat of the wagon so I could keep my dress fanned out. There was barely enough room for the three of us—my dad, me, and my hoop skirt. Rusty had to sit in the back, ha-ha-ha. He had a hard time keeping his balance while trying to film from the shaky wagon floor. *No sympathy, my friend.*

A dozen or so wagons were already parked on the circus grounds by the time we arrived. Rows of torches lined the path leading to the tent. A red, white, and blue flag waved near the ticket booth with its circle of nine stars.

I was nervous about seeing Wendell, but I was more nervous about running into Prudence. As Dad tied up the horse my eyes darted around, but she was nowhere to be seen. I spotted Wendell, standing near the booth with his brothers and his parents. I waved.

"You look beautiful," he said, as he helped me down. He wore a black bow tie with his white shirt, and a dark vest. His pants were tucked into his boots, and he wore a black hat.

"You do too. I mean, handsome."

A large crowd was forming in front of the tent. Each person was dressed in 1860's clothing, just like us. "What did the producers do?" I whispered. "Fly these people out here in private helicopters?"

Wendell laughed. "Probably an ad in the paper. Now stay in character."

As we walked toward the circus tent, Wendell pulled a small brown package out of his pocket and handed it to me. "This came for you at the Post Office."

I hadn't sent any more letters because we couldn't afford the postage, so receiving a package was as exciting as winning the lottery.

The return address was from Florida. The box inside had a little note glued to the top: "Dear Brooke, I know you can't have any contraband, but I spoke with the producers, and they told me they had these in the 1860s. Love, Grandma."

Wendell leaned over my shoulder, his warm breath on my cheek. Inside the box in a piece of tissue paper lay a silver chain with a tiny silver heart dangling from it.

"It's a locket," I said, clicking it open.

"Whose photographs are those?" Wendell asked.

"One is me when I was a little girl…the other is my mother.

We're both around five."

"You're like twins."

I hadn't shared my mom's death with Wendell, but I could tell from the softness of his eyes that he understood. Holding back tears of joy and sorrow combined, I handed him the necklace and turned my back toward him. "Clasp it for me." In a moment it was hanging around my neck. Rusty zoomed in on the locket, and I held it up for the camera.

Rebecca Lynn ran up to Wendell's brothers, and our families made our way past a peanut vendor and a lemonade stand. At the ticket booth, Dad pulled out three coins.

"No, sir," Wendell told him. "I'll pay for Brooke."

"Daddy," Rebecca Lynn said, "can I get a bag of peanuts?"

Dad handed her a penny.

Wendell's little brothers asked their father for the same. He handed over a large coin. "Don't forget to bring back my change."

When the kids came back, we stepped into the tent as a group. Already the bench seats were filling up. Above the crowd, the ceiling rose to a peak where light filtered in from open panels at the top. Oil torches were stuck in the ground around the perimeter. Most families were dressed like they were heading to the opera. Kids sucked on swirled lollipops or dug into their peanut bags. A band played from somewhere hidden, and six colorfully dressed circus members slipped in from a panel at the back of the tent. They took a bow. When they left again, the ring master, who wore a tall black top hat to match his handlebar moustache and suit, announced the show.

"Ladies and gentlemen, get ready to behold the most amazing

feats of strength, tenacity, and balance you will ever lay your eyes upon!"

I had never been to a circus so up close and personal, where the audience is part of the show. The only things that made it feel modern were the six cameras on tripods located throughout the room. But the moment the show began, I forgot all about the cameras, and fell into the fun of the circus.

The tightrope walker, a short stocky woman named Lady Regina, bounced up and down on a slack rope spread twenty feet across between two large saw horses. The rope was suspended only a few feet off the ground, but her balance was spot-on. It was hard to believe such a portly woman could be so steady. She twirled an umbrella, jumped rope, and sang funny songs, all while dancing back and forth along the rope. When she ended her routine, a drum rolled as she jumped to the ground and took a deep bow to the cheers of the audience.

Gregory, "The fastest juggler east of the Appalachians," was next. He started out by throwing five small leather balls into the audience. Wendell caught one. Gregory asked three of the people to throw the balls back, and then began juggling them. After a moment he asked the fourth person to throw back a ball. The juggler caught it, and it joined the spinning circle. Finally, the fifth ball was thrown back, and it went off to the side, but Gregory somehow caught it and tossed it into the air with the others. When he was done with the ball trick, he asked four men sitting in the front row if he could borrow their hats. Gregory threw them up so high they nearly hit the ceiling. But he never dropped one of them. He never *almost* dropped them. After tossing back the hats, he uncovered four shiny steel daggers under a cloth on the side of the stage. Into the air they went. All I could think was if something happened to him, like a dagger jamming through his skull, Doctor Hensel wouldn't be able to save him. I held my breath as he threw them into the air and caught them by their pearly handles, over and over, as though they were no more deadly than bean bags.

After his bow, I glanced around the room to watch the spectators' faces, and that's when I spotted Prudence a few rows behind. She was not looking at the ring. She was staring at Wendell and me. I wrapped my hand around the locket.

"Wendell," I whispered. "Prudence is shooting daggers at me with her eyes."

"Maybe that's her circus act," Wendell said laughing, never taking his eyes off the round stage.

When Bernard the fire-eater entered the ring, I hid behind Wendell's profile. By the time Bernard had swallowed enough flames to light up a city, and the poodles pranced around in their funny ballerina tutus, I had forgotten all about Prudence.

Prudence, however, did not forget about me.

After the performers took their final bows, our families followed the stream of happy spectators outside. Rebecca Lynn and the Murphy boys ran over to the wagon where the poodles sat at their trainer's feet, and Dad stood chatting with Wendell's parents. Camera people roamed about, but Trusty Rusty stayed closest. To our right, the crowd moved in a large wave as Prudence pushed her way through.

As if seeing me for the first time in years, she said, in a sugary-sweet Sugar Gap voice, "Oh, Brooke! How wonderful to see you. I do hope you enjoyed the show."

"Yes, I—"

"And you, Wendell Lee Murphy?"

"Yes, Prudence, thanks for asking." He turned to me. "What was your favorite, Brooke?"

"Definitely the tightrope walker."

"Really? Mine was the fire-eater."

Prudence's eyes darted back and forth between Wendell and me. She said, "I do hope you like the dress I gave you, Brooke."

"Of course I do."

My thighs did a little shimmy, making the dress rock back and forth.

"I have so many dresses, there aren't enough parties in a lifetime to show them all off." She suddenly put on a wide crazy grin. "Wendell, which of my dresses do you like most?"

"I don't know."

"Do you like the purple satin one? I can wear it to church on Sunday."

"You can wear whatever you like, Prudence."

Prudence's eyes batted wildly like she was a deranged cuckoo stuck in the opening of a clock. She said, her crazy smile never tipping, "Brooke, take a walk with me. There's something I want to show you."

"I don't think—"

"Wendell can handle himself just fine for one moment. Can't you, Wendell?"

I tried to make eye contact with Wendell but Prudence yanked my arm, and before I knew it his hand was no longer in mine, and the crowd of people had swallowed us up. She pulled me past the line of circus wagons and makeshift tents. I tried to see if Dad or Wendell was following, but she moved like a greyhound. Rusty zoomed behind us, lost us for a time, then found us again as we rounded the last wagon. I tripped in a rut and worked to regain my balance, but Prudence never let go of my arm. I had a feeling she would have kept dragging me even if I'd fallen flat on my face.

We moved beyond the cooking fires, away from the crowd, and behind the schoolhouse. We climbed up the back steps and stood under the slanted roof of the small back porch. I heard a rustle and squinted into the darkness. Rusty was suddenly on the bottom step, his camera staring at us.

"Just what do you think you're doing?" Prudence demanded.

"I wanted to tell you, but I didn't know how. Wendell asked my dad—"

"Your father? You mean the one who smells like a barn? The one who can barely pay for his purchases at the mercantile?"

Her words were hitting way too close to home. I touched the locket. "Stop talking junk about my dad."

"You deliberately stole Wendell from me."

"A person can't help who they're attracted to."

"I want my dress back."

"What?"

"Give it back," she said, pulling on the sleeve.

"You gave it to me." I jerked away from her.

"You don't deserve it."

"It isn't even the same dress. I added lace. And I'm wearing the hoop skirt Nanny made me."

"Nanny?" she asked, her eyes bulging out. "Nanny made you a hoop?"

I lifted the dress. I clicked my heels like Dorothy in *The Wizard of Oz.* "And she made me shampoo. She's creative."

"Nanny did not make you that hoop. She stole it from me."

"She did not."

"Do you know what the punishment is for a slave stealing from its owner?"

"She's not an *it.*"

"According to the law in 1861 she is. And if a slave is caught stealing, the owners can handle it any way they choose."

"You can't hurt another person for the sake of—" I wanted to say, *For the sake of reality television*, but instead, I said, "Just because you're jealous of Wendell and me."

"You took him away after I was kind enough to give you an imported dress. Then you aligned with my slave to steal things belonging to me. Well, neither of you will get away with this."

In my brain, I understood this was all bull; that nothing would happen to Nanny. In Modern Land, Prudence would be tagged a bigot, and whatever she did to Nanny would be a hate crime. Even so, I found myself getting caught up in the moment. In *all* the recent moments. Dad's sprouting garden, my lemony hair, the beautiful dress, the circus, Wendell…

It slipped out of me with a life of its own.

"Let's make a trade," I said.

She narrowed her eyes like a feral cat. "What sort of trade?"

"If you leave Nanny alone, I'll give you back your dress."

"I wouldn't dress a scarecrow in that old thing."

"You just told me you wanted it back."

"Well, I've thought better of it."

I churned other options over in my mind until Prudence's

one word cut through me.

"Wendell."

"What about him?"

"I won't turn in Nanny in exchange for Wendell."

"That's stupid," I said, laughing nervously. "You can't trade one person for another."

"Yes. Nanny for Wendell."

"Just saying you want him won't make him like you."

She chewed her cud. "One evening," she said. "I get Wendell for one evening."

"He'll never agree to it."

"I will invite him to dinner at my house. With his parents, of course. Then he won't know he's courting me."

"He won't be courting you."

"Oh, yes he will. Only he won't know it."

I knew better than to agree to something so stupid. Nanny could take care of herself. But suddenly I wanted to *prove* how much Wendell liked me, not just have him say the words. I wanted Prudence, my family, the townspeople, and even the cameras to see it. "If I give you this, you won't punish Nanny?"

"I promise with a cross against my heart," she said, sliding a gloved finger in an "x" pattern on her chest.

"Fine. One night. I'm confident Wendell will make the right choice."

"So am I," Prudence said, more to the camera than to me.

CHAPTER TWENTY-EIGHT

The Friday after the circus, Dad gave us girls a break from cooking, and I sat sewing on the front porch. Rebecca Lynn sat in the rocker next to me and watched me add lace to her dress. For over an hour, Rusty wandered in and out of the cabin, trying to find something interesting to film. The more my sister and I got into the routine of things, the less he found appealing, so when the sound of stomping hooves came up the hill from the direction of town, Rusty and his pet camera went zooming down the front porch steps. I jumped up, praying it was Wendell. It was odd dating in Yesterday World because there were no phone calls, no texts, no emails. I didn't know when I would see him again, and the only time I had any guarantee was when we took our trek into town.

I patted down my apron, retied my bonnet, and waited for the wagon to pull up out front. My sister and I watched from the railing as Wendell's wagon appeared in front of our house, but it was loaded up with Mr. and Mrs. Murphy and all four Murphy boys.

Why would the whole family be coming here? my dense brain wondered.

When they made a sharp left and headed up the Millers' long driveway, I was momentarily dumbfounded. Rusty panned the back of the clan as they made their way up the steep hill, and then he zoomed in on my sad and puzzled face.

He had finally found something worth filming.

"Are they having a party?" my sister asked.

"Something like that."

"Why weren't we invited?"

"It's not that kind of party."

Dad called us in for dinner. I could barely eat my pork strips and rice, knowing Wendell was spending time in that mansion with Prudence.

After the dishes were washed and put away, and Dad sat by lamplight rubbing his beard and reading *Harper's Weekly*, I deliberately went up to my bedroom and stayed there a while so Rusty would get bored and leave. Thirty minutes later, I motioned to Rebecca Lynn to follow me outside.

"We're going to play with Sully," I told Dad, who nodded absently, totally engrossed in the stories of the Civil War.

I grabbed a rag, tied it into a knot, and threw the toy to Sully when we got outside. For a few minutes, my sister and I wrestled with the dog, but my eyes kept wandering up the Millers' hill, and my heart was growing braver by the second, though where the courage came from I have no idea.

"Wanna take a walk?" I asked my sister.

"It's getting dark."

In the west the sun had already set behind the trees. The sky was a darkening blue with faded stripes of orange. By the time we made it up the Millers' drive, that orange tint would be gone. Millions of twinkles were already dotting the night sky.

"We can bring the porch lantern."

"I'm in my slip."

"No one will see you."

"Should we tell Daddy?"

"Probably not."

For whatever reason—maybe she saw the desperate look on my face—she didn't argue. If we'd been back at home, she would have stayed behind for the sole purpose of ratting me out. But now, wearing her slip since her dress was stuck with pins, she watched me in silence as I grabbed the lit lamp from the porch steps. We walked through the gate and out to the road. Sully tagged along at Rebecca Lynn's heels, the knotted rag hanging from his mouth.

"Stay, Sully," she ordered, patting his head as he stopped at the gate. "Good boy."

We closed the gate behind us and Sully watched us through the slats as we started up the Millers' driveway.

After walking for a minute, Rebecca Lynn asked, "Why don't you just tell Prudence you like Wendell?"

I stopped on the driveway, the lantern light flickering in the dark. The sound of frogs and crickets engulfed us. "I did."

"Oh."

We hiked to the top. Slowly I pushed open the pretty white gate. Smells of jasmine and roses swirled around us as we walked up the path to the house and up the front steps of the wraparound porch. I set the lantern on the bottom step. In our tight pointy shoes, we tiptoed to the most brightly lit window. The red velvet curtains were pulled to the sides. Large Southern ferns drooped from pots in front of the seeded glass, so we had a little bit of cover. Even so, we crouched low beneath the sill.

"There he is," Rebecca Lynn whispered.

I put a finger to my lips and nodded as we watched the scene. A bright chandelier with candles hung over the beautifully decorated dining room table, and fancy oil lamps sat on mirrored wall sconces throughout the room. The Millers and the Murphys were just finishing up dessert. Prudence wore a purple satin dress, complete with matching purple bonnet and white lace gloves. Her perfect curls looked like they were created by Katy Perry's hairdresser. Wendell wore his Sunday best. The three youngest Murphy boys and the two little Miller brothers, also dressed to the nines, ran wildly through the room before disappearing somewhere in the back. Wendell, Mr. Murphy, and Mr. Miller stood up and moved to the doorway between the dining room and one of the parlors. Mr. Miller had a cigar in his hand, and Mr. Murphy held a pipe. The three of them were chatting, but the glass windows were so thick I could barely hear the muffled voices.

Nanny appeared in the dining room, said something to Mrs. Miller, and disappeared again. Rusty stood near a corner china hutch with his camera, and Carl stood off to the side. Watching the scene from the porch was like watching a silent play, and the anticipation of what may happen next grows when the conversation can't be heard. Maybe that's because without knowing what people are saying, the brain tries to fill it in with a voice. As my imagination geared up, the window to our left was illuminated. Rusty and Carl made their way into that room, and Nanny came back into the dining room. Mrs. Miller stood up, her hands resting on her pregnant belly, and moved into the parlor with the men, leaving Prudence and Nanny in the dining room.

As Nanny started collecting the dishes, she said something to Prudence, making her laugh. Still smiling, Prudence said something back to Nanny, who then left the room with a stack of dishes. Prudence made her way to the parlor and joined the rest of the group.

By the time my sister and I crawled to the next window, the two older men had taken places by the unlit fireplace, and Mrs. Miller and Mrs. Murphy sat on a sofa facing the window. The other sofa sat opposite the first, so it helped to block us. Prudence and Wendell sat in a corner of the room in two wingback chairs facing one another. Prudence asked him a question, and Wendell smiled and nodded. Was that a real smile? Or was he merely being polite? After a moment, he glanced at the window where my sister and I lay in wait on the other side. I held my breath until he turned away again.

Josiah entered the parlor with a tray of tiny glasses, the kind my parents used to sip from at Christmas time. Each of the men, including Wendell, took one. The women did not.

Nanny came back in. In her hand she held a large potato sack that looked like it contained a small body. She laid the bundle on the sofa closest to the window, but the back of the sofa blocked us from seeing what it was. We watched as Nanny knelt down and fumbled with whatever was in the bag. The men stepped forward. The women leaned in. Prudence jumped up and clapped her hands.

I was dying to see what it was, but between the giant ferns and the high-backed sofa—

Prudence's voice shot through the glass: "Oh, yes, Wendell. Please!"

Wendell walked to the couch and bent over. He was about to pick up whatever "it" was, but glanced toward the window again. I sucked in my breath as I froze behind the fern. *Shit shit shit shit shit!* He lowered his head and extended his arms. When his hands came back into view, I was sure my mind was playing tricks on me. It was so beautiful, and it was the only thing besides Wendell I believed would save me from dying of boredom in the backcountry: the guitar from Mr. Murphy's store. *My* guitar.

Wendell picked up the instrument and sat on the sofa with his back toward the window. Prudence clapped her hands again.

I read her lips as she sat beside him: "Play something fun."

And Wendell did. He played a song on *my* guitar. The melody made its way through the closed window. It was some early American backwoods song, and it was supposed to be funny because everyone laughed as they sang along.

"Old Dan Tucker's a fine old man, washed his face in a frying pan. / Combed his hair with a wagon wheel, died of a toothache in his heel..."

Everyone cheered him on as he played, and my anger festered. The more they laughed the more I seethed. It started in my gut, rose up to my throat, and moved to the base of my skull where it pulsated like an extra heart.

"Old Dan Tucker, he come to town, riding on a Billy goat, leading a hound. / Hound dog bark and the Billy goat jump,

throwed Dan Tucker on top of a stump..."

Prudence stared at Wendell like he was a famous rocker who'd just invited her to join him on the band bus.

"Old Dan Tucker, he got drunk, fell in the fire and kicked up a chunk. / Red hot coal got in his shoe, oh my lawdy how the ashes flew!"

The anger was zooming through me now, making my ears ring in pain each time Wendell's perfect fingers moved along the strings. When the song was over, Prudence whispered something to Wendell before stepping next to the piano. She opened the lid that protected the keys, slid out the round stool and sat, fanning out her dress like a parachute. She sang alone while her fingers sprinted over the keys, her clear singing voice sliding through the window.

"How dear to my heart are the scenes of my childhood, when fond recollection presents them to view. / The orchard, the meadow, the deep tangled wildwood, and every loved spot which my infancy knew..."

Words as ancient as the piano fell from her pink lips. Her voice was not only loud, but beautiful.

"How ardent I seized it, with hands that were glowing, / and quick to the white pebbled bottom it fell. / Then soon, with the emblem of truth overflowing, / and dripping with coolness, it rose from the well. / The old oaken bucket, the iron bound bucket, the moss covered bucket that hung in the well."

I hated her stupid bucket song. I hated her. I wanted to run into the parlor and push her off the piano stool and scream to everyone to stop having such a grand old time.

Mom, what would you do? I asked silently, clasping the locket.

But I didn't need an answer. I knew what she would do. My mom, the woman who never argued because she thought arguing was a waste of time; life was short, she always said. Mom would have walked away fast and forgiven just as quickly.

Wendell played the guitar again, this time accompanying Prudence, as my mind analyzed the would-have's and should-do's. When the song ended, everyone clapped.

Something tapped my shoulder.

"Miss Brooke?"

I sprang up out of my crouched position and knocked into the fern which sat in a tall three-legged wicker basket. It rocked for a moment, but I saved it before it crashed to the floor. But catching it didn't matter. Nanny had caught me. I was exposed. The light from the parlor shone across my face. Mrs. Miller spotted me. She stood up and pointed. The guitar music stopped and Wendell turned in my direction, but Prudence didn't realize anything had happened for a moment longer. When she flipped her head around to make those stupid goo-goo eyes at Wendell, her hands froze against the keys.

Rebecca Lynn whispered, "They see us."

I was suddenly a rare specimen behind glass, and everyone inside couldn't wait to gawk. One by one they came over to the parlor window. First Mrs. Miller, then Mrs. Murphy, then the men, except for Wendell, who stood in front of the couch with his hand wrapped around the neck of the guitar. His head was cocked to the side, and he wore a strange grin. Nanny stood next to us with her knuckles against her hips like she'd discovered us with our hands buried in her piggy bank. Carl spun around with his camera toward the window. Then Rusty appeared from nowhere, filming the scene from the porch.

But it was Prudence whose face came right up to the glass, laughing.

Nanny said, "Oh, Miss Brooke and Miss Rebecca Lynn, you be in all kindsa trouble." She grabbed each of us by the wrist and brought us to the front door, where Prudence and her mother met us. "I find 'em on the porch."

"Thank you, Nanny," Mrs. Miller said.

Nanny disappeared inside.

Mrs. Miller said, "Rebecca Lynn, why are you in your slip, dear?"

"Brooke was making my dress pretty." Her lip trembled.

"Why don't we find something for you to wear in the meantime?" She put an arm around my sister's shoulders. To Prudence and me she said, "Please work out your differences like ladies." Then she took Rebecca Lynn's hand and led her up the dark steps.

Rusty's and Carl's cameras were competing to burn a hole in my cheek. But I didn't care if they saw how angry I was. If the producers didn't like what they saw, they could edit it.

"You stole my guitar," I told Prudence through the doorway.

"No one stole it, Brooke. It was paid for with cash."

"That was *my* guitar. You knew I wanted to buy it."

"With what money? It would have taken you until next year to pay for it."

"How dare you judge what I can or can't afford."

"If you listen to me, you'll understand—"

"I hate you. First you treat me like I'm manure on your shoe, and then you talk me into making a trade..."

"The trade was *your* idea."

"Yeah? Well. I saw the way you and Nanny were laughing together, so don't hand me any more crap about being true to your backstory."

Prudence said nothing.

"I want my guitar back," I said. "You can keep Wendell. How's *that* for a trade?"

"Maybe you should tell him yourself."

Wendell appeared in the doorway next to Prudence. I was reminded of a Civil War painting I'd seen once of a young girl and boy, comatose faces, their round glasslike eyes staring out from the frame.

"Brooke," Wendell said. "What are you doing here?"

"I should be asking you that question."

"Our family was invited to dinner."

"And it was so easy to say yes."

Wendell said to Prudence, "Can you leave us alone?"

Prudence glared at me before she spun on her heels in a huff and stormed back into the parlor.

Wendell came onto the porch.

"You knew I wanted that guitar," I said. "You said *someone* bought it. Why do you have it? And why were you playing it for *her*?"

"*I* bought the guitar."

"What?"

"As a gift."

"For Prudence?"

He laughed. "No. For *you*."

"Liar. You bought it for her. So I'd get angry, and I'd have one more reason to leave. You *want* me to leave. Of course you do. You want my family to get kicked out of Sweet Sugar Gap, so your family can get the money—"

"I bought the guitar for *you*. You can ask my father. I've been working extra hours at the store to pay for it."

"Why? Why would you do that for me?"

"I knew you couldn't afford it."

"You felt sorry for me?"

"I bought it so you'd have something to do out here besides complain."

Dang. A bullet to the heart. Is that how he saw me? As a big-time Debbie Downer?

"What about Prudence?" I asked.

"What about her?"

"You were having a pretty good time in there. The way you were laughing, and playing music together…"

"That's what families do in this era. They sing and laugh, tell stories, play games. I wanted to practice before I gave it to you. *You*. Not *her*."

I didn't know what to say. Here we were, standing on Prudence Miller's porch, and Wendell was offering me both the guitar and himself at the same time.

"I want to teach you some songs," he said, handing me the instrument. The neck was warm. "Modern, 1800's songs."

I hugged the instrument to my chest. "So, you're sure about this? About me?"

"I've known since before you ever came into our store."

"How?"

"Our family was the first to arrive. When I heard there was a girl moving here who was my age, I pictured you in my mind. And here you are."

"Why didn't you picture Prudence?"

"I did. It wasn't a pretty sight."

My sister appeared at the door. "Look, Brooke." She stepped onto the porch and tried to spin around in the long yellow dress, but it fell off her shoulders and bunched into a pile on the floor. "It's too big, but I told Mrs. Miller you could make it fit me. Can you?"

"I can try." I handed Rebecca Lynn the lantern from the step. "It's getting late. We should be getting home." Something inside me whispered that last word over again, for the first time without grief; a whisper that actually brought me comfort: *Home.*

Wendell walked us to the gate. He leaned toward me and kissed my cheek. He had forgiven me. Had *chosen* me. We hugged goodnight, and I carried the guitar with one hand and the back of my sister's dress with the other like a wedding train, as we made our way down the hill, back to our little homestead.

CHAPTER TWENTY-NINE

My life became that of a true blue Ingalls girl. I awoke every morning without the aid of Cuckoo Bird Clyde, whose cock-a-doodle-doo seemed to be busted half the time. Rebecca Lynn and I had the eggs collected and the animals fed before Dad came down for breakfast, and even though we were getting low on provisions, our crops were popping up like trees in a miniature train set. Baking bread and biscuits got easier, I never tired of eating freshly plucked apples and blackberries, and I hadn't burned the coffee since day one.

Mr. Murphy told Wendell he could stock shelves on Sundays after the picnic so he could visit me most weeknights. Sometimes he'd stay for dinner, other times he'd come in time for dessert. Somehow we made our food stretch enough for four.

To add to the table, Wendell brought bouquets of wildflowers—daisies were my favorite—or delicious pies his mother baked. After dinner, he told jokes about the fake war. He was so cute, sitting at the table with the firelight bouncing against his happy face, sharing stories he'd read in a journal at the store.

"A soldier, who was drunk all the time, made an announcement to the men in his company that he was swearing off drinking and told the soldiers they should quit, too. The other soldiers deliberately tried to get him to fall off the wagon by giving him whiskey every night. But every morning, the soldier would preach that alcohol was a sin. Finally, a friend said, 'You should give up the preaching, because you always end up drunk by the end of the day.' The soldier said, 'What? And give up all that free whiskey?'"

I laughed at all of his jokes, even if I didn't get the punch line.

After the dishes were washed, and Dad and Rebecca Lynn sat at the table playing cards, Wendell and I would hang out on the front porch rockers, staring at the night sky, hooting each time a shooting star whizzed across the black, or naming the frogs whose croaks we started to recognize.

And, as promised, he taught me songs on the guitar.

"Place your fingers like this," he'd say patiently with his fingers on top of mine to help locate the right chords. Sometimes while I played, Wendell would cup my cheek with a callused hand. My fingers would shake, and the lyrics would momentarily get stuck in my throat.

Rusty hung around every night, so Wendell and I got smart. We'd say goodbye next to the gate, and he'd hop onto his wagon and head over the hill. It didn't take but ten minutes for Rusty to become bored with the Decker Family After-dinner Entertainment Hour. As soon as he left for the Millers' place, Wendell would come back over the rise, and the rest of the evening was ours. Even in Yesterday World, kids knew how to pull one over.

By myself, I hadn't explored anything beyond our end of the stream, and it was hard to do in the dark, but Wendell and I discovered that our path continued to the other side of the creek, leading to a clearing with a pool the size of a small pond which always seemed to lie directly beneath the moon. We sat on the clay ledge beside the cool water, took our shoes and socks off, and let our feet dangle over the side. Fish tickled my feet.

"Trout," Wendell said.

I wiggled my toes and laughed as the fish swam around my ankles.

Beside the pool, the mosquitoes were fierce. My long dress and high shoes saved my legs, but I got countless bites on my face and the backs of my hands. Wendell brought me a jar of citronella oil from the store, and it didn't smell half as bad as the spray stuff they sell in Modern Land. Once he rubbed the oil on my clothes and hair, the bugs didn't come around at all. He also gave me a plant from his mother's garden.

"Rub a basil leaf on the bites."

I was skeptical at first, but within hours the itching had stopped. "How did you know this would work?"

"My mother is into natural remedies."

As we sat one night with our feet dangling in the dark cool water of the pool, I shimmied close to him. I lay my head on his shoulder and whispered, "I am so happy right now."

And then came the moment of truth.

He turned me toward him, grabbed my face in his hands, and planted a sweet wet kiss smack dab on my lips. I'd had lots of first kisses, but this one was the best by far. As our mouths opened against one another's, I could taste his minty tongue. It was all I could do not to devour him, right there on the bank. But he wanted to lead, so I let him.

Nearly every night we kissed under the moon with our arms around each other like we were sitting in the bleachers at a football game. Dad's constant warnings about hidden cameras frightened me, but as long as we were doing what came naturally, I didn't care. Girls and boys kissed in the 1800s. There was no way around it. And they probably started kissing a lot sooner, because people didn't live so long back then. They *had* to get started early.

The watering hole became our spot. Maybe it was the glow of the moon that never seemed to fade, the nights that were breezy and cool, or the sunsets that turned the sky into a museum painting; maybe it was the chickens who seemed to enjoy laying eggs for me, the way Willow nuzzled me each time I entered the corral, or the fact that my skin hadn't seen a pimple in weeks. I'm not really sure. Whatever it was out here in God's Country, out here in this made-up Hollywood town called Sweet Sugar Gap, I was falling hard for Wendell.

I wanted to tell him how I felt. I wanted to tell everyone. I wanted to stand up in church after the final hymn and tell the congregation. But knowing we were all just characters on a reality show, all of us vying for a million-dollar prize, I couldn't get myself to tell him just how hard I was tumbling.

It was a good thing we liked to kiss, because our conversations were limited. I couldn't share any of the things I knew before we'd met. I could not discuss my favorite modern books, like *The Hunger Games* or *Thirteen Reasons,* or classics like *To Kill a Mockingbird* or *Dandelion Wine*; or movies, since films hadn't been invented yet; or current events, unless you counted the "current" war. We couldn't discuss what I knew about science, like Pluto being demoted from planet to non-planet, the fact that I had seen Saturn's rings through a high-power telescope, or the theory of worm holes, which fascinated me. I wanted to brag about all the cutting-edge cancer treatments my mother had tried, but penicillin hadn't been discovered yet. I couldn't mention anything in history that happened between 1861 and the present day, from technology to fashion, laptops to thong bikinis.

It was frustrating to be with someone I was crazy about, but not have him know the real me. What Wendell was seeing was a modern girl, not a girl who lived over a hundred years ago. He didn't have a clue what kind of car I drove, about the panther tattoo on my lower back, or the awesome concerts I'd snuck out to see with Libby and her brothers. He knew nothing about my real house, my real friends, my real life. He only saw who I was now: a plain-faced, hairy-legged girl, barely a doppelganger of my other self. He ate my baked goods, drank my strong coffee, and complimented me on my sewing. He watched me ride Willow, balance on a log that stretched across the creek, and mend holes in my dad's wool socks.

I wanted to ask Wendell what his favorite bands were. We were stuck playing old music from his song book, filled with tunes about farmers and fair maidens and flags. I learned these songs for the sake of the show, and the money we could receive, should we make it to the end. And, of course, I was doing it for Wendell, who seemed to like the girl I was here and now, without knowing or asking about the girl I was before. All of this made me like him even more.

I was falling headfirst. Turning cartwheels in my Laura Ingalls dress down a wheat-covered hill. Spiraling out of control like a hyperactive girl who forgot to stick on her medication patch.

And because this was show business, the cameras would be there to witness the plunge, whether my dive was a perfect ten or a complete fail.

On the Fourth of July, we sat on the hill behind the church. Fireworks exploded into the air from a barge down on the river. Like the circus, the Independence Day celebration brought strangers from miles around, and we sat on blankets among dozens of spectators. The fireworks were mostly the colors of the American flag, and cast brilliant light against the dark sky that was probably seen from every hilltop in the Tar Heel State.

Prudence, who sat nearby between her brothers, glanced in our direction during the show, the colorful lights hardly brightening her sad face.

"I feel sorry for her," I told Wendell.

A little bit, anyway. Without me, she had no girlfriends. And without Wendell, she was definitely having less fun than me.

"She has enough in that big house to keep her happy" was his answer.

I was no longer jealous of her house or her toys or her dresses. What's funny is, I didn't have much, and yet I had everything I needed. I had three square meals, crops growing that my father had planted himself, a beautiful stream to bathe in, and a hottie holding my hand.

After the finale, everyone gathered up their blankets. After dropping Wendell off at his house behind the store—and sneaking a quick peck in the dark—I rode home in the back of our wagon with my sister, who fell asleep by the time we reached the schoolhouse. It was late, around ten o'clock, and the road was dark and eerie with barely a sliver of moonlight. The Millers rode in front of us, and our wagons moved slowly because of the shadowed ruts. We stayed directly behind them, since they carried two lanterns inside mirrored boxes, and we only had two small lamps.

As we made our way to the bottom of the Miller's driveway, a man's dark figure appeared in the road. He stood next to a horse and held a white sheet in his hand, waving it like a surrender flag. "Mr. Miller! Mr. Miller!"

"Josiah?" Mr. Miller called out.

We stopped our wagon. Rebecca Lynn woke up.

"It's Mrs. Miller!" Josiah shouted. "She having the baby!"

"Is Doctor Hensel with her?" Mr. Miller asked.

"No, sir. He still at the fireworks."

"Josiah," he ordered calmly, "get on down to the doctor's place. Wait for him there."

"Yes, sir."

Josiah jumped on his horse and continued down the road.

Mr. Miller's voice took on a solemn tone as it broke through the darkness. "Brooke, you need to come with us."

"What?"

"We need as many hands as possible."

"Dad?"

"Do as he asks, Brooke."

I jumped out of the wagon, climbed into Mr. Miller's, and slid next to Prudence. She was crying. I put an arm around her. I knew what she was feeling, worrying about her mother.

"Everything will be fine," I told her, not knowing if that was true.

"Can I come?" Rebecca Lynn asked.

"Yes," Mr. Miller said. "Be quick, now."

My sister crawled up and squeezed in between the two Miller boys.

"What can I do?" Dad asked.

Mr. Miller said, "Pray that Doctor Hensel makes it in time."

We left Dad behind. The Millers' two-horse team huffed as they pulled us up the pecan-ridden drive, and the two cameramen who were left to walking panted almost as loudly as they hiked with their cameras behind us.

Doctor Hensel arrived thirty minutes after us, and immediately handed out orders. I was in charge of fresh water, just like at our cabin, only at the Millers' house, a water pump was stationed near the back door. Sweat poured down my neck as back and forth I went with the bucket, first with Carl on my heels, then Rusty. Soon, I was taking bloody rags and washing them out. I wasn't sure where all the blood was coming from, but I couldn't imagine what the sight of those rags was doing to Prudence. Rebecca Lynn was in charge of putting the younger brothers to bed. Prudence and Nanny were the only two allowed in the master bedroom. Even Mr. Miller didn't go in. I wanted to ask him why he didn't want to be with his wife. Why was he just sitting there on the front porch smoking his stinky old cigar?

But I never asked. I was sure it had something to do with the era. Women working; men waiting for the work to get done.

If I'd been pregnant, I'd never have signed up for a reality show. But then, I thought, people do strange things when it comes to money. As I rushed in and out trough the kitchen door with the bucket, I wondered how many families in Sweet Sugar Gap were on the brink of losing their homes like us. Maybe Mr. Miller had lost his job, too, and that's why his family was here. It was possible that the Miller family's real life was harder than ours.

By the time the grandfather clock chimed four times, my eyes barely stayed open. I sat on the bottom step with my head against a spindle, but each time I started to doze, Mrs. Miller would let out a scream that made my heart stop. I could hear Nanny and Prudence telling her again and again that everything would be fine.

At four-thirty, Prudence came to the top of the steps. Her face was washed out and she had rings under her eyes. Her bonnet hung down around the back of her neck, her hair was flat with perspiration, and she was barefoot. "It's a girl."

The announcement sent a jolt through my core and I sobbed from a mixture of relief and exhaustion. Mr. Miller rushed past us, skipping two steps at a time.

"Come up and see," Prudence said.

Rebecca Lynn and I held hands as we made our way up the steps.

We followed Prudence into a large shadowy bedroom filled

with satiny peach textiles. Oil lamps were lit, and the curtains were drawn shut. Mrs. Miller, her face flushed, lay under a sheet in the four-poster bed, holding the baby wrapped tightly in swaddling against her chest. The newborn didn't move as Mrs. Miller rocked it gently in her arms. It didn't cry either, like some brand new babies.

Nanny wiped Mrs. Miller's brow and took the linen to a pot of water on a table.

Prudence said, as she crawled under the covers next to her mother, "We're calling her Camellia."

"That's beautiful," I said, barely hearing the name, trying to keep my eyes open as I stared down at the sleeping baby.

"Beautiful," Rebecca Lynn said.

Doctor Hensel closed his black bag. "Be sure to feed as often as possible."

"Thank you, Doctor," Mrs. Miller said.

After he left, Mr. Miller said, "I'd like to have some time with my family." He sat on the edge of the bed and placed a hand against his wife's cheek.

"Congratulations," I said.

Nanny walked Rebecca Lynn and me downstairs, out the front door, and down the porch steps. "You girls done a good job."

Still holding hands, we headed down the hill as the rising sun sent morning streaks across a dark blue sky. I barely felt my legs. My head was spinning. The fireworks from earlier seemed like a dream.

When we got back to the cabin, Dad offered us breakfast, but the two of us girls were so worn out we skipped the meal, went up the ladder, and fell into bed, our arms wrapped around one another.

CHAPTER THIRTY

Rebecca Lynn played tag with Sully, and I sat on a log cooling myself with a fan I'd made from scraps of material and twigs, while Dad split wood. When he wasn't painstakingly hand watering the field, or dragging trash to the other side of the barn, that's what he did. Chop-chop-chop. It came to be that on the days when he didn't chop, it felt like something was missing. On really hot days, like today, he chopped with his shirt off. His skinny engineer's arms had become tan and muscular.

Rusty sat on a nearby tree stump, water dripping down his cheeks and onto the collar of his Metallica T-shirt. The end of July was so hot and steamy, sweat covered every inch of my body as well. My feet boiled inside my boots.

"We need to sell some things," Dad said.

"What kinds of things?" I asked.

"I'm not sure."

"How much money do we have left?"

Dad threw the ax down on a log, splitting the wood in two, creating a pair of matching halves. "Eleven cents," he said, wiping the sweat from his neck with a dirty rag.

I picked up one half of the log and threw it onto the pile, did the same with the other, and went back to fanning myself. "Can't we sell our crops?"

"Once they come up, and as long as they produce well, they're going to have to sustain us through the rest of our time out here."

As he split the next log into pieces, I thought about ways to make money.

"Maybe you could add lace to dresses, Brooke," my sister suggested.

"I don't think women in the backcountry care about fancy dresses," Dad said.

He was right about that one, unless you included Prudence.

"Maybe I could bake goods for Wrightman's Bakery," I said. "Like bread pudding."

"We're out of sugar. And down to the dregs on flour."

The gloom in my dad's voice hovered around me for the rest of the day.

Later, after the sun had set, and Rusty had headed up to the Millers' complaining of heat exhaustion, Wendell and I sat with our feet dipped in the pool. I shared my family's dilemma.

"I overheard my father talking about the drought," Wendell said. "It's all over the state."

There was no way the producers would let us starve to death, but it was hard not to feel the genuineness of the situation.

We sat and listened to the hooting of an owl that had recently turned us into a threesome. When the owl flew over our heads for his nightly hunting, and the golden moon was high in the sky, Wendell and I headed back to the cabin and said our goodnights. From the porch I watched his wagon disappear over the hill.

One morning, after chores were nearly done, Rebecca Lynn came running into the cabin. "Look!" she shouted, jumping up on a chair and unfolding her apron. A bunch of greenish-purple grapes rolled across the table.

"Are there any more?" Dad asked.

"About a kabillion."

We grabbed a couple of baskets and followed her to the arbor sitting far off on a corner of the property. The entire trellis was covered in creeping vines, and colorful plump grapes were popping out everywhere. It only took a few minutes to fill two baskets.

"We can sell these!" I shouted, biting down on a grape. The juice was almost too amazing to bear.

"We can," Dad said, smiling as he popped one into his mouth. "As long as we don't eat them all."

Dad's trade plus the eleven cents got us a sack of white potatoes, a large bag of dried beans, a small bag of flour, a bag of chicken feed, and a bag of pig feed. The rest—a bushel of collards, a big glass jar of apple cider, and a pound of cured bacon—we put on credit.

Everything but the flour, potatoes, and beans were gone in a week.

Dad went to Mr. Miller and asked if we could leave Gretchen on their property so she could graze on their high grass. Our lot was mostly dirt and we couldn't afford any more feed or hay.

"Sure," Mr. Miller said. "Cattle ought to roam free anyway." This meant we had farther to go to milk her, and farther to carry the heavy bucket, but I knew better than to complain.

I had to get creative in the kitchen. Rebecca Lynn and I made grape juice from the grapes that continued to produce. By adding just the right amount of fresh water and a tiny bit of molasses, it was as good as Welch's. I made potato pie, potato bread, and potato soup. The soup was the best of the three, but even that seemed stale by the second meal, especially since we were rationing our salt. I used molasses instead of sugar on boiled oats for breakfast, and cooked beans every day for lunch. I switched to tea so there'd be enough coffee for Dad. With the fresh grass, Gretchen continued to produce milk, so between cheese and eggs, we were hanging in there.

Barely.

At night in bed, I prayed that our crops, especially the collards, would come up healthy. Dad said collards have the most vitamins.

Wendell started bringing goods from the store when he came for dinner; just enough to add to the meal so he wouldn't feel like he was eating us out of house and home.

On the last day of July, Dad came running into the cabin like a mad man. "Real tomatoes!" he shouted.

My sister rode piggyback on Dad's back as Sully followed us out to the field, and Rusty fought to keep up. Dad did a happy dance along the edge of the garden, grinning like he'd grown magic beanstalks. Almost overnight it seemed, a dozen or so deep red tomatoes had sprouted, hanging along the twine attached to sticks my dad jerry rigged to help the plants stand upright.

Rebecca Lynn crouched next to one of the vines. "These don't look anything like the ones at Walmart."

Dad laughed. "Because they're fresh. But we need to pick them as they ripen. Whatever we pick, we eat. We've got some cucumbers already forming over here, and check this out." He dug into one of the higher mounds and pulled up a carrot. He handed it to me.

"It's so tiny," I said, brushing off the dirt. It was the size of my pinky.

We plucked six tomatoes, one cucumber, and seven thin carrots. The collards would be ready in a few days.

"Hello there, salad," I said, staring at basket of loot. "I didn't realize how much I missed you."

We also discovered our sunflowers had sprouted on the other side of the barn, reaching high into the sky like they were trying to climb up to the clouds. Rebecca Lynn had to sit on Dad's shoulders to get to the blooms. One of the books in our kitchen said to "Carefully brush your palm over the face until the seeds fall into your hand," which is exactly what she did, except we used a jar to catch them. My sister and I followed the book's directions for drying the seeds, smoothing them out on the kitchen counter and laying packaging paper on top.

A day later, and still high from the harvest Dad called "Better'n gold," he came through the back door with three bamboo sticks. "Surprise," he said, handing each of us a stick. "All we have to do is find a great fishing spot." He stood with one hand on a hip and the other holding the longest of the rods like a cane, as though posing for a photograph. "We can take care of ourselves, just like our ancestors did. We've got milk and cheese and eggs, and God knows we have enough dried beans to last us a year. With our garden producing, all we have to do is learn how to preserve. And now we can fish. We can be autonomous."

"I've never fished before," Rebecca Lynn said.

"I haven't done it since I was a kid. But first we need to find a place to do it."

I pictured the romantic pool that Wendell and I hadn't shared with anyone, reminding myself we could go fishing in the daytime while the hooting owl slept and the moon was on the other side of the planet. It would be nothing like when Wendell and I went there. I had no choice. I had to give it away. "I know a place." I picked up the fishing rod and placed it on my shoulder like Huck Finn. "I'll take you there."

We cooked in an outdoor fire pit so the cabin wouldn't smell like fish. Dad boiled the fresh catch in a pot of rice with diced tomatoes and black pepper. Sully got a bowl of his own, his tail wagging wildly as he licked the dish clean. For dessert we ate biscuits with homemade blackberry jam. Rusty and Carl chose to eat with us, which was fine with me. I was proud of this meal. A meal we had made with things we either grew or caught on our own.

As we ate, two men in their twenties, dressed in Confederate soldier costumes and carrying satchels, appeared at our gate.

One man told us, "We're on our way to town to buy provisions, but we got no food left to get us there."

"We got nothing but hard knocks," the other one said.

Dad offered our leftovers, which wasn't much. They never offered a thank you, even after I made them coffee and gave them the last of our dessert.

The fake soldiers talked about stupid war stuff, and Dad played right along. I could see Rusty's smile of approval as they recounted attacks on various Southern forts. At first I only pretended to be interested. But the longer they sat talking, the more authentic they became, sitting next to the fire in their uniforms, with their dirty nails and worn-out boots. Soon, it was hard to believe there *wasn't* a war going on.

When the dishes were done and the sky changed colors, the two soldiers left for town as Rusty and Carl headed up the Millers' drive. We let the fire die to a tiny glow, and nighttime country sounds surrounded us as we relocated to the front porch. As I sat strumming my guitar for my tiny audience, Wendell's wagon came up the road. It was nearly dark, the sun setting earlier with autumn just around the corner.

Wendell jumped down from the wagon and came to the bottom of the porch steps. "Will you take a walk with me, Brooke?"

"Dad?" I asked.

In the dark, he looked like Abraham Lincoln. "One hour. It's been a long day."

We left Dad and Rebecca Lynn sitting on the porch rockers as we strolled around the side of the cabin.

"Why are you here so late?" I asked.

"Just wanted to see you."

"You did?"

He nodded and took my hand.

We walked along the path that weaved its way down to the pool. On the bank, he took off his boots and socks. I did the same. I told him about the fishing poles my dad made. He agreed that fishing in the pool was a great idea.

"When we fished," I said, "we stood right in the water. The bottom is like hard clay."

"Is it?"

"I'll show you." I smiled mischievously and untied my apron.

"What are you doing?"

"Isn't this the country? Aren't we back in time?" I threw my apron at him and he caught it. Next, I took off my dress, letting it fall from my shoulders and down around my bare feet.

"Brooke…"

"A little skinny dippin' nevah hurt no one no how," I said with Southern sweetness. I took off my bonnet and threw it on a stump.

"Skinny dipping?"

"Well, maybe not *all* skinny…"

I stood before him in my slip and corset, feeling sexy under the moonlight. I undid my buns, slowly, methodically, until my hair fell around my shoulders. "Untie my corset."

He slowly undid the ribbon, never taking his eyes from my own. I let the corset slide to the ground.

"You're beautiful," he said. "Like a painting."

"I'm also a good swimmer. Last one in is a big old rotten egg."

In my slip, I squatted on the edge and slid into the pool, floated in the cool water on my back, and waited. "Well?"

Wendell removed his hat and laid it on the stump next to my

bonnet. He slid his suspenders down, pulled his white shirt over his head, and took off his wool pants. Underneath he was dressed like my dad, in a one-piece shorts and tank top combination. His arms were muscular and his legs were almost as hairy as mine.

He frog-dove into the water and popped up beside me. For the better part of an hour we treaded, not speaking, just listening to our occasional giggles, as the tree tops rustled in the nighttime breeze. We swam toward each other, wrapped our arms around one another's necks, kissed, moved apart, and came together again. The ripples we made were wide and endless. If it had been up to me, we would have stayed in the pool all night.

"It's getting late," he said after a while, swimming to the edge. He pulled himself up and helped me onto the bank. When I leaned into him, he whispered, "I'm not supposed to fall for you this way." He took my face in his rough hands and tilted it back until the moonlight fell across my cheeks. He pushed my wet hair away from my forehead. He placed his soft lips against mine and held them there for what felt like eternity. He tasted minty, as he always did, and I wondered if his mother had given him peppermint leaves to chew on. I heard my thumping heartbeat underneath the singing of crickets and frogs. When the gentle kiss was over, he leaned back. A deep furrow appeared between his eyebrows, his eyes like dark emeralds. "Are you falling for me?"

I nodded, speechless. There was so much I wanted to say, so much I wanted him to know. Real things from my other life. Another life that seemed light years away from where we now stood. I wanted to tell him everything, about my mom dying, about how sad and empty I'd been. But I was afraid Wendell wouldn't care about the old Brooke; it was *this* Brooke he was falling for.

And as I fell into his kiss once again, and my heart swelled up bigger than a hot air balloon, I was suddenly confused about which Brooke was the real one.

CHAPTER THIRTY-ONE

Sully's barking startled me out of a dream of kisses and sweet talk.

I sat up in the dark. "What's wrong?"

Dad was already halfway down the ladder. "Stay here."

As soon as the front door closed, Rebecca Lynn and I pulled back the cheesecloth from the bedroom window.

Dad was shouting, "Go on, get out of here! Shoo! Shoo!"

The crack of a gun exploded through the dark, and I ran down the steps. The rifle over the mantel was gone. Out the front door I went, my sister right behind me. I held onto Rebecca Lynn's wrist so she didn't go traipsing after him, and together we waited.

His footsteps brought him back to the porch, Sully by his side.

"What happened?" I asked.

"Deer."

"Did you kill it?" Rebecca Lynn cried.

"Not *it*. *Them*. A herd. And no, I didn't kill any."

"Why did you shoot at them?" I asked.

"They were chewing on our crops."

"How bad is it?"

Dad shook his head. "Won't know until the sun comes up."

We followed him into the house and ate our tiny breakfast in the dark, waiting for daylight to show us how bad it really was.

About a third of our crops were destroyed. Sprouts were chewed to bits. Split tomatoes sat rotting on the soil. The cucumbers were mostly trampled. Holes were all that remained of the mini carrots.

Sully ran through the early morning field sniffing the deer scat as Dad plucked shredded leaves from the mist-covered earth and walked the width of the field. His loud and angry voice bounced across the lifeless garden: "What in God's name?"

My sister and I hopped over the holes and deer tracks to where Dad squatted at the field's edge.

"Corn kernels," he said.

I let a handful of dirt and kernels sift through my fingers. "But we didn't plant any corn."

The three of us followed the perimeter of the field. It was edged with corn kernels all the way to the border of the forest. Dad pulled off his hat, smoothed down his hair, and put his hat back on. "Boot tracks."

We stood near the woods, our heads cocked to the side, as if waiting for the trees to solve the puzzle.

"Someone wanted those deer to pay us a visit," Dad said. "Maybe I ought to speak to the sheriff."

As Dad and my sister went to ready the wagon, something fluttered at the corner of the field closest to the road, catching my eye. I walked over to it. It was a bonnet, caught on a stick that held one of the tomato plants. A pretty purple bonnet. I yanked it loose and held it in my hands, rubbing the material and poking my finger through the tiny hole. My gaze moved up toward the blue house, the pit in my stomach filling with rage.

It was hard to be excited about going into town after someone had sabotaged our crops, AKA our *food*. Dad had worked his ass off to make sure our garden was tended to. Every day he slaved in his field, checking the leaves, praying for rain which rarely came, dragging buckets of water from the springhouse to his seedlings.

As we headed down the road in the wagon, I glanced up at the blue house. Prudence was jealous of Wendell and me, it was that simple. Who else would have a reason for killing our crops? Our family was lucky to have been spared an eviction for my earlier stunt, but that didn't matter, since we'd be forced to leave as losers…or stay and starve to death while the Miller Family sipped tea and ate crumpets. My imagination heard laughter coming from the wraparound porch.

We passed Doctor Hensel's house, the Duffys' farm, and finally the schoolhouse. I stared at the empty building, ashamed I'd wasted most of my junior year, suddenly craving the smell of Sharpies, pink erasers, and loose-leaf paper.

We headed down the hill into the silent town, the only wagon in site. *Maybe this is where real ghost towns come from*, I thought as Dad guided Willow to a spot in front of Murphy & Sons.

Wendell looked up from behind the counter when the three

of us walked through the front door. "Brooke..."

Dad interrupted our hellos. "I need to speak with your father, Wendell."

"Yes, sir." He disappeared into the back of the store.

"Aren't we in town to see the sheriff?" I asked.

"I want to speak with Mr. Murphy first."

"About what?"

Mr. Murphy came out from the back of the store with his arms full. "Mr. Decker," he said, placing the packages on the counter.

"Mr. Murphy. I'll just get to it. Our crops are gone."

"Gone?"

"Deer."

Mr. Murphy nodded like he wasn't surprised. "Think you can manage till the end of September?"

Dad sighed. "We still have our cow, and she's producing every day. And our chickens are still laying. But...well...we have a pig. She's healthy. Got anything for trade?"

"Not unless you want some French gloves or Jane Austin books. Thanks to the drought, we haven't got any fresh stock. Not to mention the soldiers wiping us out of necessities. Had a full store a week ago, but now about all that's left are ladies' items."

"Any suggestions?"

"Could get you a butcher. He'll take part of the animal in trade, but you'll still have plenty of meat to last you."

Rebecca Lynn tugged at Dad's arm. "Daddy, no..."

Dad ignored her and continued speaking to Mr. Murphy, but I barely heard his words. I couldn't stop thinking about Bambi, the way I'd dissed her most of the time, even when she'd done nothing to deserve my cold shoulder. It wasn't her fault she was born a pig. Now I wished I'd pet her more; treated her with a little more respect. I should have played with her, the way Rebecca Lynn had. My stomach grew nauseous with guilt.

"Sounds good," Dad was saying.

"Dad," I said. "You can't."

"We need to survive, Brooke. It's how our ancestors did it."

"But we aren't our ancestors."

"Why do you think the producers gave us a pig? To dress her up and put her in a dog show?"

"She has a name, Dad...*Bambi*..."

"Bambi," Rebecca Lynn said, crying.

"Should never name your stock," Mr. Murphy said.

Pissed off, I walked out of the store. Wendell followed me.

I stood next to Willow and placed my forehead against her thick neck. "This is bullshit."

"Careful, Brooke." He nodded up to the camera sitting in the corner of the porch ceiling, then looked in the store where Rusty stood with his lens focused on my dad and Mr. Murphy. "You don't want to end up like the Duffys."

"The Duffys?"

"You didn't hear? They were sent home."

"Why?"

"For doing something...un-neighborly."

Dad came out of the store. "Heading to the sheriff's office."

Rebecca Lynn and Rusty followed him down the sidewalk, but I stayed beside Willow, stroking her mane.

"I'll be there when the butcher comes," Wendell said.

"You will?"

"Of course. Bambi will need you. But you'll need me."

The man in the leather apron knelt down in the mud while my sister and I spoke words of comfort in Bambi's ear. Wendell handed me a treat to give her, and she nibbled it and cooed. It was the first time I'd ever heard her make such sweet sounds.

It's the first time you've noticed anything besides how dirty she is.

Wendell walked over to the fence and stood by Dad. The butcher leaned toward Bambi, his long, sharp knife glistening under the sun, and for one quick second I was sure I could see fear in Bambi's eyes. But then the fear was gone. Blood poured from her neck onto the mud. She fell onto her side. A loud grunt escaped her, and then her breaths came fast, like she had just finished a race. Moments later, her breaths stopped altogether, and her eyes grew vacant.

Rebecca Lynn cried over Bambi, telling her how sorry she was, her tears dripping onto that face as round and sweet as a peach. I cried too. Sully lay down beside the pig and licked her snout. My sister and I stroked Bambi's bristly belly.

The butcher stood up and absently wiped his knife on his apron as he spoke to my dad. "Need to get her cleaned and gutted, pronto."

"Girls," Dad said, "why don't you go on into the house?"

I nodded, taking my sobbing sister by the hand. As I led her out of the pen, Wendell touched my arm. His eyes were filled with tears.

I mouthed, "Thank you," but what I really wanted to say was "I love you."

Dad and the butcher and Wendell went out to the smokehouse to make our pig safe for eating. Wendell stayed for an early supper, which I refused to cook. So Dad and Wendell took a chunk of the meat and slowly cooked it in the fireplace while Rebecca Lynn and I wandered around the property, staying clear of the empty pen, salvaging what we could of tomatoes and carrots from the garden. Soon, Dad called us in. At first, I had a hard time staring at the pieces of freshly cooked ham on my plate, but then I remembered the only other foods we could count on were beans, rice, sunflower seeds, cheese, eggs, and a piece of fish if we were lucky enough to catch one.

As I ate my meal, I thought to myself, *Thank you, Bambi. Thank you for helping us survive.*

I said this last prayer believing that eating your pet pig was just about the most horrible thing that could happen when you lived out in the backcountry. Little did I know while eating my dinner in the calm of the summer evening, things were about to get a lot worse for our little homestead.

CHAPTER THIRTY-TWO

Maybe it was the mid-August heat and lack of rain. Maybe it was the fact that our stomachs grumbled all the time, and there was Prudence up in that comfortable mansion with servants fanning her and a lifetime supply of whatever she wished for. But probably it was because what Prudence had done to us went beyond playing a part. She could play Bitchy Betty all she wanted, but messing with my dad's crops was over the top. Because we our crops were gone, Bambi had to be sacrificed. It would have been easy enough to send a message to the producers, ratting her out, but I wanted to tell her to her face what kind of loser she was. I marched up to her house with a bee in my bonnet, as the old-time ladies used to say. Rusty followed me up the hill and porch steps with a spring in his step, like there was a new bike waiting for him.

Nanny answered the door. "Hello, Miss Brooke."

"I'm here to see Prudence."

"Yes, ma'am."

As Rusty and I stood on the porch, I gazed down the

driveway. The pecan trees were eerily still, like they were waiting to see what I would do.

Footsteps approached the door. As Prudence stepped onto the porch, and before she had a chance to open her mouth, I said, "I know what you did."

"Excuse me?"

"Do you know how hard my father worked to get those crops planted and cared for? Thanks to you we're going to starve."

Carl and his camera suddenly appeared on the other side of the door. We were being filmed in stereo.

But I didn't care. Sabotaging a neighbor's crops trumped giving Prudence a piece of my mind. Besides, women back in the day got pissed off at one another. Neither anger nor jealousy was a modern concept.

"Starve?" Prudence asked. "What on earth are you talking about?"

"You stole our chance to—"

"I've never stolen a thing in my life. Not even another girl's boyfriend, in case you hadn't noticed."

"If you didn't do it, then who did?"

"Did what, exactly?"

"Scattered corn all around our garden in the middle of the night. The deer ate our crops."

"First of all, I don't go anywhere alone in the middle of the night. And secondly, you couldn't catch me in that swamp you call a garden. Besides, what reason would I have?"

"Money? Jealousy? Or maybe just because you're a—" I said as clear as a bell so the microphones would take in every ounce of that one-syllable word. "Bitch?"

"That is a foul mouth you have there, Brooke Decker."

"Yeah? Well, you have a foul attitude, Prudence Miller."

"I did not do what you accuse me of."

"Then explain this." I pulled the ripped purple bonnet from my apron pocket and held it up.

"Where did you get that?" she asked, grabbing it from my hand.

"Where do you think?"

"Nanny stole it from me."

"She did not."

"The two of you are in cahoots. You planned this together."

"I was wrong," I told her. "You're not a bitch. You're a loser, with a capital *L*."

"*L* also stands for *lady*. And if I were less of one, I'd push you right off my porch."

"Go ahead. Lady or not. Do it."

Prudence moved closer and placed her palms against my shoulders. It was like being pawed by a kitten.

I laughed. "That all you got?"

There was no time to prepare as she repositioned her hands against my corseted chest and pushed. I soared through the air backward and tumbled over the edge of the porch into a large boxwood plant. The air left me, and for a moment, with my eyes closed, I struggled to breathe. When I opened them again, the large glass eye of the camera glared down at me. My angry reflection stared back. It took everything I had not to slam that camera into Rusty's face.

I stood up and brushed off my dress. My hands had tiny bloody scratches on them from the bushes. "You want to fight?"

I asked, anger spilling into the air. "I used to hang out with mostly boys in my old neighborhood. If I can kill the enemy in a game of *Tour of Duty*, I can certainly kick *your* prissy butt."

I waited, but Prudence didn't respond.

"What's the matter? Afraid you might get dirt on your imported dress?"

The cameras were no longer poised on my face. Carl and Rusty aimed at something over my shoulder.

"What—?"

I turned around to see Wendell standing a few feet behind me on the path.

"Brooke?" he said, his head cocked to the side.

"Wendell. What are you doing here?"

"Your father told me where you were. What's going on?"

"Just came up for a visit," I said, fixing my bonnet and ineffectively smoothing out my dress. I wanted to tell him what Prudence had done to our garden, but his frowning face stopped me. "Is something the matter?"

"There's bad weather headed our way. My dad told me to warn you all."

"Bad weather?"

"Your father wants you home. I need to get back as well."

As if on cue, thunder rumbled in the distance, and the trees which had been absent of wind only minutes before, shook the branches until their leaves sprinkled down onto the driveway.

I shot Prudence a look: *Next time you won't be so lucky.* Then I followed Wendell down the driveway, hiding the tiny scratches on my hands within the folds of my dress.

By the time Wendell and Rusty and I headed across the road to the cabin, a wild gust caused the dirt to swirl up and pepper our faces. I covered my nose and mouth with my apron. My bonnet fell back from my head. Then the wind came on so strong it nearly knocked me over. Wendell held onto me as we made our way to the gate where Dad stood waiting.

"Where's your sister?"

"I don't know."

As Dad went off to find her, I walked with Wendell to his wagon. The trees lining the Millers' driveway were bending in the wind. Rusty stood in the road filming the churning sky above our farm.

"Be careful going home," I told Wendell as he grabbed the reins.

"I'll be fine. Got extra weight in the back."

A half-dozen bags of feed were laid out on the wagon floor. My mom and dad had done the same when I was little with bags of sand in the trunk of the car in our pre-SUV days.

Wendell leaned over and I stood on tiptoe as he kissed me on the lips.

"Good luck," we said at the same time.

I waved goodbye as Wendell headed down the road. I guess Rusty felt safer in the Millers' house than in our wobbly shack because he had already headed up the driveway. I highly doubted *National Geographic* would be calling him anytime soon.

As he hiked up the hill, lightning crackled a few miles in the distance, thunder exploded across the hills, and a surge of nervousness moved down my spine and into my shoes.

The sky cracked open as I stood on the front porch. A torrent of rain gushed down sideways as Dad and my sister came running across the yard. Rebecca Lynn had the milk bucket in her hand, but the wind grabbed it and chucked it off into space. Dad scooped her up and carried her, soaking wet, into the cabin.

"What about Gretchen, Daddy?" Rebecca Lynn cried as he set her down. "She's still in the corral. We need to put her in the barn with Willow!"

Dad didn't answer. "Close the upstairs shutters, Brooke. I'll get the ones down here."

I tossed my bonnet onto the table, hurried up the ladder, leaned out and grabbed the shutters outside the tiny window, and latched them closed. When I came back down, the room was dark except for the fire. Dad and Rebecca Lynn were dragging our porch rockers into the room. Our tiny cabin creaked and moaned like an arthritic old man. The wind screeched at a high pitch while we slid the bench from the table to the front door. As we pushed the bench up against it, the wind knocked against the other side, threatening to come in.

Rebecca Lynn shouted over the rain and wind. "What about Sully?" Ever since Bambi's sacrifice, Sully had hung out in the barn with Willow like he needed a new best friend. "And what if the chickens get scared?"

Dad knelt down and took Rebecca Lynn's hands in his. "We can't worry about them right now, do you understand? We need to protect ourselves."

He turned to me. "Brooke, go grab the quilts and pillows."

I did as he asked. Dad took the quilts and made up a small bed under the kitchen table. Next, he told me to gather up whatever food we had left. While Rebecca Lynn helped me fill an empty feed sack, Dad collected the lanterns and a bottle of kerosene and put them next to the makeshift bed. He tossed some wood into the fire, which blazed high and made the room bright. The wind above the chimney whistled as it sucked on the flames. I grabbed my guitar and slid it under the table.

"I'm scared, Brooke," my sister whispered.

"It'll be okay."

"Is it gonna be bad?"

"I hope not."

"When will it stop?"

"I don't know."

"I want to go find Sully."

"Dad said no."

"What if he's scared?"

"He's probably hiding in the barn."

"What if the barn flies away?"

I didn't have an answer.

Dad checked the cast iron pot in the fireplace. I had kept it filled with water since our first day in the backcountry, and Dad offered me an appreciative smile. The three of us crawled under the wooden table, huddled together, and listened to the wind. It died down for a short time and then picked up speed again, causing tree branches to reach down and claw at the roof. The rain was relentless, slapping against the sides of the cabin. The wind shook the building like a snow globe.

Mother Nature was now the main star of *Upside Down in a*

Laura Ingalls Town: Hurricane Edition. It hit me how alone we were, just the three of us, not only cut off from our neighbors, but cut off from the real world.

Nearby, there came a loud splitting like the crack of a rifle, and then the sound of a giant tree hitting the earth. Rebecca Lynn screamed as one of my two mixing bowls crashed to the floor and broke into pieces.

My favorite bowl, I thought, not realizing I'd had one until that moment.

Rebecca Lynn cried, and Dad held her. When another tree fell, like a giant falling from the top of a beanstalk, Dad didn't look like our protector anymore. He looked like a man who had deliberately set up his family for a tragedy and would soon have to deal with the consequences.

"Are we going to make it?" I asked.

He nodded, but it was only out of courtesy.

Rebecca Lynn whined, "I have to pee."

"No," Dad said.

"But I can't hold it..."

Dad crawled out from under the table and grabbed the empty dish bucket. We turned our backs as my little sister tinkled. When she came back under the table, she said, choking on her words, "I want to go home. I want Mommy."

Dad held her while my hand rubbed circles against her back.

I pictured us being picked up the next day by a limousine, Novak the producer sitting in the back smoking a fat cigar while he tells us how amazing we were for braving the elements, how he wasn't responsible for what Mother Nature had cooked up, how we would be so pleased when we saw the edited version on cable. Then the producer's mouth moved again, but this time his words were mean: "You didn't get the money," he was saying. Dad would ask him why, and he'd point to me and tell me it was all my fault. I'd performed a modern dance while holding my modern iPod and wearing modern makeup; I'd accused and even threatened another contestant when I had little proof she had done anything; and I'd spent a large fraction of air time dodging the glass eye of the camera. Novak would add, "Your family would have died out here a hundred years ago if left to your own devices."

Letting my mind get carried away with what I *thought* could happen wasn't going to help the situation. Who cared about the money right now anyway? What mattered now was my family.

We remained huddled under the table. I had to pee but held it in. Dad read loudly from *Harper's Weekly* as the storm raged. We munched on sunflower seeds and grapes, pretending we didn't hear the shingles as they peeled from the roof, or the rain as it poured into the attic and dripped through the floorboards, splashing onto the table over our heads. We pretended we didn't hear a thing as another and then another tree crashed to its death. I thought I heard Gretchen's anguished moo, but convinced myself it was only the wind. I pictured Willow, our sweet mare, with Sully cowering beside her, and prayed the barn would hold steady; the last of our carrots, still out there in the field, drowning in what was now a muddy lake; and the grapes yet to be picked flying in the wind somewhere over the Appalachians.

CHAPTER THIRTY-THREE

Our homestead was in ruins, and Rusty couldn't wait to get the footage. Nearly twenty trees had toppled, some to the ground, some against a neighboring tree. None fell on our cabin, but half the shingles were gone, and our attic bedroom sat beneath slivers of blue sky. The storm had drenched our straw beds and now they smelled like the nests in the chicken coop. The chicken coop itself was on its side. Rebecca Lynn's favorite hen, a red one with white spots, was missing. She was convinced it flew away. Later, I found the poor bird squashed underneath a large branch. I didn't have the heart to tell my sister, so I played along with her chicken-flight theory. Gretchen the cow and Clyde the rooster were still MIA. Sully had burrowed inside a pile of hay in the barn. The poor pooch was shaking like crazy. The barn had managed to stay standing, and the roof was still in tact, but Willow had nearly kicked her way through one of the barn walls, and Dad had to patch it with wood scraps.

We finally found Gretchen on the Millers' driveway next to a downed tree, her udder swollen. She seemed disoriented, but by the time we had her milked and eating fresh grass again, she was back to her same old moo. Cuckoo Bird Clyde was never seen again, much to my sister's dismay.

"Maybe he joined up with a group of hottie flamingoes," I told my sister, trying to cheer her up. But she didn't laugh.

I was way more worried about Wendell than some crazy bird, and begged Rusty to share whatever he knew, but he ignored me.

"We need to go into town," I told Dad. "To make sure everyone's okay."

"There are more important matters here, Brooke."

Unfortunately, he was right.

My sister and I followed him out to the field with a shovel, trying to salvage whatever we could. We unearthed a few carrots under a foot of mud, hardly enough to make a dent in our meals, but it was better than nothing. For four long days, we picked up branches and debris, keeping some as kindling, and dragging the rest to the trash pile to set it aflame.

The springhouse door was blocked by two feet of wet earth, so for a time I had to climb over fallen trees and branches to make my way to the creek. Along the way, I spotted something shiny near a downed locust tree. Rusty's camera watched me as I picked it up. It was an empty Miller Highlife can. I held it up to the camera.

"Someone's been dipping their hand in Modern Land," I said, taking a whiff for old time's sake. I tossed the can into the trash heap without showing it to Dad. He was already dealing with his destroyed crops and the gaping hole in our roof. I didn't want to add to his worries. Though I did wonder who the beer drinker was—Prudence? Mr. Miller? Josiah?—and whether or not they'd be kicked out of Sweet Sugar Gap because of it.

Five days after the storm, when our homestead was nearly back to normal, Dad suggested we check on the Millers.

"And the Murphys," I added, my stomach knotting at the thought of seeing Wendell.

"The Millers first."

With Rusty behind us in his high-water boots, we trudged up the Millers' driveway, climbing over large Magnolia branches and two pecan trees that had toppled, blocking our path. We straddled them and swung our legs over.

On the porch, Nanny attacked the floor with a broom.

"Morning, Nanny," Dad said.

"Mr. Decker."

"You all do okay?"

"Does it look like I did okay?" Her Southern slave accent had been replaced by an angry city voice. "Does it look like anyone but me is cleaning this mess up? It's been five days. You'd think those jackasses would send someone out to check on us."

I looked at Rusty, but his face showed no expression.

Dad said, "Maybe the roads are blocked."

"Hmph."

"Is Mr. Miller home?"

"He's out back. Staring at that orchard while my husband and I do all the work. Mr. Miller hasn't lifted one skinny finger, but he sure has a talent for staring."

She continued sweeping as the four of us made our way around the side of the house. In the back, at the edge of the orchard, Mr. Miller stood staring just as Nanny had described. Large limbs and shattered apples and other debris littered the property as far as the eye could see. The apple trees themselves seemed more like skeletons than trees. Rebecca Lynn picked up a squashed apple from the grass and examined it. Along the back of the house, a staircase led up to the second-floor hallway. Boards had peeled away from the top of the house leaving unpainted rectangular strips. The tin roof had curled along the top edge.

"Orchard's barely standing," Mr. Miller told Dad. "Six sheep are unaccounted for."

"How's your family?"

"Shaken up, of course." Mr. Miller called over to where I stood by the back staircase. "Brooke, could you go on up and talk to Prudence? I can't reason with her. She's about ready to throw in the hat."

"Don't you mean bonnet?"

"You don't need to convince her to stay," he said, ignoring my weak joke. "I just want to know she's going to be alright."

With Rusty filming the orchard and Carl somewhere in the house, I made my way up the back staircase and down the dark hallway past the closed doors. The playroom door was open a crack. I peeked through the space. Prudence stood next to the tea table. Her back was to me, and she was barefoot. Her hair was frizzy, like mine when I had performed my Modern Land Underwear Dance. One of Prudence's hands lay flat against her ear like she had an earache.

"No shit, Sherlock," she was saying.

I glanced around the room to see who she was talking to, but her only audience was her collection of creepy dolls. She had lost it, I was sure. The hurricane had pushed her over the edge.

"I know, right?" she said. "Well, I don't care anymore."

I stepped across the threshold. "Prudence?"

She whirled around, and her hand fell from her ear. As it dangled by her side, I heard a girl's tinny voice coming from Prudence's palm. Not from her palm, exactly, but what she held in her palm: "Are you there?" the voice called. "Hello? Hell-O!"

Prudence pressed a button on the cell phone and tossed it onto one of the doll beds a few feet away. "Brooke! They didn't tell me you were coming!"

"What the hell is *that*?" I pointed to the cell phone lying on the doll blanket. After all this time, it seemed alien to me, like it had been dug up from the tar pits.

"Please don't tell anyone," Prudence said, running to the miniature bed and shoving the phone under a lacy pillow. "I will get so busted." The phrase 'so busted' made Prudence sound like a Valley Girl, not a Southern Gal. "Please. If I get caught…let me give you something…" She made her way to the mantel. "One of my dolls." Then she opened the wardrobe. "Or a ball gown." She stood next to the doll bed again. "You want to borrow my cell phone?"

"No, I don't. I don't want anything from you. That's not why I'm here. Your father asked me to come up and see how you are. But it looks like you're doing just fine."

"I'm not doing fine. I don't want to do this anymore."

"Then go home. We could use the cash."

Carl came running through the doorway, his camera panning the room like there was a live dinosaur hiding among the toys.

I ignored him.

"Do you know why my family came up here today?" I asked

Prudence. "To see how you all did during the storm. To help you clean up. Isn't that neighborly of us?"

"Yes…it is…"

"Dang right, it is." I turned to leave.

"Wait!"

"What?"

She said nothing at first, only stood there looking confused. Then she lowered her voice, as if the camera wouldn't hear her whisper. "Don't you see? That storm was the final straw. Our orchard is gone. There's no more mail. No more supplies. I'm so tired." She fell onto the chair next to the tea table and placed her hands against her face.

"Tired? You haven't done anything. Oh my God, Prudence. I've had to do eight hours of chores a day. Collect chicken eggs. Milk a cow. Cook all the meals—"

"I've worked hard, too, you just don't know."

"Doing what?"

"Helping my mother with the baby—"

"Helping her do what? I've never even heard your sister cry."

"My mom keeps her in her room with the windows closed because of the pollen."

I pictured the children in the olden days who suffered from some disease or another, hidden in the attic so they wouldn't get the other family members sick.

"You and I have different ideas of what hard work means," I told her. "You've been waited on hand and foot. You get all these things to play with. Me? I have a needle for mending things. And a bucket to churn. And a Dutch oven for the cakes I bake. Or *baked,* before I ran out of baking supplies. Those are *my* toys, Prudence."

But as I said the words, a feeling crept into me that I was betraying the Brooke who did these things. Sewing was totally fun, especially when I held the finished product in my hands. The cheese we made was better than any store-bought brand in Modern Land. And before we ran out of sugar and flour, I could bake breads and cakes in a Dutch oven with my eyes closed. Wendell had taught me songs on the guitar, and we sang together, took walks, swam in the pool, and kissed until I thought my heart would melt. Wendell liked this Brooke, and so did I. Even with the freckled face and uni-brow.

"This place is hard no matter what you have," Prudence said.

"It's harder for families whose crops were sabotaged."

"I didn't hurt your crops, Brooke. I wouldn't be caught dead in the middle of a field in the middle of the night. I promise you."

Outside, Dad called my name.

"I gotta go," I told her.

"Please don't say anything about…you know…" She nodded toward the pillow where her cell phone was hidden. Carl followed her glance then put the camera back on us.

"That's your deal, Prudence, not mine. I have way more important things to worry about than the snotty rich girl who doesn't have a clue how lucky she is."

I left her at the tea table among her dolls and pretty things, and headed out to the orchard where, for the next few hours, my sister raked, Dad chopped wood, Josiah stacked it, and Nanny and I dragged large limbs into a pile. And all the while, the Miller family stayed in the pretty blue house while the rest of us brought their property back to life.

Wendell Murphy didn't wait for me to come see him. He rode up that evening, and we hugged and giggled until my sister said "yuck" for the tenth time and went inside. After eating a chicken-and-rice meal that his mom asked him to deliver, he and I played the usual game until Rusty headed up to the Millers' house.

We kissed for minutes at a time next to the wading pool. He always tasted sweet and minty, and he smelled like fresh lemons. I wondered if I tasted and smelled as wonderful to him.

"I think what you did for the Millers was awesome," he said as we sat on the bank holding hands. "Especially after finding her bonnet in your field."

"Word travels fast."

"Nanny likes to talk."

"I did find her bonnet. But honestly, I don't think she'd have the guts to sneak out in the middle of the night, especially alone."

"Maybe her little brothers did it with her."

"Possibly. Still, she seems too prissy. Besides, what's done is done. I meant to thank you, you know, for warning us about the storm. If you hadn't, things could have been a lot worse."

Our owl friend hooted from a nearby tree.

I moved my feet back and forth in the water, creating ripples. After a moment, I said, "We're sort of enemies, aren't we?"

"Enemies?"

"This is a reality show, in case you forgot."

"I don't really think about that much."

"You don't?"

"Huh-uh. Do you?"

"Sometimes..."

"Well," he said, pulling me to him and wrapping an arm around me, "if we pretend this isn't a show, we'll have way more fun. We may as well make the best of things since it's almost over."

Almost over...

The thought melted away as he kissed me. We made out until the long day got the better of me, and I nearly fell asleep in his arms. He walked me back to my cabin, where I kissed him goodnight, went inside, and fell into a deep and perfect sleep.

CHAPTER THIRTY-FOUR

A loud knock at the cabin door interrupted my dreams early the next morning. Neither Dad nor my sister budged, so I threw my dress over my slip and dragged my aching muscles down the ladder. Prudence stood on the front porch wearing a starched white apron covering a silky blue dress. A sleepy Carl with his camera on his shoulder stood behind her.

"I thought milking a cow might be fun after all," Prudence said.

Rubbing the sleep from my eyes, I said, "What are you talking about?"

"I want to pay you back for how much you helped us with the cleanup."

"That's not really why you're here, is it?"

She gave Carl's camera a sideways glance.

"This is a bribe?" I asked. "No way, *José*."

"You'd get your chores done faster."

"You won't be able to handle it."

In a singsong voice she said, "It would give you more time to spend with Wendell."

"You'll have a heart attack. Or a stroke. Or you might break a nail." I started to close the door.

She stopped it with her hand. "Please, Brooke. Give me a chance."

"Why?"

"Because I'm lonely."

I laughed. "Not my *problemo*."

"You have Wendell. I…I don't have anything."

She began to cry, right there on my porch, with the sun barely in the sky, and the camera zooming in on her wet cheeks.

I shook my head. Was I actually feeling sorry for her? "If you do this, even if it is because you're lonely, I'm not cutting you any slack. You understand? I don't want any whining because you're shoveling chicken poop instead of eating crumpets."

"No whining," Prudence said, drying her eyes with her apron. "Cross my heart."

"Stop patting down your dress," I told Princess Prudence for the millionth time. "It won't keep it from getting dirty. Trust me."

We were cleaning up after breakfast, a simple meal of eggs and tiny bits of ham. We were nearly out of coffee and I didn't want to take the chance of her wasting any, so I took care of that chore myself. After breakfast, when Dad went out to work on the roof and Rebecca Lynn went to collect whatever grapes she could find, Prudence and I headed out to milk Gretchen, who stood eating grass on the other side of the road. I carried the stool, and Prudence carried the bucket. Carl kept his camera on the two of us as I sat next to the cow. Prudence scrunched up her face when I showed her how I squirted the milk through the air and into my mouth.

"That's disgusting."

"But hormone-free."

I pushed her down on the stool and showed her how to wrap her hands around the teats. As soon as Prudence's fingers made contact, Gretchen mooed and stepped backward, knocking her off the stool.

"Why did she do that? Mean old cow." She stood up and for the millionth time brushed her hands against her dress.

"Sorry," I said. "I forgot to tell you to warm up your hands first. She's pretty sensitive to cold fingers."

I picked up the stool and pushed Prudence back onto it. She rubbed her hands together like I showed her, and then went to milk again. The milk squirted onto her apron. "Oh!"

I redirected her hands so the milk landed in the bucket. Twenty minutes later, the bucket was half full.

"I did it, I did it!" she cried, like she'd just won a spot on *American Idol.*

"Now we have to carry it to the springhouse."

It had taken my dad and me nearly a week to get all the mud away from the springhouse door. Even so, my ugly shoes and her silky slippers were completely covered in muck by the time we got there.

After pouring the cream into crocks, Prudence said, a tiny whine hiding beneath the words, "I need to use the outhouse."

"So? I'm not going to hold your hand while you do it."

Carl stayed with me as I rinsed out the bucket, and by the

time I got back to the cabin, Prudence was rocking on the front porch, like a maiden waiting for someone to bring her a mint julep and a fan.

I told her firmly, "No breaks till lunch time."

We headed to the barn. I gave her a brush and guided her hand across Willow's back and mane.

"She's so pretty," Prudence said. "But big."

When she explained she'd never ridden a horse before, I spent the next hour teaching her to ride Willow around the tiny corral. As she held the reins and moved like a goofball up and down in the saddle, she wore a funny grin on her face.

For lunch Dad made beans cooked in bacon grease.

"This is all you have for lunch?" she asked.

"Welcome to my world."

After the dishes were cleaned, Rebecca Lynn, who wanted to be part of our training program, asked Prudence to follow her to the chicken coop. She put some feed in Prudence's hand. Each time a chicken pecked at her slipper, she screamed like there were snakes in her hair. No way had she been in our field that fateful night.

"Throw the meal *away* from you," Rebecca Lynn said like a professional chicken feeder. "That way they won't peck at your feet." With my sister's help, Prudence collected six eggs, picking up each one like a rare jewel and placing it gently in the basket.

Back at the cabin, the two fake Confederate soldiers we'd met before the storm were standing with Dad by the gate.

"The store in town won't have nothing for a week or so," one of the men said. "We got nowhere to stay. Nothing to eat."

"Food's scarce as hen's teeth," the other man said. He tossed

Prudence a creepy grin, and she stared at her muddy slippers.

Dad said, "I'll give you meals and a place to sleep if you'll help repair my roof."

The men agreed. They didn't seem in any hurry to go off and fight in a real *or* make-believe war.

"This blows," I told Prudence. "We barely have anything left to feed our own family."

"What happened to your roof?"

"We lost part of it during the storm. Our mattresses got soaked. For the last week we've slept under the sky."

And under the stars. With a nice breeze. Dad told scary stories by moonlight. And I'd never slept better. Even so, our mattresses had to be refilled. I could only sleep on the hard floor so many nights, and Dad winced in pain when he woke up in the morning.

"Time to collect dried grass," I told Prudence.

She and my sister and I spent the next few hours scouring the nearby hills, taking turns cutting down the tall grass with a large scythe, and tossing the mound on top of an old horse blanket so we could haul it down. Carl followed us around until both mattresses were filled. Dad and the two soldiers—Snyder and Mitchell—dragged the mattresses up the ladder and shoved them back in their boxes.

While the men finished up the roof, I introduced Prudence to a good friend of mine. "Prudence, meet my oven."

She stared at the hearth. "That's not an oven."

"It is to me."

"I can't believe you cook over a fire."

"I know, right?" I went through the motions explaining how

the Dutch oven worked, the cookbooks I used, and the ancient tools of the trade. "We don't have any sugar left, so my baking is sort of limited."

After churning butter, collecting firewood, and grabbing another bucket of water from the stream to put near the fireplace, Prudence followed me out to the butchered garden where we stood along the edge. Carl sat on a tree stump by the cabin with his camera focused on my dad and the two men up on the roof.

"I promise you, Brooke, I would never sabotage your family," Prudence said.

"It's just that your bonnet…"

"My bonnet was missing for a while. Why do you think I'm wearing this ugly cotton one?" She stooped down and picked up a kernel of corn. "Plus, our sheep eat grass, the horses and donkeys eat hay. We never buy feed. But I do know who sells it."

"The mercantile? Duh. They're a feed store." We stood a moment, as the idea formed in my head. "A feed store," I repeated. "As in corn…"

"What are you thinking?"

"About the boot tracks we found."

"Everyone around here wears boots, except for me." She gazed across the expanse of fertile soil. "Do you know why the Duffys got kicked out Sweet Sugar Gap?"

"Wendell said they did something un-neighborly."

"He ought to know since he's the one who turned them in."

"He did? What happened?"

"Wendell made a delivery to their farm, but no one answered the door. So he looked in the barn, thinking maybe someone was out there, but no one was, and he found a cooler filled with beer.

Modern-day beer. Next thing you know, the Duffys are gone."

I remembered the beer can I'd found on my way to the stream. "Prudence, can I ask you something?"

"Uh-huh."

"Why do you think my meltdown that day didn't send us packing? Why do you think the producers forgave me?"

She shrugged. "Maybe an unbridled dance is better than beer for ratings."

I had to force away visions of Wendell sneaking onto our property in the middle of the night, his wagon loaded with feed.

No way is Wendell capable of doing something so low.

But he turned in the Duffys, argued the paranoid side of my brain.

"Let's go up to my house," Prudence said. "I want to show you something you might like."

Carl stayed with my dad and the fake soldiers as Prudence and I started up the hill.

"My back and shoulders are screaming," she said as we trudged up the incline. Most of the downed tree trunks had been cut and placed in stacks along the sides, but the mud was still slick. "I wouldn't have lasted a week if we'd traded roles."

I no longer thought of my life out here as a role I was playing, or as a contestant on a game show, because that cheapened how hard I worked. But I said nothing as we stepped through the back door of the Millers' kitchen. Rusty came in through the dining room and sat at the kitchen table while his camera rolled.

"This is called an Oberlin stove," Prudence told me.

I had seen the large, cast-iron contraption on my water runs the night Mrs. Miller had the baby, but I hadn't noticed the

1834 patent stamp until now.

"It's supposed to be more efficient than a fireplace," Prudence said. "But I wouldn't know, since Nanny is the only one allowed to do the cooking."

I checked out the rest of the kitchen. There were two connecting pipes and a chimney, and enough cook tops for a restaurant. Countless cake molds dotted the wall, and pots and pans hung from a metal rack over a long butcher-block table. The table was covered with all types of mixing bowls, and baskets filled with fruits and nuts.

The kitchen grew warm and cozy as Prudence and I baked into the evening. As efficient as their Oberlin stove was, and considering they had enough sugar and spices to get the entire town through a winter, the biscuits and cakes weren't nearly as tasty as the ones baked over a fire in a Dutch oven.

Prudence wiped her forehead, leaving behind a long streak of flour.

Nanny stepped into the kitchen. "Lawdy mercy," she said, shaking her head. "With all this food, you might need to throw a party."

"A party!" Prudence and I said at the same time.

Nanny laughed. "You all made a fine mess for me to clean. But at least the bakin' part is done did!"

After the sun had set and the cameramen were gone, Wendell and I sat next to the warm pool with our feet dangling. The storm had left a surge in the tributaries, and the water came all the way up to our knees. It was so fun coming out here without the cameras. The pool and the outhouse: the only two places I could sit for a spell without interruption.

I discussed the party particulars with Wendell, knowing I would soon steer the conversation to the more serious topic which hid just beneath my tongue. "My dad found boot tracks the night the deer ate our crops," I said, a little extra casually.

"Oh, yeah?"

"Mm-hmm."

I waited, but he said nothing. I forged ahead, my stomach in knots. "I can't help thinking…you know…that your store sells feed. A weird coincidence, I suppose."

"What is?"

"You. Working at a store that sells *corn* feed."

He leaned back. Way back. Like he was suddenly farsighted. "Are you accusing me of something?"

"You had those bags of feed in your wagon…"

"I told you. I keep them back there for the weight."

"Right. I know. And I believe you…"

"It doesn't sound like you believe me."

"I do. I'm sorry. I just…"

He stood up in a rush, speaking angrily as he hopped from one foot to the other, putting on his socks, then his boots. "You know," he said. "I had something important to share with you. Something I wanted you to know before—"

"I'm sorry." As I stood, my foot landed on a sharp twig, but I ignored the twinge. "Don't go. Please."

My stomach dropped as he walked away from me. I shouldn't have said anything. Even if he did do it, it would have only been for the money. And who was I to suggest his family was less deserving than mine? Whatever Wendell had or hadn't done, I was freaking out to think he might be breaking up with me. What would I do out here without him?

"No, Wendell. Please!"

He stopped on the path and my heart stopped as well. He looked so serious, almost anguished. There was something more he needed to tell me, something important, and I had ruined it by throwing accusations. "You know," he said, "I was just getting used to all of this. Having dinner together, sitting on your porch, coming out here, away from the cameras. Now I feel like it was all a waste of time."

"No. Not a waste of time. Please, Wendell. I was just mad about what happened. I didn't know where to direct my anger."

"God, Brooke, this isn't the time to be angry. This is the time to..." he cocked his head to the side. "Did you hear that?"

"What? No. What were you saying, Wendell? What do you have to tell me?"

He took one step toward me and stopped awkwardly, like a toddler trying to take his first step. "I'm falling for you...okay? That's what I have to tell you."

My stomach turned into an ocean with waves moving up and down, up and down. I stood frozen as he took another step.

"I didn't want to tell you," he said, grabbing both my hands.

"I'm glad you did. I feel the same way."

"But I'm not supposed—"

A loud snapping sound struck the air, and we jerked our heads toward the noise. It only took my brain a millisecond to register what I was seeing. The words barely made their way from my throat. "Oh...my...God..." The dark hairy monster stood on its hind legs six yards from where we stood, just at the water's edge across the stream from us. It let out a deep growl. Even in the dark, I could see its sharp teeth. "Wendell?"

He whispered, his voice calm, "Back up. Do it. Get onto the path."

The bear created a wave as it flopped into the pool and stood up. I was mesmerized and terrified by its height. Another deep rumble rose from its core.

"Go!" Wendell shouted.

Someone had super glued my feet to the bank.

In the water, the bear leaned forward on its haunches, dove onto its belly, and started swimming in our direction. Wendell screamed at me, but his screaming didn't matter. My ears could only hear the bear's growl and the splashing of its paws against the water, and when Wendell pulled something out of his pocket and held it up in the air, I believed *Upside Down in a Laura Ingalls Town* was no longer a family program, but a dystopian reality show where all the contestants, one by one, die a gnarly death, and he was going to be the first. He held up a red container. The bear stopped a few feet from the bank. It stood up again. Wendell took a wide step forward, his outstretched hand only a few feet from the bear's face. The bear seemed to scream as his paws suddenly slammed against his hairy face. It stumbled to the right before falling back into the water.

I was convinced Wendell was a super hero. He had waved a magic wand and willed the bear to its death. But the bear wasn't dead. It stood flailing its arms like someone had set its fur on fire. I closed my eyes, foolishly thinking that would stop the God-awful howling from reaching my ears.

Wendell took a step backward and tripped over my shoes, dropping the canister. I picked it up and squeezed my super hero's amulet in my fist as Wendell grabbed the lantern and screamed, "RUN!"

This time I obeyed.

We tore through the woods with our only light coming from the lantern I held in my sweaty hand. We both tripped. I landed hard on my knees, and Wendell skinned the side of his face. But none of that mattered. As we neared the cabin, I could smell the lit fireplace as the chimney blew smoke up and over the trees, the most wonderful smell in the world. I started bawling as we ran together up the porch steps. Within seconds my dad was rocking me in his arms, and the door was safely locked behind us.

I wanted Wendell to spend the night, but without any way to get in touch with his family, it was decided he go home. Two hours after the ordeal, Wendell and I sat on the top porch step, our eyes darting from shadow to shadow. My heart thumped erratically each time I envisioned the bear's angry eyes. In the dark beyond the railing, every chirp or twig snap convinced me there were monsters lurking.

Wendell said very little, and I knew that what had happened had shaken him to the core.

"You saved my life," I told him. "You'll probably get the money. If you do, it's because you deserve it."

He put his arm around me. I could still feel the traces of tremors. "You would have done the same for me," he said.

"This is yours." I pulled the small red canister of pepper spray from my apron pocket and handed it to him. "You were smart to sneak it in." I remembered all of the lame things I had chosen to sneak into the backcountry, back when thoughts of actual survival had never entered my mind.

"I meant what I said earlier," he whispered.

"Me too."

We sat on the step in silence until Dad told Wendell it was time to leave, and I stood at the railing until my hero's wagon disappeared into the dark.

CHAPTER THIRTY-FIVE

The blue mansion set the stage for a perfect party. Paper streamers hung from the ceilings, vases of flowers sat on every table, and there must have been a hundred candles taking up space on the three mantels. The Murphys brought cranberry tarts, Mrs. Wrightman brought a huge tray of bonbons, Reverend Clark and his wife brought nut bread, and Prudence and I baked a bunt cake and three dozen sugar cookies. Nanny popped fresh popcorn and boiled a pot of warm apple cider. It somehow seemed incomplete without the Duffy family, but we still aimed to have fun. Even the camera guys smiled like real people. The Jackie Chan lookalike filmed us in the parlor, while Rusty and Carl took turns in the other rooms. The grownups and we older kids played a game of marbles called Ringer, and the traditional Pin the Tail on the Donkey. Games that no teenager in their right mind would play in Modern Land; that only a few months earlier would have sent me running to Libby's FROG for a game of Eight-ball and a double shot of Jack.

When it was time for music, thoughts of scary beasts and

ruined crops and concluding television shows seemed far away as Wendell handed me my guitar. Everyone sang along, including my dad. His beard now hung well below his chin, and he had bathed and doused himself in cologne that smelled like a cross between lemons and parsley. Wendell had taught me "Old Dan Tucker," but I changed the words to make it about my dad instead:

"*Old Tim Decker's a fine old man, came out here to farm some land. / Never combed his hair or shaved his beard, could barely catch a fish or shoot a deer. / So get out of the way, get out of the way, get out of the way, old Tim Decker. / You're too late to git your supper!*"

Everyone was hooting and hollering. Dad's face grew beet red and he beamed like I'd just won an Olympic gold medal. So I gave him the next verse:

"*Old Tim Decker he come to the gap, ridin' on a horse while taking a nap. / Woke with a start when his horse fell asleep, landed headfirst in a nearby creek. / So get out of the way, get out of the way, get out of the way, old Tim Decker. / You're too late to git your supper!*"

Wendell took the guitar from me and accompanied Prudence on the piano, but he gave me the sugar-eye the entire time. Mrs. Miller pulled out a violin. The three of them made a pretty good band, even though the songs were more appropriate for Civil War recruits on their way to battle.

As the music played, Snyder and Mitchell, the two soldiers sleeping in our barn, showed up. They hadn't been officially invited, but in the 1860's backcountry, even party crashers were treated like neighbors. After the two men ate platefuls of dessert, they came and sat on either side of me on the sofa. A round wooden canteen appeared in Snyder's hand. He and his buddy passed it back and forth in front of me, and the room filled up with the smell of liquor.

"Want some tar water?" Snyder offered, shaking the canteen under my nose. "Apple brandy."

Except for the beer can I'd found, drinking hadn't entered my mind the entire summer. "No, thanks," I told him, relocating to a seat by the fireplace.

Soon, the two soldiers were laughing like jackasses and cussing up a storm, so my dad suggested they take their carousing outside. The men went onto the porch. After a while, Nanny went to check on them. Curious, I followed Nanny outside, and Rusty followed me.

Snyder was sitting on the porch swing. He spoke beneath the music still playing in the house, his words slurred. "My agent's an ass."

"Mine's not so bad," Mitchell said, his hand wrapped around the chain of the swing. "The last job he got me, I made residuals up the wazoo." He turned to Nanny. "Aren't you sick of being typecast?"

A usually silent Rusty said, "Guys, this is a nice party. Why don't you all go and sleep it off?"

"Why don't you go screw yourself?" was Snyder's reply.

Mitchell patted his friend on the arm. "Chill out, Snyder."

"Don't tell me to chill. They offer me a lead, and they put me out here in the sticks and pay me atmosphere wages."

For the first time that I'd ever seen, Rusty turned off his camera. It hung limply from his hand.

Snyder said, "Oh, so now you're not going to film us? Is that the way it works? We break our backs putting shingles on some farmer's roof in exchange for bad cooking, and you don't even have the courtesy to put us on camera? What do I look like, a slave?" He turned to Nanny. "No pun intended."

Nanny touched my arm, "Brooke, let's go inside."

I pulled from her grasp. I was interested in what these men were talking about, even if I didn't know exactly *what* they were talking about.

The screened door slammed as Nanny went inside.

Mitchell said, "Let it rest, Snyder."

But Snyder ignored his friend's advice and turned to me. "What about you, sweet pea?"

"What about me?" I asked, the words catching in my throat.

"You happy with what they offered you?"

Was he talking about our homestead? The opportunity to live on a farm? The money we might win?

"I guess so."

"She guesses so," Snyder said, tilting back his head to take a swig from the canteen. "You like deer?"

"Deer?"

"Seen any in your garden lately?" He laughed.

The desserts in my stomach churned into a hard clump. The only music now was the sound of Mrs. Miller's violin. Nanny came back onto the porch with Wendell and Prudence behind her.

"What's going on?" Wendell asked, standing next to me. Prudence stayed hidden behind the two of us.

"Nothing," Mitchell said, moving away from Snyder, leaving him sitting on the porch swing alone.

Snyder said, "I'm just curious as to why you all get to live in your pretty mansions, have parties, get to be the center of attention, and we fix a damn roof in exchange for crap food. I never signed up to be a Confederate soldier. Shit. My family comes from Boston. We would have fought on the Union side." He laughed again, and this time spit flew out of his mouth.

Had I ever looked that disgusting when I got drunk back in Modern Land? I prayed that I had not.

Snyder leaned to the right and saw Prudence. "Hey there, sweetheart. Haven't I seen you somewhere before?"

Snyder's lame attempt at hooking up with Prudence in front of all these people disgusted me.

"Okay, guys," Wendell said. "You both are wallpapered. Maybe you should skedaddle."

Snyder glared at Wendell. "*Wallpapered*? *Skedaddle*? That your way of saying I'm too drunk to sit here on this porch? You telling me what to do, you little blowhard?"

The violin music and laughter from inside the house had stopped. Dad stood in the doorway. Everyone except the little kids gathered around him.

"If you leave now," Rusty said, "we'll pretend this never happened."

"Your union can't tell my union what to do," Snyder told Rusty. "Actors have more clout than a stupid cameraman."

"You're an actor?" I asked Snyder, trying to decipher the difference between a *reenactor* and a *real* actor.

"Trained in London for three years. Did more Shakespeare than Shakespeare." His hand moved through the air. "Out, out brief candle! Life's but a walking shadow, full of sound and fury, blah blah blah. I worked in New York *and* Hollywood. Music videos. Commercials." He pointed at Prudence who stood just behind my shoulder and shouted, "I remember you! Sarah! You do any of those Honda commercials lately, honey? I like the one where you're sitting on the beach with your surfboard on top of the car. You look awesome in a bikini."

Prudence gasped in my ear. "Well, I never."

Dad stepped onto the porch, followed by Carl and Jackie Chan, whose cameras were still rolling. He said, "It's getting late, everyone. Maybe we should start cleaning up..."

Snyder tried to get off the porch swing but fell to the floor on his knees. The canteen dropped from his hand and fell on its side. He grunted like a bull as Mitchell pulled him up by the arm.

"Let's get you home," Mitchell said, slinging the canteen's leather strap over his shoulder.

"Home!" Snyder said, stumbling toward the stairs. "We sleep in a barn! With mice and mosquitoes and manure!" He swung a fist at Carl's camera, but missed it by a foot. "This isn't my home. This is hell!"

As Mitchell nearly carried him down the porch steps, Snyder kept rambling. "I didn't study at the Academy for nothing! I can talk like a top rail soldier who speaks real good chin music. I'm fit as a fiddle from eating my goober peas. Everything is hunkey dorey, you bunch of pie eaters. See? That's why I'm union! I'm a professional actor!"

They disappeared down the hill with Jackie Chan on their tail as the rest of us went back inside. No one mentioned what had just happened on the porch. No one said a word as we stacked dirty dishes on trays. All I could think about were Snyder's final words: "*I'm a professional actor...*"

After I carried a tray into the kitchen and placed it on the butcher block, I headed toward the back door. Rusty saw me and turned his camera in my direction.

"Rusty," I said, covering the camera's eye with the palm of my hand. "You don't need to film every little thing."

He pushed my hand from his lens.

"Please," I said. "At least let me go to the outhouse by myself. I've been holding it in for two hours."

Rusty sulked, but finally walked the camera over to Rebecca Lynn, who was playing a game of marbles in the hallway with the Miller boys, totally unaware that anything unusual had just occurred on the front porch.

I went out through the kitchen door where a collection of kerosene lamps hung from wrought iron hooks. Carl stood smoking a cigarette by the back door, the camera resting at his feet. I grabbed one of the lanterns and followed the stony path to the outhouse. It was incredibly clean inside, with a stack of white pressed linens sitting on a shelf. After I came back out, I looked toward the house. Carl was gone.

From where I stood on the path, the house really did seem to belong in a different era. In the downstairs rooms, my dad and sister and other guests milled about, and I could hear their faint voices floating from the kitchen into the backyard. The interior pre-Victorian oil lamps made the rooms behind the wavy glass seem romantic and mysterious, just like a movie.

Romantic.

Mysterious.

Just like a movie…

At the end of the path, I stopped. In front of me loomed the back staircase, leading up to the second-floor hallway. In the dark, it matched the crooked stairs from Lemony Snicket's house. With the lantern in my hand, I climbed the rickety steps, trying not to let the warped wood squeak under my shoes. At the top, the door knob turned easily under my hand. I hurried down the hall toward the playroom, and entered the dark cave. I turned up my lantern and shut the door.

With my heart pounding, I moved about the room, picking things up, peering underneath dolls in petticoats and fancy pillows and miniature china plates. I dug through the overflowing toy trunk and the wardrobe where a collection of gowns hung inside like ghosts. I moved to the daybed, leaned against it, and took a wide glance around the room.

I was paranoid. So that fake soldier was a real actor. So what? So there was a chance that Prudence had done some commercials. That's probably how she and her family got picked to come out here, because she was pretty *and* talented. Maybe she ate up the camera like Beyoncé.

I sat on the edge of the daybed, chewing on a thumbnail, scolding myself for snooping. I'd been out here in the sticks too long, like that creepy Snyder guy. He was bonkers after only a few days, so I probably was as well. Living in the middle of nowhere in a time that no longer existed could do that to a person, couldn't it?

The heel of my boot kicked the edge of something solid beneath the daybed. I bent down, lifted the bed skirt, and spotted a plastic box, the kind my mom once used for winter sweaters. I slid it out and took off the lid, figuring I'd find hats or gloves or bows. But I was wrong. Inside the box were gadgets from Modern Land. There was the cell phone I'd seen Prudence use, and a charger, though why she had one when there was no electricity was beyond me. There was an iPod, a newer version than my own. My hand burrowed beneath the gadgets and brought out a clear makeup bag, filled with Sephora products, nail polish bottles, makeup remover. My hand went even deeper and landed on something so familiar to the modern world, but so foreign to the mid-1800s, my mind had to work to distinguish between current and historic. I set the lantern next to the box and pulled out the object with two hands: a laptop.

I shook my head, unbelieving. The pale light from the lantern only added to the dreamlike effect. It was bad enough I had snuck in an iPod. But all this stuff? Did her parents know? Or the producers? If they did, why hadn't she been kicked off the show? It wasn't as if she'd hidden them in a dungeon. They were right there, under the freaking daybed, for anyone to see, including a camera if it went down low enough. I was furious with Prudence, but even angrier at myself for letting her be my friend.

With my heart threatening to jump out of my chest, I put the laptop on the floor and continued rooting through the box. I discovered a couple of Stephen King novels, a biography about some dead movie star, an itty-bitty black and white two-piece bathing suit, a bottle of Coppertone tanning oil, and a can of bug spray. How in heaven's name could anyone have snuck in all this junk? Was there a fake bottom in the buggy? Did someone meet her out in the woods like a drug dealer makes a deal in an alley? Maybe she had the contraband brought down the river. After all, if you're going to sneak in items from Modern Land to Yesterday World, you may as well keep the transportation old-school.

My fingers grabbed a hold of a sparkly picture frame with a photograph in the center. I squinted at the photo. It had been taken at Christmas time, and the people were dressed in red Santa hats and green sweaters. There was Prudence, with her parents, and a younger girl who looked like a miniature version of Prudence. I moved the lantern more closely to the photo, scrutinizing their faces better under the light. Something was wrong. Her parents. They didn't look anything like—

"Don't," Prudence said from the doorway. In her hand she held a lantern larger than mine, and the light bore its way through the room like a headlight. She shut the door behind her, turning the skeleton key to lock it.

"Don't what?" I asked.

"Don't go through my things."

"Too late."

I threw the picture frame onto the pile and stood up. "Those aren't your real parents downstairs, are they? Where's the little girl from that photo? Is she your *real* sister? Who are those boys down there?"

"I can't say anything."

"Right."

"It's in my contract."

"I don't think we signed the same contract."

She paused. "I know we didn't."

I was fearful, but not in the way a person gets when running into a bear in the woods. I was afraid the way a person gets when they realize everything they think they know is wrong. Like Mom getting cancer. That was wrong. All the long days and endless nights leading up to her death, sleeping on waiting room couches at the hospital, draining her tubes after she came home for good, saying goodbye, boxing up her clothes to bring to the homeless shelter—and everything since then—was all wrong, too.

I demanded answers. "Are there hidden cameras or microphones in here?"

"No."

"Then tell me."

"It could jeopardize everything."

"Afraid you won't win the People's Choice Award?"

"I don't mean me. I was talking about *you. Your family.*"

"My family?"

"Please, Brooke," she begged. "Don't ask me anything. This whole thing is almost over."

"I gave up my life for four months. I gave up Junior Prom, field trips to colleges, working at the beach for the summer, hanging out with my best friend…my sister could have died…we killed our pig…" I held in the tears. I was not about to give Miss America the satisfaction of seeing me cry.

"I gave things up too," Prudence said.

"Like your real family? Your real mother?"

She nodded.

"You *chose* to give them up," I told her. "I don't feel sorry for you."

"I never asked you to."

"Those soldiers...they're actors?"

"Yes."

"And you?"

"Yes."

"Is your real name Prudence?"

"No."

"Sarah?"

"Yes."

"Were you ever going to tell me?"

"No."

"I snuck in an iPod and felt like a douche bag. You snuck in the freaking Apple Company."

"I was allowed to."

"Good for you. I was allowed to wear painful shoes that give me blisters and a corset that cuts through my ribs. Looks like I win."

"This isn't a contest."

"Really? I thought that was the point of pretending—"

The doorknob jiggled.

"Go away," Prudence called.

"It's me, Carl. Let me in." He knocked hard against the door.

"I'll be out in a minute!"

The next idea hit the back of my head with such force, it nearly knocked me out of my leather boots. I don't even know why it came to me at that moment. Maybe it was the loud knocking. Maybe it was the laughter and music from earlier that evening that would have woken anyone from a deep sleep. Anyway, there it was, smacking me in the head.

"Where's the baby?" I asked.

"What?"

"Your new baby sister, Camellia. Where is she?"

"Sleeping."

"Where?"

"In my parents' room."

But those people weren't her parents.

"Why wasn't your baby sister at the party? Why does she always stay hidden away?"

"I told you. The pollen—"

"I think I'll pay her a visit." I started across the room with my lantern swinging, forming crazy shadows on the storybook walls.

"No!" she shouted, jumping like a guard in front of the locked door.

"Why not, *Sarah*?"

"Please don't call me that."

"Why can't I see the baby?"

She squeezed her lips together and shook her head.

"She's not real, is she?" I asked. "I saw her, but she's not real. That's why I haven't seen her since that first day. What is she, one of those baby dolls that freaky women buy on Creepy Fake Babies dot com? My sister and I stayed up all night for you. We thought your mother might die. God, that's sick. Pretending to have a baby. Pretending to have a family that isn't yours."

"It's for the show."

"What about the other families?" I asked. *What about Wendell?* my mind screamed. "Are they just like you?"

"I only know about *our* family. *Our* backstory. We aren't allowed to discuss anything with anyone else."

"What else does your backstory say? That you get to mess

with anyone you want? How much are they paying you to be a bitch to Nanny and Josiah? How much are they paying you to mess with me?"

"Don't…"

"My family has a backstory. A *real* one. We came out here to save our house. Did you know my mother passed away a year ago? Did you ever think for one second that I was a real person with a real life?"

"Of course. That's why I'm here."

"What do you mean, that's why you're here?"

Carl banged at the door again.

The thought of Prudence's cell phone, her iPod, and that laptop wouldn't leave my mind. I knew I should be asking important questions, questions about Wendell, the Duffys, the other families, the cameramen…so many I could have filled a book. But there was one question in particular that kept gnawing at me, and I needed to ask it: "How do you keep them charged? Your cell phone and stuff?"

She whispered, "Electricity."

It occurred to me that the only upstairs room I'd seen was the playroom, except for the five seconds I had stood over the fake baby in the fake parents' bedroom. I'd never taken a tour through the other bedrooms, or the bathrooms…

"You have indoor plumbing, don't you? You've never even used your outhouse. That's why it's so clean."

"Please, Brooke…"

The tremble in her voice was both pathetic and satisfying. I almost wished for tears to roll down her cheeks, to glisten by the light of the lantern. But she didn't cry.

"No more questions," she said. "We can't have another conversation like this one. Not until the end of the show."

The show.

Prudence was awfully good at playing her part, but I would be better. From here on out, I would play the part of a girl who has learned to be *autonomous.* A role made just for me.

"Fine, *Prudence,*" I said, opening the door. Carl stood there, the camera on his shoulder like a scientist's oversized rat. My voice was without emotion and my words were clear as I told Prudence, "Not having any more conversation with one another is the perfect way to end this venture."

I stormed down the candlelit hallway and down the stairs. Carl came after me. On the porch, Wendell and his family were saying goodnight to the fake Mr. and Mrs. Miller. Both Carl and Rusty now pinned their cameras on me like they'd caught something extraordinary on their radar.

Wendell touched my arm. "Brooke?"

I yanked it away.

"Did I do something wrong?"

"I don't know. Did you?"

"I don't understand..."

Mrs. Murphy told Wendell's younger brothers, "Get into the wagon, boys. Wendell, we'll wait for you there." She and Mr. Murphy and the boys walked over to the wagon.

The fake Miller parents went into the house and closed the door. The parlor curtains were pulled shut, leaving us in the dim light of the porch lanterns. I wondered what would happen behind those curtains. A special conference call with the producers on SKYPE?

"You know what, Wendell?" I said. "I don't understand either. And what's really funny is, I don't want to."

Dad came through the front door and onto the porch with my sister. "Brooke?"

I thumped down the porch steps and made my way down the path. Dad and Rebecca Lynn followed me, and Wendell followed them.

"Wait," Wendell called.

I kept walking.

"Brooke. Please."

Dad pulled Rebecca Lynn by the arm and led her down the driveway past me. She asked, "What's wrong, Daddy?" and Dad responded with "Don't worry about your sister. She can take care of herself."

Damn right I could.

I stopped and turned around. "I *know!*" I screamed at Wendell.

"Know what?"

I wanted to take a giant eraser and wipe that stupid confused look off his face.

"If you don't know, then lucky you. If you do know, then you're a rat. A cruel, effed-up rat."

I jerked my head upward, convinced I could spot tiny glass eyes among the pecans. I wondered if there were microphones hidden in the branches; if we were no different than the characters in *1984* or *The Hunger Games*. I wanted to run through Sweet Sugar Gap screaming that I was done playing Laura Ingalls. That what they were doing to me and my family was brutal and unfair.

"Brooke..."

But I had turned away.

Mr. Murphy called out, "Wendell, get in the wagon. It's getting late."

I heard Wendell's boots as they shuffled through the gravel away from me. I heard the horse snort, then the sound of wagon wheels. As the Murphy family made its way past, I kept my head turned in the other direction.

CHAPTER THIRTY-SIX

Snyder and Mitchell had disappeared by the next morning. Their packs were no longer in the barn. Where they went we did not know, but there was no trace of either one, though a large chunk of homemade cheese was missing from the springhouse.

Dad asked me no questions regarding what had happened at the party, probably too afraid to dig for answers, especially after the Duffys' expulsion. Anyway, Dad was a smart man who could put two and two together without trying. He didn't need any answers from me, even if I had them.

Life was easier pretending Prudence was a stranger who lived in the pretty house on the hill, pretending Rusty and Carl and all the other camera people were invisible, pretending that Wendell and I were never a thing.

Ha, I thought. *Maybe we never were.*

Nanny came down to our cabin, always the faithful servant, to tell me how upset Prudence was. But living out here in the sticks had turned me into a grumpy old mule, and I curtly told her I had nothing to say to her or Prudence. I did my chores, made do with the little bit of food we had left, and never spoke a word of what I knew. My family needed the money. And that was that.

We had morphed into exactly what the producers hoped for: a true mid-1800's family, struggling to make it in the backcountry. During the last few weeks of filming, my little sister turned into a wild child, discarding her bonnet, feeding the chickens shoeless, hiding in the barn while I washed my dirty feet in the soapy bucket. Her baby voice had vanished, too, which ironically, I missed. Dad grew super quiet, digging up whatever vegetables or roots he could from a garden that no longer made him proud. The entire Decker family felt the shift from worrying about how we appeared on camera, to where our next meal would come from.

Funny how priorities change when you're hungry all the time.

Wendell stopped visiting, which told me all I needed to know. I asked to skip church for the rest of our stay in the backcountry. Dad let me, and for that I was relieved. It was more important to worry about survival than a boy who pretends to be something he's not. We were down to living on apples, grapes, eggs, dairy products, and scraps of fatty ham. My dad wanted to go fishing, but after the bear incident, we weren't about to go near the pool. He traded some firewood with Mr. Murphy for flour and corn meal. I, however, did not make the trek to town.

On our last Sunday in Sweet Sugar Gap, Dad came home from church with an announcement: "There's going to be a September feast down on the schoolhouse grounds. An early Thanksgiving. There'll be a campfire, and food…and Brooke, everyone asks that you bring your guitar. For the final get-together."

Since that memorable night at the Millers' house, I had picked up the instrument only once. My fingers couldn't seem to arrange themselves into proper chords; my voice couldn't sing without cracking.

Rebecca Lynn pushed her greasy hair from her forehead. "What should we bring?"

"We've been asked to bring apples and grapes," Dad said. "If there's anything left."

"I'm ready for a hamburger at Spunky McDoogle's."

"One more week. Let's make this feast the finish line. Everyone is happy to pitch in."

In a pissy voice, I added, "They're only being nice because—" but I stopped myself. The lines on Dad's face had softened, either because our venture was coming to a close and there would hopefully be a check waiting for him, or because we were about to have a real feast. Either way, I didn't want to ruin that hopeful look for anything in the world.

"Because what?" he asked.

"Nothing," I said. "Rebecca Lynn, grab the basket. We've got some fruit to pick."

The leaves on the elms and oaks changed almost overnight from bright green to gold and copper, like they were dressing up for Sweet Sugar Gap's final feast.

We were last to arrive, and the sun was still warm. As we parked the wagon near the others in the schoolhouse yard, I spotted a small homemade flag sticking up from a chunk of wood in the center of the table, eleven stars instead of nine. Surrounding the flag were platters of food: a large wild turkey and a ham were the main dishes. Cranberry relish, sweet potato pie, steamed collards, turkey gravy, cornbread stuffing, pumpkin muffins, and bread pudding rounded out the meal. Dad and my sister carried our baskets to the table as I deliberately took my time at the wagon.

While Rusty and Carl and the other camera people moved around the grounds videotaping one thing or another, I spotted Wendell in the crowd and turned my head away. This wasn't going to be easy, ignoring him and Prudence, but it had to be done. If I spoke, I was bound to make a scene, much to my dad's dismay. Couldn't take that chance this late in the game. Better if I said nothing. Dine and dash.

All the townspeople, minus the Duffys, were in attendance. The minister sat at the head of the table, his wife on his right. Nanny and Josiah sat on a couple of tree stumps tending to the fire. Each child sat with his or her family along the two benches. I squeezed in between Rebecca Lynn and Dad so I wouldn't be obligated to speak to anyone. Everyone regarded my family with bright smiles and few words. Maybe they were afraid if they sparked too much conversation, I would start asking questions. Maybe they were sad the venture was nearly over.

The minister bowed his head. "We thank Thee, God, for giving us the strength to enjoy your land to the fullest, to develop cooperation and form friendships in the most unlikely of places, and to carry those friendships in our hearts forever..."

Forever? I would never see these people again, so what was he talking about forever for? I would not become besties with Prudence, who probably lived in a funky apartment over a vinyl record store in Hollywood.

As we prayed, I glanced up to find Wendell staring at me. He offered a weak smile, but I shut my eyes and tried to pay attention to the minister's words.

"And so, dear Lord, we ask in Your name that we feast today on the bounty of Your land, not for the last time, but for the first time, for every moment is a chance to begin again. Amen."

Platters and baskets made their way around the table. Meats and breads and sides quickly disappeared. For the first time in weeks, my stomach felt happy, but my heart was filled with sadness. After dessert, a bonfire threw sparks high into the air as thoughts of permanently removing my tight shoes and stiff corset settled into the modern part of my brain.

My dad went to the wagon. He brought my guitar back to the bonfire and handed it to me. At first I only stared at it, like it was as foreign to me as a cow's udder used to be. Dad said, "This is it, Brooke. We'll never have this opportunity again. Ever."

He's right. This is it. The end of the line. We can all go back to our dishwashers and HEPA filter vacuums and Facebook and Netflix. Soon we'll be staring at our computers and oversized televisions like we'd just won them on a game show, and living large in our beach condos and suburban houses.

That is, if we get to keep our house.

I tuned my guitar by rote. With all of the children sitting on the ground or on their mother's knee, and everyone silently staring into the fire, I played a song I felt was the most appropriate. It was one Wendell had taught me, one he said was his favorite, and now I believed it was my favorite, too. He watched me intently from across the fire. With the guitar in my hands, I closed my eyes. As my fingers plucked at the strings on their own, I pictured Wendell's thick hand in mine, and the way his lips felt when they kissed me, and I thought, *I can almost forgive you.*

As the heat of the bonfire warmed my face, I sang:

"*Do you remember the paths where we met? / Long, long ago, long, long ago. / Ah, yes, you told me you'd never forget, / Long, long ago, long ago. / Then to all others my smile you preferred, / Love, when you spoke, gave a charm to each word. / Still my heart treasures the phrases I heard, / Long, long ago, long ago…*"

Tears streamed down my cheeks. I was convinced I wanted to go home. But now, in this moment, singing beside the fire, I thought about Willow's sweet snort as I brushed her; Gretchen's smile after being milked; the ugly but sweet Bambi who had sacrificed her life for a family she thought was her own. I remembered burning my first pot of coffee and my silly fear of the springhouse; of Rebecca Lynn nearly slicing off her leg; of surviving the hurricane; of the way the nighttime wrapped itself around the cabin while we rocked on the porch at sunset, the crickets and bullfrogs like a chorus.

I am singing the song of the backcountry. The song of the pioneers. Of the families who moved out to the middle of nowhere to start a new life, to live off the land. To live a harder, yet, at the same time, a simpler life.

With my eyes still closed, I sang through my tears:

"*But by long absence your truth has been tried, / Still to your accents I listen with pride. / Blessed as I was when I sat by your side, / Long, long ago, long ago…*"

Wendell joined in on the chorus, his deep voice complementing my own, but it ruined the song because I didn't need any of his help. Then I felt a hand on my knee and my fingers froze. The only sound was the fire crackling. My eyes opened. Wendell sat beside me. It seemed like everyone had stopped breathing, waiting to see what I would do.

I'm sure I surprised them all when I stood up and handed Wendell the guitar. In a voice that matched the quiet of the evening, I said, "Why don't you finish it? You seem to be an expert at making things better for everyone. Why don't you just go ahead and play it yourself?" I walked away from the fire and headed to the wagon.

Wendell called from behind me, "Brooke, don't do this. It's our last night together."

I didn't respond as I grabbed a lantern from the wagon, lit it, and stroked Willow's mane. "I'll see you back at the homestead," I whispered to the horse. It was a long walk, but I knew the way. My feet would hurt, but that was alright.

By the fire, Wendell said something to my dad, handed him the guitar, and approached the wagon. "Brooke. Please."

"Please what?"

"Stay."

"Why? So you can give the producers the dramatic ending they've been waiting for?" Willow nodded her head up and down. "I'll take you home," she seemed to say. I agreed. This was a good night for a ride. Forget about walking. Dad and Rebecca Lynn can hitch a ride with the Miller clan. I climbed onto the buckboard. It was my first time at the reins with the wagon attached, but I felt confident. Four months of survival does that to a girl, whether she's ready for it or not. "Out of my way, Wendell Murphy."

He took a step back as I pulled on the reins and slowly led the wagon up the dirt path leading away from the school grounds.

Dad shouted, "Brooke!"

"I'll get her," Wendell returned.

I guided Willow onto the bumpy road. I could hear Wendell's boot steps as he ran behind us, trying to catch up. I choked the reins and sped up. As I made a left onto the road, Wendell managed to grab a hold of the side of the wagon.

"Get off!" I screamed.

He hoisted his leg over the side before falling into the back of the wagon. He stumbled back and forth as I tried to keep Willow from tripping in the ruts. He climbed over the back of the seat and landed on his rear beside me. He tried to pull the reins from my hands, but I jerked them away.

"Stop this!" he shouted. "You'll get hurt."

"Get hurt?" I laughed sarcastically.

He tried to take the reins again. "Brooke, I'm not kidding."

"Neither am I."

The wagon bounced up and down on the uneven road. My hands flew up into the air and the reins disappeared, falling into the gap along the wagon's front. Wendell leaned forward and reached down, nearly losing his balance. Willow was galloping now. I grabbed onto the back of Wenedll's shirt as he stuck his arm in the space, and pulled him back. He fell onto the buckboard and yanked hard on the reins. "Whoa!" Willow obeyed and came to a stop, snorting at the sudden change of plans.

"What are you, crazy?" Wendell scolded.

"Probably."

He grabbed my arm. "Stop acting like this."

"Leave me alone."

I pulled from his grip and jumped down from the wagon. Behind me, the bonfire had turned into a tiny star at the bottom of the hill. I could barely make out the people flitting about the flames like moths, probably deciding what to do about that crazy Decker girl.

"Take the wagon back to my dad," I told Wendell. "I'll walk home."

"You can't. It's too far in the dark."

"Then I'll run."

In my hands I collected my skirts and started running up the road. I planned to run all the way back to the cabin. What was a couple of miles? I'd worked hard these past few months, and my legs and lungs were as strong as a work horse. Maybe I'd play sports again when I got back to school. Back to My Real Life, in The Real World, if it was still there waiting for me.

I was actually moving at a good pace when I tripped and fell in a rut, landing hard on my knees, my hands too busy holding my dress to stop my fall.

"Brooke!" Wendell rushed to my side. He plunked down beside me in the middle of the road. One of my buns had unwound, and I foolishly tried to tuck the loose hair under my bonnet. The trickling of water in a tributary sounded on my right. A tiny frog jumped across the road.

"Don't cry," Wendell said, touching my back. "What can I do?"

"Say it. Say that you're a liar."

"I'm not a liar, Brooke. I'm an actor. There's a difference."

"Ha!"

"I signed a contract to—"

"Go to hell."

"Whoa. That wasn't necessary."

"Did Wendell the actor just say that? Or Wendell the sweet country bumpkin?"

"The Wendell who meant everything he told you."

"No, you didn't. Just like Prudence didn't mean everything. Or tell me everything. Like how she's done Honda commercials and has electricity."

Wendell sighed, and it came out like a whistle. "I have a different contract than the Millers."

"What about the other families?"

"They each have their own contract."

"A contract to lie."

A panting figure came up the road, but with the fire in the background, I could only make out a silhouette.

"I was instructed to make your life more bearable," Wendell said.

"And Prudence?"

The panting shape came into view. Prudence said, "My job was to make your life more difficult. To add some spice early on."

"Don't even talk to me." I stood up and brushed off my dress as if that would make things better. The road ahead disappeared into complete darkness. My rash moment of bravado waned as I remembered clearly the sharp teeth and angry eyes of the bear.

"We were only doing what we were told," Prudence said.

"If your job was to mess with me, why did you suddenly want to be my best friend?"

"It was fun at first, getting into the role of the snotty rich girl. An actress's dream, really. But I couldn't stand treating you that way. Acting job or not. And treating Nanny and Josiah like crap every time you came around. It made me sick. Then after your garden was destroyed, I called Novak myself. It wasn't easy, but I convinced him the ratings would soar if I had a change of heart. If you and I actually became friends."

"So it was all for ratings," I said.

"Not all."

"Definitely not all," Wendell added.

"Who else besides you two were hired as actors?"

Wendell said quietly, "Everyone."

I found this impossible to believe. "Even the kids? Even your brothers?"

He nodded.

"What about the Duffys? They got kicked out."

"Contract dispute."

"What about the beer you found in their barn?"

"I've never been in their barn."

I was dreaming. That had to be it. One hard shake and I'd wake up in my old bed in Modern Land. But no one shook me.

I thought about the townspeople, how they'd shown up just as I was having a meltdown; the kind women who had cooked in my kitchen like real neighbors; the doctor who had met me in his driveway, like he knew about Rebecca Lynn's accident ahead of time. Everyone had nailed their parts perfectly, like they'd had months to rehearse before our family showed up. I touched my locket, realizing how it had come to me just when I needed it most. There was Prudence and her model's skin and Broadway singing voice. Wendell and all the songs he knew from the 1800s, and his perfect dialect. Nanny and Josiah, the ideal slaves. I could just as easily have been standing on the back lot of Paramount Studios.

"You and your family are the stars of the show," Wendell was saying. "We're just the bit players."

"Are there hidden cameras everywhere?" I whispered.

"Just about."

"Even by the pool?"

Wendell nodded. "Up in a tree, about ten feet—"

"The bear."

"What?"

"Was that a fake bear? The one by the stream that night?"

"No. That was definitely an unscripted bear. Gave me nightmares for a week. The producers ate it up."

"You saved us. You saved me."

"Yes."

I turned toward Prudence in the dark, her broad skirt like the silhouette of a giant bell. "Could you leave us be?"

Prudence went back to the wagon and stood next to Willow, stroking her mane.

And then, like a swarm of bees, the questions flew out of me: "Is Wendell Murphy your real name? Where do you go to school? Where do you live? California? New York? Do you have a girlfriend?"

"I'm not allowed to share those things with you."

"But you're allowed to break my heart, is that it?"

A shooting star flew directly over our heads. I stared at the flying star through my tears as the tail grew from bright yellow to a fuzzy outline of what was no longer there.

Wendell took my hands in his. Chicken bumps covered my arms beneath my long sleeves. "Did you make any memories out here?" he asked. "Ones that *don't* include me?"

I thought of Nanny leaving me a jar of flowery shampoo and a handmade hoop skirt; of eating butter churned by Yours Truly; of the way my dad stood proudly among his freshly planted seeds, and later, his sprouting crops; of my little sister who had bravely witnessed the death of a pig she'd named and loved, and who was proud to display the long pink scar that would forever be a reminder of Sweet Sugar Gap.

"Yes," I whispered, surprised to hear my own answer.

After a moment, he said, "Let's get back to the fire, Brooke. Let's give everyone the happy ending they're expecting."

"And then what?"

"Then we go back to the real world."

"What if *this* is the real world?"

"You know that isn't possible."

We held hands as we walked to the wagon. He helped me onto the seat. Prudence climbed into the back. He took the reins, and we made our way back down the road. Rusty met us halfway, his breaths coming out in small spurts. He climbed into the back next to Prudence.

"What did I miss?" he asked.

"Not a thing," Wendell answered.

At the fire, they waited for us. All these families, these professional actors who were getting paid to be our neighbors. Had they only been kind because it was in their contracts? Or did they feel the same way I did, that I was now a part of this land, this backcountry, with its ancient oaks, sparkling streams, and rolling hills? And how would I ever know for sure, unless I asked them?

But, of course, I could not ask. My dad ran to us when we got back, but he didn't scold. He merely offered a smile of relief when he saw that Wendell and I were holding hands. And there was Rebecca Lynn, feeding bits of leftovers to Sully. How could I explain to my little sister she had sliced open her leg and killed a pet pig just to make a bunch of producers in their Ralph Lauren suits happy?

Wendell and I sat beside one another on a log near the fire. Mrs. Murphy gave me a motherly smile as the firelight reflected against the silver locket around my neck. Dad handed me my guitar, Wendell's dad handed him another, and for the next hour we sang songs of the backcountry, of battles and homecomings, damsels and soldiers, hunters and farmers, death and love.

CHAPTER THIRTY-SEVEN

What's funny is, way back in May, I had started counting down the minutes leading up to the last day. Somewhere, between then and now, the countdown had turned the tables on me. Modern Land had snuck up from behind like a professional pickpocket, about to rob me of all I had gained during the last four months. I didn't want this story to end, no matter how confused I was, or how much my heart had been tricked. I hadn't missed my tiled shower or noticed the acrid chicken poop smell since that first week. I had adapted to a different way of life. I loved the smell of baking bread and plain black coffee for breakfast, and the taste of berries plucked right from the bush, the purple juice staining my fingertips like natural tattoos.

We had said our goodbyes at the bonfire that final night. I hugged everyone, including Prudence, who whispered, "This was the coolest project I've ever been a part of. If you ever come out to Santa Monica…"

But I would never see Prudence—*Sarah*—again. She said goodbye every time a movie or TV show ended. She was a professional.

They all were.

In front of the entire town, I let Wendell kiss me with the cameras nearly pressed against our cheeks. His taste was minty fresh like all his other kisses, and I realized he tasted like Colgate toothpaste. Funny thing is, deep down inside, I always knew that's what it was. Even so, it was a sweet kiss; a Hollywood kiss; the kind romantic comedies are written for. I kissed him back. Not for ratings, but as my parting gift to Wendell.

Josiah poured a bucket of water over the flames as each "family" went to their wagons and rode off into the night for the last time. It was the last community feast, the last bonfire, the last hoorah.

I didn't cry when Wendell disappeared over the rise and into the dark. I had come to realize a broken heart isn't the hardest thing to deal with when you work to survive on a daily basis. It is hard, but not the hardest.

Now, as I stood in the stuffy attic for the last time, waiting for our ride back to Modern Land, Dad made clanking noises as he readied the morning coffee, and Sully barked as Rebecca Lynn went out the back door to feed the chickens and offer them a farewell pat on the head. I tied my bonnet in an extra pretty bow and flattened out my apron, which covered my dress, which covered my corset and slip. I fluffed up the pillows, even though no one would be sleeping on them that night. I pulled the cheesecloth curtain back from the tiny window and let the sun shine through. The mini-mirror reflected the light, and I picked it up from the wooden beam, then put it back. Maybe someone else on some future venture would need it. I would leave my iPod in the attic as well, in case some fossil hunter a thousand years from now searched for a past that included me. I climbed down the ladder, and in the still of the early morning, shared a final breakfast of coffee and scrambled eggs. My family ate in silence, each of us trapped by or lost in our own thoughts.

While Rebecca Lynn washed the dishes, I used the outhouse for the last time, washed my hands in the bucket for the last time, and headed out to the barn for the last time.

The tears wouldn't stop coming. My heart was aching—but it had little to do with Wendell.

Gretchen licked the salt from my face with her big fat tongue as she gave me her milk. I brushed Willow and told her I loved her. I said goodbye to the remaining chickens, but they only clucked like they hoped I had treats in my pocket. I walked the milk out to the springhouse and poured it into two crocks, knowing it wasn't necessary. When I came out again, Dad was standing in the middle of the field. *His* field. He stood with his back to me, his hands on his hips like he was thinking of what crop to plant in the spring. Then his head bowed, and I knew he was crying, not because his harvest had been taken from him, but because he was proud to have produced something so extraordinary with his own two hands.

Leaving him alone, I made my way back to the front of the cabin. Rusty waited near the gate, panning the quiet road. I stood on the porch, the one that leaned way too far to the right, with the crooked steps and splintered railing. Fog swirled above each and every divot between our gate and the first hill beyond.

I was afraid to come out here in the beginning, and now I was afraid to go back. My mom was everywhere I looked. She was in the gold leaves as they rustled in the wind, some of them already drifting to the ground, waiting for a winter snow to bury them. She was in the night sky filled with enough stars to light up a country. She was in the cracks and crevices of the cabin, the rocks in the creek, and the roses still growing on the fence.

I stood on the porch until the unearthly hum of Modern Land broke through the morning silence, and I shut my eyes as the vehicle approached so I wouldn't have to admit too quickly that our life in the backcountry was over.

CHAPTER THIRTY-EIGHT

The hallways were a zoo. Libby and I walked to lunch together, trying not to bump into other students as we made our way upstream. I kept meaning to bring earplugs and sunglasses to school. The slamming lockers and quivering fluorescent lights were overwhelming. I felt like I'd been living on the dark side of the moon.

Libby was working to deprogram me, like I'd been held hostage by a cult for the last four months. "You've been back a week and you've barely said a word. What exactly happened to you out there in Laura Ingalls Land?"

I wanted to say, "Why can't you wait for the season premier like everyone else?" Instead I said, "Just need some time to acclimate."

"I still can't get over how great you look," she added.

My body had found muscle definition in places I didn't know was possible. I had put on a short skirt with a pair of tall boots, and my thighs looked amazing in the full-length mirror. My deltoids belonged to a tennis player or a hairdresser. I washed my face with water and washcloth only, and my pores were clean and happy. Even though I loved the ritual of shaving, and tampons were once again my best friends, I had tossed out my eyeliner. Wild Raccoon was no longer my style. Instead of buying synthetic blush, I bought red roses from the florist. Not only did my cheeks stay pink all day, but I smelled good, too. And the tiny hole in my eyebrow had mostly closed, so I fastened Mom's hoop earring to the chain holding my locket.

"Your hair," Libby breathed.

I couldn't tell if she was complimenting me or not. My hair had grown three inches while wound up in those donuts. Instead of dyeing it two-tone, I kept it chestnut brown. It was healthy and thick and fell in waves past my shoulders. Dad kept telling me how much I looked like Mom.

"We need to get you a social calendar," Libby said as we entered the hectic cafeteria.

It's difficult to explain, even to myself, how I was more bored here than out in Sweet Sugar Gap. Gorgeous sweaters were on sale at Belk which meant that Homecoming was just around the corner. My seventeenth birthday was in a few weeks. Soon after, there'd be gobs of Halloween parties. There was Thanksgiving break, including Black Friday, followed by Christmas shopping and wrapping. There would be hayrides in Beulaville, holiday concerts at the local schools, and parties to crash at ECU. But none of that seemed to matter much. I didn't miss alcohol, had decided that pot was a total waste of time and money, and promised myself the only kissing I planned to do was with boys I actually knew—and liked. I used to think about non-stop partying during the holidays, but now all I could think about was decorating my home and Christmas tree out of things found in nature. And as far as I was concerned, I'd already had Thanksgiving.

A final photograph was taken on the last day of the venture. Dad stuck the first photo and the final one, side by side, up on the fridge. Each time I glanced at them, it was as if I was peeking into the past of some other family, one I had descended from, not one I was a part of. In the first picture, my face looked angry. In the second, a sense of peace had settled into my forehead and around my mouth. My eyes were clear and awake, my skin plain and beautiful, my shoulders relaxed.

We received an evaluation, as promised. Of course, it didn't really matter, since we were already winners from the moment we signed the contract. Out in Charlotte, Novak read the letter to us with the cameras rolling. The show's historians informed us that if our family had really lived in the backcountry in 1861, we could have survived, so long as the wood chopping continued. They said we were "...tenacious, hardworking, and gifted as creative problem solvers. A family like the Deckers is what this country was built upon. Hats off for proving that determination is the thread in the fabric of survival." Rebecca Lynn brought the letter to school for extra credit.

In the cafeteria, Libby and I slid our lunch trays along the track. The woman behind the glass served me a flat piece of meat on a bun and greasy fries on the side. I grabbed a pint of milk. Milk which tasted nothing like the kind from a smiling cow.

I handed the student cashier a five dollar bill. She handed back two dollars in change. "Three bucks?" I asked. "For *this*?"

The girl looked at me like I was an idiot.

I wanted to say, "Did you know a pound of beef was ten cents back in the 1860s?" But I held my tongue.

"Don't mind her," Libby told the cashier. "She lived in the Outback for four months."

"*Backcountry*," I corrected, shaking my head.

People came and went as we ate our lunches, some stopping by our table to ask well-meaning questions, others gawking like I'd just crawled out of a Petrie dish. Dad had advised me to "Give it some time." Of course he was right, but the feeling of living with one foot in the present and the other foot in the past made me woozy.

Since it was raining after lunch, Libby and I hung out in the gym instead of in the quad. The room was loud, over a hundred voices bouncing off the walls. Basketballs slammed against the backboards, and tennis shoes slapped against the hard floor like they belonged to a herd of cattle. I found a spot on a bleacher in the corner, opened my notebook, and skimmed over my geometry notes.

"What are you doing?" Libby asked.

I wanted to explain that when you miss the first four weeks of school, you sort of get a craving to open text books and smell highlighters. But I didn't think Libby would ever believe I was aiming for straight A's.

"Just reviewing a few things."

"I'm going to say hey to Bobby Taylor," Libby said. "I want to check out his new tat." She jumped off the bleacher and flitted across the room, her heavy backpack slapping against her spine.

I sat staring at equations, playing catch-up. As I tried to wrap my brain around postulates and theorems involving parallel lines and convex polygons, my cell phone chimed.

Dad.

Ever since returning home, he called me every day to tell me how the job hunting was going. So far, he was "Close, but no cigar." The money from the show had saved our house, but with our health benefits ending just after Thanksgiving, and Dad's severance package dwindling fast, he was sounding desperate again.

One hand grasped my locket while the other hit the button on my cell. "Hey, Dad. What's the word on the street?"

He said, like *Family Feud's* game show host, "Word on the street IS…"

I put a finger in one ear to hear him better. "Tell me."

"I got it, Brooke. I got the job."

"Oh, God, Dad, that's awesome! When do you start?"

"Right after Christmas. That will give me time to prepare…I'll be in management. What do you think? Think I can handle management?"

"Absotively."

"There's more. My new job isn't in New Bern."

"Where is it?"

"And it's a three-year contract."

The word *contract* made my stomach flip. I took in a deep breath and let it out again. "Okay. I'm ready."

"The company is in Germany."

"As in…Europe?"

I could almost see him jumping up and down in his Docksides in the kitchen. I could see him rubbing the beard he'd decided to keep—trimmed, of course—after the venture had ended.

"How could we possibly move to Germany, Dad?"

"You can go to a private school there, if you like. And college, if that's what you want. All this opportunity does is give you more choices."

"Oh." I licked my lips. I had forgotten what it was like to have choices.

"I'll understand if you're not up to it."

Bits and pieces of history classes came back to me: WWI, WWII, Hitler, the rise of democracy and the fall of the Berlin Wall. We had the famous German Bosch plant right in New Bern. We even owned one of their dishwashers. Our glasses came out spotless. I had always wanted to go to a real Oktoberfest, so that had to count for something. And I liked pretzels.

But I didn't speak German. I only spoke a little Spanish so I could chat with the waiters at El Cerro Grande: *"Este burrito es delicioso!"* Of course, it had only taken a summer to learn the language of the 1860's backcountry.

Across the gymnasium, Bobby Taylor stood with the back of his shirt lifted. Libby and a group of girls cooed over his tattoo.

Dad said, "Your grandparents offered to stay with you until—"

"No."

"No, you're not up to it?"

"No. I'm *not* telling you that I'm *not* up to it." A nervous giggle popped out of me. "I'm telling you I *am* up to it. Totally. I mean, why the hell not, right?"

I could almost see his grin; could almost hear his skin move with excitement.

"Wow," he said. "You have no idea how much this means to

me." He handed me a super long pause, and I thought he'd hung up. And then: "I have some other news, Brooke, but I'm not sure how you're going to handle it."

For four months I had swept an old shack, conducted my business in an outhouse, flipped mattresses, used sanitary napkins held in place with a belt, and wrote nineteenth-century music. I had learned how to feel comfortable in a corset, turn a plain dress into a gown, make my own butter and cheese, and like myself even when my legs belonged to a chimp. And soon I'd be moving across the Atlantic. I figured I could handle anything by now.

"Tell me."

"Wendell called. He left a message on the answering machine. Including a number. Do you want me to erase it?"

"Wendell?"

I had only watched TV a handful of times since returning to Modern Land—the high-speed images sort of freaked me out. I didn't even plan to watch the premier of *Upside Down in a Laura Ingalls Town*, much to the dismay of my classmates who thought it was effing crazy but totally awesome to be on television. Everything was already ingrained in me without the reminder of an edited version of my life that past summer.

One night, when Dad was in the family room with the television on, I was positive I'd caught Nanny playing a dead woman on an episode of *CSI*. I left the room without scrutinizing the face. On my laptop, I looked up the old Honda commercial starring Prudence-Sarah and a surfboard. There she was, barely covered by a pink bikini, her sandy blond hair blowing in the wind. And on a self-inflicted dare, I Googled Wendell. I used the

IMDB as a guide, and what do you know, Wendell was his real first name…but his real last name was Burns. Anyway, that was as much sleuthing as I cared to do. The show was over. The curtains had closed. I had left more than just the backcountry behind me.

But now Wendell had called. And our family was moving to Germany.

My life was *in flux*—a new phrase learned this week in Lit that meant "constant change." I liked the word. Planned to use it in my next essay, as a matter of fact.

"In flux."

"I'm sorry?" Dad asked.

"No. Don't erase it."

"You're sure…"

The bell rang telling me that our break was over, and it was time for class. I shoved my notebook into my backpack and stood up on the bleacher. Kids gathered up their books and packs and headed toward the doors. Like a disorganized army, the herd grew louder as tennis shoes and winter boots stomped across the gym floor. Just before Libby got swallowed up by the crowd, she turned around and waved goodbye by putting two fingers up, forming a peace sign. I peace-signed her back.

"I'm not sure of anything," I said into the phone.

But then, I thought, as a confident smile crawled across my face, *Who really is?*

Dear Reader:

I can not thank you enough for reading *Upside Down in a Laura Ingalls Town*. Although it took many years from first draft to publication, and finally into your hands, you are the one who has made the true investment. Not everyone has the desire to buy a book based on the cover or a friend's recommendation, let alone read the whole thing. So kudos to you!

Since we already know you are special, I'd like to request an itty bitty favor. Could you please leave an honest review for *Upside Down* on Amazon? You may also leave one on any site you feel would be valuable in supporting this book. Even if the book was not your style, leave a review. The only way for a writer to continue writing, and continue to get better, is for readers to leave reviews. Good or bad, they all count!

Love to you all,
Leslie

Acknowledgements:

First and foremost, I must thank my beloved husband, Jay—my personal "Almonzo"—for without his unyielding support of my perpetual writing habit, this book would never have been written. He also designs my book covers (with me looking over his shoulder as he makes the constant changes I so greedily demand), so double thanks, babe!

A mammoth thank you goes to Uwe Stender at the TriadaUS Literary Agency for reading the manuscript over and over again, and for getting this book into the hands of top editors. Without the perfect combination of expert eyes and precious advice, *Upside Down in a Laura Ingalls Town* would still be in its fetal stage. Also, Uwe, a blessed thank you for always believing in me. When the clouds remain a perpetual shade of gray, you manage to poke a hole through the gloom to let in a little sun. We make a great team, even if things aren't moving as quickly as we'd hoped. All good things...

Thanks to Mary Corning, Claire Kirby, Ashley Silver, and Mattie Keenhold—my incredible students, avid readers, and creative writers—for their invaluable guidance regarding this book's cover. Keep reading, for the journeys are boundless; keep writing, for you never know where your stories will lead you!

My gratitude goes to Marina and Jason Anderson at Polgarus Studio for their formatting expertise. You always know exactly what my novels need...sometimes before I do!

This book would not have been written if it weren't for a handful of organizations and websites to keep facts straight, so to the following I am indebted: Museum of Menstruation (Yes, this is a REAL museum!) www.mum.org; Laura Ingalls Wilder Historic Home and Museum www.lauraingallswilderhome.com; Ladies Treasury of Costume and Fashion www.tudorlinks.com; Country Doctor Museum www.countrydoctormuseum.org; Contemplations from the Marianas Trench www.contemplator.com/america/; The Prairie Homestead www.theprairiehomestead.com; North Carolina State Cooperative Extension www.craven.ces.ncsu.edu; and Bennett Place State Historic Site www.bennettplacehistoricsite.com.

Special recognition goes to Mr. C. Foy at C. Foy's Tonsorial Parlor & Barber Studio in New Bern, North Carolina, for showing me—via my husband's super smooth face—how to shave with a straight razor without causing too much injury.

Finally, thank you to all the daring pioneers, past, present, and future, for without you, the world would still be flat.

Study Guide Questions for
Upside Down in a Laura Ingalls Town

SPOILER ALERT!
DO NOT READ THESE QUESTIONS BEFORE
READING THE BOOK!

1. Discuss a time when you were thrust into a situation in which you had little control. How did you manage? Did you find it easier to buck the system, or did you try your best to acclimate?

2. Have you ever read any of the *Little House* books by Laura Ingalls Wilder? If so, which one was your favorite? How did the book(s) make you feel?

3. Have you ever watched episodes of *Little House on the Prairie*? If so, do you think the producers depicted the time period realistically? Explain.

4. Why do you think Laura Ingalls Wilder's books are still popular after all these years?

5. Has an adult ever placed you in a situation you disagreed with at first, but when all was said and done you realized he or she was right?

6. In *Upside Down in a Laura Ingalls Town,* do you believe Brooke truly falls in love with Wendell? Or do you think she

settles for him because he is the only boy in town her age?

7. One of the themes of the novel is open-mindedness. Discuss how keeping an open mind can affect a person's life.

8. I conducted three years of research for this novel, uncovering amazing facts about country living in the 1860s. Have you ever had to conduct research on a particular person or event from the past? What did you learn that surprised you?

9. Do you have what it takes to live in another time and place for four months like the Decker Family? What would be the most difficult for you to leave behind? What would you learn from the experience?

10. Discuss the ways in which Brooke Decker changes from the beginning to the end of the novel.

11. Who is your favorite minor character of the story? Who is your least favorite? Why?

12. If Brooke is the story's protagonist, who is the antagonist? Explain your reasons for choosing this person.

13. The Decker Family spends much of their time performing chores in order to survive. Compare and contrast the chores of today with the ones of yesteryear. How is life easier today? How is it more difficult?

14. What would have frightened you most about living in the backcountry over a century ago?

15. If you could write a letter to Laura Ingalls today, what questions would you ask her? What would you want her to know about yourself?

16. A pig dies in the story, just as many pigs died in the 1860s. How would you have handled this situation? Were you offended that I added the scene to the book? Explain your answer.

17. At the end of the story, Brooke discovers that Wendell has called. If you could write an additional chapter, how would you have Brooke handle this discovery? What decisions could she make that would change her life forever?

18. In what ways does Brooke use her creativity and critical thinking skills to make life in the backcountry more enjoyable? Had you been Brooke, are there things you would have done differently?

19. Colonists originally settled in the North Carolina backcountry in the mid-1700s. How do you think the landscape changed between the Revolutionary War and the Civil War? How do you think it has changed from the Civil War until now?

20. If you wrote a novel that took place in another time, which era would you choose? Why?

About the Author

Leslie Tall Manning is a Theatre Arts graduate from California State University Long Beach, where she wrote and directed her first play (soon to be a published novel). In 2003, she left the Wild West for the Sleepy South for artistic inspiration, and proudly calls North Carolina her home. As a private English tutor and writing specialist, Leslie spends her evenings working with students of all ages, and her days juggling a multitude of writing projects, including editing screenplays and working on a musical. When she isn't clacking away at the computer keys or conducting research for her adult and young adult novels, she spends quality time with her artist husband.

Feel free to visit Leslie's website where she answers readers' questions, reveals chapters of upcoming books, and offers an event calendar for book signings and guest-speaking engagements. www.leslietallmanning.com

Made in the USA
Middletown, DE
08 July 2023